Waiting for Ana

Annie Seaton

Sunshine Coast: Book 1

Originally published © 2013 by Annie Seaton Tangling with the CEO.

Second Edition: Waiting for Ana, 2021

Dedication

To my readers who love my books set in our fabulous Australian towns and country landscapes.

Acknowledgement

Thank you to Anna Welch for her accurate proofreading!

Chapter One

"Ouch." Anastasia Delaney dropped the hammer and put her thumb up to her mouth. It was sure to bruise from the thump she'd just given it. There was only one more length of decorative beading to nail up around the window frame and then she would have to leave for the meeting she was dreading so much.

The years had flown by since she and her two best friends had started the restoration department at Joe Hickey's little hardware store in Maleny, up the mountain from the Sunshine Coast. Ana had spent years in her Gramps' tool shed when she was growing up there and had a natural talent for working with wood. Sienna was the artist who worked on the delicate mouldings and painting. Her twin sister, Georgie, was the jack-of-all-trades who could turn her hand to any task. Their reputation had grown, and they always had plenty of jobs booked in the old cottages along the coast. Ana loved nothing more than working with friends she'd known since school. She blinked back a tear at the pain in her thumb and the thought that this could be their last restoration job together.

"I'll miss this so much once the takeover goes through and our department is shut down. We do damn good work, girls." Ana ran her hand lovingly over the highly polished window frame. "It's just unfair. Why does everything have to be about making money these days? We use quality materials and look at the fabulous work we do. It absolutely pees me off."

"Don't be so negative." Sienna wandered in from the balcony and stood beside Ana. "We're not going to give up until we know for sure our jobs are gone."

Georgie frowned from the top of the ladder where she was hanging curtains at the other end of the bay window. "Ana. We've got no chance if you're late for the appointment with the CEO of Home and Hardware. You should have left already. And you haven't even changed. You can't go looking like that."

"Changed?" Ana brushed the sawdust from her sleeves. "What's wrong with my work clothes? I'm a tradesperson, and I'm happy to look like one. If he judges us on the way we dress—"

"No, listen to me, girlfriend. You are a successful businesswoman and you're meeting with the top bloke from the biggest chain of home improvement stores in the country. He might also be our future boss." Sienna reached into her pocket and there was a crafty smile on her face as she held up a set of car keys. "I know what you're like, so I came prepared. Not only are you taking my car, but you will find a suit and heels waiting for you on the back seat." With a languorous wave of the paint brush she was holding in her other hand, Sienna stared at Ana. "My sporty little car will impress the hot shot executive."

Ana looked down at her paint-splattered overalls and sighed. "Maybe you should be the one to go and convince him not to shut us down. You've got the class I am sadly lacking."

And the courage, she thought to herself.

Sienna waited for Georgie to climb down the small ladder and then she put the paintbrush on the bottom rung. "Ana, we've been over this before. You knew this guy at uni, so that has to give us a bit more bargaining power."

"Blake Buchanan worshipped the dollar when we were at UQ, so I don't think we'll have any chance of him changing his mind about closing our department." Ana sat on one of the upturned buckets and looked up gratefully as Georgie passed her a bottle of water. "And I didn't mention it before, but we parted on bad terms so that will probably give us even less chance of our jobs surviving." She turned to the large window which looked out over the water. The ocean was a sheet of silver with not a breath of breeze ruffling it. Half a dozen surfers waited for waves on the point, and as she watched a pod of dolphins frolicked around them.

'Oh wow, look that means good luck!' The magnificent

view calmed her nerves a little as she sipped the cool water. She didn't want the twins to know she and Blake had been more than mere acquaintances when they'd lived in the share house at Toowong he'd owned ten years ago. Even though they'd both been studying for a business degree, their philosophies had been very different. Blake's emphasis on conservative economics had been at odds with her study of welfare economics and they'd eventually agreed to disagree when their arguments became too heated. Their discussions had been stimulating and Ana had loved sparring with him. Most evenings she would bait him with a provocative comment about her day in class just to get a rise out of him. He was so passionate about his beliefs he fell for it every time. She'd loved watching his eyes darken and his sexy mouth lift in a smile when he realised she was teasing him. She had instigated many a discussion just so she could watch his face come alive. And she'd fallen a little more in love with him the longer she stayed in the house.

"We were absolute opposites in everything, and we fought like cats and dogs," Ana explained to her friends. "He even listened to classical music. I mean, who does that when you're young. That was my heavy metal stage and it drove him crazy."

"What else?" Sienna's beautifully made up eyes were fixed on Ana's face.

"You know how I love football?" she continued. "I used to go to the games at Suncorp with the other guys and Blake would be off playing golf or something equally as snooty."

Georgie giggled. "Are you sure you aren't being too hard on him? You did go through a pretty wild stage at uni."

"It all came to a head, one night after we'd been to a State of Origin game. We came home and Blake was waiting on the porch and he read me the riot act about the state of my room. God, even Mum didn't do that."

Sienna picked up her paintbrush, her eyes narrowed.

"Maybe your mother should have?"

"Thanks, sweets." Ana shook off the criticism like water off a duck's back. She was used to being teased by the girls. She'd lived in a mess at uni when she was busy studying—and having a good time— and she still lived in chaos these days. There just wasn't enough time to run a business and finish restoring her old cottage. Keeping everything tidy didn't pay the bills.

'So what happened?' Georgie asked.

Ana pulled a face. "I'd had a couple of beers at the game, so I told Blake he had no right to be in there, called him a sexist pig and slammed the front door in his face. I locked him out of his own house." She smiled at the memory. "The other guys went to bed and Blake sat outside, cooling his heels until I let him back in. Then I got the call from the hospital about Mum the very next day and moved home. You know the rest."

Actually, they didn't.

They knew she'd given up in her final year of university to come home and nurse her mother through the final stages of breast cancer, but she'd never told anyone about that night with Blake. It was a delicious memory; one she'd pulled out and relived during the tough nights when her mother had been dying.

When she'd decided to let him back in, Blake had been sitting on the front steps looking across the road at the muddy Brisbane river and he'd ignored the open door behind him. Ana had stood quietly for a moment drinking in the sight of him before she'd called to him softly.

"Blake. I've opened the door for you." His broad shoulders strained beneath his white polo shirt and his dark hair curled over the collar. A shaft of pure longing shot through her.

Ana's fingers had itched to run through his hair, and she'd fought the urge to go and sit on the step next to him in the moonlight. It had been one of those still Brisbane nights, and was late enough that the main road was clear of the usual noisy traffic.

8

"What are you looking at?" he'd asked.

What? Did he have eyes in the back of his head?

Heat had suffused her face at the thought of being caught checking him out and she covered up her discomfort with a teasing laugh.

"I was just wondering if it was safe to let you back in. Or have I pushed your buttons again?"

Slowly, Blake had pushed himself to his feet and turned around. Ana had edged back through the door, unable to read the look on his face in the shadows, but his stance was predatory. In one swift movement, he'd jumped up the last step and before she could get inside, he'd pinned her against the wall of the porch and Ana had tried to cover up the feelings rioting through her with a nervous giggle.

"Let go." She half-heartedly tried to pull away, but he'd laced his fingers through hers and held her hands above her head.

"Anastasia, you always push my buttons, without even trying."

She'd been trapped between Blake and the wall, and when she'd looked up at him, her breasts had pressed into his hard chest. With a soft groan, he'd lowered his head and gently slid his lips across her cheek. "You drive me crazy; do you know that?"

With each word his mouth had come closer to hers and now hovered over her lips. "The way you walk, your voice, your laugh, that hippy perfume you wear. I can't get you out of my head."

She'd smiled at him and eased her arms from his loose grasp, taking his face between her hands. 'I can't stop thinking about you either, Blake," she'd whispered. "And I'm sorry I called you a sexist pig."

That first kiss they'd shared on the front porch had been slow and soft. The feel of Blake's warm mouth on hers was everything Ana had dreamed of and she'd closed her eyes as a delicious languor drifted through her. She'd sensed he was holding

9

back and that it was up to her to let him know it was okay to take it further.

Finally, she'd smiled against his mouth and murmured. "My room or yours?"

He'd lifted his head and even in the dim light she could see the laughter lines crinkle around his eyes and the warmth stirred low in her belly as he'd held her gaze.

"Is your bed clear?"

"It's made, but it's covered in . . .er . . .stuff."

"I guess it's my room then."

"So are you going to stand there daydreaming all afternoon, or are you going to go to Noosa and save our jobs?" Ana jumped when Sienna dangled the keys in front of her face.

"All right, I'm going. But be prepared for disappointment. Blake was a nice guy, but when it came to business profit, margins always came first."

Georgie rolled her eyes. "Ana, I have been trying to tell you that for years. You can't expect a small business to support every philanthropic activity."

"Well, Joe does." The owner of the local hardware store which employed them turned a blind eye to a lot of the work they never billed out to the older residents in the community. Joe's family had opened the first general store in Main Street, Maleny in the 1920s and he loved his hometown with a passion. "I can't understand why he had to sell the business anyway, *and* to a huge corporation."

Sienna stared at Ana. "Well he's almost eighty-years-old. He has no children to take over the store, and he and Magda deserve a nice retirement. She was looking at cruise brochures just the other day." She nudged Georgie and winked. "She said she might as well read something because she was sick of waiting for our accounts to come in."

10

"All right, all right. No need to be a smart arse. I'll do them tonight." Ana reached for Sienna's keys "I *will* finish them, and when Blake comes to the store, we can show him how much business we pull in. That will convince him to keep us on. Besides the community needs us."

Sienna yawned. "Two problems with that, Ana. You're the one meeting with him, and I have a feeling that may be the only meeting that happens. And do you really think a big company like Home and Hardware will care about the local community? Maybe it's time we faced reality and accept we're all going to be out of a job." She folded her arms and gazed out the window. "I have enough put away that I can manage for a few months. I've already been offered a couple of days work in the art gallery at the top of the main street."

Disappointment pressed on Ana's chest like a dead weight. It sounded like her friends had accepted that their work was about to end. "Well, whatever you decide, Georgie and I can still keep the business running." She turned toward the front door full of renewed determination. "I hate change. I really do."

Georgie cleared her throat.

Ana turned around and groaned. "Oh, no. Not you too, Georgie?"

"It's just a backup. Just in case you can't convince your Blake."

"He's not my Blake," Ana snapped. "And what plans have you made?"

"Joe told me there will be a position in the new store for me. He knows I don't mind being in the store when we don't have renovation jobs."

Ana came back across the room and draped her arms around the shoulders of the two women who were her best friends in the whole world. Since her mother had died, she had no other family and she'd filled the emptiness with her work. Sienna and

11

Georgie and her elderly friends in Maleny were her life.

"It's okay. I'm being selfish. Like I said, I hate change. But I will convince Blake to keep us on, anyway. No matter what it takes."

Sienna grinned at her with a wicked glint in her eye. "No matter what it takes?

Ana folded her arms and nodded. There was no way she was going to let her friends and the community down.

Two hours later, Ana parked Sienna's two-seater red sports coupe right outside a modern two storey house on a canal at Noosa, thanking whoever was looking out for her. A parking space here was like gold any time of day or night.

Raindrops glistened in the soft afternoon sunlight and reflected a rainbow of colours across the glass front of the house. A typical Sunshine Coast storm had hit and cleared as she'd driven down the mountain, Ana sat in the car for a moment and closed her eyes trying to calm her nerves as the memory of Blake kissing her the last time she'd seen him came storming back

She was sure she'd been a one night fling to him, but she'd followed his stellar rise in the business world with interest after he'd gone to Melbourne and finished his MBA. Okay, maybe her Internet searches were more than a passing interest, more like a hunger to fill the emptiness where her heart had once been. Last time she'd Googled him, he'd been managing a wilderness retreat in North Queensland. After that she had made herself stop cyberstalking him—it wasn't healthy, and she had plenty to fill her life without dreaming of an old unrequited love.

"Get out of the car. You're not twenty anymore." She opened her eyes and took a deep breath. All her old insecurities had come rushing back. "It doesn't matter that you don't have a degree. You're a successful businesswoman, now act like one."

So what if my dreams of a corporate career and an MBA

were history?

She'd had a precious six months with Mum before she died, and her life had turned out just fine without a bachelor's *or* master's degree. So maybe she didn't have a stellar Fortune 500 career like Blake and some of the others from their share house in Brisbane, but the little enterprise she, Georgie, and Sienna had set up was successful and fulfilling.

Who knows what might have come after our night together if I'd stayed and we'd talked?

The next morning, after Blake had gently kissed her goodbye and left for his early class, the ringing of the house phone had woken her.

"Can you come home, Ana? It's not looking good." Her mother's words were still imprinted on her mind.

My mother, my beautiful mother. Nothing else had mattered in that moment.

She'd run into her room, showered and packed; within an hour, she'd called a taxi to get her to the bus station. Overcome by worry and grief for her mother, she hadn't even left a note.

After Mum had passed, she'd briefly considered going back to uni, but by that time, she and the twins had started up their restoration business. She knew Blake had moved to Melbourne to take a position in one of the top firms in the investment business and she was determined to forget about him.

And now here she was, in her best friend's sports car dressed in a borrowed business suit, a pair of borrowed Jimmy Choos, her stomach churning, and about to confront Blake, to convince him not to close their little business as part of the takeover of the Maleny hardware store by the national corporation he represented.

"Shit." Water gushed into her shoe as she stepped out of the car straight into a puddle from an overflowing drain. Sienna would kill her. "Focus," she muttered to herself, bending to remove the

13

ruined footwear. "One wet shoe is the least of my worries." It wasn't just the thought of her friends losing their jobs that was making her feel ill.

Pull yourself together. It was just a crush. Just one night.

She'd had several short relationships over the years but none of them had stayed in her heart like that one night with Blake. She pulled her thoughts together. They were so different, it never would have worked out anyway, even if Mum hadn't got sick.

She tucked Sienna's shoes under her arm, swallowed, and pushed open the gate.

Chapter Two

Blake Buchanan sat at his small work desk in the study, annoyed that his four o'clock appointment was late. It had been a long week full of meetings with suppliers, and Zoom meetings with Mike, the owner of Home and Hardware. All he had to do now was get this last appointment out of the way and then he intended pouring a red wine from his well-stocked cellar. He was keen to shed the business suit and get into a comfortable pair of jeans. The email from his secretary had been brief and he only knew that the guy he was about to meet was a restoration specialist at the Maleny store. That whole department would go in the takeover. Blake had been Chief Executive Officer at Home and Hardware for the past three years, and shedding personnel was just another part of the job to him. Nothing to lose any sleep over.

Returning to Noosa meant being close to family—even though there was only his sister, Jeannie, her husband Rod, the local vet, and their tribe of kids left, he was determined to settle back into the town he'd grown up in. He'd had the house on the canal built last year and now he looked around it with pleasure. Glass walls across the back of the house gave him an uninterrupted view of the canal.

He couldn't help but think of Anastasia Delaney when he looked at the water. She'd grown up on the Sunshine Coast too, even though they hadn't met until they were in Brisbane at uni and she applied for a place in his share house. She'd been the only girl in the house and the most disorganised person he had ever met. She'd driven him crazy with the chaos that she'd created and her idealistic economic views.

But what a beauty she'd been, blonde and lithe. And her carefree spirit and her joyful approach to life had brought the share house alive. Blake's parents had been quiet, and if he was honest, a

15

little bit stuffy, and he knew he had been turning into a lonely and boring adult. The move back here was the time for him to change and start enjoying life.

Back in those days, he'd watched Ana from a distance as she'd gone out with the other guys and envied the fun they had together. Until that night she'd locked him out and they ended up in his bed.

The next afternoon on the way back from lectures, he'd bought a huge bunch of brightly-coloured flowers, and anticipation had filled him as he'd waited for her to come home from her part-time job at the coffee shop in Paddington. Finally, after waiting for hours, he'd checked her room, and he still remembered the hollow ache in his gut when he'd seen the stripped bed and empty closet.

When she didn't get in touch with him, the anger kicked in. She'd been toying with him and was obviously as loose with her relationships as she was in the rest of her life. Everyone in their house lost touch with her from that day.

But she stayed firmly fixed in his mind until he left for his job in Melbourne. He couldn't understand why she'd dropped out of uni so suddenly and he'd often wondered if she'd finished her degree somewhere else. And he couldn't let go of that niggling guilt that sleeping with him had caused her to flee. It hadn't made sense because she'd murmured sleepily for him to hurry back when he'd had to leave for his early lecture. And he thought she had enjoyed the night of gentle passion as much as he had.

He hadn't thought about her for a long time.

She's probably married and still lurching from one disaster to another. Maybe he could look her up now that he was back on the coast. He was determined to have a life which allowed time for some fun. His job had been boring him lately and he intended to do something about that as soon as this takeover was completed.

Blake glanced down at his watch in annoyance, and then he stood and moved across to the window as the sound of a car engine

16

reached him.

About time.

A red BMW Z3 was parked outside his house. A firm derriere and long legs with shapely calves were visible as a woman in a red suit bent down beside the car and removed her shoes. His heartbeat kicked up a notch as a cascade of silvery blonde hair swung forward hiding her face from his view. For a fleeting moment, the sight took him back ten years. The unusual silver-coloured hair reminded him of Anastasia—strange when he'd just been thinking about her. There was no way it would be her. She'd hated all the trappings of wealth. Fancy cars, exclusive addresses, and what she'd called 'fancy do dads' provided the catalyst for some of their more interesting . . . and fiery . . . debates. She'd always go on about giving back to those who didn't have as much and helping those who were unable to help themselves. He shook his head wondering what she'd done with her life and if reality had helped her outgrow her naive beliefs. He'd never been able to agree with her soft approach.

If you wanted something, you worked for it. It was as simple as that. If you didn't, you didn't get it.

He dropped the curtain, irritated with the direction of his thoughts and picked up his phone to read the headlines. Anastasia was in the past and now he would give this guy five more minutes to turn up before he missed his chance to make whatever argument he was going to try to convince Blake to keep the restoration department. The meeting was a waste of time anyway—there was no place for non-existent profit margins in the new financial model.

Just as he became engrossed in the news, the doorbell rang. Blake stood and put his phone in the charger on his desk on the way past.

About time.

Straightening his tie, he moved across to the door, and

17

glanced through the window. The BMW was still there but the Anastasia lookalike had disappeared. Schooling his face to reflect a conservative businessman, he opened the door to his late appointment. It was like a punch in the stomach and he struggled to catch his breath as the fragrance of patchouli oil drifted across from the silver-headed woman standing on the front porch.

"Hello, Blake." The sweet voice reminded him he was staring, and he gathered himself together as she reached out to grip his arm. "Blake?"

"Anastasia." He stared at her, taking in the red business suit and the designer bag tucked beneath her arm. It was a more sophisticated look than the flowing skirts and jangling bracelets of the girl who'd lived in his house, but she was still drop dead gorgeous and his heart rate took off. The hippy perfume of the share house days wafted around him, at odds with the classy outfit.

"What . . . when . . . how did you know I had moved back to Noosa? My God . . . Anastasia. What are you doing here? It must be ten years—"

"Yes, it's been ten years since I left. A long time, Blake." She removed her hand from his arm, hitched her bag onto her shoulder and looked steadily at him.

He stared at her, lost for words for a moment and then his brain kicked back into gear.

"How did you know I was back here?"

"You've come to take over the hardware store down at Maleny." Her expression was hard to read.

"You must have read the article in the *Financial Review*," he said slowly.

The paper had done an interview about his corporate success and anyone who read it would know how wealthy he was now. Experience had taught him to be wary of people who sought him out, seemingly out of the blue. Straightening his shoulders, he stepped back. "Come in. I have an appointment scheduled, but he's

18

late so he's missed out." He'd give her a few minutes to explain why she was here and then she could tell him where the hell she'd disappeared to that morning. "You know I tried to find you after you left, but no one knew where you had gone. I even tried calling all the Delaneys on the coast. Why did you just take off like that?" As much as he tried to keep his voice short and business like, he couldn't help the surge of felling that warmed him as she stood beside him. That damn perfume was taking over his senses and his head was ten years in the past, not to mention his body.

"You tried to find me?" Her voice was soft, and he lost his train of thought for a moment as her clear blue eyes gazed steadily at him.

"I owed you an apology. The way I spoke to you that night was way out of line. And then . . . the next day . . . after we . . . after that night . . . you were gone when I came home."

God, he was as tongue-tied as a teenager on his first date.

"All water under the bridge now." She smiled at him, tucking her hair behind her ear and his mood softened as her hand shook a little. "Blake, I need to talk to you. Look, I am your app—"

Before she could finish, a loud screech of tyres signalled the arrival of a familiar white SUV, which turned into the narrow driveway at the front of the house. A taxi followed and parked behind it. Blake groaned.

What the hell is Jeannie up to now?

His sister was the grand master of madcap schemes and although he loved the time he spent with her and her family, this was not the time for one of her madcap ideas. He wanted to know why Ana had come to see him, and he didn't need Jeannie's interruption.

All those thoughts flew from his head when his sister jumped out of her SUV. Her face was streaked with tears. She looked up at him wordlessly over the low gate that edged the short

19

path in front of the house.

"Excuse me." He turned to Ana before he hurried down the stairs. "Don't go anywhere."

He vaulted over the low metal gate to the driveway. By the time he reached his sister, she was handing a small suitcase to the cab driver.

"What's the matter? What are you doing?" He opened his arms to her, and Jeannie leaned into him. Her whole body was shaking.

His stomach clenched and fear crawled into his throat. He placed his hands on her arms, gently pushing her back so he could see her face. Her eyes red-rimmed and awash with tears, Jeannie passed a shaking hand through her short black curls.

"It's Rod. The light plane he's on is missing. They're out searching now." She hiccupped and caught her breath. "I just got the call."

"Where was he?"

"He was flying back to the lodge from a fishing trip with a group of guys. I'm booked on a flight to Cairns and it leaves in an hour. The kids are in the car and I threw in some food and clothes for them." She reached up and kissed him on the cheek, before handing him a set of car keys.

"I'm so glad you're here now, I don't know what I would have done if you had still been in Melbourne. I'll call you as soon as I get there."

Before he could answer, Jeannie climbed into the taxi and told the driver to hurry to the airport.

"Anything you need, just get it delivered." His sister waved to him from the open window as the taxi backed quickly out of the driveway and accelerated down the street. Blake turned to the SUV when the loud bellow of a baby came through the partially open window. Reaching for the door, he looked up when the gate squeaked.

20

"I couldn't help overhearing." Anastasia hurried over to him. "Tell me how I can help?"

Blake was used to dealing with corporate takeovers and crises in the business place but was completely at a loss standing in his own driveway with a carload of kids. He ran his hand through his hair and turned to Anastasia.

"I guess we'd better take them inside."

***

The blood had hummed in Ana's ears when Blake opened the door and she'd fought the urge to turn tail and run back to Sienna's car. He'd barely changed in ten years. His jet black hair was shorter but as dark as ever, although she'd glimpsed a sprinkle of grey when they were outside. A few little wrinkles around his eyes added maturity to his face, but apart from that he was still the Blake of her memories. She'd focused on looking calm, ignoring the heat that rushed through her fingertips when she touched his arm. The business clothes helped her confidence, although being in stockinged feet with wet shoes tucked beneath her arm did detract from the sophistication.

Her heart went out to Jeannie. Fear had been etched into her face, and her voice had broken when Blake had held her. Ana had met Jeannie briefly when she'd been at college and all her nervousness disappeared as she thought about how to help her. And if the look on Blake's face was any indication, he had no idea what to do with a crying baby.

"Unlock the door." She spoke confidently to convey the impression that she did know what to do, but, she was clueless about kids, too.

Blake double clicked the remote in his hand and all the windows of the car slid down. A combination of cries, chattering, and barks became instantly louder. A baby of an indeterminate age, strapped in a rear-facing car seat, was screaming. She had a pink T-shirt on, so Ana assumed it was a girl. Two small boys who

21

looked to be the same age were arguing over an action hero, the noise punctuated by the sharp barks of a large bloodhound whose tongue was hanging over the tops of their heads as he turned from one to the other, lathering drool across the leather seat.

"It's mine . . . give it to me." The struggle escalated as a tug-of-war battle ensued over the action figure.

"No! It's mine." The boy on the far side burst into tears as an arm pulled out of the figure's torso. "Now, look. You broke Spider-Man. I hate you."

The young girl sitting in the front seat looked up calmly from her book and spoke through the open window.

"Don't worry, Uncle Blake. He always says that, and Mummy tells him not to. So he will be in big trouble when she comes back with Daddy."

Ana blinked away the tears pricking her eyes at the certainty in the little girl's voice. Blake appeared to be incapable of moving or speaking, so she decided it was time to take over. One of the staff at the store had gone into shock one day from an allergic reaction, and Blake had the same look about him.

"Blake, you get the boys out of the back and I'll take the baby." She turned to the young girl in the front. "What's your name, sweetie?"

"Madeleine and I am eight-years-old. I'm the oldest. My twin brothers are six."

"Okay, Madeleine, can you climb out and help Uncle Blake get the boys out?"

Madeleine smiled sweetly at Ana and opened the door. The dog chose that moment to take a flying leap over two rows of seats and make a break for it.

"Get the dog." Ana yelled at Blake, grabbing helplessly at the dog's collar as it pushed past her. Blake jerked out of his stupor and tackled the dog before it could take off down the road.

Ana opened the back door and undid the baby's seat belt

22

before lifting her out. She wrinkled her nose at the smell.' Oh dear.'

One of the boys giggled. "That's why he's crying. He hates sitting in poo."

"He?" asked Ana. "I thought he was a girl."

The two boys, who Ana now realised were identical twins, giggled in unison. "Maddy dressed him. She wants a little sister and all she got were us brothers." Obviously, they both thought this was a subject of great hilarity. Maddy glared at them as she stood quietly next to the car, clutching a book in her hand.

"Come on, guys. Let's go inside." Blake attempted to brush the dirt and wet grass off his trousers with one hand while he clutched the dog's collar with the other.

"Ah, he speaks," said Ana trying to lighten the mood. She looked up at Blake and tried to give him a reassuring smile. Settling the baby on her hip, she took the hand of one of the boys. "I'll help you get everyone to the house, Uncle Blake, and then you can introduce me to these lovely children."

Blake mouthed a silent thank you to her, before turning to the gate, the dog's collar in one hand and the small hand of one twin in the other. Ana followed him, stepping carefully in her stockinged feet. The last thing she wanted was to slip on the wet path and do a face plant into the hedge, baby and all. She and the kids traipsed up the narrow stairs and they crowded onto the small glass-sided landing.

"I think it would be better if you take them in and get them settled. They don't know me, so I'll unpack the car." She passed him a disposable nappy. "This was on the seat. You change the baby while I get the food. That'll be the first thing they need, I guess?"

"Thanks. I've never changed a nappy in my life."

Ana grinned at him as she held her hand out for the car keys. "Time to learn." She ran lightly down the stairs to the

23

driveway. The afternoon sun had dried the steps and path, and she took a deep breath appreciating the salt-tanged breeze drifting up from the ocean. She opened the back of the SUV and surveyed the crates piled in front of her.

Where to start?

She reached forward to a crate jammed with groceries and jumped when the blanket to her right shifted and the music from *Baby Shark* blared out.

"Hello." A pair of large brown eyes peered out from beneath the blanket.

Ana placed her hand on her chest. That explained the empty booster seat in the third row of the SUV. He must have unbuckled himself during all the commotion.

"Oh my goodness, another one. Who are you?"

"I'm Billy. B-I-L-L-Y. I can spell my name and I'm only four and this is Fred and Wilma."

My God, how many children are in this family?

He lifted the blanket and Ana exhaled a sigh of relief at the sight of two tiny kittens curled up together in a box.

"Okay, Billy, let's get you inside."

"No. I'm going to wait here for Mummy. She's going to get my Daddy."

Ana's eyes pricked again, and she thought for a moment, for anything she could use to entice Billy out of the car. "I think the kitties would like a drink. Can you come and help me?"

"No."

"How about we go in for something to eat in Uncle Blake's house."

"No."

She reached out and tried to take the little boy's hand, but he whimpered and backed into the corner and pulled the blanket over his head, drumming his heels on the floor of the car. Ana climbed into the back of the wagon, hitched Sienna's skirt down,

24

while racking her brain for any ideas to persuade him to get out of the car. She settled in next to Billy before gently lifting the blanket and peeking beneath it. He ignored her, playing his game intently with his little fingers flying over the touch screen.

"Oh no," exclaimed Ana. "Your iPad's running out of battery, do you think we'd better go inside and plug it in?"

"Oh yes . . . only nineteen left," he said. Billy clasped the iPad to his chest and slid out of the car past her, pushing the gate open just as Blake ran through the door with a worried look on his face.

"Oh, thank goodness, I just remembered Billy."

Ana swallowed a smile as she climbed out of the car and held up the cat box. "I found him—and Fred and Wilma."

Blake took Billy and a few of the larger bags inside and Ana went back to the car. It took her a few minutes to carry an assortment of soft bags, plastic crates, a portable cot and toys and put them on the front porch. It amazed her that Jeannie had been able to remember to pack all that after getting the phone call about her husband. All was quiet inside and she assumed that Blake was feeding the children in the kitchen. Ana slid the bags and crates into the living room off the formal entry and looked around at the room with admiration.

It was very different to the house they'd shared in Brisbane. No worn carpet and mismatched furniture. No smell of sweaty shoes and gym gear and basketballs. The perpetual chaos of their college house had driven Blake crazy and he'd spent much of his time picking up after everybody. The house was very different to the old house in Brisbane and the cottage-type interiors Ana preferred, but the minimalist decorating suited Blake. The pristine white leather lounges and the gleaming hardwood floors complemented each other. The soft afternoon light streaming in through the sheer blinds reflected off the glass sculpture on the large coffee table.

Blake came in from the back of the house, a harried look on his face. "Ana, I owe you big time. Thanks so much for unpacking the car." His gaze ran over the piles of bags and crates and she could have sworn he blanched.

What the hell was Blake going to do with five children, a dog, two cats—not to mention the goldfish she'd found in a large screw top jar in one of the crates—in a spectacular home like this? It was not a home for children to run wild in, and by the look of these kids, they were keen to get moving. She grinned at him and fought the chuckle that was rising in her throat. "I suggest you find one room and keep them contained, otherwise these five little whirlwinds and their assorted pets are going to put their stamp on your house very quickly."

"I'll cope with them the best I can. Jeannie needs me."

Ana hesitated. It wasn't the right time to talk about the store, and Blake still didn't seem to realise she was his four o'clock appointment. For the sake of old times, and their old friendship, the least she could do was help him out. And who knew, helping him might go towards softening him up when she found the right time to discuss business later.

"I'm sure you'll be fine," she said. "I remember you used to be able to cope with most things back in our uni days. I'll just go out and lock Jeannie's car."

Smothering a grin at the look on Blake's face, Ana turned to the door. Mr. Hot Shot CEO had disappeared. She had a feeling he was about to transform into Mr. Mum.

"You're not leaving?" He reached out and touched her arm and she ignored the flutters in her belly.

"No, I'm not leaving."

***

Relief coursed through Blake as Anastasia headed out to lock the car. She was staying and he would have someone to help, as well as have time to talk to her. If he'd heard her correctly in all

26

the confusion, she'd said *she* was his appointment. Could his secretary have messed up his calendar somehow? There was no way Anastasia was going anywhere until they had a talk and he found out why she'd turned up on his doorstep, all dressed up and sophisticated.

Before he could get his head around the situation, two small arms grabbed his legs.

"*Unca* Blake, it's bath time." He looked down at the earnest little face of his nephew and groaned. Billy's mouth and cheeks were smeared with peanut butter. Taking a small hand in his, he led his nephew into the family room and kept a hold on him while he scooped baby Jake up from the floor. He didn't want peanut butter—or baby poo— all over the house.

"Come on you guys, Billy says it's bath time." He headed upstairs, shaking his head as the small entourage of children followed him.

He felt like the Pied Piper.

I can deal with this. As long as Rod is okay.

But a frisson of excited anticipation curled in his stomach as he waited for Ana to come back inside.

Chapter Three

Ana spent a few minutes outside to gather her thoughts after she locked the car. She would help Blake out, just as she would for any of her friends, and her own needs would be set aside in the meantime. She looked in the kitchen after she came inside but there was no sign of anyone. The sound of children giggling drew her upstairs. A trail of clothes led to a large bathroom and she peeked around the open door. Blake had discarded his tie and stood next to the bath with his sleeves rolled up; water dripped from his hair onto his white business shirt. The black and white tiled floor was awash with soap suds and Blake ducked as a stream shot out at him from a water pistol which appeared from beneath a huge mound of bubbles in the centre of the bath.

He noticed her peering around the door and grinned. Her mouth dried at the sight of his unbuttoned shirt, dark hair peeking through the V, and his chest clearly outlined by the wet silk.

She cleared her throat. "What's going on here?"

A chorus of voices from the bathtub greeted her as four little heads popped up through the deep bubbles. Ana looked around the room curiously as she walked across the floor.

"Where's the baby?"

"Asleep. The poor little guy was exhausted, and he fell asleep on me when I lifted him out of the bath. He's wrapped in a dry towel and on the floor in my room. I didn't want to wake him."

Blake smiled at her, looking quite pleased with himself.

"I'll get the others out of the bath while you go down and get the portable cot. I don't know much about babies but I'm pretty sure they need to be dressed and not left asleep on the floor."

Blake shrugged as Ana reached over to slide a towel from the warming rack beside the bath. She slipped on the soapy floor and bumped into Blake's hard chest. He grabbed her arms to steady her and her cheek brushed the wet silk.

"Thank you." She straightened and pulled away before she stared at the wet shirt in front of her nose. "But why are you bathing the rest of the children?"

She fought another chuckle as he looked at her with confusion.

"They asked for a bath," Blake said.

"We love Uncle Blake's big deep tub," said Maddy. "Mummy let us swim last time we stayed here before Uncle Blake came home."

"Guess I got conned," he said softly as his gaze locked with hers.

The heat rose in her cheeks and she turned away and picked up a towel. "I'll get some of the bubbles off this lot. When you go down for the crib, dig out some clothes for them. I left the crates in the living room and then we'll get these children dressed and fed, including that poor bub."

She helped the children out of the bath one by one into the waiting towels. A pang of sadness pierced her chest as she looked down at the four shiny clean faces looking up at her expectantly. Her biological clock had gone past the ticking stage, it was ringing an alarm, but she'd never met anyone she wanted to have a family with.

She kneeled beside the children and pointed first to Madeleine.

"Now I know Maddy . . . is it okay if I call you that?"

A shy nod came in reply.

"And I know this is Billy. I need to know three more names and we're done." She rocked back on her feet with a smile and waited for the answer, but she was met with dead silence.

Tipping her head to the side, she pointed to the first twin and then turned her palms upward. "Do I have to guess?"

"Yep . . . but you never will," said the twin on the left.

29

"Come on then, we'll go down and get you dressed and if I haven't guessed by the time dinner is ready, you'll have to tell me." She looked seriously at the twins and held out one hand to each of them. "Deal?"

Two little hands shook hers vigorously.

Twenty minutes later, with Blake's assistance and after much giggling and sharing of clothes, the four children were dressed in their pyjamas. Ana was still going through the alphabet unsuccessfully guessing names and was up to Thaddeus, much to the mirth of the twin boys.

"Uncle Blake, you are going to have to introduce me to these children," she said with a smile.

Blake pointed at the twins and screwed his face up. "Benjamin and Broderick but answer to Benny and Roddy." His face broke into a huge smile and Ana's heart skipped a beat as he held her gaze. "But I never know which is which, or rather who is who, so you'll have to work that out for yourself. The baby is Jake, and you already know Maddy and Billy."

Ana looked over at the small girl who was sitting in the large, upholstered chair in the living room, legs tucked under her and reading her book. Reaching out to Blake, she gripped his arm and inclined her head towards Maddy. Blake casually strolled over and sat on the edge of the chair next to his niece as tears welled in the little girl's eyes.

"What will happen to Daddy if his . . . if his plane fell out of the sky?" She gave a little hiccough and looked up earnestly.

Ana's throat tightened. Her business problems were nothing compared to the possibility these children may have lost their father. She looked across at Blake waiting for him to answer.

"We don't know if Daddy's plane even went up in the sky. Mummy sent a message before saying they think it is broken down at the camp and they are going through the forest to rescue them." Her chest filled with warmth as he hugged the little girl.

"Like Dora and Diego," said Billy.

The three little boys looked at him and only the noise of the game blaring from Billy's iPad broke the silence until Blake nodded and replied, "That's right, Billy. Like Dora and Diego."

What a wonderful father he would make.

At that moment, Blake looked up and smiled at her. Ana's heart sank. He still had that killer grin that used to curl her toes and it was like those ten years had never happened. She looked away. No way was she going to complicate matters by falling for him all over again. There was a lot of water under the bridge since then and she'd moved on.

Once they'd fed the children and put them to bed, she'd tell him why she was here and then make another appointment to see him later in the week.

Blake's phone rang and he jumped up to get it from the table.

"Oh, hi, Mike. No, he didn't show. No message either." He glanced at Ana and mouthed an apology before continuing with the call. "Look, I can't talk at the moment, I have a bit of a family situation."

The heat rushed to Ana's face as she realised Blake was talking about her appointment. He obviously still hadn't realised what she'd said in the melee of noise and children.

"No, Mike, I'm not going to follow up. It doesn't matter anyway. I haven't even seen the figures for that side of the business. Something smells a bit off to me. The restoration department is definitely going to go."

Ana glanced at the children watching television and headed for the kitchen. She'd heard enough. Blake's voice followed her as she stood at the sink filling a glass with cold water.

Money . . . profit . . . mergers model . . . get rid of staff. The words confirmed her suspicions. He'd not changed a bit.

And he could still talk to his boss about all that while he was worried about his brother-in-law and taking care of five kids?

"Penny for your thoughts?" His quiet voice interrupted her brooding.

"I was thinking it's time to eat and then time for me to go home," she said tersely.

"It's Friday . . . it's pizza night," Billy claimed, as he walked into the kitchen behind his uncle.

Blake frowned at her before he reached out and took her hand between his. Her traitorous nerves tingled all the way to her shoulder.

"Where is home, Anastasia?" he asked quietly. "We will have to have a little talk after dinner, just you and me. We have a lot to catch up on." He turned to the children with a grin. "But now, I'm going to order in some pizza."

"Yes, we do." She pulled her hand from his and bent down to Billy. "Let's go and play a game while Uncle Blake gets dinner."

I don't know if it will ever be the right time to talk. She squared her shoulders as she followed Billy to the living room, ignoring the curious glance Blake threw her way.

But I'll give it my best shot when the time is right.

***

Two hours later after the pizza had been demolished, Blake sat back in the family room off the kitchen, looking out at the dog whose nose was pressed up against the once-clean glass sliding door. The sun had set, and the dog was whimpering.

"No way, boy. You're not coming into my house." The cleaning service would have their work cut out for them this week without adding dog hair to the mess.

The house had descended into chaos. Toys were strewn around the room; milk had been spilled on his sofa and he'd spent the last ten minutes retrieving pizza crusts from the floor.

Ana came in from the kitchen, untying the large apron he'd

found in a drawer for her. "Remember the old dog we had in the house for a while?" Her face lit up in a wicked grin and he tried to ignore the ache that tugged at the sensitive parts of his body. "He used to eat all the food scraps."

"*You* had the dog, not we." He remembered it well. Ana had found a stray on the way home from the coffee shop one afternoon and the smelly mutt had lived in her room for a few days before Blake had caught her sneaking it out to the garden one night. "And I also remember it didn't stay very long." Blake knew his voice was short, but he couldn't cope with the chaos in front of him and deal with memories from the past at the same time.

"I lost that argument, didn't I?" Ana turned away from him and threw the apron untidily over the back of the sofa. "If you let the dog in, he'll clean up this mess in seconds." His mouth tightened as the apron slipped to the floor and she seemed blissfully unaware of the growing mess. "No way. I hate animals inside," he said. "There has to be a broom or something around here."

"So you're going to make that poor dog stay outside in the cold all night?"

"Of course, it's staying outside. There's already drool in the car and it's bad enough that the kittens are inside."

A strange feeling ran through him as Ana shook her head. It was though he was being judged and found wanting.

"He's a he, not an 'it'. Animals have feelings just like us you know." She went over to the window, and a trail of drool slid down the glass as the dog moved across to the window where Ana was standing. "He looks all lonely out there."

Maddy looked up from her book. "He'll have to come inside. Mummy got him so he made sure Billy stayed safe."

"I'll make sure Billy is safe and besides it's . . . I mean his . . . claws would scratch the floor," Blake said firmly. It was his house, and he would make sure the children stayed safe.

33

Ana reached over the back of the sofa and tugged the blanket around Billy's feet. "And that would be the end of the world... for you anyway, Blake."

##

Having Ana in his house was surreal. She'd stepped in to help without a second thought and it was like the old days again. But with five children thrown in. They'd barely had time to exchange more than a few sentences. And most of hers reeked with disapproval, but Blake tried to ignore the uncomfortable feeling that held him.

He'd spent time with the kids, but he didn't know they were so demanding. Jeannie seemed to take it all in her stride with no obvious effort.

"The house looks way more welcoming with a bit of mess." Ana tipped her head to the side and watched him as he searched for a broom. "Looks almost like the old share house days. You'd have a fit if you saw my cottage."

"I'd love to come visit you." At last she'd opened up a little.

Ana laughed and shook her head. "Trust me, Blake. You wouldn't cope."

Her face was alight with amusement and he knew she'd been teasing him about the dog. Somehow, she'd always known how to push his buttons. And he had to admit even though his house was a mess tonight, it wasn't really that bad.

The smell of pizza wafting through the living room mixed with the clean, soapy smell of the children curled up on the soft chairs overlaid the air fresheners in the power outlets low on the wall. Benny and Roddy were asleep already, curled up head to head with their legs entwined. Maddy's eyelids were drooping as she snuggled back into the chair, both kittens nestled in her lap. Blake smiled as her hand caressed their backs in her half-asleep state. Only Billy was wide awake, engrossed in a game on his iPad.

34

"I think it's time to put that away and get some sleep, Billy," he said quietly. "Time for bed, hey buddy?"

"No."

Anastasia smiled down at him and put her finger to her lips. "Leave him. It's only seven o'clock."

Blake held her gaze for a long moment and smiled at her. She'd gone quiet on him for a while before dinner, but now she seemed more relaxed. He knew nothing about her life now, but she certainly knew what to do to help him.

"Do you have children, Ana?"

"No. I've had no time for that. I have a career." She chewed on her lip as she looked back at him and she seemed preoccupied.

"I'm going to check on Jake. He was still asleep, last time I went up. You really do have the touch, Blake. His clothes were all on the right way. After that I'll get going."

Panic filled him at the thought of being left alone with the children. He sat back in his chair and sipped on a can of Coke. He'd foregone the glass of red wine he had been looking forward to since he wanted his full wits about him with a houseful of nephews, a niece, dog, cats and fish.

"Oh, damn," he said and jumped out of the chair. He hadn't fed the dog, who was still peering in through the double glass door.

"Billy, what's your dog's name?" he asked as he walked past his nephew and ruffled his hair.

"Jaws," Billy replied without lifting his eyes or fingers from the iPad.

Stepping out the back porch, he turned the light on and groaned. Jaws was aptly named. Anything that was not secured to the ground or a part of the greenery had been chewed into bits and now the stupid mutt had the nerve to lick his hand and look up at him with soulful brown eyes.

"I guess it's my fault. I should have fed you earlier." Blake

35

pointed at the mess and spoke in a stern voice. "Did you do that? Just one more reason why you belong outside."

Jaws slunk away, tail between his legs while Blake filled the food bowl with some of the dog kibble Jeannie had packed.

Bless her, he thought, she'd even remembered to pack fish food in her hurry to leave for the airport. God, he hoped Rod was okay. A hollow ache settled in his chest. He knew the wilderness up there around the lodge. If the plane had gone down, it could be days before they found it. He wished he could be up there too, helping in the search, but he was needed here.

He thought his career was busy and used all his powers of creative thinking. But tonight he discovered that was nothing compared to feeding, bathing, and caring for five children and assorted pets.

He looked out over the twinkling lights of the canal. If he leaned across to the far edge of the porch, he could just see where the river joined the ocean.

The cedar door leading out to the balcony creaked and the musky fragrance of Anastasia's perfume wafted across to him. He turned and held out his hand, but she ignored it and moved to the other side of the post he was leaning against.

"Jake is still asleep," she said softly. "He stirred a little, but I patted him and he went straight back off." She laughed. "He's out like a light."

Blake didn't answer immediately, surprised by the relief that coursed through him. He stood there trying to think of the best way to ask her to stay longer. There was no way he could cope with this by himself. Having her close by felt so natural and they had eased into a comfortable truce, despite the way they'd left things years ago. He tried to block out the way she had disappeared so suddenly since Ana didn't seem inclined to discuss it.

"Is there anyone you have to go home to?" He waited for her to answer, his stomach clenching as he waited for her to say

36

there was. With her looks and sweet personality, he would be very surprised if she didn't have a partner. They'd argued incessantly when they shared the house, but he hadn't realised how much she'd meant to him until she'd left

But no matter what her situation was, things had never been resolved between them and now he was about to call on her good nature again.

"No," she said slowly. "I live alone."

His mind whirled and his fingers itched to do a high five.

She was still single? Things were looking up.

"Will you stay the night?" He blurted it out and closed his eyes realising what he'd just asked. "Look, I don't mean that like it sounded." He reached over and took her hand, surprised by the tension in her body. "I hoped you could help me with the children overnight. I know it's not your responsibility and I know we haven't had a chance to talk. But I just want to tell you how happy I am that you sought me out and came to visit. Once we get the kids to bed, we can do some catching up.

She opened her mouth to reply but he interrupted her before she could speak.

"Honestly, Anastasia. I can't do this alone. I can run a corporation, but this situation has got me terrified. There's no one else I can call on such short notice."

She stood there looking uneasy but didn't reply and he wondered whether she was thinking about that last night they'd spent together.

"Look, I know I must have upset you somehow that last night—"

She shook her head. "No, it's got nothing to do with that. Look, I've been trying to find the right time to tell you why I'm here –"

Before she could finish, Blake's mobile pinged on the kitchen counter. He hurried inside, to read the message then ran back out to the porch to Ana.

"Fantastic news. They've found the plane and they're all okay. Jeannie is still in Cairns but she's flying out to the lodge. Apparently, the plane bucked on the runway when they were taking off. Rod has a broken leg and that's the worst of it."

"Thank God." She came over and hugged him. He put his arms around her, and her soft hair brushed against his lips. He closed his eyes as that familiar fragrance took him back ten years.

"It's a relief. The kids'll be gone, and I can concentrate on business," he said.

Disappointment filled him as Ana stiffened and dropped her arms.

"I'll help you out tonight, but I'll have to leave first thing in the morning. I've got Sunday off, so I can come back tomorrow night and help you out for one more day if you really need me to." She looked up at him, biting her lip. Her brow was creased, and she ran her hand through her hair. "If Jeannie isn't back by then you'll have to make other arrangements, because that's all I can do, Blake."

"Can you leave me your mobile number . . . just in case I have an emergency?" he asked.

She went into the kitchen and wrote it on the small message board on the wall next to the fridge. The overhead light reflected on her silver-blonde hair and he had an urge to run his fingers through the soft strands.

She came back out on the porch with an expression that was almost sad. "Happy, now?" She looked up at him "I thought turning into an important businessman would have taught you how to keep a poker face. I won't run away again, Blake." He gave in to his desire and reached out for her, but she stepped back.

Confusion filled him as he watched her walk into the house. Maybe he was moving too quickly. She'd withdrawn into herself and he didn't have a clue what he'd done to cause it.

***

Ana showered quickly and dressed in the guest bathroom downstairs, pulling on the long T-shirt Blake had found for her. She put the soft white cotton up to her nose and inhaled the clean soapy smell of his shirt. She knew it had been freshly laundered, but she kidded herself that she could still smell Blake's masculine aroma in the soft fibres.

She tugged the T-shirt down as far as it would go and then returned to the family room. The children were all asleep on the soft chairs, including Billy, who had his iPad tucked under his knees. They'd decided to leave them there and not risk disturbing them while they were sleeping.

"Poor little things," she said. "It'll be so good to let them know their daddy is okay when they wake up."

Blake was curled up in a recliner, watching over them with a football game turned low in the background. "So you're a football fan now?" She tugged self-consciously at the T-shirt as he turned to face her.

Her stomach fluttered as he held her gaze before he replied with a laugh. "What choice did I have? I got hooked into watching it because that was all that was on the TV when you lived in the share house."

"I don't remember you watching it. You never used to come to the games with us."

"You were just focused on your beloved Broncos." His eyes didn't leave hers. "When you weren't watching the game, you were doing your cheer leader routine around the living room."

Ana had forgotten about the silly things she'd done in the share house days. Life had become too serious too quickly when Mum's condition had deteriorated. "Do you want a coffee or anything before I go upstairs? I have to go to the kitchen to make up a couple of bottles." She laughed nervously. "Jake's bound to

39

wake up soon and he's going to be starving when he does."

"Yes, please." He didn't take his gaze off her and she turned into the kitchen as the heat ran up her neck.

"Still lots of cream and one sugar?"

His laugh followed her. "Black, no cream. Watching the arteries. I spend too much time at a desk these days."

She carried a tray back out with his coffee, along with two baby bottles in a warmer, ready for when Jake woke up, and a cup of peppermint tea for herself. She handed him his coffee.

"Still drinking the hippy stuff?" Blake gestured to her cup.

"I was pleased to see it in your cupboard," she replied.

"Habit." He shrugged. "Jeannie's started drinking it so now I always keep it on hand.

Ana picked up the tray and walked to the door, pausing before she headed for the stairs. For a moment, she considered raising the real reason she was here before she went up to the baby. But when she looked across at Blake, he'd dropped his head into his hands. He'd done that in college when he was stressed. Worry was etched into his forehead and he closed his eyes. It would have been wonderful, if she could have gone over to him and held him to comfort him.

Don't go there. Not the right time. For talk or comfort.

"I'll look after Jake through the night."

He lifted his head, and his forehead cleared as he smiled at her. "Good night, Ana. And . . . thanks. I really appreciate it. I'm sure this was the last thing you expected when you called in."

She walked slowly up the stairs, reluctant to leave him alone, but Jake would be awake soon and besides, she was here for business, nothing more, and she had to put her old feelings aside. Blake had the same effect on her as he had all those years ago and she didn't like that one bit. Playing happy families and looking after the kids had brought them together quickly, but she knew it was a false scenario. She *had* to talk to him about the business before the end of the week. And as soon as she raised the issues she had with the takeover, Ana just knew they would have a raging argument. Her business philosophies had firmed over the years just as Blake's had. She'd read the interview in the newspaper with dismay. He was harder now in his attitude than he had been when they'd argued back at uni. And she'd heard his response to his boss on the phone earlier.

Maybe it would be easier if she just left the store before he even knew that she was one of his employees.

No.

She stiffened her spine.

Don't go there.

She was here to convince Blake there *was* a place for a restoration department in the new store. It was needed in Maleny, no matter how modern he wanted the store to be or how much money he wanted to make for his company.

The baby's cry was a blessed interruption to her thoughts, and she hurried into the spare bedroom with a bottle. She bent down to scoop little Jake out of the portable cot and laid him down on the bed to change his nappy.

Five minutes later, she was sitting in the alcove of the bay window, with a clean, sweet smelling baby sucking contentedly on a bottle.

Nothing to it.

She gazed out over the canal and mulled over her dilemma once more, her eyelids getting heavy, as she snuggled the baby to her chest. She shut her eyes just for a brief moment . . .

***

Blake turned the television off and leaned over each sleeping child, tucking them under their light blankets. It was a mild night but he had left the air conditioning on low so the house would stay warm. He lifted the kittens off Maddy's lap and took them into the kitchen for a saucer of milk, before checking on the disgraced dog that was now curled up on a seat on the back landing. Now that he'd been fed, he'd stopped chewing everything in sight.

Although Blake thought as he looked around the demolished garden, there was nothing much left for the dog to chew. He picked up a garbage bag from the laundry room and wandered around the small garden collecting half-chewed pieces of assorted sticks and garden tools. Cursing as he stubbed his toe on a broken stick, he gave up and left the rest of the mess for the morning. He locked the back door, checked his phone for messages and then walked quietly up the stairs to check on Anastasia and Jake.

That's all I'm doing. Just making sure they're okay.
Yeah, sure it is.
Admit it. You just want to look at her and be with her.

He'd met many women over the past ten years and had a couple of half-hearted relationships, but no one had ever fired that same spark Anastasia had lit in him.

Now he wanted to know all about her. Find out about her life, where she lived, what she did. If there was a chance of them renewing their friendship, he was not going to let her slip away this time. His work just didn't satisfy him anymore. Even the thought of another new store hadn't motivated him this time. He was more excited about his move back to the Sunshine Coast. Ana walking in from the street had given him lots to think about.

Once Blake set his mind on a path, there was no stopping him until he achieved his goal. That was the way he ran his businesses and Anastasia was now firmly in his sights.

He tapped lightly on the door of the guest bedroom, but there was no answer. He opened it and poked his head in. Jake was sound asleep in the crib but there was no sign of Ana. After checking the other bedrooms, concern rippled through him.

Jeez, man, that's what you get for indulging in daydreams.

He ran quietly down the stairs, his mind working furiously.

Where the hell had she gone?

He unlocked the front door, heaving a sigh of relief when he saw the red BMW parked on the road. Resting his head against the door jamb, he took a deep breath in an attempt to calm down. He locked the door and set off on a search of the house from top to bottom. He was just checking the guest bathroom downstairs when Jake's loud cry came from upstairs. Taking the stairs two at a time, he ran along the top hall and pushed open the door of the guest bedroom where the empty cot had been. The cries got louder as he stood at the door and he could hear Ana's soft voice.

"It's okay, Jakey. Your Mummy will be back soon." There was silence for a moment and then a loud sucking sound filled the room. He tapped on the door and pushed it open. Anastasia was sitting in the bay window tucked into the large cushions and the swag curtains at the side half-obscured his view of her.

"Anastasia? Is everything okay?"

"Come in. He's just having his second bottle. I was in the bathroom when he woke up."

Blake looked down sheepishly and decided to be honest.

"What's wrong, Blake? Are the children okay?" Her voice rose and a worried expression crossed her face. "Is your brother-in-law okay?"

Staring at her, he pulled his hand though his hair and looked over her head through the window.

"I couldn't find you," he said quietly. "I thought you'd . . . left . . . again."

"And what about little Jake?" Her voice was sarcastic. "What did you think I was going to do with him? Leave him by himself and not tell you?"

"Of course not—"

"Well, we're fine up here. So you can go back down to the other children." Her voice was cold. "I'll be leaving at five a.m. I

43

have to start work early and I need to go home and get changed first."

He couldn't help himself, reaching over and lifting her chin before he changed his mind. "Where's home, Anastasia?"

"None of your damned business and for the record, I go by Ana now. So you can either call me that or Ms. Delaney." She pulled her chin out of his grip and turned her head away. "Good night, Blake. Close the door on your way out."

Chapter Four

The house was quiet when Ana tried to slip out quietly without waking anyone, including Blake. She jumped when a warm hand grasped her elbow as she reached for the front door. She turned to face Blake; his hair was sleep-tousled and his eyes were bleary. Even half asleep, he still oozed sex appeal and her heart rate kicked when he touched her, his fingers sliding down to gently encircle her wrist.

"I'm sorry I thought the worst last night. You were such a great help." Blake reached over and tucked a loose strand of hair behind her ear and she pulled away from his touch. "I owe you big time. There's no way I could have done it alone."

Let me keep my job.

She pushed the thought from her mind and decided an apology was in order.

"I'm sorry for snapping at you." Ana stared at him ignoring the warmth that stayed on her cheek where his fingers had brushed her skin. "We were both tired and you had no idea why I had to leave last time. I would never have left you with the children without letting you know I'd gone. Last time I had no choice." Her voice shook and tears pricked the backs of her eyes as she remembered the grief that had consumed her on that morning ten years ago. Seeing Blake had brought it all back. "I'll be back in the late afternoon . . . that is . . . if you still think you need me?"

"Oh yes, please. If it wasn't for the baby, I could probably manage but—"

"I'll be back," she interrupted. "Now, I'm late, so I'll see you this afternoon."

She reached down for the still damp shoes and when she straightened, Blake slid his other arm around her waist and held her before she could pull away.

"Thank you," he said softly. "I'm not going to let you get away so easily this time."

Ana tried to step back but he held her close, and a tremble ran through her as she looked up and saw the intent in his eyes. Her eyes stayed fixed on his as he slowly lowered his lips to hers and claimed her mouth in a gentle kiss.

For a moment, she closed her eyes and gave in to the feelings surging through her before she pulled back with a jerky movement.

What the hell am I doing?

"And that's a promise. Once things settle down, I'd like to renew our . . . acquaintance. I missed you, Ana.' Blake smiled down at her. "What are you working on today?"

"Just going to do my job. I have had a pretty boring life, Blake. I've stayed around here. Nothing like you. Cairns, Melbourne, Singapore." Heat surged into her cheeks as she realised she'd let slip that she'd kept tabs on his life. "Or at least that's what one of the papers said last week." She quickly covered her slip/

Ana ran down the stairs and opened the gate and didn't look back at him until she was safely in her car away from his touch. He waved and turned back into the house.

##

Ana pressed down hard on the accelerator after she turned onto the Sunshine Motorway. The feel of Blake's lips lingered on hers and she brushed her mouth with the back of her knuckles.

Why did he have to kiss me?

She'd left the house before it was light and, now that the sun had risen, she'd decided to take the coastal route home. She was heading off to a job later in the morning and had more time than she'd let on to Blake—she'd just needed to get out of the house before she blurted out to him why she was there. She needed to think more about how she was going to approach the discussion about the takeover now that they'd renewed their acquaintance on a more personal level. It was nothing like the meeting she'd planned.

Thirty minutes later, Ana cursed as she came upon roadwork at Mooloolaba. The M1 would have been the better choice but she'd needed the scenery and salt air to help clear her head. Longing for a coffee, she pulled to a stop to settle in for a lengthy wait. Closing her eyes for a moment, she put her fingers up to her lips and took a deep breath trying to block Blake—and that brief kiss—from her thoughts. Their current restoration job had to be finished up today and the last of the fine plaster work would take all of her concentration.

Ha, she thought. *You've got no chance.*

Her reaction to him was based purely on the memory of that one night and it was well known that a girl held a soft spot for her first lover.

That's all it is.

The fact that he was going to close down her department was much more complicated than any old feelings that may resurface. That was the big problem and the one she had to deal with first.

"Sienna, this moulding is perfect." Ana climbed down from the stepladder and tucked her hair behind her ear.

"Yes, I knew it would be as soon as I saw it at the store." Sienna stood back and surveyed Ana's work. "Just as well the Bennetts were happy to pay the extra. You're done and it looks great." She turned and pointed to the balcony that ran off the huge living room they were working in. "Georgie's got the coffee ready. You've got time for one now."

Ana had avoided taking a break all day because she knew the girls would be keen to know how her meeting with Blake had turned out. Working had been a convenient excuse since they'd already run over the contracted deadline for the job and promised the owners they'd be finished today. Reluctantly she pulled off her work gloves and removed her cap, shaking the rest of her hair free. No matter how hard she tried, she always managed to get plaster bits stuck in her hair.

The aroma of the much needed coffee drew her over to the worktable where her two best friends sat on upturned buckets on the balcony. The view over the ocean was spectacular as the morning sun dispersed the last fingers of sea mist lingering over the silvery surface of the water.

Sienna couldn't sit still and was trimming a piece of plaster. Georgie sat with her chin propped in her hand, her auburn curls tumbling down her shoulders as she stared out through the French doors at the ocean.

"Looks like the weather's turned for the better. That was a good storm we had yesterday." Ana closed her eyes and savoured the coffee. Wherever they worked, Georgie carried her coffeemaker and provided them with the best coffee. They were a great team and there was no way she was going to let it end just because a corporation had bought the store out.

"Forget the weather, Ana. Tell us what happened. Are we unemployed?" Sienna tapped her foot impatiently on the tiles that they had installed on the balcony a couple of weeks earlier and stared at her. "How much longer are you going to keep us hanging here?"

Ana looked away from Sienna and followed Georgie's gaze out over the ocean.

"Okay, girls, you've both have been so patient all morning and you've worked so hard to get this place finished. Once we pack up the gear, the store can bill this one out." Ana sighed and looked around the house. "I'll be sorry to leave this job. It's one of the best we've had."

Sienna stood and came around to where Ana was perched

48

on the upturned bucket.

She placed her hands on Ana's shoulders and stood there until Ana looked up at her. Sienna's hair was black and cropped short in a pixie cut. Even though they were in work clothes, her face was beautifully made up, and a bright scarf fell softly from her shoulders over her work T-shirt. But there was nothing soft about her gaze.

"Ana, spill. What the hell happened?" She stepped back and folded her arms, staring hard at Ana. Georgie turned away from looking at the ocean and sat back with an expectant look.

"Well . . . I don't exactly know yet," Ana replied slowly.

"What did he say? Is he likely to change his mind?" Sienna was persistent.

"I didn't exactly . . . er . . . get to tell him."

"Jeez, Ana. You're always too nice." Sienna tapped her hands on her arms and frowned. "What happened?"

Ana picked up her spoon and drew patterns in the fine plaster dust on the table. "That's why I don't want to go into business ourselves. You both know I'm no good at dealing with people. I'd much rather just do the work."

"There's something not quite right here." Georgie spoke for the first time and her voice was soft.

Georgie knew her all too well. She was intuitive and sensitive to feelings, whereas Sienna would crash over anyone who stood in her way. All Georgie wanted was a house and family of her own and she'd been looking for Mr. Right for years. Ana smiled as she thought of the number of times they'd heard Georgie say 'he's the one,' only to pick herself up and move on again when she was disappointed.

"I didn't get a chance to talk about the store and our work. I'm going back there to see him again tonight."

"Jeez, don't tell me Mr. Big Shot made a move on you?" Georgie's face lit up in an interested grin. "Is he a hunk? Did you go out for dinner?"

"He had a bit of a family emergency and I helped him out, that's all."

Sienna rolled her eyes. "And knowing you, Ana, you wouldn't have brought up any business to rock the boat." She stood up and gathered the cups. "I'm coming back with you tonight. Our jobs are at stake here, girlfriend, and you need to toughen up."

Ana stood next to Sienna and kept her voice firm. "No. I'll handle it. Trust me. I know what's at stake." She turned and gestured to the tools and plaster buckets lying around. "Now if we don't get this mess cleaned up, we won't have a job to fight for. Oh, and Sienna?" She grinned as Sienna frowned at her. "Can I borrow your car again? You were right, it's much faster than mine."

Sienna and Georgie packed up the worktable and tools, and carried them out to Ana's ute, loading it up while she wiped the floor to remove the last of the plaster dust. Her phone beeped in her pocket and she smiled as she pulled it out and read the short message.

Be quick. Bring food and iPad charger.

Sounded like Mr. Hot Shot CEO needed help . . . and fast.

***

Blake held Jake tucked under one arm as he tripped over a kitten and then bumped his hip on a table that shouldn't have been in his path. The twins had spent the afternoon sliding down the hallway in their socks and it had been easier to move the table out of harm's way, rather than getting them to stop. Billy had been sitting upside down on the corner of the sofa drumming his heels against the wall and squealing since his iPad had run out of charge hours ago.

Well, it'd seemed like hours.

Blake had turned the damn house upside down looking for

the charger— it seemed to be the only thing Jeannie had forgotten to pack. Toys, clothes, and half-chewed cookies covered the floor from the foyer to the kitchen. His house was starting to look very different.

And the smell.

Blake headed for the bathroom to do something about the revolting mess that was in Jake's nappy, praying that Ana was on her way.

"Maddy, if Anastasia comes to the door, can you please let her in? But no one else, okay?"

"Okay, Uncle Blake."

At least the twins were watching cartoons on the Disney channel. *The Octonauts and Baby Shark* had kept them entertained on and off all day—over and over and over— and he'd barely had time for even a twinge of guilt about the junk food he'd fed them. One day of biscuits and chips wouldn't stunt their growth, surely? Thank God Ana was going to be here soon to help him out He had tried calling every nanny service in the area, but it seemed you had to book weeks ahead for five kids.

He had to be at the store on Friday to do the handover. Surely Jeannie would be back by then. Mike was coming up from Melbourne and it was a huge deal.

Oh shit, he was supposed to be having dinner with him tomorrow night.

He ran a shallow bath and turned his head away as he stripped the baby down.

As he scrubbed Jake, Blake thought of Anastasia . . . or Ana if that's what she wanted to be called now. He owed her so much for helping him.

He was pleased she had sought him out. Even though he was the one who'd put their friendship at risk that night years ago, when he'd first kissed her, he'd been the one who got hurt when she'd ditched him the next morning. But last night the spark had rekindled between them and he hoped she was feeling it too.

Why did she come and see me?

Was it to do with his money or just for old time's sake? She looked like she'd done okay in whatever her career was. The suit and the BMW pointed to success, and she'd said she was single so there wasn't a wealthy husband in the background.

Maybe a divorce settlement?

And he'd kissed her before his brain had kicked into gear. He needed to find out all about her before he got sucked in.

"Come on, little guy. We'll get you dried off, dressed and fed and then you can fill that diaper again."

He lifted the slippery child out of the soap suds and grinned. Maybe he could get the hang of this kid thing.

***

All the way to the coast, Ana practised her pitch to Blake but any thoughts of speaking to him tonight about job security for their team disappeared when she stepped from the car. Muted screaming drifted out through the open windows. She grabbed the grocery bags, hitched her small backpack onto her shoulders, and headed quickly through the gate. The closer she got, the louder the cries became, and she realised it wasn't the baby. Her well-rehearsed speech and business plans fled from her mind as she moved the bags to one hand and pushed the buzzer. She waited for a couple of minutes before she pounded on the door.

Eventually a quiet little voice came from the other side. "Who is it?"

"It's   Ana.   Let   me   in,   Maddy."

"No, Uncle Blake said only Anastasia." The little girl's voice was firm. "What's the password?"

"What   password?   Where's   Uncle   Blake?"

"The password to get into the castle."

"Is Uncle Blake there? And who's crying?"

"Uncle Blake is up in the bathroom and Billy is crying."

"Can you please let me in? I am Anastasia." Ana put the bags down. She could see Maddy's silhouette through the opaque glass. "Why is Billy crying?"

"You're not Anastasia, you said you were Ana. And Billy's crying 'cause he's hurting."

Visions of blood and cut fingers filled her mind. If Blake was upstairs, the children could have gotten into anything. Every childhood accident she'd ever read about, kids putting cutlery into power outlets and getting into kitchen knife blocks flashed through her mind. God, what about all the poisonous detergents and stuff in the cupboards? They hadn't even thought about childproofing his house.

"Maddy, you have to let me in. Where is Billy hurting?"

"What's the password?" Maddy repeated. The door stayed firmly closed.

Ana pulled out her phone and scrolled through her contacts before she recalled she never asked Blake for his number. Then she remembered the text he'd sent earlier today, opened the message and pressed call.

The little figure disappeared from the other side of the glass. "Uncle Blake, your phone's ringing," Maddy called out.

Ana leaned against the door as Blake answered.

Thank God.

"Hello? Anast—I mean Ana. How long till—"

"Blake I'm at the door and I can't get in without a password."

"What . . . oh . . . okay, I'm on my way down."

It was only seconds before Blake appeared through the glass and opened the door. He stood there with a dripping wet and naked baby in his arms. She shoved past him, leaving the bags on the porch. His hair was tousled, and his T-shirt was soaking wet, but he was still smiling despite the screams coming from the living room.

"Is Billy hurt?" she asked urgently as she ran through the door.

Maddy was sitting primly on the sofa reading a book and didn't look up as Ana flew past, following the noisy cries to the large white sofa in the corner of the room. She kneeled down and glanced back at Blake who was close behind her.

"It's all right," he said hitching Jake up onto his shoulder. His wet T-shirt was plastered to the well-defined muscles on his chest and she was upset with herself for noticing, despite her concern for Billy. "He's not hurt," Blake reassured her.

The little boy was in the corner with a blanket over his head. Ana reached in gingerly and lifted it. The cries subsided for a moment and a tear-streaked little face looked back at her.

"Did you bring the iPad plug?" he asked.

She nodded and he smiled, before pulling the blanket back over his head. "Go and plug it in now and fix the fire fish," he said. "Please."

Ana stood up slowly and turned to Blake. The expression on his face was priceless. Both the suave businessman looks, and the sexily tousled man of this morning had been replaced with a harried face decorated with a blob of ketchup or something red above his right eye, and if she wasn't mistaken that was baby poop down the front of his T-shirt.

"Welcome to my day," he said as she fought the laughter bubbling up from her chest.

***

Blake watched as Ana pulled the iPad charger out of the large bag, led Billy over to the power outlet, and plugged it in. Billy sat down as though to settle in and watch it charge. His admiration for Ana grew as she took the little boy's hand and led him over to the twins and whispered quietly in his ear. He climbed happily onto the sofa.

She was casually dressed in a pair of loose cotton pants and

54

a cropped T-shirt which hugged her small, high breasts, and her hair was pulled back into a high ponytail. She looked like a teenager, more like the Anastasia he'd known ten years ago. Her slim body was toned, and he wondered if she worked out to keep herself fit. He knew nothing about her life now and wanted to know all about her. Needed to know. What she did, where she lived and if they could be . . . friends again.

At least friends. The last ten years had passed so quickly, but damn it, he was fascinated by her. It was as though his life in that time, had disappeared in a puff of smoke.

She cleared her throat and he realised he'd been caught staring at her. His cheeks heated and he quickly thought of a way to cover up his wandering thoughts.

"How did you persuade him to watch television?" He inclined his head to Billy, now happily snuggled between his two older siblings.

"I said I'd fix the fire fish on the iPad."

"The what?"

"Do you think he is on the computer a little too much? Or are we just spoiling him because of the situation?" Ana frowned and twirled her fingers through her ponytail. "Anyway, the fire fish is 'wireless'. He wants me to turn the wireless on. He showed me the settings folder and it needs a password! Can you believe it? How old is he? Four?"

Blake looked over at his nephew whose eyelids were now getting heavy. He had made a fort out of the sofa cushions and only his little head was visible. A surge of love rushed through his chest and he turned to Ana.

"Billy is special...or to put it in the right terminology—he's on the autism spectrum. He has the iPad for speech therapy and learning his letters, but I think we are getting conned a bit because I know there are rules about when he can play games and I'm pretty sure Jeannie leaves the Wi Fi turned off."

Ana looked back at him and wrinkled her nose and he wondered what she was going to say. She had handled Billy so well. Come to think of it, all five children had responded to her gentle, caring way. Surely, she wasn't intimidated now that she knew Billy had special needs. But a slow smile spread across her face and he waited for her to speak.

"Blake, do you know you have baby poop all over your shirt?"

"Oh, Jeez." He looked down and pulled the shirt over his head, taking care to hold the offending piece of fabric well away from his face. He turned to her and this time it was him that caught her checking *him* out. Or rather checking his abs out.

"I'm going for a shower, want to come and wash my back?" He kept his voice light as he teased her.

She lifted her head and held his gaze.

"Maddy can cook dinner. You go and start, and I'll be up in a moment," she deadpanned.

For one brief moment his heart skittered and then he burst out laughing.

"Still got your sense of humour, I see, Anast—Ana."

"It's okay, I'll answer to either. Call me whatever suits you." She smiled at him and headed for the family room. He stood for a moment, watching her as she entered into some serious negotiations with the boys about eating vegetables for dinner. It was going to be a very interesting weekend.

Chapter Five

"No, no, no." Billy slipped down from the chair and crawled beneath the table. Ana bit back a smile as Blake ran his hand through his hair. It had been sexily mussed since the children had arrived, and the neat and well-dressed businessman had been replaced by a harried uncle in jeans and a stained T-shirt. He was looking even more casual than he had back in their college days.

Billy had spent the first half of the meal refusing to eat, until Maddy pointed out that his vegetables were in the wrong order. As Roddy and Benny scarfed down their dinner to get to their dessert, Ana had rearranged Billy's vegetables until she'd hit on the right sequence of colours.

"Orange, white, orange, green." Ana turned to Blake. "You'd better write that down."

After dinner, they'd bathed the children together and Jake had obliged by going to sleep without any fuss.

Blake had grinned at her as a squirt from Benny's water pistol had soaked her shirt.

"At least I have a change of clothes with me tonight," she said. Then heat surged into her cheeks as she realised the clear outline of her nipples was visible through the wet cotton and Blake was taking in the view.

Ana folded her arms across her chest and frowned at him. "It's your turn to dry and dress them tonight."

"Spoilsport." Blake held her gaze and Ana was the first to look away.

Once they were dressed, the children settled in to watch *Octonauts*—again—and Jake woke for a quick feed. Ana tidied up the kitchen after she gave him the bottle, and Blake wandered in from the family room. He sat on a stool at the breakfast bar and Ana concentrated on rinsing the dishcloth, aware of him watching her, until he laid his head on his crossed forearms on the counter.

"You look exhausted." She wiped down the kitchen sink one last time and hung the cloth over the faucet. "I'll finish up here."

"I am," he said. "I don't know how Jeannie does it by herself. Rod spends a lot of time travelling to farms out in the western district, and she runs a web design business from home, too." Blake lifted his head from his arms and smothered a yawn.

"Superwoman," Ana replied. "How about a coffee?"

"Great. Now that it's finally quiet . . . and tidy—" Blake grinned at her and something tugged in her lower belly— "we can finally catch up. You can tell me all about your life."

"I'd probably bore you to tears. Not a lot to tell. I didn't finish uni and I stayed in my hometown."

He glanced at her with a frown. "You were never boring. Besides you need to tell me why you had that appointment with me yesterday?"

Ana gestured around the room and changed the subject ignoring his question. When they sat down with their coffee, she would come clean and tell him why she was here. "Did I tell you how much I love your house?"

Ana looked away, pretending to examine the kitchen. Actually it was worth looking at and piqued her designer interest. Brightly coloured tiles edged the huge bay window which hung over the kitchen sink and looked out over the small balcony and garden edging the canal. If she leaned forward, she could just get a glimpse of the sky too.

"I had it built when I knew I was coming home." Blake had slipped silently from the stool and moved to stand next to her. Ana turned and his broad chest filled her vision. Her fingertips began to tingle as the urge to run her fingers over the smooth fabric, over his well-toned muscles filled her. She raised her hand and took a step back, but Blake followed her, his warm masculine aroma filling her senses.

He placed his hands gently on her shoulders and she held his gaze, warmth shooting low in her belly again as his lips turned up in a sexy smile. Gradually the pressure of his fingers increased, and he pulled her closer to him.

"I'm back to stay, you know. I didn't know what I was missing out on until I came back home." He held her gaze and Ana gave in, lifting her hands to run her palms across his chest.

The warmth moved up to her chest when he drew in a quick breath as her fingers ran over the soft fabric.

"And now that we've reconnected there's even more incentive to stay here." His voice was husky, and she lowered her eyes to rest on his lips. Grasping his T-shirt between her fists she tried to fight the hunger that was overtaking her. She couldn't let this physical attraction to him get out of hand. Not until he knew the real reason for her visit. She had to convince him how valuable their business was to the store—and the community of Maleny—before anything could happen between them that would only complicate matters even more.

Her stomach churned at the thought even as his lips hovered above hers and her mind whirled in turmoil. Should she just blurt it all out?

"Oh and by the way, Blake . . . you hold my future and that of my two best friends in your hands."

If he ran a business the way he'd talked at university, the way she'd read in the papers, their jobs wouldn't matter a hoot to him if they stood in the way of profit. Even if she was sleeping with him.

"I stuck with all those ideas I had ten years ago." His warm breath puffed on her lips as his mouth moved closer to hers.

"What?" Ana squawked out the single word and tipped her head back and looked up at him as his eyes stayed locked on hers.

What was he, a mind reader?

"Building this house. It's what I used to imagine as the perfect house when we lived in that old house on the river at Toowong.'

"Oh, the house." She let go of the breath she'd been holding, and he looked down at her curiously.

"What did you think I was talking about?"

"Nothing." She stepped out of his arms and moved across to the coffeemaker, trying to steady her hands so he couldn't see how much his nearness threw her. "I found a job where I can make a difference in people's lives." She held the coffeepot under the tap. "And the community benefits from my work."

Blake moved back to the stool and she was conscious of his eyes on her as she sought the right words. Tangling with him on a sexual level was the last thing she'd expected when she'd driven here yesterday. The hard-headed businessman had morphed into the sexy man who now had his smouldering gaze locked on her. It was so hard to reconcile this Blake with the CEO of a company who was about to destroy not only her life, but that of the community as well.

But then the sexy smile turned to a cynical laugh. "Don't tell me you are still a soft touch for anyone who comes begging, Ana? Or have you become a social worker?"

Cold iced her veins and she welcomed the anger that filled her.

"Yes, Blake. I'm still a soft touch." She would not let her feelings take over what she had to say to him. "And I'm proud of it. I told you I was your four o'clock appointment yesterday, so you go figure that out." She switched the coffeemaker on and walked to the door trying to put as much distance between them as possible. "Once Jeannie's back, I'll make another appointment and we can have a business discussion without all this." She waved her hand in the air but almost gave in as his face filled with disappointment.

60

Remember, hard-headed businessman.

"I'm going to sit with the children for a while, and then I'm going to bed."

"Thanks for making the coffee." Blake's face closed and he nodded at her. "I'll see you in the morning."

##

The problems filling her mind kept Ana awake and finally she crept back out to the kitchen. All was quiet and dark, and she poured a coffee taking it outside onto the back porch before settling into the double swing. Jaws jumped up next to her and she smiled. She ran her fingers through his soft fur as he placed his head in her lap. He was simply one more example of how she and Blake were so different.

She leaned back and closed her eyes, trying to focus on the sounds of the night and to calm the thoughts scurrying around in her head. A soft shower of summer rain had just passed by and the muted croaking of frogs drifted up from the back of the garden. Ana sighed and leaned her head back.

There were so many different arguments she could use to try to convince Blake. Even though she'd seen a softer side to him as he cared for the children, she was sure the businessman wasn't far away. He had to be hard to do the sort of takeovers he did, where layoffs were a given and people lost their livelihoods.

Eventually she pushed Jaws gently off her lap and headed upstairs to bed. A little voice muttering caught her attention before she reached the top of the landing, and she turned toward the bedroom where the children were sleeping. She stood in the doorway, but the voice came from behind her in Blake's room. The door was wide open, and she stepped quietly to the entrance. Before she could tap on the door, the little voice muttered again, and she leaned forward to peek in.

Blake was sound asleep, the sheet covering him from his waist down. His arms were around Billy who was nestled into his

61

uncle's chest with one little hand tightly gripping the fabric of Blake's T-shirt. As she watched, Billy muttered in his sleep again and she stepped back quickly out of sight as Blake made a soothing sound.

Ana's chest closed and she hitched a breath as tears pricked the back of her eyelids. Maybe, just maybe if Mum hadn't got sick, she and Blake may have made a life together and he could have been holding their child.

She knew she was reading too much into their one night together, but damn it, all the feelings she'd had for him ten years ago had come rushing back and overwhelmed her.

Brushing her eyes impatiently, she tiptoed back to the guest room, before looking down into the crib at baby Jake who was sleeping soundly. Slipping off her robe, she climbed into bed and shook her head. If anyone had told her a few days ago where she'd be tonight, she would have said they were crazy.

Maybe she was...and that was the reason she hadn't given all the details to Sienna and Georgie.

##

"Don't forget the spare nappies—and the wipes." Ana called out to Blake, and grinned at him as he hitched the baby bag onto his shoulder. His brow wrinkled in a frown. Despite the way they'd ended the night last night, he'd been friendly and pleasant to her this morning. It was as though they hadn't had that conversation in the kitchen. Maybe he was trying to ignore the physical attraction between them too?

"I'll never get used to this. How much stuff do kids need?" He let the bag drop to the floor, shoved Jake at Ana and ran up the stairs. "I forgot the wipes."

Jake gurgled happily in Ana's arms and she burrowed her face into his sweet-smelling, soft hair. It was a beautiful Sunday morning and Billy had informed them that Sunday was park day, so the children were dressed, and had their shoes on. They all stood in a row on the front porch, still for the first time since breakfast. Even Billy stood calmly while he sang "Incy Wincy Spider" to Maddy, who was doing the hand actions on his arm. Ana lifted her face from Jake's hair and smiled down at them. She remembered playing house with Sienna and Georgie when they were little, but real kids were very different than baby dolls.

They did things. They made noise. They created mess.

And they required constant supervision.

After Blake returned triumphantly with the baby wipes, they set off for Peninsula Park at the end of the street. Blake led their little group with Billy as he pushed Jake's stroller. She held each of the twins' hands as Maddy walked beside them.

Ana giggled and looked up at Blake as Jaws emitted another long, howl. "We really should have brought him. He'll drive the neighbours crazy."

"Five children aren't enough to worry about?" Blake walked on, seemingly unbothered by the dog's mournful cries that accompanied them along the street.

Billy tugged on her arm with his free hand.

"Why has that house got funny windows?" he asked pointing to the old building.

Ana looked up at the house they were passing. "They're made of coloured glass."

"But why has it got funny windows?" he repeated.

"It's called leadlight. Ask Uncle Blake." She inclined her head to Blake and smiled as they crossed the road.

By the time they crossed the next road and walked along the edge of the park, Billy had forgotten about the windows and was reciting the colours of the cars as they whizzed past. They stepped up on to the elevated footpath which edged the park and Ana herded the children across the grass to the swings. The boys ran around whooping and rolling on the grass, followed by Maddy who walked along at a more sedate pace.

Ana turned and spoke to Blake. "She's a serious child."

He unbuckled Jake's seatbelt, lifted the baby from the stroller and placed him into Ana's arms. Warmth filled her chest as the little boy reached up, grabbed her hair, and cooed happily. Blake smiled at her and the heat spread to her cheeks. She buried her face in the baby's hair to hide the flush.

"She takes the responsibility of being the eldest very seriously," Blake replied as he found a place to spread the rug on the grass. "Although she was always like that, even before the boys came along."

"Tell me about Jeannie." Ana decided to keep the conversation focused on Blake's family as she settled on the rug, not giving him the opportunity to ask her any probing questions.

Blake eased down onto the rug beside her and looked at her intently. "Jeannie and Rod moved back to Noosa when Maddy was born. One of the reasons I came back was because I missed being around the family."

Ana shifted her gaze from his and glanced around. They were surrounded by families enjoying the morning sunshine in the park and dog owners who were walking a variety of breeds along the paths. A few clouds were racing high above them and the wind was ruffling the water on the canal.

"What about you, Ana? You said you live alone? Where's home?"

"Uncle Blake, Uncle Blake!" Maddy's cry of distress drifted across to them before she could reply. "Billy's stuck."

Blake jumped up and ran across the short distance to the playground where Billy was hanging upside down, his knees curled over the top rung of the jungle gym and a huge grin spread across his face.

Ana settled on the rug with the baby lying on his back beside her and watched Blake reach up to Billy who was now at the top of the slide. Her heart lurched. Just looking at him brought all the feelings she'd managed to bury for all those years came flooding back in one huge wave. She closed her eyes and drew in a deep breath.

Wake up.

It had all been immature mooning over something she would never have. And they were so different, a relationship would never have worked between them. This was getting out of hand. In addition to the complications of those stupid lovesick memories intruding in her thoughts—and that's all they were, she told herself sternly—she had her own commitments to attend to.

Her promise to help out at the community markets on Sunday had already been broken and she'd had to arrange for Georgie to pick up Thelma and Mitzi, the two elderly ladies she drove to the markets each month with their baskets and crates full of handmade goods. Even though time had been short lately, she hated letting down the local folk and it had been bad luck that Blake had needed her help on the weekend of the community market.

She'd also promised Magda all the accounts would be up to date and ready to enter into the computer last Friday, but with the trip to Noosa, the rush back to Sunshine Coast to finish the Bennett job, and now another day helping Blake with the children, the three cardboard shoe boxes shoved full of invoices and receipts were still sitting on her kitchen table. She needed to get those accounts done now more than ever as a way to show Blake how profitable their department could be.

She had to convince Blake. She just *had* to. Helping him with the children might soften him up a little but she knew it was merely postponing the inevitable clash she knew their meeting would turn into. They'd argued so ferociously at uni over social issues, she just knew he would disagree with her and she would be hard pressed to hold back what she really thought about him destroying their little community business. This peaceful existence between them was not real. Once Blake knew why she was really here, they would clash as fiercely as they had before. They were just too different and caring for the children was one of the few things they had ever agreed on.

Ana groaned and Jake turned his wide blue eyes to her. Reaching down, she tickled him under his chin and was rewarded with a huge, gummy smile.

"Okay, Jake, I'll forget about all my worries and pay you some attention. Wise advice, young man. Thank you."

The excited calls of the children drifted across to her during a lull in the traffic noise. The twins were still on the swings, Maddy was patting a small, white dog, and Billy's arm was outstretched as he pointed to a small fountain at the edge of the canal.

"But I like to swim." His little voice became louder as Blake shook his head and pointed back to the jungle gym.

"I want to swim," Billy said insistently.

Blake lifted Billy back up onto the top of the slide and turned to watch the twins. As soon as the little boy landed in the soft sand at the bottom of the slide, his little legs pumped furiously as he took off.

"Blake!" Ana pointed to Billy as he charged past the gardens and through the gum trees towards the fountain. She jumped to her feet, picked up the baby and headed for the swings.

"I'll watch them while you get Billy," she called to Blake.

But by the time Blake caught up to Billy, the little boy had removed his shoes and socks, and stood in the middle of the fountain peeling off his pants. Blake walked around the fountain reaching out to Billy as he splashed around just out of his uncle's reach. As they disappeared behind the post in the middle, Maddy and the twins jumped off the swings and ran across to Ana.

"Billy's not allowed in the water because he can't swim. Daddy says." Maddy nodded her head. "But we won't tell him because if he has a sore leg, he might get mad."

The sound of a loud splash followed by a child's giggling reached them, just before a little figure appeared from the side closet to the road and took off across the grass toward the edge of the park and the busy traffic on Shorehaven Drive. Ana's heart lodged in her throat. The park area was raised above the street and was not fenced along the footpath. It was not a huge drop, but it was high enough for a small child to take a nasty fall. She was helpless, across on the other side of the grassed area, holding the baby and with three other children beside her. Blake took the shortest route to catch Billy—straight through the shallow fountain.

"Billy, stop. Billy!" Her shrill cry was muffled by a bus as it roared past.

"Stop," she screamed again, grasping the baby to her chest and running toward Billy. But the little boy kept running, down the sloping grassy hill toward the busy street.

Parents jumped to their feet, watching in horror as Billy reached the drop to the footpath and stood there beside the busy street, his little bare legs white in the bright sunshine.

"Billy! Freeze!" Maddy's imperious voice rang out over all the cries and traffic noise. Billy stopped and turned around, teetering on the edge of the concrete wall above the footpath. Blake pushed past Ana, water dripping from his hair and shirt, from when he'd leaned into the fountain to get Billy out. Kneeling down, he put his arms around the small boy. He looked up at Ana and the look on his face brought tears to her eyes. The love for his little nephew shone from his face and Ana's heart lodged in her throat.

To have Blake look at me like that . . .

He dropped his gaze as he held the small boy close to his chest.

"Do you like to swim too, *Unca* Blake?" His voice carried

over to Ana as the little boy looked earnestly up at his uncle.

It was a slow and quiet walk back to Blake's house. The baby was sucking contentedly on a dummy in his stroller, the older children walked along holding Blake and Ana's hands, disappointed that the picnic lunch lay untouched in the basket they had packed. The only sound was the wet, squelching suck every time Blake took a step. His shoes were soaked, and his socks were wet. Billy's hand was firmly in his grasp and he had Blake's dry T-shirt around his shoulders. Ana kept her eyes off Blake's bare chest.

"No more trips to the park." His whisper was low, and Ana's heart went out to him. Blake hadn't let go of Billy since reaching him at the edge of the ledge above the sidewalk, and he'd kept his expression closed. She could imagine what was going through his mind and was sure she would have nightmares about Billy falling under a bus. They stopped at the busy intersection and Billy tried to pull away from Blake.

"Ow, let go."

Ana caught Blake's eye as she spoke to the small boy. "Do you want to have a turn holding my hand, Billy?"

Blake looked back at Ana and shook his head. "I've got him." His voice was clipped. The relaxed, carefree Blake had disappeared.

It was obvious he was in no mood to listen to her now which would only make her case harder to plead. She'd missed her chance last night by letting herself get angry with him. She would meet with him at the store when he turned up in Maleny. It would just have to wait.

***

As soon as they got inside, Ana took Billy upstairs for a bath and Blake switched the television on for the others. Then he walked the perimeter of the bottom floor, making sure every door

68

and window was locked.

If there was one thing he couldn't handle, it was being out of control. Taking the children for a picnic in the park had proved disastrous. It should have been a . . . well . . . it should have been a walk in the park.

And he'd failed.

He closed his eyes. Never again did he want to feel as helpless as he had when Billy had teetered on the edge of the busy street. God, imagine if he'd had to call Jeannie and tell her Billy was hurt . . . or worse.

"Blake." Ana's voice was quiet and firm. "Billy's okay. Everyone's safe. Don't stress."

She settled Billy onto the sofa with the other children and spread the picnic rug on the floor in front of the television before laying out their food.

"Could you get me a cold drink, please?" she said.

Blake headed to the kitchen without a word. Like him, Ana had been preoccupied since they'd left the park and he could understand why. She'd taken on the responsibility of helping him with the kids without hesitation and he'd really taken advantage of her. He'd expected a lot asking her to help him just because she'd happened to come along at the right time. He wouldn't ask her for any more help after today. He would just have to cancel the dinner with Mike and Helen if Jeannie wasn't back in time. Ana came into the kitchen, slid onto the stool on the other side of the bench and took the large mug of coffee he pushed across the shiny granite top.

"Ana." Her hair was loose around her shoulders and she reached up and flicked it back from her face as clear blue eyes gazed back at him. An uneasy feeling lodged in his throat.

A wholesome face, no makeup and plain, simple clothes. She'd shed the business suit and looked so much like the Ana of old.

Very different to the corporate, elegant women he'd taken out over the years in Melbourne.

Which was the real Ana? There was still a mystery about her appearance on his doorstep and he'd let himself get side-tracked by her last night.

But damn it, I can't keep my hands off her.

Glancing at her hands as she lifted the coffee to her lips, he noticed her long fingers had short, clipped fingernails, and were free of any adornment and he wondered once more what had brought her to his doorstep.

He cleared his throat. "Look, I've been thinking. I'm going to call a nanny service again. I'm sure they'll be able to find someone right away if I pay enough."

Her face was closed, and she nodded without speaking. Turning away from him, she stared out the window and sipped her coffee.

"Are you okay?" He felt like a heel. She was probably just as shaken by Billy's near-miss as he was.

All was quiet in the room. The muffled sound of television cartoons drifted in from the living room and Ana slipped off the stool and moved across to the door.

She glanced in at the children before looking back at him.

She swallowed and lifted her chin.

"Blake, I need to tell you something."

Chapter Six

Ana focused her gaze on the second hand of the large French provincial wall clock above the doorway. She looked at the fancy metal whorls as she struggled to find the way to tell Blake why she was really here, and what she wanted from him. In the early hours of this morning, she'd had it all planned out, but now she figured she might as well just blurt it out instead of waiting any longer.

"Fire away." Blake's gaze was fixed on her and his serious expression made her heart thud even louder. Ana gripped the side of the stool until the cold chrome bit into the sides of her palms.

"I never expected to see you again." She swallowed and sought for the right words. "That is until I decided to come on Friday."

"Yes?" He tilted his head to the side, and she stared at him. Curious eyes looked back at her, but the smile crinkles were still there. He hadn't shaved this morning and sexy stubble covered his jaw. She closed her eyes and focused on her thoughts, instead of thinking of running her lips along his rough cheek.

"So I made the appointment to see you about the store—"

"What do you mean the store?" Blake's expression tightened and Ana's stomach rolled in anticipation of his reaction.

"Do you mean, *you* were my appointment? You were sent to do the pleading for the restoration guy from Maleny? Why not tell me straight up? Still wearing your heart on your sleeve, Ana?"

Angry words rose on Ana's tongue and she bit them back.

How dare he? How could she ever have thought that he'd softened? The ring of the doorbell interrupted them before she could reply, and Blake stared at her as he walked around the counter. "Wait here. I want to hear the rest and why this loser couldn't come himself. And why was it such a big secret? Not only can he not turn a profit, but he sends someone else to do his begging?"

Ana swivelled around on the stool and watched him as he strode across the living room. She clenched her fists on her lap as the anger burned up her throat.

I tried to tell him, and he didn't listen.

"No wonder the store was ready for a takeover." Blake's words came from the living room as he disappeared into the living room heading to the front door. His denim jeans hugged his butt nicely and she closed her eyes to block the sight, but his words stuck in her head, going round and round like a mantra. She was not interested in how sexy he looked. Forget the sexy, he was still as sexist as ever.

He didn't even consider for one minute I might be the restoration guy.

"Mummy, Mummy." The excited voices of the twins and Maddy interrupted her thoughts and she opened her eyes. Blake's sister crossed the room from the front landing and bent down and dropped a kiss on the heads of her children who had jumped up to greet her.

Ana's eyes pricked as Jeannie stopped and looked down at Billy who was sound asleep on the end of the sofa. She picked up the little hand hanging down by his side, tucked it into his chest, and ran her fingers softy down the side of his face.

Jeannie followed Blake into the kitchen and smiled at Ana.

"Anastasia, it's so lovely to see you again. I was in such a panic on Friday, I didn't even recognise you."

"It has been a long time, Jeannie." Their paths had crossed only occasionally in the year Ana had lived at the house, but Blake's older sister had always been friendly to her. "I can't believe these five beautiful children belong to you."

"I couldn't stay away from them any longer." Jeannie looked across at her brother. "And I felt so bad foisting them all on

Blake. Once I knew Rod was okay, I got on the earliest flight I could."

"You should have called," Blake said. Ana looked at him, but he avoided her eyes. His cheeks were flushed, and he held his mouth tight.

Jeannie smiled at him, obviously not picking up on the tension between them. "I know how hectic it is with those five, and I didn't want to overexcite them either." She turned to Ana. "I didn't know you and Blake were still in touch?"

Blake interrupted before Ana could answer. "Ana arrived on my doorstep about two minutes before you did on Friday. She's been a wonderful help all weekend." He shot her a steely look. "She was just leaving."

Heat ran up Ana's neck and she returned Blake's unsmiling gaze. "It was my pleasure. We've discovered we are just the same people we were back in university. Isn't that so, Blake?" She bestowed a saccharine sweet smile on him and turned to Jeannie. "I was just about to say goodbye to Blake when you arrived. I have some things I really must do this afternoon."

She said a quick goodbye to Jeannie and the children and hurried to collect her overnight bag before Blake could follow and throw any more insults her way. She was so angry at his attitude, she needed to get away before she lost her temper and blew any chance of a rational conversation with him. As she closed the car door and put the key in the ignition, he ran down the steps and out to the car. He reached in and put his hand over hers on the steering wheel.

"Is he your boyfriend or did he just take advantage of your soft heart?"

Ana gritted her teeth, but she couldn't stop the angry words spilling out of her mouth. "How dare you make assumptions, Blake. As usual you are so wrong." She turned the key and the engine fired as she pressed the accelerator to the floor. "You haven't changed one bit, have you?"

"Nor have you, Ana. Still running away when things get tough."

A red mist settled in front of her eyes and she sat back with her arms folded across her chest. "Oh, but I have changed. Get in the car, Blake and I'll tell you why I'm here."

"I'm not interested. Tell your boyfriend he wasted his time sending you." Blake squatted down beside the open window and his head and shoulders filled the small space. "I think it's time you left, Ana." The afternoon sunlight gleamed off the bluish-black lights in his hair as he stared at her, a nervous tic jumping in his cheek.

So Mr Boss Man isn't as in control as he is trying to appear to be.

Ana forced a smile onto her face. She reached out and trailed her fingers down his cheek and paused on the pulse she could see beating in his cheek. "I'll make an appointment and come back when you are in a more approachable mood."

"I don't think there's any need for that." He caught her fingers in his and they stared at each other for a moment before she pulled her hand away.

"Oh, don't you worry, Blake. We'll be seeing each other again."

Blake stepped back as she put the car into gear and pulled out onto the road. Glancing in the rear-view mirror, she scowled to herself as the car reached the bottom of the hill. He was still standing on the side of the road looking her way. In the end things had ended up going exactly the way she'd expected.

***

Blake pushed the door open and stepped into the living room. Jeannie was sweeping up the crumbs by the side of the sofa

74

where Billy had eaten his lunch.

"You don't have to do that. I'll get the cleaning service in tomorrow," he said.

"Really, Blake it's just a few crumbs. Once I pack up their gear and we're gone, you'll barely know they've been here."

"Are you going to take the laundry, too?"

"Be thankful I packed the disposable nappies, little brother. I use cloth ones at home." Jeannie laughed. She looked across at him curiously. "I didn't know you'd stayed in touch with Anastasia. Things seemed a bit tense between you."

"I didn't. She just turned up here. She was just telling me why when you arrived."

Blake flopped onto the couch and put his arm along the back of the seat behind the twins, drumming his fingers on the leather. The house was starting to look like his again now that Jeannie had packed up all the toys. A soon as they left, he was going to do some investigating into this restoration guy who had sent Ana.

Jeannie shot him a curious glance as she bustled past him with an armful of toys.

"You look upset. It wasn't that bad having the kids here, was it?"

"No." Blake jumped up and hugged his sister. "Just some business worries on my mind."

By the time Billy woke, the car was packed, and the children were lined up for a hug from *'Unca'* Blake.

"I'll come over and visit later in the week," Blake promised. "I've decided to take a drive to Maleny tomorrow to check out the store."

"Does Ana still live up there?"

"I guess she does," Blake said thoughtfully. "We were so busy looking after the kids we didn't get to catch up."

"It would be sweet if you could get to know her again."

Jeannie stood beside the car as the children climbed into the back seat. "You know Ana had a crush on you back then."

"Maybe." Blake held him arms out for the baby so Jeannie could secure the children into their seats. "But mostly I was always the big bad landlord."

"You were grieving for Mum and Dad, Blake, and you always took your responsibilities so seriously." Jeannie gave him a quick hug before she opened the door. "You need to lighten up and start enjoying life."

The noisy farewell of the children stopped him from answering but his sister's soft words reduced his anger a little. He'd been very hard on Ana, but the thought of her being used by some incompetent handyman to come and plead on his behalf had stirred him up. It wasn't her fault that she wore her heart on her sleeve. She'd always been up front about the way she was.

Jeannie interrupted his musing as she lowered the car window. "I really owe you one, little brother. You have a good week."

Anticipation curled in Blake's stomach as he thought about the week ahead. He would track Ana down and get to the bottom of this. The anger burning in him had pushed away any thoughts about the store takeover which was most out of character for him.

"I intend to, sis."

Chapter Seven

On the way home Ana dropped into Thelma and Mitzi's farm to see if they still needed her help, but Georgie had visited earlier and had already moved their crates to their small shed. The two elderly ladies pressed her to stay for tea, but she'd declined. She had to find Sienna and Georgie. It was time to come clean and tell them the whole story.

"I suppose you have to mow the lawn and do your odd jobs." Thelma admonished her, wagging a finger in her face. "It's well past time you found a husband and sat home having babies."

Ana fought a giggle as a ludicrous picture of sitting in her cottage popping babies out came into her head. Then the smile faded as she remembered the feel and sweet smell of little Jake's downy head against her face.

Sure, she wanted a houseful of kids one day, but first she had to sort her work life out and make sure she could keep their business going somehow.

And besides, she needed a husband first before she could sit at home and pop babies out. She stifled another giggle. Blake popped into her mind and she tried to push their weekend together out of her mind.

Ana left the farm and drove through town to her next door neighbour's house at the bottom of the hill. Old Jerry loved looking after Mutt and walking him while she was at work, and he fed the cat and watched her house on the rare occasion she went away. In return, she mowed his lawn for him every second weekend and did odd jobs for him.

Ana whistled for Mutt to follow her and he bounded up the hill behind the car, pleased to see her home.

West of Maleny and well away from the Sunshine Coast and the dense suburban areas, Hill Cottage, her little house, was perched on a hill. Opening the gate, she called for the large clumsy dog to follow her into the garden. His head nudged her thigh as she put the key in the lock, and she reached down to scratch his head.

"Miss me, boy?" Soulful brown eyes looked up at her with adoration and she smiled at him, stepping back as he pushed past her into the kitchen. He headed for his basket by the window, totally at home inside the cottage. Blake could learn a lot from Mutt, she thought.

Huh, no pets in his house. He didn't know what he was missing out on. She squatted down beside the basket as the dog walked around three times before flopping down on the cushion. She scratched behind his ears. "Pets make a home, don't they Mutt?"

Ana stood and stretched, easing the tension from her body and trying to get Blake Buchanan out of her head. She averted her gaze from the shoe boxes on the table overflowing with papers and reached over to the kettle to brew some peppermint tea. Pouring some dog kibble into Mutt's bowl next to the door, she allowed herself a quick glance around the cottage. One day she would find the time to finish the various restoration projects she'd started here. Compared to Blake's house, her home looked like a—well, if she was completely honest—like a junk shop.

But this little cottage was hers and she loved every inch of it. As soon as she'd sorted out the problem with their jobs, finished the accounts, painted Thelma and Mitzi's kitchen like she'd promised weeks ago, she would start on the next room. She hated saying no to the old dears. It had only been a couple of months since she'd last painted it and they had decided they didn't like the colour. She had Sienna lined up for something special for them, but Ana had no idea when they were going to find the time to do the job.

There was always so much to do, and it was more important to fix the elderly folks' windows and leaky roofs than pretty up her cottage. Hers could wait, they needed to be warm and dry, and most of them couldn't afford a handyman. She frowned to herself as she thought of Blake and what he'd think of the set up.

Get out of my head, Blake. She shook her head impatiently. Two days in his company and he'd taken over her thoughts.

Her landline phone rang, and she scrambled through the paint tins and rolls of wallpaper beside the shoe boxes to pick up the old fashioned handset.

Sienna's voice greeted her. "Oh good, you're home. We're having a girl's night in—at your place. We're on the way. Is your house a mess?"

Ana looked around again and grinned. Sienna was just as bad as she was, and she wouldn't even notice the furniture covered in drop sheets. Georgie, however, would run around all night and try to clean up.

"The usual. If you're happy to perch at the kitchen table, you can help me with the accounts. Georgie can cook."

"No need. We've already ordered Indian from Raj. So there's no excuse for you. Tonight you come clean and tell us where you've been and all about this mystery man."

Ana sighed. "I was about to call you and invite you over anyhow. I think we need to make some contingency plans."

"We're on the way."

By the time Ana had a quick shower and pulled on some clean clothes, the lights of her work ute appeared at the end of her driveway. She knew it was her ute because one headlight pointed up to the trees and the other dropped down to the ground. She really had to get it fixed.

The smell of curry wafted in with Sienna and Georgie, and Ana smiled as Sienna pulled a bottle of wine from her bag.

"Spare beds are made up," she said.

"No. I'll only have one glass. I want my little red car back home safely in its own garage. That truck of yours is a heap, Ana."

Sienna twisted the cork in the wine bottle until it gave a pop. Georgie put the bag of food on the counter, shoving one of the shoe boxes to make room.

"Okay, boss. Pull out the plates and spill all your news. Where have you been? I thought you'd run away with my car." Sienna put the ute keys on the dresser.

Georgie lifted her gaze from the containers of food. "You promised you'd tell us yesterday, but you've been as close-mouthed as Joe was when he was selling the store."

"Yeah, we don't want any more surprises here. You saw the head honcho on Friday when you borrowed the fancy clothes and my killer shoes. And then you disappear. That smacks of getting lucky to me." Sienna fixed a steely gaze on her.

Ana gave a sad little laugh. "I wish. Sorry girls, Blake is way out of my league. He was ten years ago, and he still is now."

"What do you mean out of your league?" Georgie shook a finger at her. "You have to stop putting yourself down because you dropped out of uni, Ana."

"Maybe." Ana folded up the corners of the kitchen tablecloth, drew them together like a swag, and lifted the cloth and its contents onto the floor. She pulled a clean cloth out of the bottom drawer in the old dresser and flicked it over the table. Sienna opened the cabinet and passed the plates and cutlery to Ana, while Georgie put out the food containers and poured their wine.

Ana picked up her glass and held it up. "To the future . . . whatever that may be."

Sienna groaned and the three girls clinked their glasses together before serving out the curry and rice. She placed her elbows on the table and pointed her fork at Ana while she chewed. "What happened?"

Ana knew she couldn't put them off any longer.

"Blake is as sexist and purely after profit as he was ten

80

years ago. He's probably even worse. He just assumed I was there on behalf of some *guy.*"

"So what did he say when you told him it was us—three women? What did he say to that?"

"That's the problem. I was so angry I left before I blew it completely." Ana loaded her plate with a second helping and held her glass out to Sienna for more wine. Ana took a sip closed her eyes as the image of Blake's smile stayed with her. "He can really be a nice guy."

"You're not making sense, Ana. He's either a nice guy and you can trust him, or he's not." Georgie sipped her wine and frowned.

"So just how close were you two in this share house?" Sienna's beautifully made up eyes were fixed on Ana's face. "There's something you aren't telling us."

Lifting her wine glass, Ana held it up and twirled it, and didn't meet Sienna's gaze. What had happened back then was between her and Blake and she wasn't going to share it. "We were just friends. I'll make an appointment to see him as soon as he hits town, okay?"

And I'll keep my temper this time. Waiting another couple of days wasn't going to make a difference. He'd either listen to her or they'd be out of a job.

Chapter Eight

Blake tucked his hands deep into his pockets and stood on the corner of Hastings Street waiting for the lights to change. He glanced over at the ocean, he could hear the hiss and roar do the waves from his house tonight. He'd bring Billy here one night; the little guy was fascinated by ocean. He was focused on his sea creatures.

Blake had managed to shake most of the fear that had stayed with him since Billy had teetered over that busy road, but now he shivered. One of the reasons he'd come back to Noosa was to be close to Jeannie and Rod and the kids. But when he had kids, there was no way he would stay in busy suburbia with its traffic and hidden dangers.

He blinked with surprise.

Where had that come from?

He had too much on his mind and his thoughts were skewing in a crazy direction. He needed to get them on track before he sat down with Mike.

Ana had been firmly fixed in his mind since she'd driven away this afternoon and now it was time to turn his thoughts to business. He had barely given the takeover a thought since he'd put his laptop away on Friday afternoon. For the life of him, he couldn't understand why she had come to plead the restoration guy's case. As soon as he arrived in Maleny, he was going to find her and get to the bottom of it.

And if he was honest, he owed her an apology. He'd been so shaken by what happened with Billy, he'd taken it out on her.

A cool breeze blew up the narrow street from the beach. When there was a lull in the traffic. Blake hurried down the hill and turned into the restaurant strip, looking for Fish Divine. He almost walked past—it was a tiny building on the corner, nothing like the restaurants in Melbourne where Mike usually held court. Pushing open the door, he looked around and spotted Mike and Helen sitting at a table tucked into the corner window overlooking the street.

"Blake." Mike's loud voice boomed out across the small space and some of the other diners smiled as he stood and enfolded Blake into a tight hug. "Great to see you, boy. What do you think of Noosa?"

Blake laughed and caught Helen's smile. "Hasn't changed much. Remember I grew up here, Mike?"

If it had nothing to do with making money, information didn't stay in Mike's head for very long. Before Blake could squeeze into the narrow space on the other side of the table, the bell on the door rang as it opened.

"Here's Jack!" Helen stood and waited for her son to cross the small restaurant before folding him into a tight embrace.

"Hey, mate." Blake reached over and shook Jack's hand when he'd extricated himself from his mother's arms. "What are you doing on the coast?"

"I'm moving to Noosa." Jack nodded at his father who sat tight-lipped, looking out the window, apparently engrossed in the traffic. "Dad."

Mike looked back at his son as Jack squeezed into the other side of the table next to Blake. "Son."

There was an uncomfortable silence for a few seconds until Blake turned to Jack. They'd met a couple of years ago and hit it off instantly over a few rounds of golf at the exclusive Royal Park Golf course in Melbourne where Mike was a member. Last Blake had heard, Jack had been commissioned to do a series of paintings for the club.

"So why the move to the coast?" he asked.

"I'm buying a gallery in Noosa. And I'll have peace and quiet to paint. Melbourne interferes with my creative process."

83

Mike gave a loud harrumph noise and picked up the menu. "Time to order, and then Blake and I have business to discuss."

After a few moments of casual conversation, Mike left to go to the rest room and Helen turned to Blake with an apologetic smile.

"Just ignore this pair. Mike is still cross that Jack doesn't love the business like he does. You know what he's like." Helen looked across at her son. "And Jack likes pushing his buttons."

"He'll get over it," Jack shrugged. "And if he doesn't, I don't really give a shit."

"Jack!" Helen glared at him and turned to Blake.

"Now before you get buried in business talk, tell me about your place here,' Jack asked. 'Are you going to drive to Maleny every day?'

"I'd like to stay in my house, but I suppose it will depend on the drive and"—he glanced across at Mike who was walking back to the table— "and the hours I'll have to put in to get the store up and running."

"Knowing Dad, he'll expect twenty-four seven." Jack glanced at his father who had stopped at the small bar on the other side of the restaurant.

"The takeover of the Maleny store was really a bonus for me. I'd planned on moving back home to Noosa anyway. It was time for a change," Blake said.

"Don't let Dad hear you say that," said Jack. "You're his golden boy."

"Hear what?" Mike sat back down and grinned. "Don't use the restroom, it's made for midgets." He patted his large girth with a huge hand. "And I'm no midget."

They all laughed and the atmosphere gradually lightened as they ordered and enjoyed their seafood meals. Jack and Blake caught up on the two years since they'd last met and even Mike appeared interested in some of his son's stories. After they'd finished their coffee, Mike summoned the waiter again.

"Who's going to join me in a port?"

Helen glanced across at her son. "Jack, would you walk me back to the hotel while these two talk business?"

As they said goodbye, Blake shook Jack's hand. "Want to come for a drive with me tomorrow? I'm heading down to Maleny to have a look around the area. We might throw the golf clubs in. What do you think?"

"Sure, give me a call in the morning."

Once they'd left, Mike turned to Blake and lifted his glass of port.

"To success in the latest Home and Hardware venture."

They clinked their glasses and Mike frowned. "So, how did it go with the guy who was coming to beg to save his department?"

"He didn't show. He sent someone else to plead his case, but we didn't have time to talk."

"Oh, well. He was going to get a big no, anyway, no matter who he sent. Stupid idea running tradesmen from a store. Just the cost of insurance alone would eat into any profits it made." Mike refilled their glasses. Blake knew where Mike's huge girth came from—he was a connoisseur of fine food and wine. Even though he was a member of the exclusive golf club, he'd never once seen him out on the course. "There's no place for softness in our business. If we listened to all the soft hearts, we would never make a dollar. And we can't have that, can we, son?

Blake cringed. He hated it when Mike called him 'son'. Even though he admired his boss for the successful corporation he'd built up, he thought Mike's priorities were a bit screwed. Seeing the way Mike treated his own son tonight had showed him how hard his boss could be.

"There's no place for any personal relationships in business. All those stores we've taken over, all those stores that wanted to be family businesses." Mike shook his head and took a

85

gulp of his wine. "Bound to fail. There's no friendship in business. You remember that, son. As soon as friendship comes in the door, profit flies out the window."

Mike's loud voice drowned out the soft conversations in the small room and Blake flinched when he called him son again. A picture flashed through his head. If he devoted himself to Mike's philosophies, he could end up just like Mike.

Look what it had done for him. He was pretty much estranged from his own son and focused solely on chasing new business and bigger profits every year.

"The restoration guy was probably some old-timer, probably too old to drive himself into the city to see you. Joe, the owner, told me most of the staff is past retirement age." Mike's deep laugh boomed out and the restaurant went quiet as conversations paused while everyone looked at Mike. Blake looked down at his wine glass as discomfort crept through him.

"I have a mental picture of all the staff pushing themselves around the store on walkers. They can all be pensioned off and you can hire some fresh, young blood." Mike slammed his glass down onto the table and belched.

Blake folded his napkin and stood. He'd heard enough. "I'm going to the store tomorrow, just to get a feel for the place."

"Don't let them know who you are. Just wander in as a customer." Mike's hearty laugh boomed out. "Like one of those secret shoppers."

"Maybe. It's a good way to see how a place really works." Blake waited while Mike signed the bill. "Thanks for dinner. I'll call you after the handover on Friday."

Mike stood and eased his huge girth around the tables as he followed Blake to the door. "You'll have no trouble turning it around. Once we do the shop refit and turn it into a proper store, the folks down on the coast will come in droves. It's all about profit, profit, profit, boy."

86

Blake frowned at Mike's words. He had enjoyed the challenge of working with Mike's company and had supervised the takeover of several of the other stores but always from his office in Melbourne. This was the first time he'd actually been out on the frontline of a takeover and he wondered if Mike had taken the logistics of the small town atmosphere into account, particularly when there were local jobs being shed. It was the sort of thing he and Ana had argued about at uni.

"What do you mean by a proper store?"

Mike shook his head and frowned.

"Apparently Joe Hickey has owned it forever—like sixty years. He brags about how he's kept it looking like something from the last century. Nothing modern, not even checkouts at the front of the store." He shook his head and disbelief was written all over his face. "He's proud that they've never remodelled. They even have a slogan, if you can believe it in this day and age—a store slogan!"

"Which is?" Blake had never seen Mike so stirred up and uncertainty began to filter through him. It sounded like this takeover was going to involve a lot more changes than implementing policies and updating the storefront. His gut churned as he wondered what he was going to find down in this small community, and an uneasy feeling crept up his spine as he wondered if it was an old guy Ana was helping out. If he was honest with himself, it was jealousy that had pushed him into being so hard on her. Now it was beginning to sound like the Ana of old. Helping out the needy and not worrying about money.

"*Whatchamacallits, thingamajigs, and doohickies for every need.*" Mike choked on the words as he laughed, and Blake thumped him on the back.

"Interesting," Blake said. If he'd known all this about the store, he may have reconsidered the move and looked for another corporate position in Brisbane. He could have commuted from

Noosa. As he always did, he'd looked at the figures and profit margins and he'd never had anything to do with human resources before. Maybe it was time he changed the way he thought, but he'd given his word to Mike and he'd see this deal through. The thought of seeing Ana again sweetened the deal considerably.

Chapter Nine

Joe had asked them to take inventory of the store so Magda could enter the stock into the computer. The renovation section area in the back was the only department waiting to be finalised.

Along with the accounts still sitting in the shoeboxes on her kitchen counter. Ana found it so hard to say no to anyone who needed help and it constantly put her behind. Balancing the accounts was the job she always put last because she knew the numbers never showed quite as much profit as they hoped to bring in. And definitely not as much as Blake would be expecting.

They'd ended up finishing the bottle of wine last night and when Sienna and Georgie had finally roared off in Sienna's little red sports car, Ana lit the candles on her bathroom windowsill and soaked in a deep bath. By the time she'd gotten out, she'd stumbled sleepily to bed.

Tonight. She'd do them tonight after the three of them helped out in the store.

"Well, looky here." Sienna drawled.

Ana lifted her head from the box of brass curtain hooks and frowned at Sienna. "What? Oh drat." She dropped the handful of hooks back into the box. "Now I've lost count." She looked up crossly at Sienna. "Look at what?"

"Three o'clock."

Ana put the box on the dusty concrete floor. "Are you going to stop talking in riddles? What's on at three o'clock?"

"Eye candy at three o'clock," Sienna dropped her voice to a husky murmur. "Georgie will be running for the wedding magazines when she sees this pair."

Ana rolled her eyes. "Are you going to help me count this stuff or do I have to do it all myself?"

"You are getting so boring. I think they might be movie

89

stars or something. Oh, mama, huge and hunky. I heard there's a movie being made in the hinterland I wonder if they'd like to be shown around town. I'm just the girl for it."

"Sienna, you are supposed to be helping me, not planning your sex life." Ana sighed and pushed herself to her feet as Sienna reached for her phone.

God knows what she was texting. Sienna could be quite irreverent when the mood took her. A ripple of laughter came from Georgie in the next aisle and Ana craned over to read what Sienna had texted to her sister.

Sex on legs relief for those in need heading your way.
"You are so bad."

"Bad girls have more fun, don't you know that?"

Georgie appeared around the end of the aisle with a big grin on her face.

"Yes, I am in need. Where's the solution?"

She walked on her tiptoes in the direction her sister pointed and stood behind a pile of plastic wheelbarrows stacked almost to the ceiling.

"Oh. My. God." Georgie turned to Ana and beckoned her come over.

She wasn't going to get any peace until she looked at this eye candy of Sienna's and made the girls happy. Ana walked slowly to the end of the aisle and put her hand on Georgie's shoulder as she peered around the wheelbarrows.

"Oh, my God."

Georgie turned to her with a grin which died quickly when she looked at Ana.

Ana's world was about to come crashing down sooner than she'd planned unless she got out of there mighty quick. She recognised the jacket; she knew the hair and more than anything she recognised the butt she'd checked out thoroughly in the park yesterday.

What the hell is Blake doing here?

There was no way she was ready for this meeting with him today, not in front of everyone. The back door was at the end of the aisle where they were standing. If she could get to it before Blake—and whoever he was with—turned around, she could go out and hide until he left.

As she spun around to make a quick exit, her shoulder knocked one of the wheelbarrows and it tipped slowly.

"Georgie, look out," she whispered urgently. But Georgie had turned to look at the two guys and didn't see the teetering pile tipping toward her. Ana shoved her out of the way just as the tower of wheelbarrows slid to the right and fell with a huge crash. As soon as she could see through the clouds of dust rising from the concrete floor, Ana checked that Georgie was okay and then she took off back down the aisle toward Sienna, who was standing next to the boxes of curtain accessories with her mouth wide open.

Gesturing madly to Sienna to open the back door, Ana didn't see the box in front of her and before she knew it, she sprawled headlong onto the floor. The hard concrete jolted against her ribs and took her breath away. She closed her eyes and buried her head in her arms, praying that no one would notice her spreadeagled on the floor while she tried to get her breath back.

The cold concrete pressed into her cheek and she slowly opened her eyes.

"Ana, are you okay?" Georgie crouched beside her and ran her hands up and down her back. "Ana, talk to me."

"I'm okay." She lifted her head and groaned as two pairs of jean-clad legs hurried down the aisle towards them.

***

As he and Jack approached the store, Blake wondered how much research Mike had done into the location. The village atmosphere of the small town seemed to be a real tourist attraction. It was certainly not the right place for a modern hardware store.

Other stores surrounding it had been done up to retain the history of the place. Once they entered the dark and musty store, Blake had muttered and sworn under his breath at the mess. Piles of goods blocked fire exits, stock that looked to be decades old lay covered in dust on the shelves and the staff—God, Mike was right—Blake hadn't seen anyone under seventy yet.

"Why the hell did your father buy this place?" he whispered to Jack as they'd moved half a dozen large garden forks completely blocking one aisle. "He's got rocks in his head."

Jack grinned. "You're not telling me anything new there, mate."

"It needs demolishing." Blake ran his fingers through his hair in frustration. "How the hell—"

The crash of the wheelbarrows and the woman lying on the floor were all Blake's nightmares about this store coming to life. He and Jack took off at a run and were soon lifting the wheelbarrows to clear a space to the aisle.

A potential lawsuit already. Then he breathed a quick sigh of relief, they hadn't signed the paperwork yet.

Jack followed him and in the middle of the aisle, a woman was crouched down beside a prone figure face down on the ground with a silver blonde ponytail poking through a baseball cap. Blake hurried down past the piles of garden tools and crouched down beside her. He groaned. He must be hallucinating.

"Ana?" She rolled over to her back and looked up at him. Her jeans were filthy, and her dark jacket was covered in fine, grey concrete dust. A small bruise was darkening on her chin and he prayed she had no broken bones or concussion.

"Help me up, please."

"No, we have to make sure nothing's broken."

"I'm okay." She put her hands on the filthy floor and pushed herself up.

Blake looked around and spoke to the young woman
92

crouched beside him. "Call an ambulance, please."

Before the woman could answer him, Ana interrupted crossly, "No, don't. I'm all right." Blake took her arm to steady her as she stood.

"Thank you. Now I'm in a hurry—I was just leaving." She pulled her jacket closed and stepped away.

"Wait, you can't just go. You have to give your details to the store so they can do a report." Blake held tightly to her arm. "You might have a concussion."

"I'm alright, Blake. Now I really have to go. I have more shopping to do."

The young woman beside him made a peculiar noise and he turned to her.

"Are you with Ana?"

"Er, yes. You could say that." The woman frowned at him. "I'm Georgie. And you're Blake?"

Blake nodded absently as he watched Ana hurry down the aisle toward the entrance of the store. "Tell her I'll call her."

Georgie waved to a woman standing at the other end of the aisle. "We'll pick you up later, Sienna . . . after we finish our *shopping*." She hurried out the door after Ana, while the woman she'd called Sienna sauntered up to them.

"Gentlemen, is there something I can help you with?"

Blake noticed the writing across the front of her T-shirt as she unfolded her arms. '*Whatchamacallits, thingamajigs, and doohickies for every need*'

"You work here?"

She nodded and stared at him. "Surely do. Now what can I help you gentlemen with?" Jack stood beside him not saying anything but paying close attention to their conversation.

Blake shook his head. "Ah, nothing. We were just leaving." Before he turned away, he cleared his throat. "You know Ana?"

"Yes, I do." The frown on the woman's face deepened and

93

he could have sworn she was scowling at him.

God, were they all crazy in this town?

"So you know where she lives?" he asked.

"Yes, I do." She refolded her arms across her chest.

"Will you give me her address? So I can go check on her?"

"No, I won't. She's fine."

Blake shrugged and walked away as Jack followed.

If she wouldn't tell him, he might be quick enough to see Ana's red BMW parked outside and catch her before she left. He strode down the cluttered aisles as quickly as he could and stepped out into the spring sunshine. It was a pleasure to take in a deep breath of fresh air after the mustiness of the dark, cluttered store.

"Come on, Jack. I need a drink. I've got a lot of thinking to do."

There was no sign of Ana or her car, so they headed towards the hotel on the corner. While Jack found a table, Blake bought them a couple of beers from the bar and ordered a bowl of wedges.

He joined Jack at the table by the window, pulled out his phone, and sent a quick text to Ana's number asking her if she was okay.

"Who's Ana?" Jack asked curiously.

"An old friend from uni. I actually caught up with her over the weekend."

"Well, you must have made a great impression, mate. She couldn't wait to get away from you."

"Hmm." Blake stared into his beer and thought about the coincidence. Ana was connected to the store somehow and she'd let him believe she was on a social call until she'd come clean about being his appointment.

Read about me in the paper? He didn't believe a word of it. There was something smelly about the whole situation and he was going to get to the bottom of it.

94

"If you squeeze that glass much harder, it's going to pop. Waste of a good beer." Jack was looking at him curiously. "What's got you so upset? Not happy that the little cutie took off? I might get her phone number from you when I move down here."

Blake's head snapped up and he glared at Jack.

"Ah, so that's the way the land lies." Jack gave a quiet laugh. "Don't tell Dad you're interested in one of the staff."

"Staff?" Blake frowned. "What do you mean?"

Jack shrugged. "I might be wrong, but she had the same shirt on as the other girl who worked there. I noticed it before she pulled her jacket together."

***

Ana pulled Georgie along behind her as she crept around to the back entry of the store. "You go in first and check that they've gone. I don't want Blake to know that I work here, just yet."

"Why not? What on earth are you up to, Ana?" Georgie sighed. "And who's the hunky guy with your Blake?"

"I didn't want to talk to Blake yet. It really threw me when I saw him in the store." Ana replied sheepishly. "And he is not *my* Blake . . . and I don't know the other guy."

Georgie grinned. "Could have fooled me. You're acting like a crazy teenager."

She waited outside until Georgie came back and called to her in a melodramatic whisper.

"Coast's clear."

Sienna was waiting inside the door and held her hands out to Ana. "Are you okay? That was a nasty fall you took." She reached up and touched her chin lightly. "Why the subterfuge?"

"I'm fine, just my pride was hurt. I was not going to have it out with him with an audience. And I'm angry."

"Because the wheelbarrows fell on you?" Sienna frowned at her. "I told Joe he had them stacked up too high when he bought so many last year."

"No, no." Ana put her hands on her hips. "I'm angry because that lowlife came sneaking around the store, checking it out. And did you notice? He didn't even go and see Joe. Joe obviously had no idea he was here, or who he was."

She stomped off toward the office. "I'm going to tell him."

Before she could get to the end of the aisle, Sienna caught up with her and grabbed her arm.

"And what's that going to achieve? You're overreacting." Sienna frowned at her.

"Don't go upsetting Joe and Magda. Let's go and grab some lunch and we'll work out what needs to be done."

Sienna glanced over at Georgie who was restacking the wheelbarrows into three piles instead of one high one. "Go grab our bags. I'll check if the street's clear."

As they walked through the store, Ana looked around her, trying to see the store through Blake's eyes. She'd worked here for ten years and was used to the dark and dusty interior. In fact, she even thought it added to its quaint charm. Blake would see it totally differently; he would see the clutter and chaos that she had always thought was quaint.

Georgie caught up to them as they stepped out into the street. The late morning sun was warm, and Ana shrugged off her jacket and brushed the remaining concrete dust off her store T-shirt. The street was busy as tourists meandered down the wide walkway between the old shops. It was a wonder the town wasn't under a heritage order. This town had been settled in the early twentieth century by Italian immigrants who had planted acres of vegetables to supply the Brisbane market, and it still had a distinctly European feel.

At the end of the street was a bar run by Sienna and Georgie's Uncle Renzo. Georgie disappeared into the kitchen to order their lunch and Sienna snagged them three stools at the counter.

"Drinks, girls?" Uncle Renzo called out.

"Just coffee, thanks. We're still at work." Sienna answered.

Ana propped her chin in one hand and gingerly probed her jaw with the other. She winced as her fingers encountered a tender spot.

Sienna took a quick breath beside her and Ana glanced up to see what was wrong. Reflected in the mirror behind the bar, she and Sienna were dressed in their dark work shirts with *whatchamacallits, thingamajigs, and doohickie for every need* emblazoned across their chests. Ana lifted her gaze higher and drew in a shaky breath before she turned slowly to face Blake who stood behind her with his arms folded across his broad chest.

"Hello, Ana."

"Hello, Blake."

"I take it you work at the hardware store?"

Beside them, Sienna's head turned from one to the other as they spoke.

"I do. And I take it you were creeping around spying before you take it over on Friday?" She kept her voice level.

Blake's eyes narrowed. "And I take it you're from the restoration department, and visited me to try and keep your job?"

If Ana had been royalty, she couldn't have inclined her head more gracefully then she did in response to his question. Ice-cold anger was building inside her and she fought to keep her temper under control.

"I was. However I saw a greater need and filled that."

'You haven't changed.' Blake gave a bitter laugh. "Always the do-gooder."

"And you are always the capitalist," she replied, holding his gaze without moving.

"Hey, you guys, time out." Sienna waved her hands between their faces, breaking their deadlocked gaze. Georgie came out from the kitchen and Blake stared at her T-shirt.

"All three of you work in restoration?"

"Yup." Sienna leaned in close to his face. "Hurt one, hurt all of us."

Ana frowned. "I can handle this, Sienna."

The guy who'd been with Blake in the store wandered over from the bar where he had been watching the exchange between Blake and Ana.

"Can I buy you a drink, ladies?"

"Are you going to introduce us to your *colleague,* Blake?" Ana asked.

"Not a colleague, just a friend out for an afternoon drive." The guy held his hand out to Ana. "Seeing as my pal here is so lacking in manners, I'm Jack."

She took his hand and introduced the two girls before sliding off the chair and pushing past Blake.

"Well, enough of the niceties. I'm going to call it a day. I'm feeling a bit . . . off." She glared at Blake as she turned to the twins. "I'll see you two tomorrow."

Ana turned on her heel and muttered 'nice to meet you' to Jack as she headed to the door.

Chapter Ten

Ana crunched through the gears and floored the accelerator of her ute—not that it made one scrap of difference. The old heap was ready for the wreckers and the engine groaned up the last hill to her cottage. Mutt was sitting at the back door waiting for her, as she stepped out and pushed open the gate to the cottage garden. She sat next to the big dog and put her arm around his neck. A sloppy, wet lick up the side of her cheek brought the first glimmer of her good humour back to her since she'd left the store.

"It's true what they say, boy. Pets lower the blood pressure. Would do Blake a load of good." She laughed as Mutt put his paw on her knee and tried to burrow his head under her arm. "You're certainly good for the soul." She ruffled his ears and stared out over the mountains. A huge bank of cloud was sitting above the horizon and a slight breeze was puffing wisps of cloud closer to the Glasshouse Mountains. The movement of the air was stirring the flowers in the garden and the sweet smell of orange blossom drifted in from the orchard on the hill across the fence.

Ana pushed herself to her feet, threw her bag on the old wooden bench outside the back door, and walked down to the small garden shed. Slipping on her gloves, she picked up the secateurs and headed into the orchard. Gardening was food for her soul and the combination of the view of the ocean and her pretty garden would bring her temper back to within normal range.

She even allowed herself a smile. She'd almost clocked Blake when he had called her a do-gooder. He hadn't changed one bit—he was still more interested in money and profits than people and that didn't bode well for their little hardware store. The compassionate, caring Blake she'd seen with the children was only what she'd wanted to see. He was as hard as nails. There was no hope for them.

Ana wandered around the orchard, clipping off dead branches and gathering a spray of blossoms to put in the kitchen. Holding the white flowers to her chest, she inhaled their sweet fragrance and stood on the cliff top as thoughts flitted in and out of her mind. The bright pink of the pig face plant at the top of the cliff years ago was a riot of colour and further brightened her mood.

Change was coming—as surely as the clouds would roll in over the hills this afternoon. There was no doubt about that. It was just a matter of making the right decision and adapting to the change. The soft purr of a vehicle reached her ears, and she knew it was Blake before she even looked. Happiness flitted briefly through her briefly at the memories of their uni days. Their arguments may have been heated but inevitably one of them would seek the other out and apologise before the day was over.

With a deep sigh, she walked slowly across the orchard and stood at the gate watching as a sleek grey Mercedes drove up her rutted driveway. With the bouquet grasped in front of her, she waited while Blake parked the car.

He stepped out and walked across the lawn and looked past her to the mountains. "Nice view."

"Suits me fine," she replied, keeping her voice cold. "Who told you where to find me? Georgie?"

He nodded.

Ana sighed and shook her head. "Well then, now you're here, you'd better come in so we can have that chat."

She passed him the blossoms and smothered a smile as he stood there holding them while she pulled her gloves off. Taking them back, she turned and led him through the gate into the house garden. Mutt came up and sniffed around the back of the hand Blake offered him, before licking it and flopping back down in the shade.

"I guess that means one of you accepts me." His face was serious, and she found it hard to read his expression.

100

"It's nothing personal, Blake. We have business to discuss. We gave up the personal stuff ten years ago. A one night stand doesn't make us friends." Ana pushed open the back door. "We have nothing in common. And we never did."

She could feel his gaze on her as she walked into the kitchen. Crossing to the sink, she filled a large glass jug with water, put the orange blossoms in it, and carried it over to the table by the window.

"Sit down." She gestured to the only chair that wasn't covered with tools and rolls of wallpaper. "I'm renovating, so I won't apologise for the mess."

She stared at him, daring him to make a comment about the chaos surrounding them. Pressing fingertips to her forehead, she waited for the smart remark, but he surprised her with an apology instead.

"I'm sorry I was rude to you at lunchtime, Ana, especially in front of your friends."

Moving away, she bent down and cleared the other chair before replying. "I'm sorry, too. I was out of line."

Blake walked across and sat down. He leaned forward and dangled his hands between his knees, looking down at the floor. The sun broke through the clouds and shone into the room, illuminating the dust disturbed when Ana had cleared the chair. She watched him for a while without speaking, drinking in the sight of his broad shoulders, outlined by the snug T-shirt. A warmth she didn't want to feel, filled her chest and anger seeped into her voice as an attempt to disguise it. "Seeing as we are going to have a business meeting, we could probably do with some coffee? I know I could."

Blake went to stand, and she shook her head.

"No, stay there." Her mood softened marginally. "But thanks for offering."

While the coffee brewed, she reached up to the cupboard

101

for two clean coffee mugs, but they were all in the dishwasher, which she hadn't run for a couple of days. She reached to the back of the cupboard and pulled out two fine china cups and saucers. It was a business meeting, so she would act like it was the usual way she entertained her clients. Ana looked across at Blake, the cups rattling as her hands shook. He was watching her with an intense expression on his face. His lips were straight and frown lines creased his forehead. Looking away, she filled the tray and added some of the ANZAC bikkies Thelma had sent home with her on Sunday.

Placing the tray on the floor between the two chairs, she sat and waited for him to break the silence. When Blake didn't speak, she bit her lip and reached down to the tray, ignoring the thudding of her heart. The silence continued as she passed him a black coffee and placed a cookie on the saucer.

Finally she couldn't stand it any longer and took a sip of her coffee before blurting out, "So where do we start?"

Blake put his cup down and folded his arms. "You made the appointment with me last week, so I'll listen to what you have to say. I'll be fair and give you the same consideration you would have had"—his voice was cold— "in your business suit and high heels."

Ana took a deep breath and relaxed into the soft sofa, reassured by his apparent willingness to hear her out but her heart was still pounding heavily.

"Okay." She met his steady gaze. "This town is very special. Down on the coast is the commercial centre where businesses like Home and Hardware should go. Maleny is for people have lived here all their lives, and for those who retire here for a slower—more old-fashioned, I suppose you could say—lifestyle. It has created a unique place that tourists love, and flock to."

She looked down and that ever present shiver when he was
102

around trickled down her back. She rubbed her arms to dispel the goose bumps.

"The renovation department, specifically Georgie, Sienna and I, provide a service. It's so important to keep the old homes true to their original state, and we've combined our skills to restore them." She jumped out of the chair as a thought struck her. "Finish your coffee. We're going for a drive so I can show you some of the houses we've done."

Blake shook his head and her spirits plummeted.

"I'm sure the work you do is great. But I need to see how much money it makes."

Ana couldn't stop herself from glancing at the shoe boxes full of invoices. The goose bumps disappeared as heat crept up her neck. She dropped her head and her hair fell over her face as she attempted to hide the tell-tale red flush she knew would be staining her fair skin. All was quiet for a moment and she fought to regain her composure. Lifting her head, she dug deep for the anger she'd felt the other day when he'd made assumptions about her.

"You could give us the courtesy of looking at our work. You obviously don't think women are capable of doing it. Then if—"

"Whoa. Stop right there." Blake came over and crouched in front of her. "Where did you get that idea from?"

Ana pushed to her feet and crossed to the window. When he was near her, she couldn't think straight and her whole future—and that of her friends—hung in the balance.

"Ana, look at me." She lifted her gaze to meet his and to her distress a single tear spilled over on to her cheek. Blake followed her and he lifted one hand and wiped it away with the pad of his thumb. "What makes you think I am such a sexist? Surely not that silly argument we had back in college?"

"No . . . well, yes. I suppose that was part of it. And then you made that comment about a guy sending me on Friday to plead

103

his case. You automatically assumed it would have been a man."

Blake's voice was patient. "No, Ana. My secretary told me *a guy* was coming for the appointment. There was obviously a mix-up because I made no such assumption."

"Coming to see you was going to be our—or rather my — final attempt to save our jobs. Joe had already told the staff which departments would be going and who would probably be out of work. I thought I'd appeal to you—and maybe your commitment to the community. I knew how important your family home was to you and I thought you might understand."

"Business doesn't run on kindness . . . or friendships." Blake smiled and ran his fingers down the side of her face. "Ana, you always were a softie. Going into a competitive industry where it's all about pleasing shareholders never would have suited you."

"But Blake, why does it have to be like that? We've managed here this way for a long time." She reached for his hand. "You've seen the store now, and you've seen our little town. You have to see that it isn't the type of place that a big shiny store will fit in."

"If you had asked me the same question on Friday at my place, I wouldn't have understood. Now I've been to Maleny and seen the store, I get more of a sense of where you are coming from."

He looked at her intently and she swallowed, desperately trying to keep her gaze from his lips. She tried to let go of his hands, but he gripped hers tightly.

"Look, I'm probably going to regret this, and I can't promise anything, but I'd like to sit down with you and have a look at the numbers from your department. I don't remember seeing them in the spreadsheets Mike sent me."

She shook her head. "No," she said slowly." Magda is just waiting for me to get last . . . er . . . the last couple of month's figures to her."

"Are they on your computer? We could have a quick look at them now." He patted his shirt pocket and pulled out a flash drive. "I can take them with me and add them in with the others."

Ana couldn't help the bubble of laughter coming up from her chest and past her lips. Blake tipped his head to the side.

"What? Is it so funny I carry a flash drive around?"

"No." She pointed to the table. "I don't think you can transfer shoe boxes to a flash drive."

Blake looked to where she was pointing at the three overflowing containers. He turned back to her and smiled, the laughter lines crinkling around his blue eyes.

"Oh, Ana, you haven't changed a bit, have you?"

Ana caught her breath, the feelings she had been trying to push away since she'd first seen him last Friday rolled over her in waves, and she closed her eyes to block his face from her view. She tried to summon up a semblance of control as her nerve endings went into a tailspin as he stood close to her. There was silence for a moment and then gentle fingers gripped her chin again. She opened her eyes slowly.

"It's going to be okay, Ana."

Ana heard what he was saying but the words didn't really sink in. The expression on his face told her he wasn't really thinking business either. Silence stretched between them and she wondered if the same tingles were running up and down his arms as he held her gaze in his.

Don't get excited.

She wasn't going to get her hopes up because dreams didn't come true like that. He was just being kind.

"Right, then. Let's talk business," she said briskly smoothing her hands down the front of her jeans. "That's really the only thing we're here for, isn't it?" She crossed the room and picked up the first box.

***

The fact that Ana reminded him of their business relationship brought Blake solidly back to earth. Years of making high stake deals in boardrooms had taught him how to keep his expression bland. But when Ana stood in front of him grasping a blasted shoe box against the 'whatchamacallits' and 'doohickies' T-shirt, the sweet smile on her face sent all his resolve crumbling.

"Come outside with me. The table on the porch is clear."

While he waited on the porch, Ana made more coffee for them. By the look of things they would be here a while. It was only fair to listen to her. She'd put her life aside for him over the weekend and helped him with Jeannie's kids, so it was one way he could repay her a little bit. And besides, he loved being with her. Once she'd left, his house had seemed sterile and empty. Her enthusiasm for her work and the local community was infectious and he was prepared to listen to what she had to say.

No promises, but he'd listen.

He knew Mike would be immovable on changing the store structure. Every Home and Hardware store across the country was identical. The stock, the layout, the staff structure, and their uniforms—he'd argued a few times with Mike about the need to do a demographic study, but in his usual bull-headed form, the man wouldn't listen.

"Shit." Thinking about Mike reminded Blake of Jack waiting for him in town. He glanced down at his watch. It was just after two o'clock. Pulling out his phone, he scrolled through to Jack's number and pressed call.

"Hey, Blake."

"Sorry, Jack. I got caught up with some business. Do you mind if we skip that round of golf?"

"No problem. Georgie here—" Blake heard a feminine chuckle in the background— "has offered to show me around. I was just about to call and see how much longer you'd be."

"Great. I'll call you in a couple of hours when we finish."

"Sounds like a plan. See you later, mate."

The smell of freshly brewed coffee wafted out to Blake as he put the phone back into his pocket. He drew a deep breath and settled back into the comfortable chair. He grinned to himself—the porch was neat and tidy in contrast to the inside of the cottage. A deep planter running along the balcony was filled with a profusion of sweet-smelling herbs. Wind chimes hung on each side of the steps and as the afternoon breeze puffed in, the gentle tinkle of chimes overlaid the sound of the birds trilling from the bush.

The door pushed open and he jumped up to take the tray from Ana.

"I'll just get the boxes." She grinned at him and disappeared inside, reappearing with her arms laded with the three boxes.

"How long have you lived here, Ana?" Blake gestured around to the cottage.

"Do you mean in the cottage? I bought it about nine years ago after my mum—with a small inheritance, but it was in such a state of disrepair I didn't move in for a few months. Sienna and Georgie helped me do the kitchen and bathroom, so it was liveable."

"So you've been friends for a while?"

"Since the first day of school when we were five-years-old."

"I owe you a couple of apologies, you know." He looked out over the ocean searching for the right words.

"When my parents died in the accident, Jeannie and I were left in that huge old house in Toowong." He shook his head and reached for his coffee. "I knew Jeannie was going off to Sydney uni and I was terrified of being alone. So I filled the house with you guys and watched you all have a great time."

"You never really did join in with us," Ana said quietly. "I always felt we weren't good enough for you."

107

Blake stared down at his feet and scrubbed a hand through his hair. "I just didn't know how to connect with you all. So I guess I overplayed the landlord role a bit and, in the process, I really screwed things up."

He lifted his head and turned to face Ana. "I'm sorry about that last night. I always wondered if you left so suddenly because we slept together."

"Oh no, don't ever think that. I was upset and I didn't even think to leave you a note or anything."

"So why did you go?"

"I came back here to Maleny. I got a call. My mum was ill—dying. I left without thinking about anything else."

Blake wasn't aware he'd been holding his breath and now he let it out a light exhale. "For ten years, I thought you left uni because of me." He put his hand on her arm as distress filled her face.

"No, Blake. You couldn't be more wrong. That night was special for me and it stayed with me through some pretty tough times. I was young and Mum was all I had. I guess I didn't know how to handle my grief. And after she passed, the twins and I started up the business and it grew from there."

She leaned across and picked up a business card that was in the box with the receipts and invoices. "I'll never have the academic credentials you do, and I don't lead a glamorous corporate life, but we work hard, and we do okay." She passed him the business card and smiled at him. Her face came alight as she looked up at him and it was like a punch to his stomach. For a moment, he just looked at her, the light in her face as she told him about the business.

"We had so much work when our reputation began to build, Joe offered us the chance to run our own department out of the store. Georgie had worked there since she'd left school and Joe did the billing and the accounting, while Sienna pulled in the jobs. And

108

we all did the restoration work."

Blake shook his head slightly. "I don't understand. If they do the business side, why do you have all this?" He gestured to the boxes.

Ana darted a sideways glance at him as she turned the pages. "The accounts that go through the store are the ones where we make the money. These other accounts are for the jobs that the store . . . er . . . subsidises. But is shows you how many jobs we have. Between the two types of jobs, and um . . . and the great profit the store makes on the other ones, these kind of—."

"Kind of what?"

Ana jutted out her chin. "Look, Blake. It's the sort of thing that happens in small towns where members of the community look out for each other."

"I'm not arguing. I just don't understand what you're saying." A prickle of unease trickled down his neck. He had a feeling he wasn't going to like her explanation.

"Okay, it's like this. We have two types of clients. There are the long-term locals who need work done to maintain their homes, and there are the outsiders who buy up the old houses to flip them. You know, they get us to renovate them and they make a profit."

"So you charge them differently?"

"One side of the business funds the other. The people who hire us to restore their houses so that they can flip them are happy. They make up for the money we spend on the old folks' maintenance jobs. Joe supplies the materials from the store, and we charge them at cost."

He scratched at his head. "So where's the profit come from?"

"Well," she said slowly. "There isn't a lot."

"And Joe was happy with this setup?"

Ana folded her arms. "Yes, he was. And he is."

"And what do you get out of it?"

Ana pursed her lips obviously trying to keep her response polite. He recognised the signs of her temper building from the old days.

"Apart from the satisfaction of helping people. I get a wage." She pushed herself to her feet and waved a hand over the boxes. "I'm not doing a good job of explaining here." She went back inside and came out with her car keys. "Come with me."

Blake followed her as she strode across to the old work ute beside his Mercedes and he thoughtfully climbed into the passenger seat.

Ana didn't speak as she backed down the steep driveway. Blake bounced in the seat as the wheels hit a rut and his head hit the roof of the car. He reached for his seat belt as they turned out onto the main road.

"Where are we going?"

"You'll see."

Chapter Eleven

Ana's heart was pounding, and heat was flushing through her body. She'd really messed that up. It had been ten years since she'd written all those great essays on welfare economics, and all the terminology could still roll off her tongue. But here she was talking to a corporate executive who had always bettered her in any argument.

Her hands gripped the steering wheel and she stared ahead at the road as it wound north towards the township, and then turned down to the coast. Blake didn't speak as she guided the car around the sweeping bends of the highway, and she focused on her breathing. Showing him the Bennett place was going to demonstrate how good their work was, but deep in her heart she worried it wasn't going to make the slightest bit of difference to his decision.

As they rounded the last curve, the house appeared in front of them, situated majestically at the top of a sweeping lawn with the real estate agent's for sale sign perched in the middle.

"Hmm," said Blake. "That's an exclusive agency. They're one of the best in the Noosa area."

"This is an exclusive house." Ana pulled up beside the fountain in the middle of the circular driveway and reached into the glove compartment for the house keys.

She put the key into the lock of the main entry conscious of him standing so close behind her, she could almost feel the warmth of his body. Smiling to herself, she turned her attention to his reaction to the house. He was about to get his socks blown off.

But when she turned to him, Blake wasn't looking at the house. His gaze was fixed on her and her heartbeat kicked up. Reaching out, he brushed a stray lock of hair back from her face. More heat surged through her. At this rate she'd look like she had a bad case of sunburn.

No matter how much she tried to convince herself they were too different, his touch sent her nerves jangling.

"So why are we here?"

"You'll see."

The Bennetts had employed a landscaping firm and staged the house with rented furniture. The only room without furniture was the ballroom where she and the girls had just recently completed the decorative plasterwork.

"This is why I couldn't help you out on Saturday. We had to finish up here." With one hand casually anchored on her hip, she led him through to the large room leading out to the balcony and swallowed a satisfied smile when he looked around.

Ana straightened her shoulders as she looked around with satisfaction. "Did a good job, didn't we?"

"What exactly did you do?"

"Everything." She spread her hands wide. "Plasterwork, painting, tiling, cupboards, varnishing—" Her voice trailed off as Blake walked into the kitchen and she followed him.

"The only thing we don't do is the plumbing and the electrics, but Joe's two nephews take care of that."

Blake walked over to the bench top and ran his hand along the gleaming granite before turning to her. "You, Sienna, and Georgie did *all* of this?"

"Yep."

"This is amazing. It's as good as anything I've ever seen." Slowly shaking his head, Blake turned back to her.

"Why wouldn't it be?" Ana laughed at the disbelief on his face. "Why do you look so surprised? And be careful of any sexist comment you might be thinking of making."

She studied him, standing in the room where she had worked her butt off for the past three months. A lurch in her belly hit her like a sucker punch. No matter what he thought of her, no matter what he said, she wanted him as much as she ever had. Despite their differences, his presence surrounded her and filled her senses. All the old feelings came rushing back and she tried to ignore the feelings flooding through her, but then Blake looked over and smiled at her.

"I can't believe you do this for a salary. Joe must be making a killing on this. He's obviously more astute than we gave him credit for."

Her happiness fizzled as if he had thrown a bucket of cold water over her. Just when she'd thought he was seeing the worth and beauty of their work, he had to bring it back to profit and balance sheets. He would never understand why they did it.

Always Mr. Cold and Calculating putting the dollar first.

Nothing had changed, she'd been kidding herself. He was still the same hard-nosed businessman chasing a dollar. He would never understand her.

For the life of her, Ana couldn't understand this damn attraction to him. It had to be just lust, because she didn't like one little thing about his attitude. She deliberately blocked out his kindness to his niece and nephews and his explanation about his loneliness when his parents died. It was all about money for him and it always had been. She couldn't believe she thought she was falling for him.

"No," she said coldly. "Joe gives back to the community."

"How?"

Turning on her heel, Ana strode to the door and flung it open. "Come on, I have something else to show you. It might not be as upscale as you're used to, but the work that goes into it is worth ten times more to me than something like this."

She'd shown him what she did and told him how Joe worked. Showing him Thelma and Mitzi's house might kill any chance of him taking her seriously, but she was going to be honest about what drove her to do the work she did.

And then the ball would be firmly in his business court.

***

Blake was sure Ana had an ulterior motive for showing him this job. The two elderly ladies fussed over him as he held a fragile teacup between his fingers and balanced a plate of cake in his other hand. Ana sat back with a smug smile.

"And we must show you the chicken coop too." The smaller of the two ladies reached over and held his arm—he thought it was Mitzi— and he couldn't move for fear of dropping his plate.

"Ana built it for us last winter. She is very clever, you know." The old dear dropped her voice to a whisper and he nodded, glancing across at Ana as a stifled chuckle came from her direction.

"Did we tell you she fixed our fence too?" the other woman added.

"And our roof was leaking, and she came out in the middle of the night, climbed up on the old wooden ladder to fix it while it was still storming." Blake's head turned from one to the other as they finished each other's sentences.

"And there was the time—"

"Mr. Buchanan has seen plenty of the house," Ana interrupted. "As soon as he finishes his tea, we'll have to go. He's very important." Blake narrowed his eyes as Ana smiled at him sweetly. "He's the new owner of Joe's store, you know."

The two old dears squealed with delight and sat on either side of him on the floral sofa.

"How wonderful! So you are going to be a part of our town." The one called Thelma patted his hand.

"You can come to the weekend markets. Do you do any woodwork or make things?" You could set up a stall." Mitzi hung on to his other arm. "And you will have to come to dinner with

114

us."

Blake glanced across at Ana as she stifled a laugh.

"Thank you, I'll keep you to that." He smiled as Ana looked obviously surprised at his easy acceptance of the elderly women. "And I'm not the owner, just the manager and I'll be living in Noosa."

"Oh, no." Thelma grabbed his hand and shook her head. "Living there is too lonely. A nice young man like you needs to be part of a wonderful community like ours." She shot a smile at Ana. "If you are working here you will need to live close by. And you'll need to mix with other young people."

"And if you live close by you can come to dinner with us more often." Mitzi squeezed his hand. "Isn't that so, Ana? You tell him what wonderful cooks we are."

Ana caught his eye and grinned at him as she nodded. He had a feeling he was the centre of a matchmaking plot being hatched by the two women. But despite the teasing, he was surprised to find he was enjoying himself. "I would be delighted to come for dinner and try your home cooking. I don't see a lot of that. My sister has five children and when I eat at her house, we generally eat the same meal as the children." Blake couldn't remember the last time he'd spoken to anyone about his family. In fact, he doubted if any of his work colleagues even knew he had family back in Noosa. "I usually eat out at restaurants."

"That's dreadful! We'll have to take you under our wing." Thelma said.

"Like we did with Ana." Mitzi said looking across at Ana with a smile. "She eats with us often, don't you sweetie? After her poor mum passed on, we all made sure she looked after herself." Mitzi pulled a lace hanky from her pocket and wiped her eyes. "And now she's like a granddaughter to us."

"Not only us, she takes care of the whole community." Thelma stared at him. "I hope things won't change. It would be dreadful if Ana couldn't help us out." Discomfort filled Blake at the thought of the changes that were about to happen. He'd had no idea what Ana had meant when she'd talked about the jobs she did for the elderly folk, and he knew his answer wasn't what they wanted to hear. "Don't worry, Home and Hardware won't let you down."

Thelma reached for her walking stick and pushed herself to her feet. "Mitzi, give Mr. Buchanan another slice of cake." She turned to Ana. "Come into the kitchen, dear. We've chosen the new colours for the walls."

Blake glanced at Ana as Mitzi refilled his teacup and passed him another slice of cake. He knew Ana was enjoying herself. They left him sitting in the parlour—the room filled with old-fashioned furniture and knickknacks couldn't be called anything else—while the two women dragged Ana into the kitchen. Leaning back on the sofa, Blake closed his eyes trying to come to terms with everything he'd seen today.

He'd known Ana was kind—and generous. She'd put her own responsibilities on hold for a couple of days to help him out with the kids, but he hadn't realised this was how she lived her life. All of the philosophies she'd espoused at college were here in front of him, in flesh and blood, in real life, and Blake didn't know what to make of it.

She was important to these two women and by the sound of things, there were many more old folk who relied on her. This town seemed to be all about building relationships and giving back. And Ana was at the centre of it. It was alien to anything he'd ever experienced before. Jeannie had never called for his help before last weekend and really if he thought about it, he wasn't needed by anyone. An emptiness sat uncomfortably in his stomach and it had nothing to do with the food he'd eaten.

"Ssh, he's having a little nap." Blake's eyes flew open as the three of them came in laughing from the kitchen and he caught

Ana's gaze fixed on him. Desire hit him fair and square as he caught a fleeting glimpse of hunger in her eyes.

He stood and turned to the two elderly women. "Thank you for showing me your cottage. Your home. It's delightful."

Blake followed Ana to the car as they waved them off. He was looking forward to getting home and thinking this through. The feeling that Mike was making a huge mistake was growing and he wasn't sure he wanted to be a part of it anymore.

***

The sight of Ana striding along the tiled floor toward the front door of that magnificent house stayed with Blake all week. Her cute little behind outlined by her snugly fitting jeans came into his head at the strangest times. And the feel of her lips beneath his. He shook his head to clear his thoughts—he had to focus on the Zoom meeting.

Mike was talking about profit margins and standardised stores, and all he could think about was how well Ana filled out her jeans.

"Blake? What do you think about that?" Mike's voice interrupted his musing,

"Sorry." Blake turned his attention back to his boss whose ruddy face filled his screen. "About what?"

"What's wrong with you? Don't tell me I've made a mistake sending you out there."

Blake balled his hands into fists at his side, biting down on the angry response that sprung to his lips.

"No, Mike. You didn't send me. I chose to move back here. Remember?"

Blake could see Mike's eyes narrow on his screen.

"You been spending time with Jack?"

"No. He's gone back to Melbourne. Why?"

"Thought it might explain why you weren't focused. Thought you might have been out partying."

Although he was loyal to the company, his boss's attitude was starting to piss him off big time.

Blake injected coldness into his voice and his words came out like steel pellets as anger burned through his chest. "I have been doing some research into this takeover and I think we might be making a mistake up here."

"Why?"

"Mike, have you even been to Maleny?"

"No need, the team sussed it all out. It's a prime site for future growth. I know it's not going to be a big store for a while, but Sunshine Coast is growing. In a few years, Maleny will be a suburb like any other and we'll already be established there, waiting for all the new homeowners to come and spend their money."

And what a shame that would be.

Blake swallowed. He couldn't believe the direction his thoughts were taking. Ever since Ana had shown him around the small community and he'd met Thelma and Mitzi, he'd become more uncomfortable about the takeover of the store.

"Blake, don't you worry about it. The figures have been run hundreds of times. There's enough business already to make the wait worthwhile. Once the area develops, it will take off big time. You just have to go in there tomorrow and get going. It won't be pretty, but that's the way we make money."

Blake lifted his head and stared at the screen. Mike's jowls were sagging, and his neck was pinched where the sides of his shirt struggled to meet beneath his chin. The veins on his cheeks were broken and contributed to the ruddiness of his complexion.

"There's just one more thing I want to run by you before we sign off." Blake kept his voice firm. "Have you thought any more about the restoration department? I've had a good look around the area and it's a huge business down here. *Spark and Burns Realty* has the market sewn up and the hardware store does most of the work on the restorations."

"No." Mike shook his head emphatically. "A standard store set up, remember? You go and sort out the human resources and the refit team will arrive in a couple of weeks."

A couple of weeks. And then a couple of dozen people would be out of a job, and Ana would be taken away from the work she loved.

Piece of cake.

The following morning, Blake dressed in his business suit and exited the hotel to his car. It had rained overnight, and the heavy grey sky matched his mood. Rolling down his window, he let the cool air blow in and listened to the swishing of the tires on the road, trying to concentrate as he drove from Noosa to Maleny. Joe had organised for him to talk to the whole staff before the store opened and then he had back-to-back appointments with individual staff members.

And he wasn't looking forward to any of it.

His stomach was in knots as he focused on the road ahead of him. Every time he thought about how to tell the staff about the upcoming changes, all he could picture was Ana's face when he had to tell her the restoration department was gone.

The street was jam-packed with cars when he pulled up outside the small hardware store. Stepping from the car, he avoided the puddles in the gutter and even that made him think of Ana and the wet shoes she'd carried into his place only a week ago. He schooled his face into a pleasant expression as an elderly man in a suit stepped from the store with his hand outstretched.

"Blake Buchanan?"

He took the proffered hand and shook it, appreciating the strong grip that grasped his hand in welcome. "Joe Hickey? Great to finally meet you in person."

And immediately his professional confidence came back, and he breathed a sigh of relief. It was time he got over this mooning around and focus on the job in hand.

Joe chatted to him as they made their way up the stairs to the office overlooking the store. The walls only went halfway to the ceiling and the noise of the store as the staff prepared to open for the day drifted up to them. A small, motorised trolley purred along one aisle and another elderly man swept with a straw broom, stirring up clouds of dust.

"We're very lucky here." Joe looked at him from beneath beetling brows. "When I told the staff about the meeting, they all came in early so the store could still open on time."

"Great." Blake rubbed his hands together briskly and peered down into the store. It was cool up here in this open-walled office and there appeared to be no heating in the old building. A quick glance down to the store below showed no sign of Ana yet.

"Here's the list of your appointments for the day."

Joe handed Blake a handwritten list of names and chuckled. "I hope you can read my wife's writing. She doesn't like to use a computer much—says they're too impersonal."

Blake ran down the list twice, but he didn't see Ana or Sienna on it.

"Is this complete?

"Yes," replied Joe. "Two of our girls resigned yesterday so you don't need to meet with them."

Chapter Twelve

The damp seeped through her jeans as Ana kneeled on the wet earth. She'd left her gloves in the shed and had intended to use the garden fork to turn over the soil in her vegetable garden. But the weeds had beckoned and now she sat back on her heels with wet knees and black soil covering her hands. Breathing in the smell of rain, she tipped her head back and let the light mist caress her face. Despite the weather, it was restful being outside catching up on her chores. The garden had been well and truly neglected since they'd started work on the Bennett house and the weeds had overtaken the vegetable patch. She grinned to herself. It was usually only the inside of her cottage that was chaotic.

And with the way things had turned out, her garden was going to be even more neglected from now on. If Home and Hardware wouldn't keep them on, then she and Sienna would just do the work themselves. It might be a little slower as they waited for materials instead of using the store's inventory, but they would still have jobs they loved.

She hummed to herself as she worked until the sound of a car coming up the drive interrupted her thoughts.

She wiped her hands on her jeans and wandered over to wait by the side of the driveway as Blake parked next to her ute.

At least I won't have to wait for Georgie to report in now.

Ana lifted her hands to give her hair a quick finger comb and remembered just in time that she had dirt all over them. Pausing with her hands in mid-air, she wondered what it was about Blake that always put her in such turmoil. It wasn't so hard to admit that just being around him excited her.

It always had been.

He stepped out of the car and tucked the keys into his suit pocket. Her nerves were jangling by the time he reached her.

"Hello, Ana."

"Hello, Blake." She stood and drank in the sight of him in his suit, trying to keep her expression solemn. "This is a surprise. I thought you'd be busy at the store?"

"I'm on my way back to Noosa and I just wanted to check on you." He frowned as he looked down at her. "Why did you resign so suddenly?"

Ignoring his question, she turned her back to him and headed inside. "Come in." He followed her and as she washed her hands, she watched as he lifted her cat from the sofa in the living room and sat down. Instead of putting the cat on the rug, he lifted Sooky into his lap and patted her.

The traitor lifted her head back between his hands and purred.

"You'll get cat hair on your suit."

He shrugged. "I've been thinking about getting a pet. Can't decide between a cat or a dog." He shot her a grin, but she didn't take the bait.

"That will be good for you."

"Yes, it probably will. Look, come over here and talk to me." Blake held her gaze until she shrugged her shoulders and sat at the far end of the sofa.

"Why did you resign?"

"Did anything change? Did management have a sudden change of direction?" Ana lifted her chin and waited for his reply.

"No."

"Then I did the right thing. No point staying where I'm not wanted."

Blake cleared his throat and she smiled. She was enjoying seeing him squirm.

"You have to understand, Ana. I did try."

"Oh, I'm sure you did, Blake. Once you'd seen the potential of our work, I'm sure the dollar signs went *ka-ching*."

"I really do admire your work."

"What? The moneymaking potential of what we do?" She held his gaze and held her resolve firm as he ran his fingers through his hair. She was starting to recognise his gestures and what they meant. "Don't you worry about us. We've taken our future in our own hands. Sienna and I are opening our own little business and we are going to be just fine."

"What do you mean?"

"Watching how you operate and listening to your endless talk of profit made me realise I wouldn't work for you even if you wanted us to stay. You have no care or respect for the community—for our people—and that's a given for us."

Blake slid across the sofa in one swift movement and grabbed her hands. "You're wrong about me, Ana. You have to understand I work for a large corporation and as such I have to remain loyal to the business direction, even if I may not agree with it."

"As such"—Ana mimicked his phrase— "you are selling your soul for something you don't believe in." She looked up and was encouraged by the uncertainty in his expression. "Why do you stay there, Blake? If you don't agree with what's happening?"

His eyes held hers and he frowned. "Up until the Maleny store, I've always worked in front of a computer. I've never had anything to do with the community, or the people in the store. It's never been real."

Ana pulled her hands away from his clasp, ignoring the need to stay holding onto him. She stood and moved across to the window. "Sounds like you've got some thinking to do then. Everything is real, we are real." She placed her hands on her heart. "The people you've met. Joe, Mitzi, Thelma and there are many more in this wonderful town—they're all real people with needs and feelings."

"Tell me about what you're going to do." He stood and put

Sooky down carefully on the chair, but she shook her head.

"No way. You're the competition now." She smiled sweetly at him. "I'd hate to put you in a difficult position."

"Oh, for goodness sake, Ana. I'm here as your friend."

"Blake, we were never friends. You barely tolerated me at college. We slept together once, you used me when you needed help last weekend, and you were about to take my job away from me today. If that's what you call being friends, I'd hate to be your enemy."

"If that's how you feel, there's no point in me hanging around. I was going to see if you wanted to come back to town with me and have dinner."

She laughed bitterly. "What? You were going to fire me and then take me out to dinner? Now that does remind me of a sexist pig I used to know."

Blake turned on his heel without a word and walked out to the car. He didn't look back once as he climbed in and drove down the driveway and out of her life.

##

By the time Sienna and Georgie arrived to recap the day, Ana had wiped away her tears and washed her face. She tried to block out all the feelings that had resurfaced since last weekend. If she was honest, they'd always been there, and she'd buried them when she'd left Blake's house ten years ago. But this last week had proven that they were still opposites in every way that mattered, and a relationship just wouldn't work even if he did reciprocate her feelings.

She spent half an hour roaming around the house, packing up and putting away things that had been lying around for months.

Amazing what you could achieve in one day.

Garden weeded, living room and kitchen tidy, and the love of her life banished with a couple of unkind words.

Love of my life? Jeez, where did that come from?

By the time the girls came through the front door, a bottle of champagne in Sienna's hand, Ana was calm and composed. Sienna went straight to the cupboard and peered inside.

"Champagne glasses? I'm not drinking French champagne out of a vegemite glass, Ana."

"In the living room." She waved one hand in the direction of the old Welsh dresser.

A loud pop followed by the gushing of froth from the top of the bottle had Georgie running over with a glass. "Ugh, don't waste it. It's *Moet.*"

Ana frowned at Sienna. "A tad extravagant, considering we've only got one job lined up so far?"

"But we have news." Sienna grinned at her and Georgie clapped her hands. "Lots of news."

"Okay, spill. The news, not the wine." Ana grinned and tried to ignore the regret that was still tugging at her. She'd been perfectly happy before she'd met Blake again and she was going to be happy again.

Sienna poured the wine slowly, and Ana tapped her hands on the back of the chair impatiently. "Come on, girls, don't keep me in suspense."

Sienna handed her a glass and lifted hers for a toast. "Here's to the new *Sunshine Coast Reno Service*—" she paused and put out one hand in a dramatic flourish— "and to the feature of the Bennett's house in *Ocean Home* magazine."

Ana gasped. "Are you kidding me?"

Sienna nodded smugly.

"Oh, my God." Ana waved her hand in front of her face as a feeling of light headedness stole over her. "Either this champagne is potent, or I'm overwhelmed."

Sienna put her glass down and hugged her. "See, Ana. I told you it would all work out. Change is not all bad. The Bennetts want us to sign the contract for the restoration of a second house

125

next week. And Georgie has news from the store, too."

"It was a good day, Ana. It's a shame you didn't stay for it." Georgie tipped her head to one side. "Blake's a honey. If he wasn't taken, I'd be going for him myself."

Ana's head flew up and she stared at Georgie. "Taken?"

Georgie laughed and nodded with a knowing glance at her sister. "Anyone can see you are head over heels, and we saw the way he looked at you in the bar the other day."

The heat started in the pit of Ana's stomach and travelled up her neck to her cheeks. She waved her hand in front of her face again as both girls laughed.

"It's the champagne." She glared at them. "Why was it such a good day?"

"Generous payouts for the staff who are going. Pay raises and great benefits for those who stay. Joe and Magda didn't stop smiling all day."

"That's good. I'm so happy for the staff—and you too, Georgie. Ana reached over and hugged her friend. "But our department was still destined to go. I'm just pleased the Bennetts made the offer before we got fired." She picked up the bottle and topped up her champagne. "Sounds like Blake was a hit."

"He was great. He talked about how he believes the store should keep its local identity and how he would work hard to keep that."

"I'll believe that when I see it."

"You're too hard on him, Ana. What did he ever do to you?" Georgie frowned at her. A ripple of guilt flickered through Ana. Georgie always saw the good in every situation. Or maybe Blake was coming around? Maybe he'd begun to understand what their community was like? And what it meant to her?

Ana wandered over to the window and spread her fingers on the cool glass. The rain had cleared, and the sun was hovering above the horizon as the day came to an end. Soft pink and gold hues filled the western sky and tinged the mountains with a soft light. She sipped at her champagne and the bubbles tickled her nose.

"You're right, you know. He's just doing his job." She turned back to the twins. "After we see the Bennetts on Monday, I'll go into the store to see him." Going over to the table, she tapped the lid off one of the shoeboxes. "Besides, I promised Joe I'd get these invoices to Blake by then."

Sienna looked at the boxes on the table and laughed. "I'll believe that when I see it."

"I have every intention of clearing the backlog before Monday." Ana put her champagne glass down. "That's my weekend plan."

Chapter Thirteen

Ana sat back in her chair and lifted her arms above her head, stretching her neck from side to side, trying to ignore the beautiful day outside. The mid-morning sun was streaming through the kitchen window heralding the onset of summer, the birds were screeching in the bush and Mutt sat at her feet, his big brown eyes telling her he would love a walk in the hills.

"One more box to go and we'll go for a walk," she promised. His tail thumped on the floor and she reached down to rub his head. "But there'll be a lot more time spent doing the books from now on, boy."

She'd not slept well. After the girls had gone home, she'd worried about the huge step she and Sienna had taken. From now on, they would be on their own, and excitement warred with common sense in Ana's thoughts. She had a horrible feeling their decision to start their own renovation company had been made in haste and if it hadn't been for Blake's comment about Joe making a killing on the Bennett job, they would have waited to see what ensued in the meeting with him at the store.

He just didn't understand.

Ana fought back the thought that maybe—just maybe— what they'd been doing for the past few years hadn't been good business. But when she looked at Thelma and Mitzi, and the other locals they'd helped out, they'd done a damn good job and made a lot of people happy.

They would never have been able to afford to do the work for the community without Joe's generosity, and their hard work. Could they fund it all on their own? Perhaps not right away, but eventually? She reached for the final box and lifted out a handful of papers. Mutt jumped to his feet and ran to the door and for a moment, she thought he'd given up waiting and was asking to go out.

And then she heard the purr of a motor. The same sound of the car that had been driven out of her driveway so abruptly yesterday.

Prickly heat ran up and down her body as she looked down at her pyjamas. Standing up quickly, the antique Hitchcock chair crashed to the floor behind her and she shut and locked the front door before scurrying back to pick the chair up.

Oh God, she'd already insulted him. Now he'd think she was slamming the door in his face. Ana opened the door again, peering around the side.

What on earth is he doing here?

Blake walked around the back of the car and opened the passenger door. Ana watched with fascination as he held his hand out and Maddy emerged from the back seat, the ever-present book tucked beneath her arm.

Ana turned and ran up the stairs to her bedroom pulling off her pyjama top along the way. By the time she was in her room and searching desperately for a clean T-shirt and a pair of jeans, a knock sounded at the front door.

"Be down in a minute," she called out.

Low voices drifted up to her as she quickly washed her face and pulled a brush through her hair. Finally, she slipped on a pair of flat shoes and walked slowly down the stairs, to catch her breath and compose herself.

When she stepped out onto the porch, Blake was sitting in one of the rocking chairs with Sooky who was once again on his lap. Maddy was crouched in front of him stroking the cat's long, silky fur.

"Well, hello, Maddy." Ana threw a guarded glance toward Blake. "This is a lovely surprise."

"Hello, Ana." Maddy stood and clasped her hands together in front of her chest. "Uncle Blake and I are going on a picnic. Will

129

you come with us? Please?"

Before she could answer, the little girl rushed on. "We didn't have one when Billy was naughty in the park when Mummy was helping Daddy in the rainforest and Mummy said we could have another one today and Billy could stay home, and Benny and Roddy are at soccer and—"

Blake placed his hand on Maddy's shoulder and interrupted his niece. "And Uncle Blake thought it would be a really good way to show Ana how friends can have a good time together?" He lifted his sunglasses and met Ana's gaze. "Even after they argue?"

"Well . . ." Ana eyed Blake for a moment and a pleasant shiver ran down her back as he held her gaze steadily.

"We are still friends, aren't we?" he asked. His head was tipped to the side and he raised his eyebrows. More often than not he'd been the one to initiate the peace between them in the past, and it looked like he was trying to make amends now. The laugh lines around his eyes deepened as he smiled. He was still the Blake she'd held close in her heart and the ice around her heart cracked a little more. She looked away from him reluctantly, and down into Maddy's earnest little face. "I guess we are."

Maddy gave a whoop of delight and turned her attention back to the cat.

A tentative smile tipped the corners of Blake's mouth up. "Maddy was really excited to see you again. You made a big impression last weekend."

Blake glanced at his niece and then he walked along the porch to Ana. "I wanted to see you too, but I wasn't sure what sort of reception I would get." He kept his voice low and Ana inclined her head for him to follow her into the house.

She stepped inside and waited as he closed the screen door behind him.

"Blake—"

"Ana—"

They both spoke at the same time and Ana smiled.

"Me first," she said. Blake leaned on the door frame and waited for her to speak.

Blake smiled at her and she tried to ignore the trembling that shot down her legs. It was only because she'd run up and down the stairs in about twenty seconds.

That was all.

"I shouldn't have left the store without talking to you. That was rude." He'd made the first move and she was happy to give a little.

Blake held up his hands. "Let's call a truce for the day. There's a little girl out there who's had a bit of a tough week."

"Oh, no. What happened?"

Blake took a step back and looked out to check on Maddy. "It's been a big week for the whole family, with Rod's accident. And on top of everything, some kids at school gave Maddy a hard time. Jeannie thought a change of scenery would do her good." He held his hands out and said simply. "So here we both are. Two needy souls."

Ana burst out laughing at the plaintive look on Blake's face. "That's the last thing I'd call you, Blake. You're the most self-sufficient person I know."

Blake grinned back at her and then caught sight of the invoices spread out over the table. He raised a quizzical brow at Ana. "You know you don't have to do them anymore."

"I promised I would finish them. No regrets and no hard feelings."

Blake stepped closer to her and the fresh smell of soap filled her senses as she dropped her gaze. His denim jeans were faded but neatly pressed with a sharp crease running down each leg. He reached over and tipped a finger beneath her chin and tilted her head up gently.

For a moment, she thought he was going to kiss her again

and she was disappointed when he spoke instead.

"We still need to talk about work, but not today, I promise. Today is for having some fun." The crinkles around Blake's eyes deepened as he smiled at her. "And catching up on that picnic Maddy missed out on."

"Sounds good to me, where are we going?"

"The Fairy Pools in the National Park. Lots of tidal pools there for Maddy."

Ana looked down at her clothes. The heat rose in her neck as she realised her T-shirt was on inside out and her jeans were crumpled from being on the bedroom floor all week.

"Just give me a minute?"

***

As they travelled down the highway, Maddy showed off her excellent reading skills. Blake glanced back affectionately as her little voice confidently read the words about the littlest lighthouse keeper. A soft marshmallow feeling lodged in his chest as he glanced across at Ana. She was quiet, and she looked out at the ocean as he steered the car along the coast road. When she'd come back downstairs, his breath had caught in his throat. She'd changed into some sort of loose, floaty dress and her silvery blonde hair was down around her shoulders. It was just as though they'd gone back ten years and the hippy college student had come back.

"I thought we'd go to the beach first and have our picnic before we go for a walk. Maddy would like to collect some shells too." He turned the car into the National Park car park. "Okay with you girls?"

"That's fine with me. I'm just tagging along as a guest." Ana smiled at him and stretched her head back to look at Maddy who had finished reading the story. "This is a great beach, Maddy. Have you been here before?"

The little girl shook her head. "We don't go to the beach very much because the boys can't swim, and Mummy says you

132

need too many eyes." Maddy counted on her fingers. You would need six pairs of eyes to watch us." She was quiet for a moment as she kept counting on her fingers and then looked at Ana with wide eyes. "Wow, that is twelve eyes plus ours. That makes twenty two eyes all together. So that would be all of us kids and Mummy and Daddy and you and Uncle Blake and we would still need two more grownups to get enough eyes."

Blake glanced across at Ana and grinned. Her eyes were almost as wide as Maddy's.

"Do you know why you need so many eyes, Ana?" He laughed when she shook her head. "One pair for each child and a spare—just in case."

Ana opened the door and waited by the car as Blake helped Maddy out, before he opened the trunk and lifted out a huge picnic basket and a rug.

He passed the rug to Ana. "Maddy, you hold Ana's hand. I need both hands to carry this basket. I think Mummy thought that all the eyes would be coming when she packed our lunch."

As Ana turned to his niece and held out her hand, the light wind lifted her hair. The neckline of her dress was scooped and a tantalizing glimpse of the soft swell of her breast peeked out. Blake forced himself to look away and hefted the basket up.

"Come on, girls. Time to go exploring." His voice was gruff and when he glanced back, he caught Ana's eye. For a moment nothing more was said. Clear hazel eyes looked back at him, calmly assessing. Perhaps seeing more than he'd wanted her to see until they'd sorted out what was happening between them—without the complication of the store takeover making things difficult.

That damned patchouli she wore wafted around him when she moved, and it reminded him of that night they'd had together. If he closed his eyes, he could still feel her silken skin beneath his fingers. It had been such a long time ago.

133

Too long.

"Uncle Blake, why are your eyes shut?"

"Ah, I was just having a rest." He turned to Maddy. "Come on, there's lots of starfish, urchins, and hermit crabs for us to look for."

When he and Jeannie had been small, their parents had brought them here to the rockpools on many weekends and it was fun to be doing it again with Ana and Maddy. He had a wonderful memory of swimming to his dad unaided for the first time as a six-year-old in the big pool and calling triumphantly to this mother and Jeannie who watched from the rocks. That was what he wanted from life.

Those moments of love and sharing of happiness.

The restlessness of his corporate life didn't compare to moments like that. For years he'd kidded himself that Jeannie and Rod and their kids were enough family for him. But when Ana's clear assessing gaze locked with his, the certainty of the future he'd mapped out for himself faded.

Ever since he'd kissed her the other morning, his world had shifted, and he was going to do his damnedest to convince her he wasn't the greedy businessman she seemed to think he was.

Slow and steady.

All he had to do was convince her of that.

They walked down along the bush track to the beach before the pools, and Maddy shrieked with delight as the velvety sand squeaked between her toes. Blake found a sunny spot sheltered from the wind off the sea, tucked the picnic basket beneath an overhanging rock, and covered it with the rug. The morning sea mist had burned off, and the sun was warm on his back as he followed Maddy and Ana along to the Fairy Pools. Ana's dress blew against her slender figure and he watched her, wondering if there was a possibility of a future together. He stood back and looked north as Maddy led Ana from one tidal pool to another and the little girl's excited chatter didn't stop.

Blake dropped to a crouch and waited for them to come back to him with their bounty. He looked curiously at the crustaceans Maddy held in her cupped hands, before looking up at Ana. Her fair cheeks were flushed, and her expression, contented.

"Ready to eat?"

She nodded and walked back to their picnic spot while he took Maddy back to the water to carefully place all the creatures back in the pools. By the time they got back to the sheltered spot beneath the bluff, Ana had spread out the picnic rug and was peeking in the basket.

"Oh, yum. I forgot to have breakfast." She grinned up at him. "Too busy playing with shoeboxes."

Her sense of humour filled him with anticipation. Maybe she wasn't going hold a grudge. Reaching into the basket, she passed him three picnic plates before lifting out some sealed containers.

"Potato salad, green salad, quiche and oh, I wonder who this is for? A peanut butter and jelly sandwich?"

Ana handed the sandwich to his niece and Blake grinned.

Maddy giggled. "No, that's for Uncle Blake."

Ana shook her head and passed over the sandwich with a laugh. "Had me fooled."

Blake leaned back against the rock and the warmth seeped through his T-shirt as he munched on his sandwich. "I've got more places for us to see, girls."

'Where to?' Maddy asked.

'Not far from here,' he said.

'You sound like you remember the area well.' Ana said.

"I do. What would you say to me becoming more of a local than just running the store?"

"How?"

He spoke slowly and kept his attention totally focused on

her reaction. His future happiness—and hers if things went as he planned—depended on how she took his news.

"I plan on living here for more than twenty-five years. I'm keeping my house on the canal, but I'm moving to Maleny."

Chapter Fourteen

The gloss of the day rubbed off a little for Ana after Blake dropped his news during their picnic lunch. Up until then she'd managed to put all thoughts of work out of her mind. They were just two friends and a little girl having a fun day out together.

Blake put the picnic basket and rug back in the car after they finished lunch and they strolled along the track back to the car park and crossed to the other side of the next bluff. A large pod of dolphins frolicked in the waves and Maddy's delight made the long walk worthwhile. As the path became a little rough, Blake held his hand out to Ana. She tried to ignore the frisson of nerves that travelled up her arm at his touch.

As they watched the dolphins, Blake held Maddy up high and Ana held her phone up until the little girl stopped squealing.

"Smile, Maddy," she called, taking longer than necessary to capture the shot.

No man should be so good-looking. Standing in front of the brilliant blue water, he looked so strong and sexy. His plain white T-shirt hugged his broad chest and his faded jeans clung snugly to muscular thighs. By the time Maddy insisted on taking one of Blake and Ana, Ana was well and truly flustered, and she stood stiffly in the circle of Blake's arm, pasting a smile on her face. His hand rested low on her back and as they stood, waiting for Maddy to take the photograph, the light pressure of his fingers sent a delicious shiver down Ana's spine. As she trembled, Blake's fingers began a slow caress on her lower back and by the time Maddy yelled 'smile', he had moved his hand around her and pulled her close against him.

"Have to make sure we're both in the frame for Maddy's photo." His warm breath whispered close to her ear.

"Another one," Maddy yelled as she stepped closer to

them.

After Maddy had taken the photo and walked back to them, Blake kept his arm loosely around Ana's shoulder and she had relaxed against him.

Maddy nodded off to sleep as they headed back to town.

"Do you want to go for a coffee after we drop Maddy home?" Blake asked quietly.

Ana glanced at her watch. "Drop me off first. I need to get home. I'd like to take Mutt for a walk before the sun goes down."

"Okay. I've got an appointment in town tonight."

An appointment or a date?

Ana wondered which it was, but Blake didn't say any more.

Rich. Good looking. A great house—make that *two* great houses. She was sure the women would be falling over his doorstep to hook up with him.

Maddy was still asleep in the back when they reached Hill Cottage and Ana quickly exited the car.

"Don't get out, Blake." She walked around to the driver's side and he slid his window down, reached out and took her hand. Ana looked down at his strong fingers wrapped around hers.

She squeezed his fingers lightly despite wanting to pull back as confusion filled her. "Thanks for a fun day."

"What are you doing tomorrow?" Blake lifted her hand and brushed it against his lips.

The question surprised her. "Why?"

"I'd like to drive back up and see you. There are a few things I still need to talk to you about."

"Oh. What sort of things?" Excitement rippled through her at the thought of him wanting to see her again so soon.

"I'd rather leave it till tomorrow when we can have a proper talk."

"I'll call you. I'm not quite sure what my plans are yet."

"Okay. I'll be down at the store anyway, so I'll look

forward to your call." He dropped her hand and then turned to her again. "Watch that Mutt dog of yours, while I back out."

Ana bent down and picked up Sooky before whistling for Mutt.

"And Ana? Thanks for your company. Maddy was really excited you came along with us." After a final wave from him, the window slid up and he backed slowly down the drive.

Ana stood with her hands on her hips watching until he turned the car onto the highway, and they disappeared. She walked slowly inside.

It had been such a great day. Not one cross word spoken, and she'd enjoyed his teasing. She'd seen yet another side to Blake today and wondered if that was the real Blake that had been buried under the business exterior. When he'd dropped the bombshell the was moving to Maleny her thoughts had been in turmoil. He'd be close by, and living in such a small community, she'd be sure to run into him often.

It was going to be hard to remember he was the new boss at Home and Hardware.

##

As it turned out, the next day didn't go as planned. A frantic call from Joe's cousin, Maria, sent Ana hurrying into town to help with the shingling of their roof. Her elderly husband, Aldo, had started the job while Maria was at church and she had come home to a fallen ladder, a husband stuck up on the roof, and a great gaping hole above her kitchen.

Ana packed the ute, slipped on her dungarees, tool belt, and work boots and drove the short distance into Maleny.

Maria was waiting for her outside and folded her in a grandmotherly hug.

"Thank you, Ana. Look at the silly old fool. I told him to call and get you to do it."

With her hands on her hips, Ana called up to Aldo.

"Having a bit of trouble up there?"

A frown and a grunt were all she got in return.

"Let the silly old man sit up on the roof for a while. Come in for some *biscotti* and lemonade." Maria bustled ahead of her toward the front porch, but Ana shook her head.

"No, I'll get up there and help before he hurts himself. It shouldn't take too long." Ana picked up the ladder and wedged it firmly against the edge of the garden before joining Aldo up on the roof. The morning fog had been heavy, so Ana took extra care as she slid over the slippery roof shingles toward the elderly man.

She grinned. Below them, the gaping hole opened to the kitchen and she could see Maria at the stove as the tempting aroma of minestrone came wafting up.

"Morning, young Ana." Aldo's voice was gruff.

"What seems to be the problem?" Ana looked across the tops of the houses toward the hardware store on Main Street. At least if she needed any gear to help Aldo she could go and get it.

No, she corrected herself. She would have to go and buy it. Her work was no longer a part of the store and that was going to take some getting used to.

"I've loosened all the old glue, but I can't lift the shingles around the edge of the hole." Ana looked down at Aldo's old gnarled, arthritic fingers, not surprised he couldn't get a firm grip on the material.

"No matter, I'm here now with my tools and we'll get it done in no time."

Aldo insisted on climbing up and down the ladder to get the replacement shingles two at a time and Ana bit her lip in worry each time he disappeared over the edge of the roof. It took four hours to glue the new material in place. Maria insisted they come down for lunch and that had added another hour to the day.

The final shingle was placed, and she wiped the last bit of excess glue with a rag. She turned to follow Aldo across the roof as

Blake's car slowed to a stop and parked behind her.

Her heart gave a funny little flip when he stepped out and leaned against the bonnet of the Mercedes. She sat on the peak of the roof and waited as Aldo climbed down the ladder.

Blake grinned up at her. "Are you coming down or should I come up there?"

Here she was sitting on a roof in her old work clothes, and all it took was the sound of Blake's voice to make her heart beat faster. She seriously needed to get over this . . . and him.

"I'm coming down now," she said.

She could see the grin on his face, and she closed her eyes to block out the sight. He strolled leisurely across the pavement to the ladder and put his hand out to help Aldo down the last few rungs. Ana was acutely aware of her bottom at his eye level as she climbed down the ladder and ignored the jolt that ran up her arm as he took her hand to help her down. It was bad enough that her legs turned to jelly when he'd pulled up, now her arms were all tingly from where he'd touched her. She jumped down onto the concrete path, her work boots making a resounding thud as she landed.

"Aldo, this is Blake Buchanan. He's the new manager of Joe's store."

The two men shook hands before Aldo disappeared inside to wash the glue off his hands.

"Well . . ." Blake said.

Ana stared at him. He was dressed in his faded jeans teamed with a black T-shirt today, and it highlighted his dark hair. Sunglasses covered his eyes, and his lips were turned up slightly, but he didn't seem happy now.

"Well, what?" She stood with her hands on her hips. "Is something wrong/"

"Is this how you usually spend your weekends?"

"More often than not. Do you have a problem with that?"

"You work too hard." He finally lifted his sunglasses, and

141

she returned his look with the same intent that was in his.

"I don't class it as work. I like to help my friends."

"So it's not a paying job?

"I don't think that's any of your business. I don't work for the store anymore, remember?"

"Truce?" Blake held his hands up in front of him. "Honestly. I was just interested."

Ana relaxed her stance and slid her hands from her hips as he went back to his car and opened a rear door. Turning away she unclipped her tool belt and slipped it off, before walking to the ute and shoving the belt through the open window onto the front seat. She took a deep breath and composed herself before turning back to him. She gasped in surprise and raised her fingers to her lips as Blake handed her a posy of violets wrapped in mauve tissue paper. She raised them to her face and inhaled the sweet fragrance.

"I saw these as I drove into town and I thought of you. A peace offering?"

Warmth surged through Ana and she kept her eyes down, for fear he'd see the hunger in her gaze. "Thank you, that was very thoughtful." She placed them carefully on the front seat. "I just have to say goodbye to Maria and Aldo and then we can have our chat."

"Can I follow you back to your place?"

"Okay."

Ana's stomach grumbled as Maria pressed a pot of soup and a cob of freshly baked bread into her hands. "Thank you so much."

The old, wrinkled face beamed at her. "You are a good girl."

Ana hugged Maria. The women in the community had banded together when her mother had passed away and had looked after her. It was like having a huge family of elderley aunts—and uncles—and she was always glad to help them out. She glanced up to see Blake watching them with a kind smile. Hope filled her and she held her breath.

He is beginning to understand. Please.

She followed Blake's car along the road until they both turned up her driveway. Anticipation and doubt about talking to him warred for supremacy in her mind.

After today, she probably wouldn't see much of him.

And it wouldn't bother her one bit.

Really.

He would be immersed in running the store, and once she and Sienna signed the contract with the Bennetts, they would be busy with the next house.

Blake was waiting for her on the driveway as she pulled up and he walked over and opened her car door.

"Thank you."

He didn't speak. Mutt ran over to greet them both and Sooky nudged Blake's leg as they walked along the porch together and he gave her a quick pat.

"Come in." Ana unlocked the door and gestured for Blake to follow her inside. He stepped in past her and she pushed the door shut. Before she could speak, Blake moved in close and put his hands on the door behind either side of her head. Her heartbeat quickened with anticipation as he held her gaze.

He lowered his head slowly and his mouth touched hers lightly. She hadn't known her body could feel so alive until his soft and coaxing lips claimed hers and she clung to his shoulders and kissed him right back. His T-shirt was bunched in her fists and heat spread from her fingertips. It coursed through her, and the slow, steady flame grew until she felt she would burn from the heat filling her entire body.

All her thinking, and worrying, and doubt disappeared for a moment as their lips met and clung.

And then the doubts crept back in and reason damped the

heat.

Reason which was cold and empty.

Ana stiffened and pulled back and Blake loosened his grip. Running her hands through her hair, she looked up at him, surprised to see his cheeks flushed and his eyes hazy. She was sure she looked the same.

"I've wanted to kiss you again since last weekend," he said softly. "It's all I can think about."

"Why?"

Ana swallowed and lifted her head to meet his intent gaze. He grinned at her and she clasped her hands to her chest.

"Because I can't get you out of my mind." He shook his head. "I'm supposed to be concentrating on this move— horrendous as it is—all I can think about is you."

"Horrendous? Which move? The store or the house you bought?" Ana dropped her arms as the warmth dissipated as quickly as it had filled her. "You didn't have to do either, you know. Things could have stayed the way they were."

Blake crossed the room and stood at the large window overlooking the ocean. "Change can be good, Ana."

She followed him over and stood next to the antique rocking chair which she had positioned to take in the view.

"How? Why can it be good?" She knew she sounded like a petulant child, but her emotions were in turmoil and she didn't want him to know how her blood was still zinging from his kiss.

"Life moves on. People change. Our needs change." The earnest expression on his face was the same as when they'd argued in college. But this time, she was listening to him . . . just a little bit.

"You have to be honest and really think about what it is you want out of life. Too often we get caught on the work treadmill. I know I did. The move here—reconnecting with my family—has been the best thing for me. When my parents died, I

144

thought making my fortune would fill the gap I felt. But I was wrong." He shrugged and held his hands out to her. "It didn't. The move home and meeting up with you again—that's shown me what's important. . .and what I want. What I need."

He stretched his hands out to her and she stared at them for a moment before wiping her palms on the front of her dungarees. Her own hands were dirty, and her nails were broken from pulling the shingles off the roof. Slowly, she reached out with one of hers, as tentative acceptance of his words. He raised it to his lips, and she couldn't help the smile tugging at her mouth.

"Let's take it slow. Let's start afresh and get to know each other again. No baggage, no past?" Blake tipped his head to the side and he quirked an eyebrow. "We've had the truce, now we'll make a deal."

"Before we start talking mergers?" She chuckled at the look on his face. "Always the businessman, Blake?"

"All depends on what sort of . . . er . . . mergers you are talking about. I can think of a few pleasurable ones myself."

Her face heated as Blake slid his hands along her arms and pulled her close. She snuggled into his warmth and sighed with pleasure as he leaned his forehead against hers. His warm breath puffed on her cheeks for a moment before he slid his lips slowly down her cheek until they teased at the corner of her mouth. Ana shivered, her lips parted, and she waited for his mouth to claim hers again. The thought of a 'merger' sent spirals of heat shooting through her limbs.

Her eyes flew open as his phone rang stridently. Blake pulled back reluctantly and lightly touched her face.

"I'm sorry. I'm expecting a call that's going to make a big difference to things." He brushed his lips across hers. "Hold that mood?"

Ana stepped back and pointed upstairs before he took the call. "That's fine. I'll have a shower and get changed. Would you like to stay for some of that minestrone and bread Maria sent home?" He smiled and nodded before turning away to speak into the phone.

Ana went out to the car to bring in the food and put the gas on low beneath the soup pot. She glanced across at Blake as she headed for the shower, but he was frowning and intent on his conversation.

Standing beneath the hot jets, Ana could barely contain her excitement as she scrubbed at her hands to remove the dirt and dried glue. She quickly rinsed her hair, before exiting the shower and drying herself off. She wrapped the towel around her as she searched for something to wear.

Muttering to herself, she discarded the underwear at the top of the basket in her closet and dug deep for a pink lacy push-up bra and matching panties. A soft pink cashmere sweater and a draping skirt completed the outfit. A quick spray of her patchouli perfume and a dash of lip gloss, and she was ready to go back down. Her stomach fluttered and she looked in the mirror again. Her eyes were bright, and her lips were softly parted.

Yes, this is right, and you will give it your best shot.

A merger. Hmmm.

Walking slowly down the stairs, her legs trembled with anticipation and she listened for Blake's voice, but all was quiet—it seemed his call was finished. She hurried into the kitchen and turned the soup down and placed the loaf of bread in the oven to warm.

"Almost ready," she called.

He didn't answer. Ana walked into the living room, but the room was empty. Smiling to herself, she opened the front door and called out to the porch. "Are you hungry?"

All was quiet. Mutt lifted his head and flopped his tail on the tiled porch and Sooky ran over and wrapped herself around Ana's legs, meowing for her dinner.

The space beside her ute where Blake had parked was empty. Disappointment filled her chest as she walked back inside. A note was propped up against the shoe boxes on the table.

'Sorry something came up. Will call.'

And that was why they would never be any good together, she thought sadly. Business had always come first with Blake—and it always would. He couldn't even wait for her to come downstairs to tell her he had to leave.

Chapter Fifteen

Three days passed and there was no call or visit from Blake. Ana tried to tell herself she didn't have time to think about it, that she didn't care.

On Monday, she and Sienna met with the Bennetts and came to an agreement for two more restoration jobs. On Tuesday, they spent the day at the houses, measuring and making lists. Today, she and Sienna were back at her cottage, planning out their work and ordering the supplies they would need.

Ana moved to the table which was now clear of shoeboxes and picked up their new order book. She'd dropped the boxes at Georgie's house on Sunday night and asked her to take them into the store for her on Monday. It was the worry of the new business venture that was keeping her awake at nights and waiting for the phone to ring through the day.

And constantly checking that her phone was not turned off.

Nothing to do with Blake.

She was waiting for jobs to come in. That was all.

"We can only order exactly what we need," Sienna commented. They were at Ana's cottage and stood at the window looking out over the hills. "We don't have the luxury of everything at our fingertips anymore."

Ana nodded absently. She glanced down at the phone and resisted picking it up to check for messages.

"You okay, Ana?"

"Yes, why?"

"I thought you'd be happier." Sienna looked at her expectantly.

"Why?"

"Oh, just that Maria was telling Georgie about the hunky guy who came to see you when you were fixing Aldo's roof."

Sienna tipped her head to the side. "And he gave you flowers?"

Ana looked at the posy of violets on the kitchen windowsill. They were starting to wilt. "Oh that? Blake just stopped by to say thanks. For helping him out."

She'd been all excited about telling Georgie and Sienna how things were panning out with Blake until he'd disappeared. Now she wasn't game to put what she felt into words in case she'd read him all wrong.

"Yes. And?"

"And nothing."

"Why should there be an 'and?'"

"Because I know you very well and there's something bugging you. Is it because Blake's gone away?"

Ana's head flew up. "Gone away?

"Yes, he went to Melbourne first thing on Sunday night. The takeover's been put off for another week. Didn't he tell you?"

"He doesn't have to tell me anything, Sienna. I don't work there and I'm nothing to him."

Obviously.

"Ah. . . so that's the way the wind blows." Sienna smiled. "Georgie will be upset if you beat her to a wedding."

"Oh for goodness' sake, Sienna. Stop talking nonsense." Ana pushed some catalogues across the table to her friend who was looking at her too intently. "Sit down and start looking for some ideas for the Bennett's beach house. If we are going to make this business a success, we have to make this project spectacular."

Sienna looked at her from under her lashes. "And if we are going to make this business a success, you have to do away with shoebox accounting."

Ana swatted one of the catalogues in her direction and laughed when Sienna ducked.

***

Blake stood outside Mike's executive suite in the building

near Federation Square and cursed himself for the umpteenth time. He couldn't believe he'd left his mobile in his car at home before he'd caught the taxi to the airport. He'd tried everything he could think of how to find Ana's number but none of his attempts had come to fruition. He couldn't call Joe's store and ask for her number because negotiations were at such a delicate stage. He didn't know Georgie and Sienna's last name so he couldn't look them up. And Ana's number still wasn't listed, just like it hadn't been ten years ago. Damn it all.

He pushed open the door of Mike's suite. The secretary gestured to a chair. He felt bad about leaving Ana's place while she was in the shower. The note he'd left for her had been brief but when the call came in from Mike, he'd only had an hour to get to the airport. His whole attention had to be on the meeting ahead— any chance of a future with Ana hinged on the next few minutes. If things went as planned, he would have plenty of time to make up for the way he'd left her.

She'd be fine.

She'd forgive him.

He hoped.

"Come on in, Buchanan." Mike's voice boomed through the door and his secretary jumped. "Are you waiting for an invitation?"

Mike sat behind his huge cherrywood desk and glowered at Blake as he entered the office. Being called by his surname did not bode well. Mike steepled his fingers in front of his chin and stared at him.

"Sit down."

Blake nodded at the man who had been his boss for the past three years. "Thanks for seeing me at such short notice."

"I'm disappointed in you, Blake."

"I appreciate you considering my proposal, Mike."

"I think you're crazy, you know. You had a bright future

with this company." Mike shook his head. "In fact, I'd even hoped you might buy me out when I was ready to retire. That son of mine doesn't want it."

"You never know, he might change his mind," Blake responded kindly, though in truth he knew Jack was happy with his sculpture.

Mike reached over and stabbed at the buzzer on his desk. When there was no response he yelled through the open door. "Grace, bring those papers in here." Then he stood up and called out loudly. "Please."

"Of course, sir." The secretary walked in and placed a file on Mike's desk. "Will there be anything else, Mr. Devereaux?"

Blake smothered a smile. It wasn't just him who found Mike difficult. Grace went back out to her desk.

"Coffee, Blake?"

"No thanks, Mike. I've got a plane to catch."

"Don't know what's gotten into you, boy." His soon-to-be former boss shook his head and hollered through the door again. "Grace. Get Jim to come up, will you. We need a lawyer to witness this."

Ten minutes later, the papers were signed and as Blake walked to the door, Mike stood and threw his arm around his shoulder.

"Anytime you want to come back here, there'll be a job waiting for you."

"I'm pretty settled out on the Sunshine Coast now, but thanks for the vote of confidence." Blake punched Mike playfully on his burly shoulder. "And anytime you want to come and visit, I've got that great big house on the canal at Noosa. Lots of guest rooms.'

He didn't want to mention the move to Maleny in case it jinxed things.

151

Mike turned to him, his face sombre. "Seriously, Blake I hope it all works out for you. You never were one to take things slow. And I guess Helen will want to go up and visit Jack, so I might take you up on that offer one day."

Blake stepped out on the street and whistled for a taxi. As he headed to the airport for his return flight, he felt lighter than he had in years.

Ten years to be precise. And it felt so good, it was worth the wait. And his life was about to get even better.

Chapter Sixteen

According to Georgie's grapevine, Blake was still away, and Joe was stomping around the store like a cranky old man. Ana spent the whole week running from one place to another in the whirlwind of the new business and her house descended back into its normal mess. Sienna and Georgie had dragged her into Caloundra to purchase a laptop that was now set up in the small room off her kitchen. A ceremonial burning of the shoe boxes, which Georgie returned *sans* accounts, took place out in the garden on Thursday night with a bottle of wine to toast the signing of the Bennett contract.

This morning was spent at Thelma and Mitzi's house where Ana finally finished painting their kitchen. Sienna painted a *trompe l'oeil* of a cow in a field on the bottom half of their kitchen door and they all stood back to admire it.

Ana giggled, and whispered behind her hand to Sienna as the elderly ladies stepped closer and pored over it. "It's awful."

"Ssh," Sienna hissed. "It's what they wanted."

"It's the eyelashes." Ana kept a straight face as Sienna elbowed her and they were both smiling a few minutes later as they walked to the ute.

"Give me a lift home? I walked down," Sienna said.

Thelma and Mitzi stood at the door and waved to them as Ana backed down their driveway.

"Say hello to your young man for us, Ana." Mitzi called out.

"Bring him over to see us soon," Thelma added.

Ana put on a dramatic eye roll for Sienna's benefit and tooted the horn at the old dears. "I love this town, but it has a crazy rumour mill. There is nothing between Blake and me."

"Oh, come on, Ana. You are so transparent. You've been

153

mooning around all week like a lovesick cow, and as soon as someone mentions Blake's name you are at instant attention. That's what gave me the idea for the cow's eyelashes." Sienna laughed. "I love it. I'm trying my hand at sculpture too, life's been a bit boring lately."

Ana didn't reply and turned down Main Street toward Sienna's house. She was desperate to know when Blake would be back but didn't want to give Sienna more reason to tease her. Finally she couldn't hold back any longer.

"I wonder when Blake will be back from Melbourne. Do you know what it's all about?" She kept her attention on the road in front of them, trying to inject a casual interest into her voice.

"Georgie said something's going on at the store but it's all a big mystery. The takeover was supposed to be signed off by now, but everyone has just been told to come to work as normal until Blake gets back, even those who got their notice." She looked at Ana with a sly grin. "And no, I don't know when that will be."

"Okay. You're right, I'll admit it. I am attracted to him. I always have been but it's not going anywhere because we are too different."

"Opposites attract, you know." Sienna crossed her arms and sighed. "Don't let him go because of a foolish belief."

"It's not foolish. Blake has always put business first. I never have. So I have to get over him and move on."

"Just because your views lean toward the charitable side, don't judge him too harshly.

Ana thought over Sienna's words after she dropped her off at her house. Before she headed out to the cottage, she decided to stop by the store and see Joe. It was strange not to be there every day to pick up gear. It had been her second home for ten years and the staff were like her family.

She parked the ute in the back and hoped Blake's grey Mercedes might be there, too, but there was no sign of it. After she saw Joe and Magda, she was going home for a long walk in the hills with Mutt. Sienna's words had stuck in her mind and she knew she had a lot of thinking to do.

Maybe Blake had taken off in a tearing hurry the other day because he'd regretted kissing her.

Maybe he'd given their relationship a lot of thought, too, and recognised how different they were.

Maybe he'd looked around her cottage when she was upstairs and realised they were poles apart. Her mess would frighten anyone away.

Slamming the ute door shut, she pulled herself up short.

Forget the maybes. From now on, she would take things as they came and when she went for a walk this afternoon, she'd figure out just what she was going to do and how she'd greet Blake when he came back home.

If he even came to see her.

But he had kissed her, and her insides went to jelly as she remembered that kiss. She grinned to herself. Sienna was right. It was just like being back in high school.

Ana slipped in the back door of the shop and greeted Herb, the security man, who was dozing in a chair by the back counter. If she was honest, there were a few places where the store could be improved.

Maybe it *was* time for change.

Georgie was manning the cash register and raised her eyebrows at Ana.

"Blake's not back yet."

Ana let out a soft groan.

"How many times do I have to tell everyone, there is nothing between Blake and me?" She pointed up the stairs to Joe's office. "Are Joe and Magda upstairs?"

"Yes, they're just back from lunch at Renzo's."

Ana was three steps up when Georgie called out to her.

155

"Ana?"

She paused and looked back to a broad grin on Georgie's face. "Yeah?"

"Don't pick pink for my bridesmaid's dress. It clashes with my red hair."

Ana stomped up the stairs and ignored the laughter coming from the counter below. Magda was sitting at the small front desk and she bustled around and embraced Ana in a close hug.

"Ana, my dear. We have missed you." She called into the office through the open door. "Joe, we have a visitor."

Ana stepped back and shrugged. "It's only been a week."

"But it's not the same without you and Sienna popping in all the time to pick up things and helping out. Is it, Joe?" She turned to her husband who had come to the doorway. He held his hand out to Ana and she followed him into the office,

"It is good to see you. Come in and tell me all your news." He winked at her and tapped his nose. "I believe you have some."

"Oh, not you too, Joe." Ana's face burned with embarrassment.

He tipped his head to the side quizzically with a gentle smile. "I heard something about the Bennetts. Is there something else?"

"Oh. No. That's all. Sienna and I have signed the contract so it's public knowledge."

"Ah, that is good." He nodded. "There have been a lot of enquiries about your work since the Bennett place was sold."

"That's right."

"Blake was very impressed with your work, I hear."

"So he is still taking over the store?"

Joe sighed and ran his hand over his bald head. "Yes, the store takeover is going ahead." He smiled at her. "But it's all good news and I can tell you, there will be a lot of happy people in our town—including you, Ana."

Before she could ask the questions forming in her mind, the telephone on Joe's desk rang. When he ignored it, Magda called out from the small office.

"Joe, pick up. It's Blake and it sounds important."

Joe's eyes widened and he reached for the telephone. "Blake. Has it fallen through? Ah, I see. Yes. I can do better than that." He looked across at Ana and his brow creased. "Just a moment."

Joe turned to Ana with his hand over the hand piece.

"He wants your phone number." The old man frowned. "It sounds urgent."

Ana caught her breath and held her hand out for the phone. "I'll talk to him."

"Blake?"

"Oh, Ana. Thank God, I found you." Ana's legs trembled as Blake's voice broke. "I need you. Can you come to Noosa?"

She gripped the phone to her ear and her hand shook.

"What is it, Blake?" Her voice cracked as a dozen scenarios flicked through her mind. "What's wrong?"

"Billy's missing."

Chapter Seventeen

Before they disconnected, Blake gave Ana Jeannie's address. His flight from Melbourne had just landed and there had been a message for him. He'd made a frantic call to Rod; Billy had been missing for two hours.

As the taxi headed for Jeannie's house, all Blake could think of was the fear that had gripped him when Billy had run to the edge of the road at the park. He knew Billy's fascination with water. He stared out the window and clenched his jaw, trying not to think of all the lagoons near Jeannie and Rod's house. "I like to swim, *Unca* Blake." His throat clogged with emotion as he remembered Billy's determination.

Blake closed his eyes. As soon as the initial shock of Rod's call had subsided, a deep need to have Ana with him had filled him. He'd done a lot of thinking on the flight and he'd already decided to go and see her as soon as he got home to tell her his news.

Now that was all unimportant and he just wanted her by his side as they searched for Billy. Nothing mattered except Billy being found safe—and soon.

The taxi pulled to a halt outside Jeannie and Rod's house. Rod was home with the children and Jeannie was out searching with the neighbours. Two police cars blocked the driveway, and a news van was parked on the sidewalk. Neighbours stood in small groups talking quietly. The driver parked behind the news van and Blake grabbed his bag from the trunk before sprinting for the front door.

Rod must have been watching because the door opened before Blake was up the steps. His face was white, and he inclined his head to the living room.

"The kids are watching TV with one of the neighbours."

158

Rod used his crutches to limp through the living room to the kitchen and Blake followed. Two women were in the kitchen making sandwiches and Rod smiled briefly.

"Bronwyn, Vivienne. This is my brother-in-law, Blake."

Blake nodded at the two women as Rod shut the door to the living room. "I don't want the kids listening. Maddy is really distressed. She blames herself because she was on the deck reading when he went through the side gate from the back garden."

"Tell me what's happening. Where should we look?" Blake pulled out a chair for Rod and took the crutches from him as he sat down.

"I feel so useless with this leg." Rod rubbed the back of his neck, his anxiety obvious in every movement. "Jeannie and two of the neighbours headed off to the paths along each side of the canal while I called the police. There's been no sign of him yet."

"The other kids are all here?" Blake hadn't even taken notice of who was in the living room as they walked through.

"Yes, but there is one good thing." Rod gripped the side of the table and his knuckles were white. "Jaws is missing, too. So we're just praying he's with Billy."

"Which gate did he get through?"

"One of the side gates was open. The one closest to the canal."

Blake swallowed. "You've searched the house?"

"Yes, and the yard and the neighbours' yards. Now we're waiting for the police with the search dogs to arrive."

"Where do you want me? Here with the kids or out looking?"

Rod dropped his head in his hands. "How about you drive me around? My keys are on the hook next to the garage door. You get the SUV out and I'll meet you out front."

Blake passed him the crutches and headed for the garage. He opened the garage door with the remote control on the wall and slid into the driver's seat. Backing the car out slowly, he parked it in the driveway. Rod was standing next to a policeman who was talking into a radio and for a brief moment, Blake hoped there might be news. He turned the car off and stepped out onto the driveway and waited for Rod to finish talking, his stomach churning.

A familiar sound of a rattly diesel reached his ears and he looked up as Ana's ute rumbled down the wide street. She parked it and ran across the lawn to him. Blake held out his arms and she ran into them.

He buried his head in her hair and the familiar patchouli fragrance filled him with comfort.

"Oh Blake, have they found him yet?"

Blake shook his head, unable to speak for a moment. "No, not yet." He cleared his throat and kept his arm tightly around Ana as Rod limped over to them on his crutches.

"Rod, this is my. . . friend. . . Ana. She's here to help."

Rod reached over, briefly shook Ana's hand, and then looked at Blake. "Are you ready?"

Ana stepped out of Blake's embrace "Where's Maddy and the boys? Would you like me to stay with them?"

Rod nodded and pointed inside without speaking before he handed Blake his crutches and stepped up into the car.

"Thank you for coming." Blake looked down at Ana and despite his worry, her presence calmed him. She stood in front of him chewing on her lip, her work dungarees covered with paint and more splotches of bright green paint on her hands.

"I'm so happy you called me."

"I need you, Ana. But we'll talk about that later." He dropped his head and kissed her hard, before throwing the crutches in the back of the car and jumping in beside Rod.

***

Ana walked past the colourful shrubs in the front garden

160

and hurried up the stairs. She pushed open the front door and followed the sounds of the television. A middle-aged woman was sitting on the sofa cuddling a sleeping Jake. Ana walked over and lightly touched the baby's head.

"Hello, I'm Ana. I'm a friend of the family," she said quietly.

"Hi, I'm Sophie. I'm from next door."

"How are the children doing?" Ana whispered.

"Maddy's really the only one who knows what's going on. She wanted to go with Jeannie, but Rod asked her to stay here and help me with the boys. Now that you're here, I'll take Jake upstairs to his cot."

Ana slipped onto the sofa next to Maddy. "Hey sweetie."

Maddy looked up at Ana. Her eyes were wide, and her little chin was shaking. "Hello, Ana. I lost Billy."

The little girl's guilt broke her heart. "Oh no, you didn't Maddy. It's not your fault."

"I shouldn't have been reading my sea creatures book."

Ana held her arms open and Maddy slid over the sofa and nestled into her chest. The twins lay on the floor still engrossed in the cartoons on the television.

"You smell funny."

"I've been painting. My friend and I painted a cow on a door. I'll take you to see it one day. How would you like that?"

Maddy nodded. "How about today? As soon as Billy comes home?"

The backs of Ana's eyes ached with the tears she was holding back. "Well, we'll have to see what Mummy says."

Maddy nodded. "Can we go and play outside? Billy might have come back?"

Ana looked down at the twins. "As long as we all go outside together. It's my job to look after you while Mummy and Daddy and Uncle Blake are out. . . finding Billy."

"It won't take long," Maddy said. "He's got Jaws and he's got his iPad. They'll be able to hear them and then they can bring him home."

Ana squeezed the little girl closer to her. "That's really good thinking, Maddy."

"Can we look outside, too?"

"We sure can." Anything to keep Maddy occupied would help the little girl stop worrying about her little brother.

Please God let them find him before dark.

Ana switched the television off with the remote control and was met with a duo of disappointed cries.

"Come on, boys, we're going outside to have an adventure."

"How about a picnic?" Benny asked.

"Sure, let's see what we can find in the kitchen."

"All right, I s'pose that's okay." Roddy reluctantly pushed himself to his feet. "Can we have Coke at our picnic?"

"We'll see. You'll have to show me the way out to the back garden."

"It's not the garden. It's the jungle." Roddy's little voice piped up. "I'm going to be an explorer. Benny, you have to be the lion."

Ana averted the brewing disagreement as Benny opened his mouth to protest.

"Come and show me the jungle," she said.

The children led Ana through to the kitchen and she met a couple of neighbours who were making sandwiches for the search teams. Sophie had come down from the baby's room and was pouring coffee into mugs on a tray.

"We'll bring your picnic out." One of the women called as the children ran ahead to the door. Then she dropped her voice to a whisper. "No news?"

Ana shook her head as she turned toward the door. The

162

back of the house was just above ground level with a huge wooden deck from one side to the other. The twins jumped down the two low steps and disappeared into the garden where thick bushes and high shrubs screened the high back fence. Soon their excited cries reached Ana and Maddy.

"Do you think it would be all right if I sit in the hammock and read?" Maddy looked up at Ana with her big brown eyes wide and her face serious. Ana's eyes pricked with tears and she pulled her sunglasses from the top of her head to cover them before Maddy could see she was upset.

"That would be fine."

Ana crossed to the edge of the deck and listened for the boys as they darted in and out of the bushes. She kept an eye on Maddy who quickly became absorbed in her book. Behind the fence she could hear the drone of traffic on the nearby bridge. A faint but familiar sound hummed beneath the traffic and then stopped. Ana cocked her head to listen but all she could hear was the traffic and the twins yelling in the garden.

"Maddy?"

"Yes?" The little girl gazed across at her.

"Did you say Billy had his iPad?" she asked softly.

"Yes. Why?" Maddy's voice was wary.

"Come on over here and sit down here with me? Tell me what   you   can   hear?" Maddy slipped out of the hammock, her book dropping unheeded to the floor as she came over to Ana who had dropped to her knees. She lay down and placed her ear against the wood deck. Maddy kneeled beside her and together they listened. After a moment, the faint sounds of *Baby Shark* music drifted up.

And then it stopped.

"Maddy, is there a way to get underneath here?" Ana asked urgently. She bit down on the excitement filling her chest, not wanting to get Maddy's hopes up.

163

"There used to be a door, but Daddy locked it. Jaws took his bones under there and they smelled bad."

"Can you show me where?"

Maddy led her down the steps and around to the side of the house. A small shed filled the gap between the side of the house and the fence but Maddy pointed around to the back of the shed.

"It's behind there."

Ana squeezed through the narrow gap and bent down until she could see the small door. She pushed it, and it opened with a squeak. Turning to Maddy who was close behind her, she grasped the little girl's shoulders and held her gaze.

"Maddy, I have a very important job for you. Run inside and get Sophie and ask her to come straight out and watch Benny and Roddy until I come out."

Maddy looked at her and nodded.

"Can you do that for me now? Run fast." Maddy ran and Ana dropped to the ground and pushed through the small space. It was so narrow she had to turn her shoulders to squeeze through, but she was soon rewarded by the sound of a deep, low woof. As her eyes adjusted to the dark, a faint light flickered ahead of her in the far corner. A loud swish and a rush of air preceded the licking of her face by a rough tongue.

***

Blake and Rod had driven around every street within a two mile radius. Just before the bridge, they came across Jeannie, striding ahead of a group of volunteer searchers.

"Pull over, please," Rod asked. "Make her come home with us. She'll be exhausted. There are plenty of teams out there now."

Blake stopped the car and jumped out. "Jeannie."

His sister ran across to him and Blake's heart clenched. Her face was streaked with tears and he wiped a smudge of dirt from her forehead.

"Have they found him?" Her voice broke and he held his

arms out to her.

"You need to come home with us. Rod's in the car. There are plenty of search teams out. You should be home so you're there when they find him and bring him back." He kept his voice upbeat, but Jeannie looked up at him and shook her head.

"He's in the water somewhere, Blake. He would have headed straight for the water."

Her legs gave way and Blake caught her and helped her across to the car before opening the back door for her.

Blake clenched his jaw and tried to block out Jeannie's sobs as he drove them back to the house. The feeling pressing on his chest was a hundred times worse than when he had watched Billy teetering over the traffic on the edge of Peninsula Park. He pulled into the driveway and retrieved Rod's crutches from the back seat before going across to check in with the police coordinator on the front lawn. The policeman simply shook his head and Blake turned to the house, following his sister and her husband.

The living room was empty, and Jeannie called to the children.

"They're probably out back. Don't panic." Rod said.

She clutched the kitchen bench and doubled over. "Oh, God, where is he. . .?"

Rod limped to her and his crutch clattered onto the floor as he held her close.

Blake walked to the sliding door that opened to the back deck, surprised to see the three women gathered on the back deck and peering around the corner. There was no sign of Ana or the children.

"Rod." He frowned and kept his voice quiet. "I'm just going out to see Ana and check on the kids."

The twins were on the swing set and there was no sign of Maddy or Ana.

He walked up behind one of the women he'd been introduced to before. He didn't remember her name and he smiled apologetically. "Where's Ana?"

"She's under the house." The woman's voice was full of excitement. "Bronwyn's just run around the front to get the police."

"Rod, Jeannie, come quickly." Blake called through the door before he jumped down the two steps and went around the side of the house. Maddy was peering into a small gap behind the shed and as he watched, Ana wiggled out bottom-first and lay on the ground with her arms stretched out through the small gap.

Joy filled him, and he blinked away the wetness in his eyes as her soft voice reached him. "If you pass it out to me, I'll go and plug it in, and you can play *Octonauts* inside."

Billy's head poked through the gap and he handed the iPad to Ana. He crawled out closely followed by Jaws.

He looked up at Blake and called out.

"Hello, *Unca* Blake. Can we go to the park while my iPad's charging?"

Behind him, Jeannie shrieked and pushed past Blake, grabbing Billy in her arms, and folding to the ground. Blake swallowed as she cried and buried her face in Billy's hair. Rod limped over and stood behind them reaching down to touch his little boy's head.

Ana slowly pushed herself to her feet and walked toward Blake. Jeannie grasped her hand as she walked past and looked up at her, her face full of gratitude and her eyes awash with tears. Blake held her unwavering gaze as she walked slowly over to him. Her paint-splattered dungarees were filthy where she'd lain in the dirt beneath the deck and there was a wet streak of dog slobber on her cheek.

He'd never seen anyone more beautiful in his whole life.

He held out his arms and Ana stepped into them. Holding

166

her close, her body curved into his and he captured her lips, not caring who was watching. He had never wanted anything more in his life than he wanted Ana at that moment. Her soft lips opened beneath his and she took what he offered. Something passed between then, something so elemental he couldn't put into words. Deeply moved, he cupped his hands around her damp cheeks and deepened the kiss.

Slowly she pulled back, and looked up at him, smiling. When she gazed up at him like that, a lump filled his throat as happiness surged through him.

He knew they would be okay.

***

Ana looked at Blake and took a deep breath. Two hours had passed since she had found Billy. The police had packed up and gone, the TV news team had their feel good story, and the neighbours had all drifted back to their respective homes. Jeannie was sitting on the sofa, still holding Billy close. To his dismay, his mummy had followed him around and had not left his side since he'd crawled out from beneath the house. He glared up at her.

Blake had stayed close to Ana, even following her into the bathroom while she'd scrubbed the dog drool off her face. "I guess I should think about heading home," she said softly.

"I was hoping you might drive me back to my place so I could pick up my car and some clean clothes. I'm going back up to the hotel at Maleny and my car's at home."

"Do you want to come with me to keep me company? I could drive you back down to Noosa at the end of the week." Ana looked down, embarrassed as Jeannie nudged Rod and smiled. This was all too new for her to take in. She looked down at her hands and picked at the bright green paint that was still stuck to her fingers.

"I guess I could do that."

Maddy came running over. "Can I come too and see the

cow now?"

Ana reached out and hugged the little girl.

"How about tomorrow?" She looked across at Rod and Jeannie. "How about you all come? It's Saturday and we could have that picnic we keep missing out on?"

It was agreed, and Blake and Ana headed outside after making their goodbyes. Blake glanced across at Ana with a grin as she crunched through the gears.

"I need to talk to you," he said. "I have some big news for you."

"Not while I'm driving. Can it wait till we get back to my cottage?"

Blake reached over and rested his hand on her knee. "I can wait for however long it takes."

Chapter Eighteen

Ana waited in her ute while Blake grabbed some things from his house. He'd asked her to come inside but she preferred to stay in the car, scared they'd get side-tracked if she went with him. When they finally got around to having this talk, she wanted to be at her cottage. Being on her own ground would add to her confidence.

"Are you sure you don't want to take my car?" Blake threw a small bag onto the ute tray.

"No, I'll need the ute over the weekend. I promised—" she let her voice trail off— she knew how Blake felt about her doing odd jobs for the old folk.

"Keep going," he said. "You promised?"

"Doesn't matter."

He shrugged and held up his mobile. "Were you upset when I didn't call?"

"No," she lied through her teeth. "I thought you must be busy."

"Ana, we need to be totally honest with each other. Otherwise we have no chance."

"Blake, I don't want to talk in the car. I need to concentrate on driving." She reached over and turned the radio on.

"Well, just so you know. I left my mobile in my car before I went to Melbourne and I didn't have your number. That's why I didn't call."

She smothered a smile as relief shot through her.

The silence was comfortable as she headed up the mountain road, the rush of the wind through the open window and the loud music blaring from the radio covering up the usual roar of the old diesel ute as it laboured up the hills. Every so often, Blake would look across at her and smile. Anticipation curled in her stomach.

169

"Do you want to come back to my place before I drive you to the hotel?" Ana leaned over and turned the music off as they approached Maleny.

Blake reached over and took her hand with a smile.

"I'd love to."

Mutt greeted them as the ute trundled slowly up the driveway and sniffed her legs curiously as she stepped from the car. Ana reached down to fondle his ears.

"It's okay, boy. You're still my number one dog."

Her heart was pounding as Blake followed her along the porch. She opened the door and turned, drinking in the sight of him as he smiled down at her.

"If I go up and have a shower will you promise you'll be here when I come down?" She looked at him from beneath lowered lashes as shyness filled her.

"I promise." A smile lit up his whole face and she ran upstairs to the shower before her legs could turn to jelly.

The same pink lacy bra, the matching panties, the pink cashmere sweater, and the soft floaty skirt completed her outfit. Her hand shook as she pulled her damp hair back into a ponytail and applied a dash of lip gloss. She walked slowly down the stairs.

Blake stood by the window waiting for her. "All set?"

She nodded and sat primly in the chair beside the window, her back straight and her knees together. He crouched down and kneeled in front of her.

"Ana, I've got two things to tell you and then I want to ask you something."

Ana's heart was pounding, and her lips were dry. She resisted the urge to lick them and focused on his face instead as he looked up at her.

He reached for her hand and she was surprised to feel his hand trembling slightly.

"I have some big news and I think you'll be very happy."

It was like looking through a rosy haze and Ana giggled. "I think you could tell me anything now and it wouldn't upset me."

"First, I went to Melbourne this week."

"I know."

"I met with Mike and he agreed not to take over the store."

Dismay filled her. "Oh, no. Joe will be so disappointed—and Magda won't be able to go on her cruise."

Blake held her close and his lips pressed against her forehead. "That's one of the things I love most about you, you know. You are such a giving person. You always think of everyone else before yourself."

Ana shook her head. "So what's happening? Are you out of a job? Oh no, you've bought the house here. Where will you work? Where will you live? What are—?"

"Sssh." Blake put his fingers on her lips again. "Listen to me."

Ana frowned and considered all the implications of the non-takeover. "But—"

"I bought the store."

"You what?" For a moment she thought Blake said he'd bought the store.

"I bought the store. Joe and I are signing the papers on Monday."

"You bought the store?"

Blake beamed down at her. "Yes."

"You bought the store?" Ana's breath hitched as she repeated the question.

"You've already asked me that. I'm looking for someone to do a renovation job for me. Someone who can bring it into the twenty-first century but keep that old hardware store atmosphere. Do you know anyone who might be able to do that?"

"Oh my God." Ana gazed up at Blake as she struggled to keep her voice steady. She was so happy she couldn't understand

171

why tears were pricking at her eyes. "How does Sunshine Coast Renos Service fit into the scheme of things? Will a local firm fit the bill?"

"I think they'll fit in very well," he said, and his smile got wider. "I think in a community like ours. . ." Blake paused, and joy shot through Ana as he made himself a part of her community. "In a community like ours we have to stay local."

She grabbed his hands and brought them up to her face unable to put her joy into words. Blake raised her fingers to his lips as he held her eyes with a true and steady gaze.

"Ana, I let you go ten years ago without realising how I felt. I've searched for happiness since then, but I was always unsettled. As soon as we met again, my life felt complete." He held her gaze. "The second thing I want to tell you is the most important. What I want to tell you. . . is how much I love you."

She drew in a quick breath and opened her mouth to speak but Blake placed his fingers gently over her lips.

"Let me finish. What I want to ask you is. . ."

Ana closed her eyes, as the joy and love for this man surged through her. For the first time, she was able to accept her feelings and knew they were returned in full.

"Open your eyes."

Slowly she met his gaze and smiled as her heart settled into a slow steady beat, as steady as the love shining from his face.

"Will you marry me, please, Ana?"

Nothing could overcome the love she had for this man.

She met his gaze full on. "If you'd asked me the same question ten years ago, I would have said no. If you'd asked me a week ago, I would have been slow to answer. But..."

She leaned forward to let her lips touch his, her heart aching with love, with need, wanting to feel him against her. Against his mouth, she murmured the words in her heart. "But now. . . no hesitation, no second thoughts . . . yes, Blake. I'll marry you."

He leaned in and kissed her, and a thrill coursed through her as his arms pulled her close. She'd waited a long time for this moment, but it had been worth the wait.

Epilogue

Mutt and Jaws hit it off as soon as Rod opened the back of the SUV in Blake and Ana's garden and the bloodhound had jumped out, ears swinging in the breeze. It was a warm October afternoon and the sun shone from a brilliant blue sky with not a sign of cloud on the mountains. The whisper of the wind stole ruffled gently through the trees and Maddy and Rod were down on the lawn throwing sticks to the dogs.

Sienna lounged in a garden chair while Georgie bustled around offering drinks to the guests sitting at the tables scattered through the orchard. Thelma and Mitzi had made lemonade for the ceremony.

"Roddy! Benny! Get down at once." Jeannie called out to the twins as they climbed high in one of the orange trees. She hurried over and stood beneath the tree, one hand grasping Billy's shoulder, the other holding on to Jake who was toddling along beside her.

One final car came up the driveway and Joe and Magda, and Maria and Aldo walked through the gate. Georgie ushered them through to the orchard.

Georgie called out to Rod and Maddy and they walked up the cliff path. Rod's hand was on his daughter's shoulder and Maddy had a huge grin on her face.

Maddy ran into the house along the porch.

"Everyone's here now," she called happily. "You can come out."

The door opened and Blake stepped out first, closely followed by Ana who was holding the newest resident of Maleny close to her chest.

They walked slowly to the orchard and Blake looked down at his wife of eleven months with a huge grin rivalling that of the

174

bloodhound who was lolling on the end of the porch. A laugh rippled through the small crowd as the celebrant met them at the gate and held her hands out for the baby dressed in little dungarees with a pink ribbon in her hair.

"Welcome, Faith Anastasia Buchanan."

THE END

.

The Trouble with Jack

Annie Seaton

Sunshine Coast Series: Book 2

Chapter One

The door of the Sea View Gallery at Noosa Heads shut with a satisfying *click* behind the last customer of the day, and Sienna Sacchi turned the closed sign around on the glass door.

"I thought she'd never leave." She yawned as she looked over to the electrician who was waiting to show her the new lighting he'd installed in the front corner of the gallery.

"But she was loaded with bags with the gallery insignia on them, if I'm not mistaken?" Jeremy waited for her to come over to the counter. "You were wasted in restoration, Sienna. You're a born saleswoman."

Sienna had been friends with Jeremy since school; the other business Sienna was involved with hired him for the electrical work. The restoration business—or house flipping as Georgie preferred to call it—was shared with Georgie, her twin sister, and their best friend, Ana, up the mountain at Maleny. As well as working with the girls until recently, Sienna had also worked part-time in a small gallery up the mountain until she'd seen the ad for the gallery down here at Noosa.

"And a talented artist, too, don't forget." Sienna grinned at him as satisfaction coursed through her. A sale like the one she'd just made reassured her that her decision to be a silent partner in the reno business and move on to focus on her art and buy this gallery had been the right one. She would be her own boss once again; working for someone else stifled her creativity. "And yes, she loved my enamelled frogs, and bought one for each of her friends back in Sydney."

The sale had been one of the biggest Sienna had made since she'd taken over the management of the gallery a month ago. Her hiring had been done by email with the company and she hadn't even met the owner—the soon-to-be former owner; the gallery administration operated under a company name. Once she owned the place, she would have final say in how it was run. She couldn't wait to tell the girls; she'd told Georgie she had news but wouldn't give any clues away.

"That's the sort of customer you want." Jeremy looked at her with a grin. "Holy Dooley, I saw the price tag on your frogs when I was running the electrical wires under the shelves."

Sienna nodded with a smile. "So, are you done?"

"I am. Are you ready to be bedazzled?"

"I am." Sienna had filled the corner at the front of the gallery with her own work. She waited as Jeremy stepped behind the elegant glass table she used as a counter, reached down, and flicked a switch.

Sienna gasped and put her hands to her lips as she surveyed the once-dark corner. The various little creatures came to life on the display shelves along the side wall. Colourful frogs peeked from behind small pieces of wood softly lit by downlights hidden beneath the higher shelves, and copper grasshoppers gleamed in the corners. She had been working day and night to finish her sculpted metal creatures for her upcoming exhibition, but she still had a lot of work ahead.

"Happy with the job then, sweets?"

"Happy? I'm delighted. It's like fairyland." The small creatures she had enamelled in bright primary colours were highlighted by the carefully placed lighting. She stepped closer and twirled around, looking at the lights as they twinkled, and was hard pressed not to yell out in delight. "You've worked magic, Jeremy. Thank you so much."

"My pleasure." He picked up his toolbox and crossed to the door. "I won't bill the company until I finish the whole room for your exhibition. Let me know when you want me to come back."

After he left, Sienna wandered around, barely able to keep the smile off her face. The gallery looked very different from when she'd taken over as manager, with an option to purchase, only four weeks ago. The last email from a secretary at the company advised that any changes she made before the contract was signed must be approved and then would be billed out to the company. It had taken three weeks to get the approval to go ahead with the lighting, and she'd worried it wouldn't be complete before her exhibition. As soon as she'd received an email giving her the go-ahead, she'd called Jeremy to come in to do the work, and he'd turned up within an hour.

There'd been no reply from her solicitor about the contract of sale when she'd checked her email at lunchtime; she glanced down at her watch. Hopefully it would settle next week, and then the gallery would be all hers with the freedom to do as she wanted before her first exhibition. Having to get permission to make any change, no matter how small, was a pain in the proverbial.

There was no time to check her email before she left for the restaurant. As usual Sienna was running late, and she knew the girls would tease her about being late for her own birthday dinner.

She grabbed her iPad and her bag from beneath the counter, and with one last satisfied smile at the beautifully lit display, she flicked the lights off and headed for the back door.

Chapter Two

The waiter leaned over the table and the cork popped out of the champagne bottle flying over the heads of the patrons in the noisy, crowded restaurant. Sienna laughed and leaned forward, holding her glass to catch the cascading bubbles.

"Happy birthday!" Ana took Sienna's glass as wine frothed over the top onto the checked tablecloth.

Georgie mopped at the damp cloth with her napkin and smiled at Sienna. "Happy birthday, sis."

"You too, Georgie." Sienna grinned back, wondering for the millionth time how they could be so different. Even though they were fraternal twins, in twenty-nine years she had never been able to find one glimmer of similarity between them.

Looks, personality, interests, or attitudes. About the only thing they shared was their birthday.

"So, Machu Picchu is still the plan for next year's big thirty?" Ana, their best friend since primary school up the mountain at Maleny, sipped her wine. Sienna and Georgie had always promised themselves a special trip for their thirtieth birthday, even if they were married with kids. But that hadn't happened for either of them—intentionally for Sienna, and not so intentionally for Georgie.

Sienna shook her head and looked across at her twin. Georgie was leaning into her latest boyfriend, Cal . . . or something? Kel?

She couldn't keep up with the men in Georgie's life. Her sister always tried so hard to find Mr. Right. Each time a guy sensed Georgie was after the wedding dress dream, he took off and she was left nursing another broken heart.

She should know by now relationships rarely work out, and she needs to toughen up, Sienna thought, but kept her thoughts to herself

Georgie caught her eye and smiled. "No, Sienna will be too busy. Are you going to tell us your news, sis?

Sienna rose to her feet and tapped her glass with a spoon, but the hum of noise from the other patrons in Fish Divine overlooking the beach at Noosa covered the sound. She sat back down with a grin and waited until she had the attention of the small group at the table. Leaning back on her chair, she lifted her glass and sipped before she announced in a dramatic voice, "I *almost* have news."

"Come on, don't keep us in suspense." Ana leaned forward and placed her elbows on the table. Sienna hadn't caught up with the girls since she'd moved to the gallery at Noosa.

"You know how much I loved working at the gallery at Maleny?" she said.

Ana nodded, and Georgie smiled.

"Well, I quit." Sienna knew she had a flair for drama; Georgie had always said she should go into the movies.

"What?" Ana frowned. "I thought you were about to have an exhibition of your sculptures?"

"I was, but my sculptures and I have moved to the Sea View Gallery up the road here." Sienna picked up her glass and sipped. "And the big news is—I'm about to buy it. I will have my very own gallery. I'm just waiting to hear when I sign the contract."

She waited for their congratulations, but Ana looked at her with a strange expression on her face, almost disbelief. "Did you say the Sea View Gallery?"

"Yes. It's in a much better location than Maleny. I mean I know there were a lot of tourists up the mountain, but this so much busier. I'm really excited. You know I've always dreamed about having my own gallery. All that hard work in our restoration business has paid off. I'll have my own place where I can show my work. And I can run it how *I* want."

Still no flurry of congratulations.

"And you'll all get a special invitation to my first show at the end of the month."

It wasn't like Ana to be so quiet. Sienna frowned at her across the table.

"What's wrong, Ana? Aren't you just a little bit excited for me?"

Ana reached out across the table and grabbed Sienna's hand. "Sweetie, there's something you need to—"

"Is this a private party, or can anyone join?"

Sienna froze and her heartbeat kicked up a notch before she turned slowly. She'd know that voice anywhere. A delicious shiver ran down her back as she looked up at Jack Montgomery who was standing behind her chair. Ever since she'd first met him last year when he was visiting the area with Blake, Ana's partner, her interest had increased each time they'd run into each other.

Blake had ended up buying the Maleny hardware store and Jack had been a visitor for a while, but he'd never stayed long enough to take Sienna out for dinner like he'd mentioned a few times. Last she'd heard from Ana, he was in Melbourne looking after the family company. His bad-boy reputation had piqued her interest, although Ana assured her, he had settled down since his dad had been ill.

"I told Blake I was coming to town, and he invited me to join you." Jack looked around with a frown. "Where is he?"

"Blake had to cancel." Ana gestured to the chair beside her and Sienna bit her lip, as a ripple of disappointment ran through her; she'd been about to invite Jack to sit beside her.

"There was a crisis at the store, and he asked me to look out for you, Jack," Ana said.

"So, he hasn't changed his workaholic ways yet? Even though he's moved from big business to a small store of his own? I think I've won a bet there." Jack pulled out the chair and sat beside Ana, but his intent gaze was fixed on Sienna, and her heart felt like it was doing backflips in her chest.

"I'll have to line him up for a game of golf or two." Jack didn't take his eyes from her.

She swallowed and flicked her scarf back over her shoulder, trying to regain her composure. He was the only man who ever made her nervous. "How are you, Jack? You haven't been up this way for a while," she said trying to look calmer than she felt.

"I'm well, thanks." Jack kept his green-eyed gaze on her, and his sexy grin sent another shiver down her back. "Especially now that I'm moving here for good. We must catch up."

"We must." She smiled and a frisson of anticipation shot through her in a lazy swirl.

Woo hoo. Life's looking good. Jack's back on the scene; I'll have my own gallery and an exhibition coming up.

Ana put her hand over her mouth and cleared her throat loudly before Jack answered.

Her brow was wrinkled in a frown and she stared at Sienna.

What's going on?

The noise of the conversations in the restaurant washed over her as Sienna moved her gaze from Ana back to Jack. He would make a good subject for a portrait; her fingers tingled with the urge to capture his face on canvas. It would be a happy portrait of a man at ease in his own skin. Jack always had that sexy grin on his face. He had high, sharply defined cheekbones, and sensuous lips that were tilted up in a smile as he looked back at her. His sun-streaked hair flopped onto his forehead, and the come-hither eyes fixed on her were enough to give her palpitations. Having him back on the coast might prove to be very interesting…and a lot of fun.

"Sienna?" Ana's soft voice pulled her from her dreamy musing. "Come for a walk with me?" Ana looked across at Jack apologetically. "Please excuse us for a minute."

"Excuse me." Sienna pushed her chair back and caught Jack's eye. This time the tingle that ran through her was warm and settled nicely in her tummy. "I'm pleased you were able to come tonight." She ran her hand lightly down his arm as she passed by his chair, and his warm skin beneath her fingers kept those tingles going.

This is going to be fun. I'm overdue for some, that's for sure.

As she followed Ana to the ladies' room, thoughts of Jack and the launch she'd planned once the gallery was hers filled her head. She'd invite him . . .

Ana kept walking past the ladies' room before she pushed open the door of the restaurant that led out onto Hastings Street.

"What's up? Where are we going?" Sienna followed her until they reached the gap between the buildings where there was an excellent view of the beach.

Ana leaned against the white timber wall, her back to the view. She grabbed Sienna's hands; unease caught in her throat as Ana held them. "I need to tell you something before you put your foot in it with Jack."

"What do you mean? What's wrong?"

"I so wish you'd told me you were at the Sea View Gallery and wanting to buy it. I know you keep things close to your chest, you always have, but you are going to be so disappointed."

"What on earth are you talking about? Stop talking in riddles." She stared at Ana.

"The gallery's not for sale anymore."

186

"How could you possibly know that?"

"Jack called Blake last night. Now that his father has recovered, Jack can hand the family business back over. He never wanted to be there in the first place." Ana held Sienna's gaze and squeezed her hands. "He's moved here to run another business *his* company bought a couple of years ago. An art gallery. The *Sea View* Gallery."

***

Jack leaned back in his chair and watched as Sienna and Ana headed for the door. Sienna was even prettier than he'd remembered. She was wearing a tight-fitting black top tucked into a coloured floaty skirt. A matching scarf hung around her long slender neck His blood zinged in appreciation. Sienna had fascinated him from the moment they met, and he knew the attraction was mutual. He'd always intended on asking her out but getting called back to Melbourne when his father got sick had put that on hold. Tonight, he'd pick up where he'd left off last year.

"So, you're really here to stay this time?" Georgie smiled at him, and Jack shot a glance at the guy who was sitting on the other side of her. He held his hand out across the table.

"Jack Montgomery."

"Sorry, how rude of me. I didn't introduce you." Georgie said. "This is my friend Cole. He just started work at the hardware store in Maleny."

Cole shot him a sullen look as Jack shook his hand.

What's his problem?

Jack turned away from the guy with the death stare to speak to Georgie. "It's good to be back on the Sunny Coast. When I told Blake I was arriving today, he said you'd all be down here tonight."

"We came to celebrate our birthday. Sienna and I, that is." Georgie shot him a grin. "Where are you staying? In Noosa?"

"Yes, in my gallery. I swung by there and threw my bag in

187

on the way. There's a sofa at the back of the studio, and that'll do for a while. At least I hope there is. I only had a quick look at the place when I bought it. It's been managed by Dad's company for a couple of years." Jack stifled a yawn. "Sorry. I left Melbourne the day before yesterday, and I rode my bike up from Sydney today. Left at the crack of dawn."

"That's a long haul. What kind of bike have you got?" Cole took his arm from around Georgie's shoulder and leaned forward.

"A BMW K1600GT. Best one I've ever had." He glanced at Georgie as she moved her chair a little closer to his. "And I've had a few."

The guy was giving him bad vibes.

"What gallery are you talking about?" she asked.

"The Sea View Gallery in Hastings Drive. I bought it around the same time that Ana hooked up with Blake." Jack settled back in his chair and glanced around, wondering where Sienna and Ana had disappeared to. "I had it on the market, but now I've decided to move here and use it as my base. Try my hand with my own gallery and doing something I love."

Georgie's eyes widened and she grabbed Jack's arm. "Did you say the Sea View Gallery? Here? In Noosa?"

"I did. Why? Is something wrong?"

"Oh, shit," she said.

Ana held the door open and Sienna strode in. Her black hair was cut short, framing her face in a pixie cut. Her dark brown eyes looked huge, outlined with that black pencil stuff she always wore. She flopped into her chair and sat back with her arms folded and stared across the table at Jack.

Her gaze was not friendly, and tension fair radiated off her. Jack looked from Sienna and back to Georgie, unsure of the vibes he was picking up.

"Happy birthday. If I'd known this was a birthday party, I wouldn't have intruded." He looked around for the waiter. "The least I can do is buy a bottle of champagne."

"I'll get it. The waitress is busy." Sienna stood and pushed her chair back hard. It hit the low windowsill behind her with a loud *crack*.

Jack slid his chair back and followed her to the bar at the other end of the restaurant. She was edgy, and it seemed as though she was trying to get away from him. It was strange because five minutes ago she'd been smiling back at him. As they waited behind another couple, he took hold of her arm. "Would you like to tell me what I've done to upset you?"

"No, I wouldn't." Sienna stared up at him without a smile. He could have sworn her voice broke slightly, and she turned away from him and stared through the window. The sun had slipped below the horizon, and fingers of mist were settling over the street as the sky darkened.

Jack shrugged and gave his order to the barman. The tension rolling off Sienna was enough to make him fidget as he waited for the bartender to open the champagne. Finally, the bottle was on the bar in front of him. "Coming?" He grabbed the bottle and waited for her to follow.

"I'll be there in a minute." It was quite clear she didn't want to be in his company.

"Fair enough." Jack shrugged.

On his way back to the table, Cole pushed past him as he headed for the bar. Jack placed the bottle in the wine bucket and glanced back just in time to see the guy lean into Sienna. He put his hand on her waist, and she shoved it away. Jack's fists curled as words were exchanged, and Cole glared at her for a few seconds before he pushed past her and headed for the door. Georgie and Ana, deep in conversation, missed the whole interaction.

Sienna walked back to the table, a flush on her cheeks.

"Everything okay?" Jack kept his voice low as she returned to her chair, a surge of protection rising in him.

189

"Bloody perfect." She waited until Georgie looked across at her. "Your friend had to leave suddenly. I'll explain later."

Jack was bemused when conversation turned to the hardware store.

"Magda came in the other day." Georgie held out her glass for a top-up and smiled at him. "She and Joe are leaving for a Pacific cruise next week."

Ana turned to Jack to include him in the conversation. "Did you ever meet them? They are the sweetest old couple. They've lived in Maleny forever. Blake bought the hardware store from them when he left your father's company."

Jack shook his head.

"How many cruises have Joe and Magda been on now?" Ana asked Georgie.

The conversation buzzed around Jack and it was as though he'd imagined the prickly atmosphere when Ana and Sienna came inside, and the interaction he'd just witnessed at the bar. He sat back, interested to catch up with all their news. He hadn't been north for over a year. He'd stayed in Melbourne to support his mother after his father's heart attack. To his surprise, she stepped in to help him with the company while Dad went through a series of heart operations and a massive lifestyle change. In the end, to his great relief, Jack had only had to play a minor role in the business, and he'd spent a lot of time with his father. Dad had disapproved of his casual attitude and frowned at the playboy lifestyle he thought Jack led. They'd had a few rocky years, and finally made their peace after Dad finally understood that Jack's creative nature didn't lend itself to being in big business, and Jack had spent more time on his art and less time hitting the clubs.

When Dad had offered for his company to manage the gallery for him, Jack had viewed it merely as Dad investing in something Jack loved. Now he had a chance, once and for all, to prove to his father that art was not a hobby, but his lifetime career.

190

Getting the commission for his sculptures in a new building in Sydney had built Jack's confidence, but until he'd finished them and met the deadline, he was not going to tell anyone why he'd moved here. He would prove to everyone that he was a true artist and that the commission had not been a fluke, no matter what Dad said. There had been an offer to buy the gallery last month, but he'd told the management company to tell the buyer it was no longer for sale. He had something to prove to himself.

This was Jack's big chance to make something of himself in the art world.

Something that hasn't been given to me.

There was no way he would ever get sucked into letting money rule *his* life. Chasing the dollar almost killed his father, and he had no life outside of his work.

Not for me. No way.

"Sir?" Jack looked up at the waitress who was standing beside him, with her order pad ready.

"I'll just have the seafood chowder, thanks." Jack stifled a yawn. "Sorry. I need to have an early night and grab some sleep."

He caught Sienna looking at him as he reached for his water glass. If he drank any wine, he'd probably fall asleep at the table.

"You do look tired." Her voice had lost the icy edge and the angry colour on her cheekbones had faded. Maybe it was that other guy who had been bugging her.

"Yeah, I love riding my bike, but the last two days were pretty hectic. I wanted to get up to the coast to—"

"Well, it's good to see you here." Sienna cut him off before he could finish. "I'm sure we'll be catching up some more."

"Hope so. Are you still working in Maleny?" He'd assumed that Sienna still worked in the hardware store where they'd first met.

"No," she said slowly. "I've moved jobs down this way."

She held his gaze, her beautiful dark eyes fixed on his.

He lowered his voice. "I'll give you a call later in the week when I get settled. Same number?"

Sienna looked at him over the top of her glass, but her expression was guarded as she nodded slowly. "Same number."

Georgie cleared her throat loudly, and he reluctantly broke eye contact with Sienna and settled back in his chair.

"Don't drown like our great-grandmother. That was one of Uncle Renzo's favourite stories," Georgie said. Jack looked across the table at her as her laugh rang out, before he switched his gaze back to Sienna. Damn it, he couldn't take his eyes off her. Sienna had a wry grin on her face.

"And you, as gullible as usual, always fell for Uncle Renzo's story," she said, nudging Georgie with her elbow.

Jack must have looked confused, and Sienna leaned closer to him as she explained. Her perfume was sharp and floral, and he took a deep breath, enjoying the fresh fragrance after a day on the road smelling dust and bitumen.

"When we were in high school, Uncle Renzo brought us down here to the beach at Noosa for a birthday dinner, and he told Georgie a story about his grandmother falling asleep at the table when he was a little boy and drowning in her seafood chowder."

Jack grinned as Sienna continued the story. "He had her sucked in, hook, line and sinker, for the whole night until she started to cry, and then he took pity on her."

Sienna smiled as she looked at Jack. Her long, delicate neck arched gracefully as her head turned slowly from side to side, and he got another whiff of her perfume. Her eyes were hooded, and Jack sensed she was waiting for something.

Or someone, maybe?

He couldn't smother the next yawn that overtook him when he finished his meal. Jack pushed his plate away and put his hand over his mouth. "Sorry."

"Boring you, are we?" Sienna smiled, and he held her gaze for a long time before she looked down again. Her long dark lashes hid her expression.

"Not in the least, but I'll have to get some sleep, or I'll drown in the chowder too." He joked to lighten the tension between them; you could almost hear the attraction crackling between them. He was looking forward to spending time with her, as soon as he got himself organised.

"I hear you've been in business back in Melbourne." Sienna tipped her head on the side and narrowed her eyes.

"Yeah, I have been. But it wasn't really my scene. I'm sure I'm going to like the Sunshine Coast much better than the hectic pace of Melbourne."

"It can get hectic here too," she said, and there was something strange in her tone, as though she was trying to talk him out of the move. Jack racked his brains trying to think how much Blake knew of his reasons for coming down here. He knew he owned the gallery but nothing else. No one else knew about his commission.

"So, you didn't like being the boss? You're going to do that sort of thing down here?" Sienna sounded interested.

"No, I'm not." Jack shrugged. "I intend on finding a good manager for my business and I'll look for a place to live near the beach. I'm sure I'll get plenty of time to go surfing."

"I hear it's hard to get good staff down this way." Sienna glanced at him and he had the feeling she disapproved of his plans.

Jack narrowed his eyes; he didn't need anyone else judging him. "Is it? I'm sure I'll find an agency to help me." It was as though they were playing a game, but he didn't have a clue what it was.

"So, bring me up to date. Are you all still in the restoration business?"

Ana and Georgie shook their heads, but it was Sienna who

answered him.

"I suppose you could call my *work* that. I still work with 'doohickeys' of a sort." She sat up straight in her chair and her voice was still a bit snarky. He wasn't imagining it; she was playing games with him and he didn't like it. Maybe he wouldn't call her after all. He didn't need any unnecessary complications taking up his time.

Jack put a civil smile on his face. "That's right. I'd forgotten the slogan for that hardware store that Blake bought. What was it again?"

"*Whatchamacallits, thingamajigs, and doohickeys for every need*," Georgie piped up. She and Ana had been watching the interaction between Jack and Sienna with interest.

Why did he get the feeling that everyone else knew what was going on? It was hard to concentrate because he was so tired from the long ride today.

Jack pushed his chair back and stood slowly, but Sienna's eyes stayed on him. "Time I hit the road. You'll have to excuse me. I've had a long day." Jack turned to Ana and Georgie and smiled. "I'm sure we'll catch up in Maleny. I'll be up to see Blake in the next couple of weeks. As soon as I get settled, I'll give him a call."

Sienna lifted her wineglass to her lips and sipped slowly, regarding him over the rim.

"I'll give you a call too, Sienna." Jack's eyes fixed on her rosy lips until her next words dripped from them.

"I'll look forward to it." But her terse tone belied the words. Jack turned to ask for the bill, but Sienna's next words stopped him.

"Tell me, Jack, whatever possessed you to buy an art gallery when you've had nothing to do with the art world?"

So, she wanted to be smart. Well, he could play the same game. He turned slowly to face her.

"A gallery just sells a different type of product. Business is business whatever is sold. Paintings, pottery, furniture, wheelbarrows, stocks and shares…even doohickeys"—he flicked a glance at her— "or whatever it was you were in charge of in that hardware store. As long as you have a buyer and decent staff, there's money to be made. No knowledge of art required."

They were his father's words, and although Jack didn't believe them for a moment, he made them his. Sienna had really pushed his buttons with her "nothing to do with the art world" comment.

Her eyes flashed at him as her cheeks coloured a deep red. "Well, Jack, I'm sure your *staff* will look after your gallery and make lots of money for you while you're off surfing."

"That's all I can hope for." He caught the waitress's eye and asked for the check before turning back to the table. "I'll get the bill—that's my gift to you both. I hope you had a happy birthday, ladies."

The scowl on Sienna's face said otherwise.

Chapter Three

"What did you say to Cole to upset him?" Georgie stood outside the door of the restaurant with Sienna, while Ana went to the ladies. "Why did he leave?"

"Why would you think it was me who upset *him*?" Sienna didn't let the hurt show in her tone. She kept her voice firm as she faced her sister. "He made a move on me."

"I can really pick 'em, can't I?" Georgie frowned. "I can't believe he hit on you on our second date. I'm destined to be a spinster. I might as well move in with the surrogate great-aunts now.

Sienna shook her head with a small smile before she looped her arm around her twin's shoulder. "I don't think you're quite ready for crocheting coat hangers with Thelma and Mitzi just yet. You just have to toughen up."

"You're not as tough as you make out." Georgie gave her a sideways glance. "I saw the way you were trying to act mean with Jack, but you can't fool me. You're as soft as marshmallow inside. I'll just focus on my job for a while, pay off my apartment, and then I'm going to travel. We might make Machu Picchu together yet." She punched Sienna lightly on the top of her arm. "And then when I get back, we can both move in with the aunts and you can paint the toilet roll holders."

"Very funny," Sienna said drily. "I've got grander plans than that for my art." She stifled a giggle. "Although I suppose the toilet roll holders are products too. A bit quirky. Maybe we could ask Jack to sell them in the gallery. After all, what did he say? Wheelbarrows, stocks and shares…even doohickeys."

"I'm pleased to see your sense of humour is back," Georgie

said. She turned to Ana. "I guess I need a lift home, seeing as my sweet sister here sent my driver home without me. Can you drop me off?"

Ana nodded and the three girls headed off along Hastings Street together in a comfortable silence. The air was crisp as the chill of the autumn air settled, and Sienna took a deep breath when the salt-tanged breeze drifted across from the beach. She opened her bag and pulled out her keys. "I'll see you all next weekend?"

"Whoa, not so fast." Ana grabbed her arm. "We need to talk."

"What about?" Sienna wanted to get home and think about the bombshell that Ana had dropped about Jack being the owner of the gallery . . . *her* gallery.

"Are you okay? About the gallery?" Ana frowned.

"Yes, I'm okay."

The gut-wrenching disappointment that had hit her when Ana told her about Jack owning the gallery, and changing his mind about selling, settled in Sienna's stomach like a stone. She worried about the schedule for her exhibition. She needed to keep using the studio to finish her pieces in time. She'd done so much preparation; the exhibition couldn't be put back. To make matters worse was the jolt that hit her nerve endings, *everywhere,* every time Jack looked at her or opened his mouth to speak and let that sexy voice pour over her. If he was going to be her boss, seeing him was out of the question. Besides, all her energy right now had to go into finishing her pieces and setting up the exhibition. She had no time for a social life—and didn't want to ruin her reputation in the art community by going out with the boss. Funny that, until she'd found out Jack owned the gallery, she had looked forward to catching up and having some fun.

Sea View Gallery was perfect for her, and the building had everything that she wanted. This afternoon seemed like a dream now; she'd had such plans for the place. It had the best position—

on one of the busiest tourist streets in Queensland. As well as that it was a great building: it had the best layout, with a kiln room underneath, it was across from the beach; and she'd already started to change the interior. And not only that, she was using the studio at the back for her work. She'd even slept on the sofa in the studio a few nights when she was too tired to drive to the lake. She'd been planning on spending all day there tomorrow to do some more enamelling of her frogs.

But she didn't want to worry Georgie and Ana. "It's okay. Another space will come up for sale eventually."

"I was worried you'd be really disappointed." Ana reached over and kissed her cheek. "We'll catch up soon. I'd better hurry up and pick Faith up. She'll have worn out the old dears by now. I know Thelma and Mitzi love her, but they spoil that daughter of ours dreadfully. They wanted to know if we were ever getting married so she could be the flower girl. Would you believe they started pulling out dresses from *their* grandmother's time?"

"So . . . is there going to be a wedding?" Sienna smiled at her friend.

"Of course there is . . . one day. And you two will be the first to find out when." Ana grinned, and then headed for her car.

"I'll be there in a minute." Georgie waited with Sienna and turned to her with a frown. "You're devastated about the gallery, aren't you? I know you very well, sister dear."

Sienna linked her arm through her twin's. "That's a bit over the top. Not devastated, but I am disappointed. I had such big plans for it."

"I could see the sparks snapping between you and Jack. I told the soup story to kill the sexual tension that was hanging over the table. Now you have to work for him."

"If he won't sell to me, I'll find something else. I haven't given up on the idea." Sienna sighed. "I don't want to have to ask approval for everything I do. I just hope I can still have my exhibition at the end of the month. Maybe I can find a vacant shop in Caloundra or Mooloolaba."

Georgie stared at her. "Noosa is the artsy capital of the Queensland coast. Don't give up so easily. Maybe he won't come in and change things."

"I'll think about it." Sienna leaned over and hugged Georgie. "Between sleazy Cole and sexy Jack, we certainly had an eventful birthday."

"Just don't make any hasty decisions. I know how much time you've invested in this exhibition." A phone beeped loudly. Georgie unzipped her bag and scrabbled around in it. "Blasted phone. It always gets lost in this bag. Got you, you little sucker." She blew Sienna a kiss before she hitched her bag back onto her shoulder and glanced down at the screen.

"A text from Cole." She shoved the phone back in her bag and turned toward Ana's car.

"Georgie?" Sienna put her hand on her sister's arm as she moved away.

"Uh-oh." Georgie rolled her eyes. "You've got the big-sister lecture face on."

"I know we joke about it, but promise me you'll be a little bit more . . . er . . . careful when you accept a date next time?"

"I know, he was a sleaze but—"

"Stop trying so hard. There's no such thing as happy ever after." Sienna crossed her arms, waiting for Georgie's reaction.

"You are so cynical. I do worry about you." Georgie frowned and rubbed her forehead with her hand. "Romance is alive and well. Look at Ana and Blake. Look at all the lovely old couples in Malcny who've been married for a hundred years."

"A hundred?" Sienna looked away at the fog rolling in from the sea. "Ana and Blake, well, they're one in a million. You've got to stop going out with losers just to try to find something that doesn't exist."

"Just because our mother made bad choices doesn't mean we can't find love. *You* have to learn to trust."

Sienna pushed away the sympathy that rose in her chest when she saw tears well up in Georgie's eyes. Her twin was going to end up hurt . . . again.

"I don't *need* to be loved by a man. It's not what I want. I love what I do and I'm really happy with my life the way it is." She shook her head as the disappointment of the night's events resurfaced. "If it hadn't been for Jack changing his mind about selling the gallery, I would have been well on my way to being settled. But I'll find something else."

"Well, we're going to have to agree to disagree again." Georgie's face was closed, and she turned away. "I'd better hurry, Ana's waiting. So no hasty decisions about the gallery, especially if Jack lets you keep the date for the show. Okay?"

Sienna waved as she walked over to her car parked two rows away.

"I promise," she said.

She would have to catch up with Jack first thing on Monday and find out what was happening. It was strange that no one from the company had even contacted her to say he was coming.

Chapter Four

Jack rolled the BMW up to the kerb a couple of doors up the street from the gallery. He knew there was a garage behind the building, but he only had a key to the front door. The rest of the keys had always been with the manager.

He let himself in and felt around for a light switch. There was a full moon to help light his way; the streetlight was outside the dress shop next door. He flicked the switch and shelves were bathed in a soft light; a brighter spotlight highlighted a colourful display in the window. The space was well laid out and looked very different from when he'd first bought the place. He'd run the numbers, ducked into the gallery for a quick look, and realised the property would appreciate in value. Its location was one of the best in the street. So he'd bought it and left it in the hands of Dad's company, which looked after a few of his interests.

Whoever was managing it now was doing it well. He hoped the current manager would stay on. He didn't want a full-time role running the place. His deadline was coming up fast, and he was itching to get back to his sculpting when his stuff arrived next week.

A stack of work to do before I can get those pieces finished.

Jack grabbed the bag he'd thrown in the door earlier and wandered around, picking up the occasional piece on display. Vases, bowls, all with a motif of small animals and insects, as well as an eclectic array of pieces, filled the shelves. And the colour followed a pattern that appealed to his sense of order. Everything in the window facing the street was in bright primary colours and bathed in the strongest light. As he let his gaze wander down along the shelves to the back of the gallery, he appreciated the skill that had gone into the placement of the pieces by colour. Mid-range yellows and greens filled the middle shelves and were lit with a fading light. At the back of the gallery, set in an alcove, white bowls were set off by a soft light shining down from beneath the low ceiling. Candles and bowls of flower petals placed discreetly between the artwork gave off a soft floral fragrance.

Very nicely done. It was well balanced. If the manger was that good, he might even think about a pay rise.

Jack yawned and a muscle tightened between his shoulders. He tipped his head to the side to stretch his neck. If he didn't get some sleep, he'd be useless tomorrow. At least it was Sunday and the gallery would be closed, according to the discreet sign on the glass counter near the door. He switched off the lights and pushed open the door at the back, which opened into a small kitchen. Two more doors were at the back of the kitchen. Jack pushed open the first, nodding with satisfaction as he took in a small bathroom.

Putting his bag on the floor, he pulled his T-shirt over his head and ran water over his face in the small sink. He wiped his face and hands on his T-shirt before he pushed open the last door. It opened into a studio filled with shadows, but the moonlight streaming in through the large bay window facing north hinted at the light that would fill the room in the daytime.

Too tired to turn on the light and lift all the drop sheets covering the shelves to see what was beneath them, Jack headed over to the sofa tucked into the back corner of the room. Thank goodness he didn't have to crash on the floor, although he was so tired, he could have slept anywhere. He threw his T-shirt onto the floor before he stepped out of his jeans and kicked them aside.

A blanket was draped over the back of the sofa, and he sank gratefully into the soft cushions and closed his eyes. As sleep overtook him, he forgot about the gallery and all his plans; his artist's eye took him back to Sienna, with her large dark eyes made bigger by black kohl, accentuated by the short feathery hair just touching the fair skin on her forehead. Her high cheekbones had worn a soft flush throughout dinner, and a sexy smile had tilted her rosebud lips before her mood had changed. Jack drifted off and sleep overtook him with Sienna's face planted firmly in his thoughts. He could even smell her perfume.

Jack couldn't be sure if it was the light streaming through the bay window or the need for coffee that roused him from a deep sleep hours later. He swung his legs over the sofa and leaned forward, rubbing his hands over his stubbled chin. He'd go in search of that much-needed coffee as soon as he shaved and showered. He looked down at his watch. It was only seven o'clock; he was sure he'd find an open restaurant close by in a tourist town like Noosa.

Coffee . . . and eggs. Or pancakes. Or both. With bacon.

Jack lifted his head at the sound of dishes, and he realised he really could smell coffee.

It's not just wishful thinking.

He quickly retrieved his jeans from the floor and stepped into them before he walked across to the door. He lifted his hand to turn the knob, but the door opened in front of him before he reached it.

"Shit a brick," he exclaimed.

A hot cup of coffee hit his bare chest at the same time Sienna's squeal reached his ears. He jumped back when the mug tipped over and hot coffee spilled all over the wooden floor. The cup bounced without breaking.

"What on earth are you doing here? And bringing me coffee? Are you a mind reader?" He rubbed his eyes and looked at Sienna, trying to figure out what the hell she was doing here. "Or am I still dreaming?"

"What?" Sienna gawked back at him.

"How did you know I was here?" Jack racked his brain trying to remember the conversation last night. "And how did you get in? Did I forget to lock the door?" He rubbed his hands over his eyes again trying to wake up. He stepped across the room and picked up his T-shirt and pulled it over his head. Sienna just stood there looking at him, not saying a word.

He walked back over and took her arm. "Sorry. You woke me up. I didn't even check to see if you were okay. That coffee didn't burn you, did it?"

"No, I'm fine." She pulled back from him and folded her arms. Jack looked down, following the direction of her gaze. He grinned and zipped up his jeans over his black boxers before he reached out and gently held her shoulders.

"It was very sweet of you to bring me coffee. Did Georgie tell you I was here?"

Beneath his hands, Sienna put her shoulders back. Her muscles tensed when she took a deep breath. "Let's just get one thing clear, mister. One thing I am not . . . is sweet."

"But you brought me coffee?" He grinned at her.

"In your dreams." But a smile hovered at the corner of her mouth.

Jack dropped his hands and shook his head in confusion. "So what are you doing here?"

He stepped back to give her some space, taking care to avoid the puddle of coffee on the floor around them.

Sienna looked him up and down, her expression serious. "I manage the gallery. Or at least I did. It depends on what the *owner*"—emphasis on the word, and she lifted her chin— "wants to do now that he has a sudden interest in the place."

"You're my manager? You're going to be working for *me*? Are you serious? Why didn't you tell me that last night?" Jack narrowed his eyes and grabbed her hand. "What are you doing here on a Sunday? The gallery is closed, isn't it"

"Which of your twenty questions will I answer first?" Sienna tipped her head to the side and she regarded him steadily.

204

"Don't make assumptions about me. I'm more than a shop assistant. I manage everything about the gallery, and I work here in the studio. And I *was* in the middle of purchasing the place." Sienna pulled her hand away and flicked a graceful hand around the studio. "This is—or was—my studio. I've always been an artist even when I worked for the hardware store, and when I worked with the girls Oh, and yes . . . we are closed Sundays."

He stared back; she really had the dirts this morning. "I'm sorry. I seem to have made more than one wrong assumption." Jack ran his hand through his hair. "Didn't you know I own the place? Ah"—he tapped his hand on his forehead— "that's what was wrong with you at dinner last night."

"I only found out last night. I'd emailed my lawyer to take up the option to buy and I was waiting to hear back. No one told me you owned it and were coming back. Ana told me when you arrived."

"That explains why you were so snaky last night." Jack pulled out his best killer smile, but it didn't seem to work. Sienna stood next to the door, her arms folded, and her beautiful face darkened by that same scowl.

"There's obviously been a mix-up. I'm sorry." Jack shrugged. There wasn't a lot more he could do.

"Obviously," she said.

"Look, can we start again?" Jack held out his hand, but Sienna ignored it. He had no idea what she was thinking. The serious face in front of him was nothing like the sweet one that had filled his mind as he'd gone to sleep last night. Then her words filtered through to his sluggish brain. "What sort of artist?"

"Later." Sienna turned on her heel and waved her hand as she headed to the door. "Have a shower or whatever. I'll clean up that coffee, and then you can tell me your plans for the place."

The door closed behind her with a loud *click* and Jack shook his head, totally bemused.

An artist? And she said she'd been going to buy the gallery. Something was amiss. Jack walked back to the sofa and sat down. He ran a hand across his eyes, trying to dispel the feeling that things had gone awry, before he grabbed a towel from his bag and headed for a shower. Maybe it'd clear his head a bit. Tomorrow, he'd make some calls and find out where the stuff up had happened.

There was no sign of Sienna when he went through the kitchen on the way to the small bathroom. Jack stood beneath the water, turning the temperature to cool, trying to wake up. If she was using the studio here, there were going to have to be changes. He needed this studio for his work, and his deadline meant he needed it as soon as his pieces and tools arrived.

They *did* have some talking and sorting out to do.

Chapter Five

As soon as she heard the shower running, Sienna grabbed an old rag from the storeroom and hurried back into the studio to wipe up the coffee on the floor before going back out to the gallery.

She groaned. She'd seen the big road bike parked beneath the tree up the street before she drove her car around the corner to the small parking lot at the back of the gallery but hadn't given a thought to it being Jack's. She'd planned to work on the next batch of frogs for her show all day, and now her plans had been thrown into disarray with his arrival. Her show was only three weekends away, and managing the gallery took up most of her time. Now Jack would slow her down even more. Meeting with him, showing him around and seeing exactly what he wanted her role to be—if indeed she still had a job, let alone an exhibition—was going to take up time. Assuming he would come by when the shop was open had been stupid. He *was* the gallery owner. He could come in any time he liked. And it looked like he was planning on staying here, too.

Of course he'd come in on the weekend.

She just hadn't expected him to be here this morning. All she could hope was that bunking here was a temporary arrangement, because it would interfere with her preparation for her exhibition until she could find another studio to work in. She looked around with a sigh. It had taken her an entire week to move her equipment and pieces from Mountain View, and she wasn't looking forward to moving it all again. And the kilns downstairs were perfect for her work.

Why would a businessman from Melbourne even want to own an art gallery in Queensland? Products, he'd said!

She tried to remember what Ana had told her about Jack when he'd come down for Faith's christening last year. All she could remember was that he didn't work in the same company Blake had, and that he had a reputation for liking a good time.

Because his family was loaded.

Last year at the christening, they'd indulged in a bit of flirting at Ana's cottage, but he'd left before dinner. And she hadn't seen him again until he'd walked into Fish Divine last night.

He'd looked good then, and he looked even better this morning. His hair was rumpled, and the dark stubble on his jaw tempted her fingers. She'd dropped her gaze to a muscled bare chest and refused to acknowledge the little flip low in her tummy. Closing her eyes, Sienna recalled the cheeky grin on his face as he'd zipped his jeans over the black boxers she saw before looking away. She remembered the first time she'd seen him up in Maleny a couple of years back. She'd told Ana two gorgeous guys were in the store and sent Georgie a text message about sex on legs or something.

Well, he certainly was that, and she was going to have to forget it until she found out what his intentions were for the gallery. Her exhibition was booked, and all the flyers were about to go up all over town. Noosa Heads was ready for her show.

I have to be ready too.

Chapter Six

Giovanni's Café was the best eatery in the area; Sienna was a regular customer. She had an appointment with them tomorrow to go over catering for her launch.

"Just a black coffee, thanks, Sophie."

Sienna glanced up at the waitress who stood between them, waiting for Jack to finish looking at the menu. Once he'd come out of the bathroom, showered, and dressed in jeans and a T-shirt, she led him down Hastings Street to her favourite coffee shop. Now Sophie was ogling Jack and the broad shoulders beneath his T-shirt. Sienna tried to ignore the tight shirt moulded to his shoulders and chest, and the way his hair flopped onto his forehead when he'd wandered out to the gallery after his shower. The smell of the citrus aftershave that wafted over her when she'd locked the front door of the gallery hadn't helped, either.

Ignore it. Jack is my boss. This is a professional relationship.

"Pancakes, bacon, and fried eggs." He grinned up at Sophie, and Sienna could swear the girl was turning to jelly as she took the order. He was so happy and carefree, as though he didn't have a worry in the world.

Okay, so he's easy on the eye. I'll admit that. And he's got a sexy voice.

"Coffee?" Sophie held his gaze and he nodded before he glanced at Sienna.

"You're not eating?" he asked.

"No, just coffee for me." She glanced down at her watch and frowned. Her stomach was in knots—there was no way she could eat until she knew what was going to happen. "As soon as our meeting is done, I need to get back to the studio. I have a lot of

209

work planned for today."

Jack nodded, and the waitress headed to the kitchen. Sienna followed his gaze as he looked around the small courtyard that was located at the side of the shop. There were only two other customers there so early in the day. Old wooden wine casks were scattered among the tables and on either side of the doors, filled with the last of the summer flowers. Asters, zinnias, and dahlias spilled over the edges of the wooden tubs in a profusion of colours. The paving was weathered and covered with moss in the shaded corners. In the distance, the sound of the surf added to the relaxing atmosphere.

The low rumble of Jack's sexy voice drew her attention back from the flowers and to her current problem. "This is a pretty place. Very trendy," he said. "And there are a lot of galleries in the shopping area. I didn't know there were so many here."

So he didn't know much about the place.

"What made you decide to buy the gallery?" Her voice was short, and Sienna studied him while she waited for him to answer.

Jack put his elbows on the table and linked his fingers beneath his chin. "Promise not to laugh?"

"Not until I hear what you have to say."

"I'm a movie fanatic. I bought the gallery because so many movie stars live here on the coast."

"What? Where did you hear that?" Sienna felt her mouth drop open. She closed it and reached for the coffee Sophie put on the table. 'I think you've got Noosa confused with Byron Bay.'

He put his hands up. "No, just joking. I've always been interested in art, so I decided to buy a gallery and host exhibitions. Noosa seemed as good a place as any. A wealthy, retired clientele who are looking to build up their art collections live here." He stared into the distance and Sienna sensed there was more to the story. She wasn't going to press him. It wasn't his past she was interested in; it was *her* future.

210

"I saw Sea View Gallery in one of the art magazines I subscribe to."

"So you bought it, had it managed, and then you decided to sell it a couple of months ago? And then you changed your mind again." Sienna frowned. It sounded as though Jack didn't know what he wanted. Her entire future was at stake because a flirty playboy with time on his hands and money to burn bought a gallery he didn't even seem much interested in. "And now you're going to take it over?"

Buy. Sell. Keep. Move in. Why would he do that? It was the bottom line that mattered. All *his* choices were affecting *her* plans.

Jack leaned back casually and put his hands behind his head, turning his face up to the sunshine that had begun to bathe the courtyard. "I thought I'd be in Melbourne for good after my dad got sick, but, well…here I am." The corded muscles in his neck and his toned biceps didn't look they belonged to a businessman, but more like the gym junkie she'd first mistaken him for. Now Sienna stared at him, waiting for him to keep talking and spill his plans for the gallery.

"Look, there's been a mix-up. I'm sorry. I'll have to call Dad's secretary. I told her to take the gallery off the market when I—"

She waited for Jack to continue, but he cut off his sentence. After a couple of minutes of silence, she couldn't wait any longer. "We need to sort out what's happened, and you need to tell me what you are going to do."

Jack nodded. "We do. And soon."

"How about now? I have to make plans." Sienna fought her rising temper. "Perhaps I was a bit hasty making plans before the sale was final. I have my first exhibition opening in three weeks. I had no idea you would change your mind. In fact, remember, I didn't even know it was you selling to me."

"Would that have made a difference if you had?" Jack

211

narrowed his eyes.

"Why would it? I barely know you." Sienna waved her hand dismissively. "I haven't given you another thought since you took my number."

Liar.

She had, and she still remembered how disappointed she'd been when he left Faith's christening early, and then never called her. Despite what she'd said to Georgie, there was still a place in her life for going out with men and having a good time. Just because she didn't want the commitment-and-wedding deal like Georgie didn't mean she was going to live a nun's life. She'd just been too busy to go out, building up the gallery's business and her reputation as an artist. And now Jack had to turn up and own the damn gallery. Too complicated.

"Until last night I thought the contract of sale would go ahead. I've made plans, and, yes, maybe I was a bit premature, but I'm not known for being patient." Sienna put her cup down and folded her arms across her chest. "If I had known this was going to happen, I would have stayed at Mountain View Gallery."

"So you haven't been at my gallery for very long?"

Sienna shook her head and gritted her teeth. *His* gallery. God, he didn't even know what was happening before he waltzed in to take over. Was he serious about the business? She couldn't work for someone with such a casual attitude. Sienna needed to be organised, and everything she did was planned ahead.

"I've only been there a couple of months. My…your…gallery had been closed for a few months after the other manager left town. You didn't even know that?" She tried to keep her voice even. No point upsetting him although she'd probably done that already.

Jack shrugged and a frown wrinkled his brow. For the first time he seemed a little uncomfortable. "No…no, I'm sorry, but I had no idea. I have a lot of business interests that Dad's company looks after for me. Maybe I should have paid more attention." He leaned back as Sophie put a plate overflowing with food in front of him. It seemed as though the discomfort she had glimpsed a moment ago disappeared. "Looks great, thanks."

Sienna sat back and watched Jack dig into the meal, as she weighed the pros and cons of what her choices were. Her stomach grumbled, and he grinned at her as the heat warmed her neck.

"You should eat something. You're too thin."

Now her temper really began to boil. "I eat plenty. I'm petite, not thin."

"What did you have for breakfast?"

She pointed to her coffee.

Jack sighed and used his fork to lift a pancake and a slice of bacon onto the small plate that held his toast. He slid it over to her. "Eat. We have a lot of talking to do."

"Thank you." Sienna nibbled at the edge of the pancake and stared at him. "So start."

"Start what?"

God, he was laidback. She spoke through her teeth with forced restraint. "Start talking."

He grinned and kept eating without saying a word, until his plate was clear. "That was great." Finally, he picked up the napkin and wiped his mouth. "Okay, tell me what *your* plans are."

"You're the owner. You tell me." Sienna kept her voice patient and held his gaze.

"But *you* did have plans?" Jack's green eyes crinkled when he smiled, and her stomach did a little flip.

Hunger and not enough coffee.

She caught Sophie's eye when the waitress walked past and pointed to her empty cup.

"Well, yes, I did. Like I said, I like to know what's ahead, and I plan for it. This has thrown me a curveball, and I need to rethink where I am...and where I'll go."

213

"Maybe you don't have to go anywhere." Jack leaned forward and propped his elbows on the table as he held her gaze.

"I need to know…are you going to be hands-on, or are you going to be an owner who only comes in occasionally?"

Jack stared back at her, and his eyes were full of mirth. "Definitely not hands-on, not in the gallery anyway."

The subtext in his words was clear by the grin on his face. Despite the pleasant shiver that ran down Sienna's back, she gritted her teeth to hold back a rude retort. He was trying to push her buttons. Why did he take it off the market if he didn't want to work in it?

"So you'll support any exhibitions I've already booked, including mine?"

"Yours?"

God, the man was casual.

"Yes, I told you before. I'm an artist. I'm planning my first show at the end of the month." She spoke slowly as she stared at him. "And I have advertised it, so I need to know right away if I need to find another gallery, seeing as I won't have my own now."

Jack returned her stare. "You're a bit out of sorts this morning."

Finally, she was getting through to him.

"This is me. I like to be organised." She forced a smile to her face, and it was at odds with the temper she was barely hanging on to. "I need to know what you're going to do. It might be hard for someone as…for someone like you to understand, but this is my livelihood." She couldn't help herself and her temper finally spilled over. "Anyone who buys a gallery because they think movie stars live in town, and then leaves it in the hands of a manager who leaves and he doesn't even know it sits there all closed up—"

"Whoa…right there." Jack held his hand up again. "You've got yourself all worked up. Look, I'm sorry the sale fell through,

214

but I have my reasons. And what do you mean by someone like me?"

She pursed her lips, arms still folded. "Nothing." She'd been forthright enough already. "Okay, my plans…if you are happy for the first exhibition—mine—to go ahead, I need three things to happen."

"Okay. Tell me."

"One. Do you need a manager, someone to do the day-to-day gallery stuff?"

He held her gaze and nodded without speaking.

"Two, can I still hold my exhibition in the gallery the week I've advertised?"

"Yes." He nodded again as relief flooded through Sienna. Now his arms were folded across his chest. "And three?"

So far, so good.

This was the one she really needed him to agree to. There was no way Sienna could move her stuff to another studio and have her pieces ready in time. And there was no formal agreement in her employment contract for the manager to use the studio. She swallowed and her fingers bit into the skin on her arms.

"Three, can I keep using the studio?"

"No."

Chapter Seven

Jack looked across the table at Sienna. The twin spots of colour were back on her cheeks, and he could tell she was about to lose her cool. Beneath the table she was tapping her foot against the cobblestones.

"I'm going to stay in the studio until I find somewhere permanent to live, so you'll have to find somewhere else to work." He leaned back in his chair. He wasn't ready to tell her that he planned to use it for his work, too.

Not just yet.

He was still trying to figure her out, and he wasn't ready to share his private work with her. When they had first met, he'd thought she was a little distant because she was being protective of Ana, and he'd admired that.

She shrugged. "Can't do."

"Can't do what?" Now her attitude was starting to get under his skin.

"If I have to move to another studio, I won't be ready for the show. And I certainly wouldn't have the time to manage the gallery for you. So, we have a catch-22."

"Maybe we'll have to look for a compromise?" The last thing Jack wanted was to have to manage the gallery himself, and he didn't want to have to find a new manager. It wouldn't be a good look for the business to close the place again so soon after it had been shut for a few months. He needed to keep Sienna in place as manager. Maybe he could postpone his work on his own pieces for a couple of weeks. If she would stay, maybe he could give a little. "What if you could use the studio for the next two weeks and then find somewhere else after that?" He could afford to give her two weeks, but that was all.

"Two weeks. I could possibly do that. Any other conditions attached? Like a rental fee?"

"God, no. You can just use the space. As long as there's room for me to store my stuff somewhere when it arrives, and you can work around it."

"How much stuff?" She tapped her finger against her lips.

He hadn't noticed her hands before. Her nails were short and square cut and didn't match the rest of her flamboyant style. Long, painted nails would match the colourful scarves and the dangling earrings. *But she is an artist.* So that explained the functional look of her hands.

"A lot."

"How long were you planning on living in the studio? I can't work if you're sleeping there."

"That's true. That could be a problem." Jack frowned. He wasn't ready to find a place of his own here yet. He rubbed the back of his neck. He didn't want to let her down, but things were getting complicated now.

"The sooner you find somewhere to live, the sooner I can get back to work." Sienna kept her fingers against her lips as she looked at him thoughtfully. "There's a real shortage of rentals here in Noosa…and it's really expensive. You might have to move to a hotel."

Jack bit back the niggle of temper that tugged at him. She might like to be organised and call the shots, but there was no way she was going to send him to a hotel when he owned a perfectly good studio to sleep in. He kept his voice even. "I hate hotel living."

"Even for two weeks?"

"Even for one night. It's not an option I'd consider."

Sienna stared at him and frowned. Her fingers drummed on the table, and she held his gaze. Her expression changed, and a slight smile tipped her lips. Jack looked at her mouth and was surprised by the rush of feeling that ran through him. She looked at him thoughtfully.

"I might have a solution. I have a proposition for you." Her smile was wider.

The thoughts running through Jack's mind had nothing to do with where he was going to live, and he forced himself to concentrate on what she was saying.

"There's a small apartment in the back of my cottage. Near the lake. You could have that until you find something better. You could move in today, and I could keep working in the studio. Two weeks. What do you think?" Her eyes were wide and her expression hopeful. His return to take over the gallery had really put a hole in her plans.

"I'll take a look at it and think about it." He didn't know how interested he was in her offer. Sure, he could see she'd only offered because it meant she could get back into the studio. But as far as working with her in the gallery, and living in her house…well, he didn't know how he felt about that. He wanted to date her, but living and working in the same place? That was a bit too much.

"How about we go now and you can look at it? Then I can get to work as soon as we get back."

A strong desire to reach across the table and put his hand around the back of her long, slender neck and pull Sienna to him so he could kiss those lips overtook him.

Whoa, not yet. Let's get the first problem sorted out.

"Okay. Won't hurt to take a look." Jack knew his voice was gruff, but he was fighting the feelings tugging him back and forward. He stood, pushed his chair in, and walked across the courtyard to the cash register. He'd check out this apartment of hers, but it would be better if he found a place of his own. Maybe he'd make some calls after he looked at it and see if he could find somewhere else to live for a while.

And quickly.

He needed somewhere he could have his own space—somewhere to put her at a distance. Jack needed privacy and solitude for the muse to kick in. And he couldn't afford to risk it—his deadline was fast approaching. He didn't want anything to dent his confidence; God knows, Dad had a big enough go at doing that. Living in close proximity to Sienna would complicate matters even more, and if there was one thing he didn't want, it was to make it hard to focus on his sculptures because his head was somewhere else. He'd been living with his parents since his father's heart attack and was more than ready to live alone again.

That was just *one* of the reasons he wasn't too keen on taking up Sienna's offer. The other one was that she was just too damn appealing, and he didn't want to put himself near her just yet. They had to keep a professional relationship now that they would be working closely together. Sex complicated matters. He'd been down that road before…and more than once. His last girlfriend had read him wrong, and Arielle had mapped out a whole future for them before he'd pulled back. He wasn't going to risk it again, especially when they had this business connection. If it were just a fun relationship, they could move on—with mutual agreement—when it burned out. Jack wanted no complications; having the gallery connection would complicate matters. Let alone living in the same place. Twenty-four-seven. No way.

"Come on, we'll take my car." She strode ahead of him, and he was surprised by how quickly she moved. Sienna barely reached his shoulder, but he had to step up his pace to catch her.

The streets had filled with tourists and locals alike since they'd been in the coffee shop, and he looked around with interest. Sienna slowed down and shot him a grin. "Looking for movie stars?"

It was the same droll humour that had appealed to him

219

when they'd first met.

"Nah, just checking out my new town." The place had a fresh feel. After his time in the hectic world of business in Melbourne, he was looking forward to the change. A relaxed lifestyle. A slower pace. A place where integrity and honesty could exist without someone trying to make money from his hard work. Or better him in a deal.

She walked along beside him. "You know *anybody* you pass on the street could be a *somebody* here. But there is a code of anonymity in Noosa. Even if you pass Chris Hemsworth…you just keep on walkin'."

"I'm sure." If he saw Chris Hemsworth, he'd probably gawk like a fan.

"I'll teach you the Noosa way." She'd relaxed a bit, probably because of the possibility of getting her workspace back, and that made him uncomfortable. He felt as though she was happy because things might work out her way, not because she was enjoying his company. He was sure if it hadn't meant being able to stay working in the studio, she would never have offered to show him the apartment. She kept walking past the gallery, then turned into a back lane.

"You keep your car back here?" he asked.

"Yes, there's just enough space for it."

Sienna walked over to a red BMW Z3 parked in a small paved area and leaned over to unlock the door. Jack felt that small tug of desire pull at him again as her loose pants clung to her legs. He lifted his gaze and ran it down the car instead. "Nice car."

"I love it," she said with a smile. "Especially when I drive back up the mountain to visit Georgie and Ana, and the weather's good enough to keep the top down."

'Which lake do you live near?'

'Lake Weyba. It's only a short drive from here.'

He opened the passenger door, slid in next to her, and

watched as she reached up and pushed the front part of the top up, before turning the key and pressing the electronic control to open the roof. It slid back silently, and they were bathed in warm sunshine.

"Almost as good as riding a bike," he said.

"Might as well enjoy the day. Sunny days can be few and far between here along this stretch of the coast."

The wind blew strongly as Sienna drove out through town and took the turnoff at Noosaville. Jack dropped his shades over his eyes when they turned south. He took in the scenery and recognised the golf course where he'd played with Blake a couple of years ago. When they passed Noosa Hills, Sienna swung a right onto Eumarella Road. "Pretty exclusive area," he said.

"The average listing is over two million," she said.

Jack narrowed his gaze. She must be doing okay if she had a place here *and* was going to buy the gallery too. Maybe she could find herself another studio and he wouldn't feel so bad about moving her out.

"You are easy to read, you know." Sienna turned and grinned at him as she swung into a driveway and drove past a huge home between some tall pines. "I said the average." He appreciated her smile; she'd looked thoughtful as they'd driven through town and hadn't said much to him.

She slowed in front of a huge house built in pink concrete, with large circular windows on each side of a tall entry that towered over an expanse of green manicured lawn. He waited for Sienna to turn into the circular driveway at the front, but she kept going. A little farther down the road, the lake glimmered through the trees and she swung left into a narrow driveway. A small cottage sat on a rise at the end of the road with a garage beside it.

"Home sweet home." She stopped in front of the cottage and turned the car off.

"Nice." Jack let out a low whistle when he stepped out and

221

took in the view of the lake. "Very nice. Lived here long?" It was exactly the sort of place he'd love to find down here along the coast. He'd thought of having ocean views, but this small lake, hidden among the trees, was beautiful.

"When I was first working with Georgie and Ana in our restoration business, it was one of the first old places we bought. It used to be the boat cottage of the estate up the road. It was going for a song because it was in such poor condition." Sienna walked up the three steps, and Jack followed her to the porch. "We pooled what we had and it was our first restoration."

The view was even better from the porch. The cottage was so far from the road there was no traffic noise. Jack closed his eyes and listened to the wind sighing through the trees. He could move in here right now. His fingers tingled with the urge to get working.

"Local gossip says the estate once belonged to an American movie star, and this was his love cottage." She grinned at him and her face came alive. "We learned a lot doing the renovation. And we had so much fun. Because it was so far from Maleny, we'd stay overnight, camping in the forest." She pointed to a low fence with a gate at the side of the cottage. "When we finished the restoration, we rented it out, and then when we closed the business, I bought the girls' share and I moved down here last year." She put the key in the front door and led him through the small cottage. "The only downside to the apartment is that it shares a common entry with the house. That's why I haven't rented it out before. It's got everything else, but it's really tiny."

"Show me." As he followed her down a wide timber-lined hallway, Jack watched her walk. Her movements were graceful, and he regretted not having the opportunity to follow up that promise of calling her.

Too late now, especially if he was going to be her boss…and her tenant.

Chapter Eight

"So, what do you think?"

Jack stood at the window of the small living room. The apartment at the back of the cottage had an uninterrupted view of the lake. Sienna smiled to herself. There hadn't been any view until she, Ana, and Georgie had cleared the overgrown garden. The house and its garden were one of the best restorations they'd done. That's why they never sold it.

"This light is amazing."

She jumped when Jack turned to her, his face alight with enthusiasm. "Have you ever thought of adding a studio to the back here? The aspect is perfect."

"I did, but I can't afford it." She looked at him thoughtfully. "I saved everything to buy a gallery, but that's not such a bad idea. Now that the sale's not going ahead."

"Have you ever thought about selling?"

"The apartment?" She tipped her head to the side, unsure of what he was saying.

"No, the whole property." His eyes were bright with interest, and he came over and held her arms gently. Sienna tried to ignore the jolt of warmth that shot up her shoulders and settled in her chest when his fingers brushed down her arms before stopping at her wrists.

"Maybe we could do a deal with the gallery?"

She bit back her frustration at his attitude. She had so wanted that gallery for her own; Jack had it and didn't really want it. And now he wanted her house, too?

"Uh-uh. I'm settled here." She kept her voice bland.

He stared down at her and the warmth fluttered to her

stomach. His gaze held hers, and she let go of a little of her anger. How could she not when that sexy grin homed in on her?

"Well, give me some thought if you ever do decide to sell it."

"I guess this means you'll take the apartment…for the two weeks anyway, while I get my exhibition ready?" She tried to steer the conversation back to their original problem and ignore the crazy feelings racing through her from where his fingers were touching her skin.

"Yeah, but you can only have the studio for two weeks. Do you think you could be ready by then?"

She looked at him thoughtfully and tapped her finger to her lips. "Maybe."

"You have to."

Sienna looked at him. He had let go of her and had an intense look on his face. He was flexing his fingers as he walked around. "Okay. If I work every night, I can do it in two."

Jack stopped in front of her and held his hand out. "We have a deal then."

Sienna took a deep breath and took his hand as relief zinged through her.

Maybe this will work out okay. After all, Jack owed her nothing really, and he *was* letting her have the studio in town and hold her exhibition. The only thing in it for him was having someone to manage the gallery for him just like she'd been doing already.

"Come on. I'll show you the garage. There's room in there if you want to store your stuff when it arrives." Sienna stepped away from his loose hold and headed back through the house and out onto the porch, conscious of him close behind her. God, she was acting like a teenager. She'd never let a man affect her like that before, and she wasn't about to start now. Men had a role in her life. She went on dates, she had the occasional fling, and she didn't let any of them close enough to hurt her. She swallowed and straightened her shoulders.

And I won't now. I'm not Georgie.

Between Georgie and their mother, there was enough hurt to last them all a lifetime. Sienna didn't intend on adding to it.

"In here," she said briskly as she opened the swinging wooden doors to the empty garage. "Can you fit all your stuff in here?"

Jack walked in, his thumbs tucked into his jeans, and looked around. "It'll be fine. I'll put my personal stuff here and the big stuff can go into the space at the back of the gallery."

He must be planning on storing his furniture too.

Sienna didn't care what he put in there as long as it meant she could use the studio. She went inside to get the spare key to the front door and the padlock for the garage, while Jack walked over and waited by the car.

God, she hoped she wasn't making a huge mistake. Working with him and living in the same house meant she would have to try twice as hard to keep him at a distance. She'd had a lot of practice being tough, and she was about to invoke it now. That soft feeling that had crept through her bones earlier was banished to a place she never let see the light of day. She hadn't been out with anyone for a while. She'd have the same reaction to any good-looking guy who came along.

Yeah, sure.

The little voice in her head let the doubts creep in. It had been in the back of her mind since she'd first met Jack, and now the attraction whooshed straight back in with a vengeance.

As soon as they got back to the gallery, Jack packed up his bag, ready to head out to the apartment. He said he had some calls to make to get the delivery address for his gear changed. Sienna drew a deep breath of relief when he finally roared off on his bike. Her mind was in turmoil, and she needed to get into the studio and do what she loved.

And figure out what I'm going to do. How to fit the gallery in through the day and get four weeks' worth of work done in two. She couldn't understand why he would only give her the two weeks? Maybe he was just being ornery and had to show her who was the boss? But that didn't fit what she'd seen of Jack's casual character.

Sienna lifted a drop sheet and picked up a plastic crate full of her copper frogs. They were shaped and ready for enamelling. She lifted the roller door at the back of the gallery and walked down the ramp to the bricked-in room beneath, and she wondered if Jack knew the room with the kilns was there.

Sienna shrugged and tried to clear her mind as she fired the kiln and reached for a small container of ground enamel.

***

Jack unpacked the panniers and the one bag he'd carried on the bike from Melbourne before he made his calls. He really needed to harness the ideas that were flowing through him. He pulled out a notebook and did a couple of quick sketches of the pictures in his mind before he lost them. Then he called the moving company, and now he was calling home to check on his father. As the phone rang, he looked around the small apartment. Every colour and every piece of furniture reminded him of Sienna—her vibrancy. It would be a good place to chill while he thought about the work ahead of him.

"Hey, Jack!" His dad's voice boomed across the connection. "Great to hear from you, son." Jack grinned. At least having a life-threatening heart attack had given Mike Montgomery a whole new perspective on life. They'd fought for years, about how Jack didn't want to work in the family business, and his mother, Helen, was caught in the middle. His laid-back attitude really got under his workaholic father's skin. Life was too short, and his father had

226

finally realised that point with his heart attack. It had given him a huge wake-up call.

"How are you, Dad?"

"All good. Can't talk long. I'm getting picked up for golf in a minute."

"Mum there?"

"No, she's at the office."

"On a Sunday?" Jack frowned. He hoped his mother wasn't going to step into the shoes his father had vacated.

"Yeah, the sooner Blake gets up here the better." His father cleared his throat. "Uh-oh, scratch that. I wasn't supposed to say anything."

"Blake?"

"He'll tell you what's happening. Forget I said anything. How's that deadline looking?"

Jack bit back a terse reply. "Fine, fine. Remember I only arrived here last night." He hated the fact that he felt it necessary to make excuses to his father.

After he disconnected the call, Jack walked thoughtfully into the small bedroom. Sienna had told him where to find some sheets, and after he'd made up the bed, he lay back with his hands behind his head, going over the events of the day. Nothing had really panned out like he'd expected, but that was the way he liked life to be. He wasn't going to get trapped on the treadmill of predictability where he always knew what the day would bring, with too many people depending on him. Look what it had done to his father. Although when he'd been in Melbourne, his own need to control what was happening in the company had surfaced a little and unsettled him. He worried he had more of his father in him than he thought. Maybe that's why they clashed for so long.

So once he'd signed the contract for the sculptures, he'd hightailed it out of the business and out of the city. Now he'd have all day to work on his sculpture, focus his creativity, and do what he loved. The only small problem was the deadline on the contract he'd signed, but that didn't bother him as much as not being able to work for two weeks. In a way, he already regretted saying Sienna could use the studio. He would have to be firm and stick to the timeline he'd given her. Then he'd move in there, finish his commissions, and start work on the ideas crowding his thoughts.

When he had more done, he could think about his own exhibition.

As long as Sienna would keep managing the gallery.

If she was happy to stay at the gallery after her exhibition, that was fine. If she did choose to move on, he'd have to deal with it. And he wasn't going to complicate matters with a personal relationship. As much as he would have liked to start up something between them, things had to stay on a business footing.

He closed his eyes and frowned as her face continued to fill his thoughts. He rolled over and punched the pillow. This had to stop. He focused on where he would get the truck to deliver his stuff. He'd have to split it when it arrived and decide what would go where.

It'd be crazy to move even one sculpture twice, but it had put a dent in his plans having to wait a couple of weeks before he could start work. There was enough space and light here to do some of his modelling, but he needed the kilns, so he'd wait out the two weeks. He ignored the little voice telling him that he was worried his work wouldn't measure up.

But he'd made a deal with Sienna and he'd stick to his word. He wouldn't let being at loose ends interfere with his decision to keep her at arm's length. If he got bored just hanging around and not working, he'd go out and explore the district. Go up and visit Blake. Play some golf. Catch a wave. He'd leave Sienna in peace until she'd finished her own work, and then he'd get to know about the gallery when she wasn't so busy.

The problem was that wasn't the way his thoughts were

taking him. Finally, he drifted off and awoke refreshed a short time later. The afternoon stretched ahead, and Jack decided to go for a walk around the lake. When he opened the front door, he noticed the *Noosa News* lying on the table on the porch, and he tucked it beneath his arm as he set off.

***

By the time Sienna finished enamelling the batch of frogs, it was after dark. She pushed her helmet up and rubbed her eyes. It was hot down here with the kilns on, and her clothes were damp from perspiration. Her stomach was grumbling; she'd only snatched a quick lunch once she'd finished the first batch of frogs and hadn't eaten since. As soon as she got home, a shower, a meal, and a glass of wine on her back porch would complete the day. She put her hand up to her eyes and rubbed.

She arranged the frogs on the shelves and stood back. Satisfaction rippled through her. They were good. In fact, they were better than good.

They're fabulous. If I say so myself.

The red one with his leg dangling inches below the green enamelled log she'd wrapped him around was her favourite. It was one of the best pieces she'd done yet. Three more batches to enamel and she'd be ready for the show. But tomorrow she had planned to focus on publicity and organising event logistics. There weren't enough hours to get everything done. She had some more media sheets to send out, and she had back-to-back appointments with artists wanting to book their own shows, as well as meeting with the caterers for her first-night launch event.

Where will Jack fit into all this?

Even though they discussed the studio and his living arrangements, they hadn't discussed anything about her day-to-day running of the gallery now that he was here. He was so casual about it. Did he really want the gallery to succeed or not? She shrugged, flicked on the night-light to leave the gallery softly lit, and pulled the door shut behind her. She'd keep doing things her way until he told her to change them.

Fifteen minutes later, she drove her sports car into the small carport next to her cottage. The house was in darkness, although she noticed that the padlock on the garage doors was locked. Jack was likely home and in bed already. Sienna let herself in quietly, slipped off her shoes and padded barefoot along to her bathroom. She threw her clothes into the linen basket and turned the shower on hot. The hard jets of water soothed her neck and refreshed her, and once she was dry, she tucked a towel around her breasts and wandered into her bedroom. Maybe it hadn't been such a good idea, jumping in and offering him the apartment. It was going to be hard getting used to having someone else around. No more wandering around half dressed. She slipped on some underwear and tied a loose sarong around her before she headed out to the kitchen.

It won't be for long.

Once she finished the last batch of firing in the kiln in two weeks, she could start looking for a studio. Then she had to decide whether she was going to stay working for him or look for some other place to buy. She bit her lip. Jack's idea about building a studio on the back of the cottage had given her something to think about. If she stayed managing his gallery, and could work on her sculptures from home, it could be the ideal solution. She just had to find the money to do it.

His decision to take the gallery off the market had created a lot of problems for her. Her thoughts whirled around as she made a grilled cheese sandwich and poured a glass of wine. Maybe, just maybe, she could build herself a studio out here on the lake. Using her shoulder to push open the back door, she headed out to the porch.

"You're home late."

Sienna jumped and grabbed for the plate before it slipped

from her hand. Jack unfolded himself from her hammock, crossed the porch, and took the plate from her.

She put her hand on her chest as her heart thudded. "You scared me. I'm not used to company."

"Sorry. I was sitting out here enjoying the quiet." He pulled out a chair and put her plate on the table. "You don't eat properly."

Sienna bit down on the smart retort that hovered on her lips and forced a smile in his direction. He really brought out the worst in her.

What is it to him what I do or what I eat?

"I had a good lunch."

"That's okay, then."

She couldn't help herself, despite her intention to keep things non-emotional. "I'm so pleased you approve." Putting her elbows on the table, she glared at him in the soft moonlight. She'd left the outside light off deliberately to keep the insects away before she'd come outside. Despite the cool breeze, Jack was wearing running shorts and no shirt, and her reaction to the sight of his broad, muscular chest bugged her even more. She pushed away the flare of desire that sparked inside her. "Aren't you cold?"

"No, I went for a run around the lake after I ate. I miss my gym equipment. I'll have to find a place to work out around here."

Sienna reached over and picked up the small lighter she kept on the table and lit the vanilla candle in the glass bowl in the centre. She drew a deep breath and held her hand steady, surprised by the tremble his proximity caused. The candle threw a flickering light over Jack's bare skin and she caught her breath. Tipping her head back, she looked up at the stars. It was only his natural beauty that she found appealing. Her artistic eye was drawn by beauty.

Nothing else.

She dropped her head and looked out over the lake shimmering in the moonlight. The low branches of the trees surrounding the cottage bowed elegantly in the light breeze, their

231

leaves forming long, draping sweeps illuminated by the soft light.

"It's beautiful here." Jack's voice was a whisper, and a shiver snaked up her spine.

Maybe she should do something about this feeling? Let this attraction run its course? What did they say about only living once?

Not worth the risk.

"Yes, it is."

"Did you get your work done? You put in a long day."

Pleased to get her mind off the bare, muscular shoulders across the table, Sienna nodded. "Yes, I got a good amount done. I should be able to finish in the two weeks if I put in the next couple of weekends as well as every night."

"Do you always work this hard?"

She nodded. "Not usually every night. But what has to be done, will be. And I love my work. I lose myself in it." She looked up at him. Maybe it would be hard for a businessman—and one with such a casual attitude—to understand what she was saying about the creative process.

"Where do you do your enamelling?" Jack held her gaze steadily with his. He seemed genuinely interested, so she kept talking.

She looked back at him. "Did you look at my frogs in the gallery today?"

All Sienna's confidence in her work faded in that instant and she bit her lip. Then her temper kicked at the thought of Jack looking at them without her. Her mood seesawed back and forth. "Frogs? No, I read about your upcoming exhibition in the local paper."

"Oh. I forgot about that."

"According to the journalist, you're quite the up-and-coming artist in the area...and you work in enamel?"

"They say the same thing about everyone they interview."

"Tell me about your work. About the processes you use. Do the kilns beneath the gallery work?" Sienna was surprised at his level of interest and his knowledge of the process.

"I wondered if you knew there was a brick room beneath the gallery. I use those kilns." She shook her head. "You really didn't know what you bought, did you?"

Jack certainly wasn't a hands-on manager, and if that was the way he worked maybe she would be able to stay at the gallery with him as owner. He could let her run it the way she wanted and keep out of her way. As long as Jack found somewhere to live, maybe life could go on the way it was. It would just mean the gallery wouldn't belong to her, but that wouldn't be the end of the world. The money she'd set aside for the deposit could go toward adding on to her house and building her own studio, while she continued to work in the studio at the gallery. For the life of her, she couldn't understand why he wanted it. If he wasn't going to be involved, what was he going to do with his days?

"I really liked the feel of the town. Before I even ran the numbers, I decided to buy it."

The opposite of her. Sienna had everything planned down to the last detail in all her life. Jack grinned at her, and the flickering candlelight played over his bare chest.

This is altogether too romantic a setting out here. She needed to break the mood. If she was going to run his gallery, she needed to know a little bit more about the direction he wanted to go.

"What sort of art do you enjoy?"

"Oh, I have eclectic tastes. I have a few contemporary paintings in my apartment in Melbourne. Some are being shipped out, and some I'll leave there till I find a place to live. I often spend my weekends cruising galleries."

Sienna finished her wine and put the glass down. How nice would it be to be able to afford to collect art? And to have the time to wander around the galleries? When she got the chance—and that was not very often—she loved visiting art museums and other galleries. Maybe they did have something in common after all? She pushed that thought away. There'd be no sparks crackling around the table tonight if she had any say in the matter. She couldn't help but grin when she remembered last night. There was no Georgie here with family stories to dispel the tension tonight.

"Great." Jack was staring at her, and she dropped her gaze as she stood and pushed her chair back. "You found everything you needed? I'm going to bed. We've got a busy day ahead of us in the gallery tomorrow. We'll have to spend some time sorting out my role now that you've arrived."

He stood and followed her to the door, and as she turned to say good night, he held her arm. The heat running up her skin rivalled the heat of the kiln this afternoon.

"I meant to tell you; your phone rang a few times tonight." Jack looked down at her and held her gaze.

"Thanks." Sienna moved away and pushed the door open, turning the light on before she crossed to the phone. Three missed calls from Ana flashed on the screen.

All from the same number. "It's Ana. I wonder why she didn't call my cell?"

Jack grinned at her. "Maybe because you left it at home? I could hear it ringing from the front of the cottage."

"I can be a bit forgetful when I'm immersed in my work." Sienna pulled a face at him as she glanced down at her watch. "I didn't realise I'd left it here."

It was late, but she wouldn't sleep until she knew what was wrong. She pressed the return call button. "And she hasn't left any messages."

Ana's phone rang for a while and Sienna waited to leave a message, but Ana finally picked up.

"Hi, Sienna. Sorry, I was just putting Faith down. Little

miss hates going to bed."

"What's wrong? Jack said you tried to call all afternoon."

"Jack?"

"Yeah, he's staying here for a while."

"Ooh-la-la. You didn't waste any time picking up where you left off."

"No, *la la*. And there was nothing to leave off, anyway." Sienna kept her voice low and flicked a glance at Jack. He was standing, looking out over the lake, and had his back turned to her. His skin was tanned, and his smooth shoulders tapered down nicely to a narrow waist above his running shorts. She swallowed and looked away before her gaze could continue down his bare thighs. "Jack's staying here only until we sort some things out with the gallery. Now what's wrong? Why were you trying to get me?"

"I called mainly to check that you were okay."

"I'm fine. Nothing to worry about, everything's good. I'll fill you in on the weekend."

"And that's another reason I called, to remind you about Faith's birthday party in two weeks. And it's a dress-up party." Ana's giggle made Sienna smile. Ana had taken to motherhood with lots of support. As well as having Georgie and Sienna as surrogate aunties, and Thelma and Mitzi as surrogate great-aunts, little Faith had most of the elderly community of Maleny as surrogate grandparents.

"Oh, dress-up. Love it."

"It's a fairy-tale theme. Have you still got your fairy costume? Wear that. Jeannie and Rod are bringing the kids down for the party." Excitement filled Ana's voice. "You should see how excited Blake is. He's putting on the biggest party ever!"

Sienna laughed. "What about Georgie? Another chance to wear pink? I know how much she loves it."

Ana chuckled. "Did you always torment her about her red hair?"

235

"Sure did, and she bit every time. Don't you worry, though, she tormented me right back."

Ana's laugh ended and her voice sobered. "I was a bit worried about her today. She took a call when I was at the store this afternoon and she got really upset."

"Is that sleaze-bucket Cole bothering her?"

"No, he was at the store for the Sunday shift too. He was over talking to Blake when her phone rang. I don't know who it was, but I'm sure she was crying. She wouldn't tell me what was going on."

"I'll call her."

"I have to go. Faith's calling me. And, Sienna, invite Jack to the party, please? Blake was going to call him, but you can pass the invitation on instead. Seeing as he's at your place." Ana's voice was full of mirth once more. "Okay?"

"Okay, I'll pass it on, but don't go getting the wrong idea."

Ana's laugh rang out as Sienna disconnected.

"Everything's fine." She hung up the phone, cleared the messages on the screen, and turned to him with a grin. "Have you got a pair of tights?"

"What? Tights?"

"You've been invited to a birthday party." Sienna put her fingers to her lips and looked him up and down. "I think you'd make a lovely Prince Charming. You remind me of the one in *Shrek*."

Sienna chuckled to herself as she headed up the hall to her room and Jack's voice followed her.

"I don't think he was the hero, though, was he?"

"No, he wasn't." She held her door and peered around before she shut it. "I'll see you in the morning. Good night, Jack."

Sienna closed the door and leaned against it for a moment. She looked at the clock beside her bed. It was too late to call Georgie, especially since she'd worked at the store today. She'd call her first thing in the morning. Sienna was wired now and not a bit tired. Crossing to the window, she slid the curtains open, sat on the wide sill, and looked out over the lake. A slight breeze ruffled the waters, and there was a smell of rain in the air.

The day had ended up turning out better than she'd expected. Now to see what the week ahead would bring.

Chapter Nine

Jack reached for the antique phone receiver on the glass counter at the front of the gallery. It was at least the tenth time he'd answered it in the past half hour. Sienna was showing some tall guy around, and they were standing at the back of the room, head to head, deep in conversation. An unfamiliar shaft of jealousy hit Jack's chest as he watched the guy loop his arm casually over Sienna's shoulder. As he answered the question on the phone, a deliveryman pushed through the front door carrying two large boxes with FRAGILE stickers plastered over them and dumped the boxes on the desk beside the phone. He shoved the electronic delivery screen in front of Jack's nose.

"Hurry up, mate. My truck's parked outside."

Jack reached for the pen and scrawled his signature, without a clue as to what was in the boxes he was signing for. All he could hope was that whatever was in them was not broken.

"I'll have to take your number and get someone to call you back. Okay?" He took down the name and number of the artist on the other end of the phone and ended the call. Then he lifted the boxes carefully and put them on the floor behind the stool at the desk. When he got up from his haunches, his eyes were level with two pairs of legs, clad in sheer black stockings. His gaze travelled higher. Similar tight black skirts, frilly shirts, and business jackets. He stood and smiled, and the shorter woman held out her hands with a warm smile.

"Welcome to Noosa. Ms. Sacchi tells us you've bought the gallery? Is she available?" The taller woman spoke with a slight European accent. "We have an appointment."

"Who?" He had no idea who she was talking about. Then it dawned on him that he didn't even know Sienna's last name. She'd always been...well...just Sienna. "Thanks...yes, I have. Take a seat." He pointed to the curved black-and-white-striped love seat by the door. "I'll let Ms. Sacchi know you are here."

Jack walked to the back of the gallery and grinned. He felt like a secretary. How the heck did she do this by herself all day? Why wasn't there more staff?

The smooth, tall guy was standing too close to Sienna for Jack's liking, and he took great delight in interrupting them.

"Excuse me, Ms. Sacchi." He dropped the grin and put on his best business voice. "Your next appointment is waiting for you."

Sienna's head flew up and she narrowed her eyes. "Thank you. I'll be there in a moment." She took the guy's arm and turned away from Jack, and he felt summarily dismissed.

"Perhaps you'd like to offer them a drink while they wait?" He glanced back and her wide dark eyes were dancing with mischief. She knew exactly how he was feeling, and he shot her a grin.

"Of course, Ms. Sacchi. Is there anything else you'd like me to do?"

"Perhaps you could dust the shelves, and then go to the post office and get the mail?" Jack could see the smile playing around her lips.

"Of course." He nodded. "If you could just direct me to the post office?"

"It's down past the coffee shop we went to." Her face broke into an impish grin and his heart kicked up a beat as her dark eyes held his gaze a little too long before she looked away.

What the hell is going on here?

Turning back to the front of the store, Jack caught sight of his reflection in the mirrored wall behind the shelves holding an

239

array of coloured bowls. He certainly didn't look like an art gallery assistant. His jeans had a rip in one knee, and the clean T-shirt he'd grabbed this morning stated *Less work. More golf.* He'd intended to look around the gallery and then sit down with Sienna to discuss what they were going to do, but the morning had been hectic, so he'd pitched in. And had enjoyed every minute. Jack shrugged and headed back to the two women waiting at the front of the store. After he'd offered them a drink, it was time to get out of here for a while.

***

"Who's the new hunk?"

Sienna turned to Jeremy, who'd come back to finish the lighting for her show.

"Would you believe he owns this place?"

"Get real! True?" Jeremy watched as Jack left through the front door. "Not gay, is he?" he asked hopefully.

"Don't think so." Sienna glanced at her watch. "If we're done here, I have another appointment with the caterers."

"Sure, I'll be in touch." Jeremy air-kissed both her cheeks. "I'm looking forward to finishing this job. Even more now that I've checked out the new eye candy in the gallery."

The morning had been busier than usual, and Sienna was pleased. Maybe it would give Jack a different perspective on how the place worked. She couldn't figure him out, and it was messing with her head. At least it got her mind off this morning's conversation with Georgie. Her twin had tried to hide how upset she was, but Sienna could read her like a book. She'd always been able to, and she'd protected Georgie from the time they were small.

Marjorie, their mother, had called. Somehow, she'd finally gotten wind of them selling the restoration business and had hit Georgie up for money. She knew better than to call Sienna.

"Don't...don't even think about giving her a cent." Sienna

had been so angry she'd had trouble getting the words out.

"She's our mother. And she needs it."

"She's not our mother. She took off and left us with Uncle Renzo."

"I feel sorry for her. Her partner's ill and she needs the money for his operation."

"Partner number what? Six? Seven?" Sienna had swallowed and tried to inject calm into her voice. "Georgie, listen to me. How long since we last heard from her? You think about it."

There had been a long silence at the other end of the phone. "Not for a while."

"That's right. Not since Uncle Renzo sold his business and had some spare cash. When he wouldn't listen to her, she came to get us to do her dirty work. Remember? There was a *sick* partner back then too."

"I remember." Georgie's voice had broken, and Sienna tried hard not to soften.

"Where is she now?"

"She's in Sydney, but she said she's going to come up and visit."

"If she does, I'll deal with her. Now promise me you won't do anything."

"All right. I promise. Maybe we'll catch up this weekend?"

"Probably not. I've got a stack of work to do in the studio, if I want to be free the next Sunday for Faith's birthday." Sienna had tried to lighten the conversation. "Have you got your fairy dress out?"

"Ha ha."

"Ana wants us all to wear the pink set. Did she tell you?"

"Yes, she told me. I think you're all mean to me." Georgie had laughed, to Sienna's relief. She'd ended up with the red hair and they teased her about it. "So, what's happening with the gallery?"

241

"I'll fill you in at the party. You're not bringing that Cal sleazebag, are you?"

"It's Cole, and no, I am not bringing him." Georgie had sighed. "But I have met this other guy—"

"That was quick."

"He's—"

"I have to go to work, talk later." Sienna knew if Georgie got started on the new guy, they'd be on the phone for ages, so she ended the call. Sometimes it was hard staying strong, but Georgie was soft-hearted, and she couldn't see when someone was trying to use her. She hadn't listened to what Sienna had tried to tell her the other night. At least she'd found something else to focus her energy on besides worrying about their mother. Hopefully the new guy she'd met wasn't another user—usually, they saw Georgie's goodness and homed straight in.

Sienna shook away the thoughts and walked to the front of the store. She greeted Gina and Carla, the caterers who worked out of Giovanni's coffee shop, and they sat down to work out the details for the launch supper at her exhibition.

The morning flew by as it always did, and as the tourists hit the streets, the gallery filled, and Sienna was pleased with the sales she made. Jack didn't reappear for a couple of hours, and she looked up as he pushed the door open with his shoulder, carrying a small plastic crate full of mail, two paper bags, and two cups of coffee.

He looked around the empty gallery, moved across to the door, and locked it. "We're closed for lunch."

"Are we?" Sienna raised her eyebrows at him.

"Yes, we are. I'm the boss, remember?" He lightened the words with a big smile and put the mail on the desk before carrying the crate to the door leading to the studio. He looked over his shoulder at her before he opened the door to the studio. "I hope you like chicken."

Sienna turned the closed sign around on the front door and reluctantly followed him. "It's a shame to close now. The streets are full of tourists."

"They have to stop for lunch, too." Jack put the crate on the floor and moved the blanket from the sofa to clear a space for Sienna. "You have to eat. You run around and use up so much energy. I don't know how you do it."

Sienna sat beside him, keeping some space between them, and looked at the heart-stoppingly-gorgeous man leaning casually back on the sofa as though he didn't have a care in the world. Picking up her coffee, she looked at him over the rim of her cup. "Telling me what to do again, Jack?" She shook her head with a half-smile. "You're going to learn the hard way, and it won't be pretty."

One corner of his mouth quirked. "I'm tough. And you do work too hard."

She avoided looking at his broad shoulders and the T-shirt straining over them. He picked up one of the bags and looked inside before handing it to her.

"Thanks." She shot him a grin. "You worked hard this morning too, Mr. Assistant."

"Totally out of my work ethic." Jack took a bite of his sandwich and his gaze settled on her as he chewed. "The gallery had a good buzz, though."

Sienna dropped her gaze, ignoring the little shiver that prickled her skin, and looked inside the sandwich bag he'd handed her. "What do you mean? Out of your work ethic?"

"I saw what working too hard did to my father." She lifted her eyes to meet his and found it hard to hold his gaze. She dropped her eyes. The fluttery feelings running around her insides were something she wasn't used to *and* something she didn't like.

Hunger. It was the smell of the fresh bread doing it to her. She unwrapped the sandwich and broke off a small piece of bread

243

and put it in her mouth. She glanced up again, and her stomach clenched as his gaze dropped to her lips and stayed there as she chewed.

Right. Enough was enough. She pushed up to her feet and stood in front of him with her hands on her hips.

***

"What's wrong?" Jack sat up straighter. "You don't like your sandwich?"

"Will you be serious for one minute?" Sienna stomped her foot, but the soft flat pump made no noise on the wooden floor. Jack put his sandwich down. He gave her his full attention before she lost her temper. She'd worked hard this morning, and he had to remember that he was the one making the most money from the gallery, her planning and hard work, and the sales she made. He must check how much his company was paying her. He'd thought of that as she'd flitted around this morning. She looked like a butterfly darting from one end of the gallery to the other, as colourful as the pieces she had so artfully arranged on the shelves. Flat black shoes and shiny leggings sat beneath a loose multi-coloured sheer top draping down to her elbows. Her feistiness, her energy, and her volatility hid how petite she actually was. Her personality was big enough to more than make up for her lack of size, and she was absolutely beautiful.

"Stop gawking at me. It makes me uncomfortable." She glared at him, and those spots of colour appeared high on her cheeks again. Her dark eyes glittered.

"Sorry." He hadn't meant to make her uncomfortable, but he *was* enjoying the view. "Did I ever tell you that you remind me of my Aunt Caroline?"

"No." She frowned, wondering what he was going to say.

"She's…what's the right word? She's prickly."

"So I'm prickly? What's that supposed to mean?" Sienna pursed her lips for a moment as she thought about his comment. If

244

he meant she was strong, she could live with that.

"It means you're always hiding your softness beneath a prickly shell. Sometimes I feel like if I put my hand out and touched you, I'd get scratched.

"But Aunt Caroline...hmm... I think you'd really get along with her. She's as soft as butter inside." Jack reached for his sandwich and leaned back on the sofa, munching as he watched myriad expressions cross Sienna's face. "And just like her face, yours is like an open book. When I was a kid, I stayed with her when my parents were travelling overseas, and I knew when to stay out of her way. You're the same—I can tell what you're thinking by the angle of your mouth and the depth of pink on your cheeks."

"You're making some huge jumps in your thinking there, Jack." Her foot tapped the floor again. "And not only that. You haven't got a clue what's happening here. You bowl into town. I find out you own this place and that you've changed your mind about selling it to me. Then you rock up here this morning looking like a bum surfer type, you play at being *my assistant*, you disappear for a couple of hours, and now not only do you tell me you haven't got a work ethic, but you know exactly what I'm thinking?"

"Anything else bugging you?" He lifted a brow.

"Yes, you're right. There is something else bugging me. You sure got that right. You look at me...like that... and I don't like it."

"I like looking at you." He kept his voice low, and the red in her cheeks deepened. "And I like the way you look back at me."

"Well, I've got news for you. We had our chance to get to know each other a couple of years back, but we've both moved on. You turning up here has put a big question mark over my future, and I don't like not knowing what's happening. And that's not a good basis for starting up anything."

"Anything?"

"Going out, getting together, having that date. Whatever you want to call it." Sienna turned and walked to the window across from the sofa and stared outside. "No matter that I might find you attractive, it's my exhibition and the gallery that are important to me. I'm not going to compromise my future for anyone. So stop the looking and lose any idea of getting together for that date. I have more important things on my mind."

A shot of warmth hit his chest and lingered. The spark *was* mutual, she'd as much as admitted it. Maybe they needed to do something about it?

"I *do* admire your work ethic, but don't expect the same from me. That's not why I'm here, or why I bought the place." He balled up the sandwich bag and tossed it into the crate on the floor, stood, and came across to join her at the window. "I've told you more than once already I'm not here to run the gallery or have anything to do with the day-to-day business."

She looked up at him, and her eyes were full of uncertainty. "So why are you here?"

The confident, brash Sienna had disappeared, and her hesitation planted some doubts in Jack's mind. He'd really messed up her plans. He ran his hand through his hair as he wondered whether to tell her about his own work, but he held back. It wasn't time, and he wasn't ready yet. Frustration with the situation burned in his gut.

Maybe I should just sell her the place and move on. Find another studio.

He looked around.

No. It was perfect for his work, and the truck was arriving in the morning with all his sculptures. He was itching to get to work and didn't want to wait. He'd checked out the space, and there was room in the shed to store his pieces while Sienna finished off the metal sculptures for *her* exhibition. And he had a deadline to stick to.

And he wanted to be in Noosa. Contrary to what he'd told her, he hadn't just shown up here by chance. He'd researched the place thoroughly before he'd bought the gallery two years ago, and this was where he wanted to be. As soon as he spent some time here, he intended buying a place of his own. Shame she wouldn't sell hers.

And it's where I want to work. To create the sculptures that are in my head.

He just wasn't going to let being in the gallery suck him into being involved in business. It was in his genes, and he'd fought against being like his father his whole life. He wasn't going to replicate the mess his father had made of everyone's life. He was going to focus on his art and make a successful career. If the gallery was successful, that would be a bonus.

Jack had no commitment to anything or anyone, apart from the completion date for his sculptures. He was an artist, and he'd come here to create and show his work. He had his first big commission, and that was the reason he needed to stay here and sort out what he was going to do with Sienna.

He huffed out a breath. "Okay, let's be honest here."

Her eyes were wide, and if he looked closely, he suspected there was a glimmer of a tear in the corner of one.

Damn, he was a sucker for tears. He took her hands gently in his. It was time to come clean. If Sienna was going to be working for him and managing the gallery, he'd be honest with her.

"How about you stay to run the place, but we hire an assistant for you. Then after your exhibition, we'll see how it works out? I'll move out of your place and find my own apartment and the only thing you'll have to do is find a studio…or build your own?" He shot her a grin. "I'll be busy once my stuff arrives, and as much as I enjoyed playing secretary"—he straightened his shoulders and spoke confidently— "I'll be busy finishing off my pieces."

"Your what?"

"My pieces."

"What sort of pieces?" She pulled her hands away from his and stared at him.

"For my contract. I'm a sculptor. That's why I bought the gallery and the studio."

Sienna held his gaze, and her dark eyes were wide.

"That's why I said I was surprised when I read about you in the local paper. We work in the same medium. After I finish the pieces that are contracted, I'm going to start work on another series and hold my first exhibition here."

Chapter Ten

Sienna got through the afternoon—barely. Jack's bombshell about being an artist had thrown her in a spin. Luckily, there was a steady stream of tourists through the gallery, and she tried to concentrate on them. Jack's being an artist didn't bother her—not really. In a way, it added to his attraction, but the knowledge put his ownership of the gallery in a whole new light. He had contracted pieces, so he must be good. Why the hell hadn't Ana mentioned it, or did he keep his art private? Jack Montgomery? She knew the art world...but she hadn't come across his name before. Had he been hiding the truth from her deliberately? And if he had, why would he?

Who is the real Jack?

The laid-back guy she'd seen this week who wasn't fazed by anything? The wealthy playboy from Melbourne? Or an artist committed to his work? Lost in her thoughts, she tried to focus on the customers milling about the gallery. It was a busy afternoon, and she needed to concentrate on that. There was still work to be done no matter what problems she was trying to sort in her head.

A couple of times Sienna noticed Jack stroll casually through the shop, but she was busy with a customer each time. She straightened her back and continued to describe the enamelling process to an older tourist who loved the frog displays.

"What do you think?" The lady was looking up at her with an expectant smile.

"Sorry. What was that?" Sienna pushed thoughts of enigmatic Jack away.

"One of each. Shipped to Perth for me."

"One of each of this set?" They were standing in front a set of her frogs lying on different-shaped pieces of timber, carved into small logs.

The lady smiled at her. "No. I want one of each of your frog sets." Her wrinkled face lit up in a grin. "I love them all and it has been a magical visit and I want a memento of Noosa when I get home." She grabbed Sienna's arm and whispered. "You'll never guess who was having lunch where I ate."

Her excitement was infectious, and Sienna smiled back at her, delighted with the sale and the customer's enthusiasm.

"No, do tell."

"Chris Hemsworth! It has been the most amazing day."

Sienna looked around for Jack, but he was nowhere to be seen. She'd love to tell him that piece of news.

Later. In the meantime, she had about twenty-five frogs to package up and ship to Western Australia. Not a bad day's work.

***

Jack spent the afternoon visiting local stores to pick up some supplies to keep him going until the truck arrived with his stuff. It was due tomorrow, so he checked out the garage and the kiln room beneath the gallery. It was perfect for what he wanted. He'd passed through the gallery a couple of times through the afternoon and Sienna was as busy as ever, and ignored him each time he walked past her. He didn't need to read the expression on her face or see the depth of colour in her cheeks. Her back was ramrod straight, and something was bothering her.

He shook his head. Maybe telling her about his sculptures hadn't been such a good idea. She'd obviously thought he'd bought the gallery as an investment, which he had in a way. As much as he tried to convince himself and his father that he was a free spirit and his art was all that mattered, Jack knew he needed stability in his life. The contract and the thought of working in the studio here grounded him.

He'd also have to check out how much he was paying

Sienna to run the place.

She was working her butt off, and as he'd walked around the village today, he'd realised that Sea View Gallery was by far the busiest gallery in the small town. Sienna had done a great job setting it up and getting it going in the short time she'd been here.

At five o'clock, he wandered back with a couple of packages in hand. Sienna was behind the glass desk looking at her iPad.

"A *very* good day." Her voice was soft, and her expression was wary.

There had been a shift in their relationship since he'd told her about being a sculptor, and he wasn't sure how to respond to her.

"We had a lot more customers in today," she said, her eyes still on the figures on the small tablet screen in front of her. "And excellent sales too. I've got a lot of work ahead. I sold quite a few of the frogs I'd planned to use for my exhibition."

"But won't that mean more work for you to replace them?

Sienna nodded absently before she lifted her head and looked at him with a frown. "Yes, it will but it was a good sale. Good for the gallery…and good for me."

Jack looked down at his clothes with a grin. Maybe he could dress up a bit if he was going to spend a bit of time in the place.

Keep it casual. "Nothing like a bum surfer look to pull the women in."

Sienna pulled a face and huffed. "I think it had more to do with Chris Hemsworth being in town today."

"Chris Hemsworth's here? And I missed him?" He laughed. "But thanks for the vote of confidence. Wait till you see *me* in my Prince Charming costume."

Her eyes widened, and he was glad to finally see her smiling. "You bought one?" She pointed to the packages he was

251

carrying. "Really?"

"Yup. Nice tights, too." Jack grinned. "And I'm looking forward to the party."

"Me too." Sienna yawned and turned off the iPad.

"How about we go out for dinner to seal our agreement?" Jack wasn't sure how she'd take that, so he continued before she could refuse. "There are a couple more things we probably should discuss. The truck will be here in the morning with my stuff and I've had a look around. I just want to run it by you."

"It's your gallery. You can put things where you want."

"Whoa. You're in charge here. Remember?" He held his hands up. "And we compromise. I'm a nice guy."

Sienna snapped the cover of the iPad closed and stood. "I guess you are. I'm just being me. You'll get used to it."

And being her was a big act as far as he could tell. He'd like to get to know the Sienna beneath the prickly surface she showed him.

"So dinner? My treat."

"I suppose." She smiled again, and he relaxed as her face lit up.

"I'd like a shower. I've been poking about in the kilns. Let's go home first." A strange feeling filled him as the words came out and Sienna frowned. He quirked an eyebrow and smiled at her. "I mean, let's go to your place."

***

Jack rode his bike back to the cottage, and Sienna followed in her car. It had been a strange day, and she was a little unsettled. Dinner out somewhere lively might snap her out of this mood she was in. She'd get up early and do some enamelling before she opened in the morning. Throughout the day she'd moved from uncertainty, not knowing what her future was going to hold, and finally settled in a place where the worry landed deeper as the day wore on. The agreement with Jack about the gallery pleased her, even though she

252

was going to have to find somewhere else to work, but the conversation with Georgie this morning wouldn't go away and stuck in her chest like a stone. She flicked on the radio and tried to let the music lift her. By the time she turned into the drive, the rock music had the desired effect, and she was feeling better even though she had to work out whether Jack had been lying to her, or if he just hadn't bothered to mention being an artist. He was so casual and friendly he sucked her right in. Somehow, he had the ability to get past the defences she usually had in place.

Things would work out. She would make sure they did. Planning and organisation were the key. Knowing she had to replace the pieces she'd sold today meant she had to make the best use of her time. Dinner with Jack was a luxury she probably couldn't afford time-wise, but no matter how hard she tried to resist him, his sexy grin sucked her in.

Jack was waiting for her outside the cottage, and he'd put his bike away. "Can we go back into town in your car?"

She unlocked the door and shot him a grin over her shoulder. "Bit misty for you here on the coast?" She pointed to the wet helmet in his hand.

"No, I'm used to Melbourne weather." That damned perpetual grin was still on his face.

Did nothing ruffle the man?

"I just thought it would be nice to travel in together. We could always go on the bike." His smile did something to her, and her heart gave a funny little flip as she pushed opened the door.

"This isn't a date, okay?"

"No. It's a business meeting, but we're leaving from the same place to go to the same place, so it makes sense to travel in the same car...or on the same bike?"

She put her hands on her hips. "All right. You win. It makes sense, I suppose. But it's not a date...and I don't like bikes, so we'll take my car."

"It's not a date." He repeated her words solemnly and she shot him a look. "You'll have to pick somewhere because I don't know my way around the area yet." He put his bike helmet down inside the door. "I've only got jeans or bike leathers."

"Do you like Italian?"

"I'll eat anything."

She was sure he would. "There's a nice Italian at Coolum. Great food and a live jazz band. And it's only ten minutes from the lake." She needed some music and crowds around her to snap her out of the doldrums. Whenever she let the worry take over, the muse disappeared, and her work suffered. And she couldn't afford to have much downtime this week after that sale.

"Sounds great. Half hour?" Jack stood there looking at her, and Sienna snapped her thoughts back to present.

"You might be able to get ready in half an hour, but I'm going to have a soak in a deep bubble bath before we go anywhere." As soon as the words were out, she regretted them. The grin got wider; he was obviously using his imagination. Sienna gave him a little shove. "You go to *your* apartment and leave me in peace. I'll knock on your door when I'm ready."

"Yes, ma'am." With a final grin he disappeared down the hall, and Sienna didn't relax until she heard his door open and close.

The restaurant was crowded and noisy, and the band was playing. Jack held her chair out for her after they were shown to a discreet corner table away from the band.

"At least it's quieter here." Sienna put her bag on the floor. "We can talk. I made a list of things I want to sort out with you."

"Water?" The drinks waiter stood beside the table.

"Yes, please." Sienna pulled out her iPad. She'd taken it into the bath with her and made a list as she'd soaked in the bubbles.

Straight to business. This was *not* a date.

"We've sorted out the studio and your storage. Now we need you to make some decisions on the day-to-day running of the gallery.

"Put it away."

"What?"

"The iPad." Jack pointed to the computer on the table in front of her. "I told you, I don't want to run the gallery. Do what you want." For the first time today, he looked serious.

"But—"

"You've been doing fine. I'm happy for things to go on the way they are. Like I said earlier, we'll see what happens after your show. Then *you* decide if you want to stay, or if you want out."

Sienna frowned at him. "But—"

"If you want out at the end of the month, I'll find another manager. Now let's enjoy dinner."

"So we didn't need a *business* dinner after all?"

"No, but we will talk salary before we order. I looked into how much we've been paying you and it's not enough. The gallery has been doing so well, you need to be compensated more."

Sienna lifted her glass and sipped her water. "Well, that is very kind. I won't object." With a higher salary and selling more frogs, she would be in a better position to look around for her own place...and maybe build her studio.

"Nothing kind. Good business."

For a moment, she caught a glimpse of the businessman beneath the casual facade. He was a chameleon, that was for sure. Then his wide grin reappeared, and Jack leaned back in his chair. "Business is over now. We need dinner and you need some time out."

"What do you mean I need time out?"

Jack reached over and put his finger beneath her chin, and she pulled back a little as a tingle ran down her neck to her back. "I

255

told you this afternoon. You have the most expressive face."

"Stop right there. Read my lips." She folded her arms to cover the thudding of her heart. "This. Is. Not. A. Date."

He held his hands out in front of him innocently. "Did I say it was?"

Sienna tilted her head to the side and studied him, and she couldn't stop the smile that was tugging at her lips. "Are you always so happy?"

He grinned at her and she rolled her eyes. He'd worn a black polo shirt with his black jeans, and if it was possible, the dark colour added to his sex appeal. She was going to have to work very hard to keep him at a distance. "Tell me about Melbourne. You said you went back to help out in the family business. That's where you know Blake from?"

Jack leaned back in his chair. "Yeah. I grew up in a wealthy family, went to the best schools, and was expected to follow the family path. My father had big plans for me. So when I dropped out of college and took off to art school, you could say he was less than impressed."

"But why the move out here?" She watched as his green eyes lit up. "You could have bought a gallery back there."

"I guess I got the idea from Blake. I met him when he worked for Dad at Home and Hardware and we clicked. A few games of golf, and he told me about his home in Queensland, and how much he loved the Sunny Coast. I came out on a trip and caught up with him. I actually bought the gallery the same week I met you at that doohickey place."

Sienna fought the rising panic that welled in her throat. She remembered how she'd been so attracted to him back then. Now his smile was sending constant shivers down her back, contrasting with the hot feeling in her chest.

"The time that Ana and Blake finally got together," she said weakly.

Fight it.

"So enough about me. Tell me about you. You and Georgie grew up here?" His green-eyed gaze locked with hers, and Sienna focused on her breathing. The shaky feeling disappeared a little as she thought of her background, and she met his gaze squarely.

"Yes. We were born in Sydney but grew up in Maleny. Our father ran off when we were little, and our mother chased after him and brought us to Queensland. Her brother and his wife took us in." Jack's eyes were fixed on hers, unblinking. She looked down. Jack's fingers were rubbing the inside of her wrist. She hadn't even been aware of him picking up her hand.

"Did you have a happy childhood after that?"

"We did. Uncle Renzo and Aunt Lucia gave us all the love we needed." She stared over his shoulder and couldn't keep the bitterness out of her voice. "Now our mother only ever comes back when she wants something."

"Parents can be a trial. I guess I was the opposite. My father smothered me, tried to put what he thought I should do over what I wanted."

She held her breath as Jack's deep voice washed over her. "That's why I'd never have children."

Well, that's one thing we agree on. "Me either."

Sienna picked up her water glass and took a long drink.

"Wine?" Jack called the waiter over. "If we have one glass you can still drive. Or if you'll trust me, I could drive that snazzy little car home."

Home?

Jack had settled in a bit too quickly for her liking. She was in *his* gallery, he was in *her* apartment, and now they were having a too-cosy dinner. And Sienna knew the riot of feelings and the trembling of her legs had more to do with his presence across the table than the hunger gnawing at her stomach. She didn't answer him, and she watched as the waiter opened the bottle. When the

257

ruby-red liquid filled her glass, she held it up to the light, fascinated by the depth of colour. "Do you know how hard it is to replicate that ruby red?"

When he nodded, she looked at him curiously. "Tell me about your work, about your art."

Jack stared past her, and she wondered for a moment what he was thinking about. He lifted the glass to his lips and Sienna looked away. Coming out to dinner, no matter that he said it wasn't a date, had not been a good idea. She was altogether too attracted to him. Ana and Georgie were the only two people she ever let into her heart. Even Uncle Renzo and Aunt Lucia were kept at a distance; she could never quite trust. She kept her heart locked up tight, and there was no way she was going to leave herself open to be hurt. She'd fostered the prickly exterior and kept people at a distance, and she didn't like the way Jack was able to get past it. He drilled right past her defences and unsettled her. He was way too observant for her liking…and way too interested in *her*.

And I'm way too attracted to him. I'm going to have to be very careful here. She needed to brush him off a little.

His next words brought her back to the present, and she focused on what he was saying.

"I'm not sure what you'll think about it. And I have a feeling it might impact your decision to stay in the gallery."

"Why?" She tipped her head to the side. It was the most serious she'd seen him be.

"Your exhibition."

"What's it got to do with my exhibition?" Unease snaked its way to her stomach, and she picked up the wine and took a sip to cover her uncertainty. He'd seen way too much of that already over one dinner.

"Because of what I do."

"What do you mean?" It was a strange moment. Jack's expression was so intense she couldn't read him.

258

"In a way, our work might complement each other's."

"Jack, get to the point." Sienna lowered her voice and put her hands beneath her chin. "Will you stop beating around the bush and tell me what you're trying to say?"

"Is this the first time you've experimented with vitreous enamel? Do you have anything bigger than the frogs?" His gaze was fixed on her.

"Not in enamel," she said. "Only my paintings."

His shoulders dropped and he let out a breath as she watched.

"My enamel work is all based on small creatures. Frogs, mice, snails...sort of cutesy stuff. My first few pieces were really popular. That's why I decided to do a range of creatures," she said as he held her gaze. Jack was worrying her with his intense interest in the nature of her pieces. She had a feeling he was about to drop something she didn't like.

"That's excellent, then." He nodded.

"What are you trying to say?" Sienna tipped her head to the side waiting for his explanation.

"It *is* a coincidence, because I haven't even seen it in galleries in Melbourne recently."

She stared at him, and he hurried on. "I sculpt in copper and bronze too, and I use enamel to create pictures on my sculptures."

Sienna shook her head slowly and frowned. "So you were worried about having the same type of exhibition?" It was a coincidence. When she'd researched the process, she'd found few other artists who were using the same process. And she hadn't come across his name at all. She would have recognised it if she had. Her heart plummeted. Or maybe this was what the dinner and softening her up was all about. Maybe he'd changed his mind about her exhibition? If she was honest, she hoped he enjoyed being with her. The problem was, she found him so damned attractive, and no matter what his intentions were, all she could think about was getting close to him. Even when she was so unsure of what he wanted for the gallery, and her role in it, all she could think of was how it would feel to be held by him. If she looked into his eyes, she was a goner. She firmed her voice to push away the unwanted riot of feelings racing though her.

"Are you trying to tell me that you don't want my pieces exhibited in your gallery because it will take away the impact of yours when you have your own?" She narrowed her eyes as she thought of something else. "Wait, it's more than that. Do you think I've copied your ideas?"

Shit.

Chapter Eleven

"Of course not." Jack reached for Sienna's hand, but she pulled back.

Sienna was the most unpredictable woman he'd ever met. He'd had plenty of girlfriends, and he thought he knew his way around women pretty well. He'd learned when to say the right thing, and when to shut his mouth, and when to nod and not speak, but he was having trouble reading the mixed signals Sienna was giving out. Despite the complication of the gallery and their art, and living in the same place, he had this overwhelming need to kiss her. And he wanted her in his bed.

"Just get to the point, Jack. If you've changed your mind, spit it out." Her cheeks were flushed, and as he watched she crossed her arms in front of her chest and glared at him. "But don't lie to me."

"Settle down. There's no need to get upset."

"Well, I am. These past few days have been unnerving, and now you're about to tell me I have to find somewhere else to have my exhibition in *your* gallery, because *my* work is the same as yours?"

He shook his head. "Calm down. Where did you ever get the idea I was going to cancel your show?" He straightened in his chair. "I gave you my word that you could have it there, and I don't go back on my word."

"Well, you'd be the first man I've ever met who hasn't." Sienna's voice was sad and the look on her face dispelled the anger that had been building in his chest. "Look, this whole thing is getting complicated. Let's forget the month and the show. I'll pull out and leave your gallery all to you. You obviously have some concerns about our work being too similar?"

"No, I think it will be great for the gallery. We'll really establish a theme with the bronze and the enamelling." This time, he took her hands in both of his and held on tightly when she tried to pull back. "I've already sold my pieces, and I don't need to have an exhibition. They'll be on display in the building. You have yours organised, and I'll have my first show when I do some more work."

"No." She shook her head slowly.

"No, what? I'm not going to get angry, but you are beginning to piss me off with the little Miss Hard Done By act."

"No…I'm not being difficult. Do you really think it will work? This changes things even more."

Her cheeks flushed more deeply as he held on to her. "Nothing has changed, apart from you jumping to conclusions. All I really wanted to tell you…or all I wanted to do, was make sure you knew that I work in the same medium before the truck arrived with my stuff tomorrow and you jumped to the wrong conclusion when you saw it."

He got a glimpse of her dark eyes before she looked down.

"Your reaction tonight, when I'm trying to be honest, tells me if you'd seen my pieces unloaded tomorrow and I hadn't told you we work in the same medium, you probably would have walked."

"You're getting to know me." She shrugged. "I probably would have."

"Sienna, do you always think the worst of people?" She was hard work, but he was determined to get closer to her.

She nodded. "Until they prove themselves to me. Yes, I do."

###

The walk from the restaurant to Sienna's car was quiet. For the rest of the meal they'd discussed the techniques they each used, and

Jack was pleased that Sienna seemed keen to see his work. She had relaxed a lot after he'd told her a bit more about his commission, and her interest was pleasing. He held the driver's door open for her before walking around to the passenger side and sliding in.

"As much as I love your car, it really is made for midgets." His knees were cramped between the seat and the dashboard. "Next time we go on a non-date, we'll take the bike. You'll love it."

And so would I. The thought of Sienna pressed up close behind him sent a pleasurable zing through his body. Jack leaned back and closed his eyes and waited for her to start the engine, but she took her time.

"Dratted car," she muttered.

Eventually there was a loud *click*, and she cursed again. Jack opened his eyes, and realised she'd been trying to start the car while he'd had his head back and his eyes closed, daydreaming about her in his arms.

He shot her a teasing glance. "Don't tell me we're going to have to walk home. We should have come on my bike."

"She's been doing this on and off for a couple of weeks. I keep meaning to get the motor looked at, but I haven't had the time. I've spent every spare minute with my frogs."

"What's wrong with it?"

"Her." Sienna shot him a cheeky glance. "It's a she, and she's old and cranky. Like I will be one day."

"Is that where I'm supposed to say you'll be a sweet old lady? And I suppose you're also hoping I know something about engines?"

"Do you?" Her lips parted as she smiled at him, and a rush of need coiled through Jack's chest. She was flirting with him.

"The very basics." He opened his door, enjoying the need that had moved and was now firmly lodged in every nerve ending in his body.

Every nerve ending.

"Open the hood and I'll see if any parts look like they're in the wrong place."

"That fills me with hope." The sarcasm was back, and he grinned. Better than the quiet tones that had touched him over dinner.

Sienna unlocked the hood using the lever inside the car, and then she followed him around to the front. He lifted the hood and held it up with one hand as he looked for the metal prop to hold it up.

"Sorry, it's broken. I'll hold it up while you look."

Luckily, they were parked beneath a streetlight, and he was able to see into the engine in front of him, but nothing stood out as being disconnected, covered with oil or water, or in the wrong place. That was about the limit of his mechanical knowledge. Sienna stood beside him quietly, stretched on her toes, holding the hood above his head. He ducked beneath her arm as he peered at the back of the engine, and the warmth of her body touched his skin. The need built higher and hotter, and he closed his eyes for a moment before he leaned forward, acting like he was still checking the engine. Standing so close without her pulling away was enticing. He muttered a few "ahs" and "hmms", so he sounded a little knowledgeable before he reached up and took the weight from her as he eased the hood down.

"Everything looks fine to me." He shrugged. "I guess we're stuck here until a mechanic shows up."

Sienna looked up at him without speaking and her dark eyes widened even further, filled with a hunger that echoed what was churning inside him. From the first time he'd laid eyes on her in that "doohickeys" shirt from the hardware store two years ago, he'd known this moment would come.

Something elemental shifted in him as his control fell away. He reached for Sienna without hesitation and turned her, lifting her to sit on the hood of the car so that her face was level with his. For a long moment, he stared into her eyes and she looked back at him, holding his gaze.

Wordless. But a thousand words passed silently between them. Jack moved, and her stifled gasp puffed gently on his lips as he cradled her small, delicate face between his hands. He brushed his thumb gently over her full bottom lip.

"I know we're not on a date, and I know you have an issue with me being your boss, but I would very much like to kiss you." Her gaze locked with his and still she didn't speak. Jack waited. He wasn't going to take what he thought she was offering until he knew for sure.

Damn the woman. He'd been reading her wrong all day and he didn't want to make the wrong call now. Sienna leaned into him and laced her fingers behind his neck. Her eyes, full of mystery and promise, remained locked on his. Her short hair, dark as the shadows of the still night around them, caught the moonlight. Her skin was warm, and the sweet fragrance of her perfume drifted across to him.

He lowered his lips and lightly touched her mouth with his. That first kiss was gentle, full of promise, and her unexpected sweetness hit him like a punch to the solar plexus. This was not the Sienna she presented to the world. Jack gathered her even closer to him, running his fingers through her silky short hair as the need to protect and comfort her sprang from some unfamiliar place deep inside him. Somehow in that kiss he felt her confusion, and her willingness to give, despite the tough exterior she showed the world.

***

Sienna shivered as a fire raced through her. Never in her life had she felt such a need, and it frightened her. She pulled back with a jerk and stared at Jack, fighting to keep her expression bland. Her response to his kiss had come without thought, and now she tried

265

to force herself to be strong, and not lean back into him like her traitorous body was demanding.

"Well, considering we're not on a real date, that was a bit of a surprise." She tried to put a level of sophistication she wasn't feeling into her words, but it didn't come out like that. She knew her uncertainty sounded in her voice, with a hint of wariness mixed in, which was probably just as good.

"A nice one, though." Jack's face was shadowed, but she had felt his heart thudding hard against her chest as he'd held her.

Sienna slid down from the hood of the car and forced a casual smile onto her face. "It was. But now I need to do something about this car, seeing as your mechanical skills leave a bit to be desired."

This time her grin was genuine, because it had been obvious all along that he knew nothing about cars. "One more try." She opened the car door and slid into the driver's seat, relieved in one way to put some distance between them. Her heart was still thudding, and she ached to be back in Jack's arms, but she was going to listen to logic.

"Come on, start," she muttered. "Please." On the first turn of the key the engine fired. "I knew you could do it, old girl. Quick, Jack, get in before she changes her mind."

Jack climbed into the passenger seat. "Changes her mind?" He flicked a glance in her direction, and she knew he wasn't talking about the car.

"I need to get home. I have a lot of emails to send tonight. It was so busy in the gallery today, the work's piled up."

"Can't let the work wait, then." Jack settled back in the seat and she eased the car out onto the road. His tone was light, but the look he sent her was full of respect and a warm feeling filled her.

The roads were quiet, and Sienna was grateful for the monotonous swishing of the windshield wipers when a light shower of rain began to fall. She took the route along the coast that went through Peregian Beach before she turned off to the lake. The moonlight bathing the water glistened eerily through the fog. As they passed the sign for the beach, Jack turned to her and she wondered what he was going to say for a moment.

"It's a beautiful coastline. Great inspiration for the creative soul."

"It is." Sienna took a deep breath and gripped the steering wheel tightly. A connection had been forged between them tonight. Not just the kiss they'd shared, but the conversation they'd had when Jack had opened up about his sculptures. She was looking forward to seeing them.

"Thanks for tonight…and dinner." Sienna switched off the ignition after she parked in the carport next to the cottage. "I enjoyed myself."

Unsure of what Jack expected, she fumbled with the car door handle and turned to him.

"Well, I hope she starts tomorrow so I can get her to the mechanic."

"I'll have to give you a lift to the gallery if *she* won't."

Sienna's toes almost curled when Jack shot a cheeky grin in her direction. The interior of her little sports car was small, and he was way too close for comfort now that she wasn't focused on driving. She pushed the door open and grabbed her bag off the floor.

"You're determined to get me on that bike." She smiled at him as he followed her up the steps to the small porch. "But I've never been on one and I don't intend to start now."

"Where's your spirit of adventure, Sienna?" Jack was so close his breath brushed the back of her neck. She stepped away from him with a small sigh of relief when the door opened.

Thank God. She needed some time by herself to restore her equilibrium and remind herself why a fling with Jack—the boss—was out of the question.

"I put all of *my* spirit into my work."

"And I get to reap the benefits of your hard work." Jack's voice was thoughtful, and Sienna wasn't sure what he was referring to. His words had echoed her thoughts. She turned to him as he followed her to her bedroom door and looked at him from beneath her lashes. She didn't want to risk heady eye contact, not trusting the nervous little flutters running through her stomach. Sienna lowered her voice as she held the door half shut.

"What are your plans tomorrow? Are you coming into the gallery?" She lifted her chin and forced herself to look up at him, gripping the edge of the door between her fingers.

Jack held her gaze with those deep green eyes for a long moment before he smiled at her. "I'm not sure. Depends on what time the delivery truck gets here."

She'd forgotten his stuff was arriving tomorrow.

"Okay, then. I'm going in early, so I'll be at the gallery when you need to get in."

"I do have a key, remember?" His grin got wider, but his words had the effect she needed. The urge to grab his shirt and pull him into her room behind her faded as her boss spoke.

"Of course. Silly me. How could I forget? You own the gallery, don't you?" She turned away and nodded at him as she pulled the door shut. "Good night, Jack."

Chapter Twelve

Jack lay for a long time staring at the shadows on the ceiling before he went to sleep. The window was open, and the rustling of the leaves drifted in on the soft night breeze. Events of the last couple of days looped through his head like scenes from a movie, and Sienna was centre stage in every shot.

For the first time in his life, he'd really let a woman get under his skin, and the feeling bothered him. Everything she did stayed with him. He enjoyed sparring with Sienna; he loved watching the way she walked, the expressive gestures she made with her tiny hands when she was talking. And her low, husky voice was enticing.

He would love to see her sculpting—to watch those hands involved in the process of creation. There was so much at stake now that he knew how vulnerable she was. Sienna wanted the same things he did; they came from different backgrounds and were following different paths to get there. He knew the attraction was mutual. She'd said it in so many words yesterday, and the kiss they'd shared had shown him exactly how she felt. It was a shame he hadn't followed through on that date a couple of years back. There was no place for commitment or settling down in either of their lives. They could have had fun, gotten it out of their systems, and moved on. He could be the boss and she his employee without the flirting, and the skirting around the attraction between them.

And he still had to sort out the problem of them both needing the studio to work.

He had his sculptures and his deadline to worry about, and he owned the gallery. There was no way he was going to get into a relationship or tied down to a career and end up running the business himself.

Look what it did for Dad.

Jack woke to bright sunlight shining on his face. He yawned, swung his legs out of the bed, and wandered over to the open window. The lake was a brilliant blue, reflecting the cloudless sky above. He glanced down at his watch and grunted with surprise when he saw that it was after nine o'clock. Even after sorting out his thoughts last night, he'd still had a lot of trouble getting to sleep.

Damn. He wondered if Sienna's car had started. She should have left for the gallery by now. He sat back down on the side of the bed and listened, but there was no sound coming from the house. If she'd needed him, she would have come knocking— wouldn't she?

Jack made himself a coffee before strolling out to the back porch. Last night's light rain had washed everything clean; it was a glorious morning.

Perfect for a run.

But before he went back in for his running shoes, he couldn't help himself. He strolled down the steps and around the side of the house. There was no sign of Sienna's car.

Great. The car must have started okay and he could forget about her and focus on waiting for the truck and getting his stuff unpacked.

A quick call to the delivery company, and the driver told him he was just coming up the motorway and would meet him within the hour. He would have time for a short run before the truck arrived. He looked up at the little cottage as he stretched before his run. It was a shame Sienna wouldn't consider selling this place to him. The longer he stayed, and the more he looked around, the more he was convinced he could live here and build a studio. He could understand why she had bought it from the others; for the first time in his life he had found a place where he could combine work and home.

He'd try again. It would give her more money to buy her own gallery and studio somewhere, which seemed to be what she wanted. Maybe they could come to a deal. Money talked. He'd found that all his life.

***

"What are you doing down here?" Sienna smiled at her sister. She was surprised to see Georgie walk through the front door of the gallery. She narrowed her eyes as she took in the redness around her twin's eyes before she led her to the privacy of the studio. Luckily, the place was quiet. It was early and the tourists hadn't filled the street yet.

"Sit on the sofa. Coffee?" Sienna got Georgie settled and went back through the gallery and flicked the closed sign over before going into the small kitchen to pour them both a coffee. Georgie's voice came through the door.

"Mum came to see me last night."

"Mum? You mean Marjorie?" Sienna walked out to the studio and put the two cups on the floor next to the sofa. She'd spread her latest batch of enamelling on the coffee table and covered it with a drop sheet when she'd arrived earlier.

"Our mother." A little hiccough escaped Georgie's lips and she dug in her bag.

"Here." Sienna had a clean tissue in her pocket and thrust it at her sister. She should have guessed what brought this on. "Aunt Lucia is our mother."

Sienna took a step back, narrowly missing the coffee cups as Georgie glared at her.

"If you're not careful, you'll end up just like her." Georgie snapped out the words, her voice different.

"What?" Sienna stared at Georgie. "What the heck are you

talking about?"

"You're so hard on her. She had her reasons for leaving us. She had to be hard…and in a way you're as bad as she is for not listening to her."

"How much money does she want this time?" Sienna was determined to hide how her sister's words cut her like a knife. She and Georgie rarely fought, but if her twin insisted on taking their mother's side, she wasn't going to hold back now. "I told you to tell her to call me if she contacted you again."

"She's dying." Georgie dropped her face into her hands and burst into tears. Sienna turned away, running her hands though her hair. Her chest closed and her breath hitched as she fought the tears that ached behind her eyes.

If it's true…

She stared through the window, trying to think of the right words to say, holding in her reaction. She didn't want to upset her sister anymore. The sound of the front door closing reached her, and Jack called out.

"Are you out the back, Sienna? Do you want me to keep the closed sign up?"

He peered around the door and looked into the studio.

"Morning. Your car started okay for you then? You left before I woke up. I didn't even hear you go."

Georgie leaned around Sienna with a surprised look and a sniff. "Interesting."

Jack turned to her with a broad smile. "Hello, Georgie, I didn't see you there."

"It's not what it sounds like." Sienna managed to compose herself before turning to Jack. "Look, we're having a private conversation here. Can you leave us alone?" She softened her tone and gave him a small smile. It wasn't his fault. "Please?"

"No problem. The delivery truck followed me into town, so I'll head out the back. Where would I find the key to the back

272

garage?"

"It's on the hook beside the kitchen light switch, the one with the red tag." Sienna put her hands on her hips and waited for him to leave, but he stood there—all six feet of him, pure male testosterone, in running shorts and a tank top. Sex appeal oozing out of every pore.

"Everything okay here?"

Sienna's mouth dried. Jack lifted his hand and ran it though his damp hair. The muscles rippled beneath his tight shirt.

"Fine." She knew her voice was husky, and she waited for him to leave. Hell, she could barely catch her breath.

He smiled at her and disappeared through the door.

"That was quick." Georgie wiped her eyes and looked at Sienna. "What's going on?"

"Nothing." Sienna walked over to the sofa and slumped beside her twin. "Don't jump to conclusions. He's staying in the apartment at the back of the cottage while I use the studio. Just for a couple of weeks." She looked up at the shelves with a frown and muttered half under her breath. "If I ever get time to work."

"It would be a bit distracting having him around to look at all day." Georgie wiped her eyes and a smile crossed her face.

"That's not what I meant. I'm just...busy. And I've got a lot on my mind." Sienna sat straight and tucked her leg beneath her. "Now tell me what else *she* said that you had to drive all the way down here to tell me."

"I had to come down here anyway. And it's not the sort of thing I wanted to talk about on the phone." Georgie patted the bag beside her. "Blake was supposed to come down to Noosa to get some papers signed, but I offered to come so I could see you on the way." She dabbed at her eyes again with the tissues. "Now I have to clean myself up a bit before I meet this guy. He's the solicitor for some famous author that the store is doing a renovation for."

Sienna folded her arms. "I know you think I'm hard, but

273

Marjorie knows you're a soft touch. Did she ask you for money?"

"Well—"

The sound of a truck beeping as it backed up the back driveway interrupted Georgie's words.

Sienna rolled her eyes. "Whatever happened to my peaceful life?" She pushed herself to her feet and crossed to the kitchen door before pushing it open. "Jack, your truck's here."

He wandered through casually, cup of coffee in hand, and headed out to meet the truck driver.

"He's going to drive me crazy. I guess that's what being wealthy does for you. Nothing ever seems to bother him. He is so laidback." Sienna shook her head and held her hand out to Georgie. "Come on. Let's get out of here and grab a real coffee, and we'll figure out what to do."

Sienna moved to the door and tried to push away that feeling that her life was about to change.

By the time Sienna got back to the gallery and flicked the sign on the door to open, there was no sign of Jack or the truck, and she heaved a sigh of relief. She had enough to think about— a gallery to run, her frogs to get finished in two weeks, and an exhibition to organise, and dealing with the riot of feelings Jack set afire in her. And the only way she'd managed to calm Georgie was to promise to see Marjorie when she was in Montville for Faith's birthday party, the weekend after next. Apparently, their dear mother had moved back to the area and needed money for medical treatment.

Or so she said.

What if their mother really was ill?

Sienna rubbed a weary hand over her eyes. This time last week she'd been full of excitement about buying the gallery and her upcoming exhibition. She got through the afternoon, sold a few big pieces, interviewed two artists who were looking for a venue for a show, and took a dozen phone calls. She couldn't wait until

Katy, a young artist, started work as her assistant. That had been one of the positive changes in the past week.

Jack had lightened the load by getting the mail and bringing her coffee. If only she could forget about how good he looked.

There had been no sign of him since this morning, which should have suited her just fine. But she hadn't stopped looking up eagerly every time the door opened. At five o'clock, she closed the gallery and headed downstairs to turn the kilns on. She was going to spend a few hours on her pieces. She'd promised Georgie she'd stay overnight after Faith's party, so that would be another day out of her preparation time. As she walked down the steps she flicked a curious glance toward the garage. There was a shiny new padlock on the door. It would be interesting to see Jack's work. She had been curious about his methods since he'd described them at dinner the other night. As soon as he came back from wherever he'd gone, she'd ask him to show her, but in the meantime, she had work to do.

Five hours later with her hands on her hips, Sienna studied the array of pieces on the studio shelves. A row of frogs in a variety of positions in bright hues of green, red, and blue looked back at her. She yawned and debated whether to go down and enamel the last of tonight's batch, but before she could decide, the sound of a motorcycle pulling up at the back of the building caught her attention.

Her heartbeat picked up and she smoothed her hair down. She'd been perspiring in the heat of the small bricked-in room, and her hair was plastered to her head. Heading for the bathroom to clean up, she pulled off her thick work apron and then stopped before she got to the door.

What the heck am I doing?

She turned and crossed the room to the door to the back of the building. Jack was walking across to her, with his helmet in his

275

hand.

"Are you okay?" He put his helmet on the ground, held the top of her arms and frowned down at her. "When it got so late, I was worried about you."

A strange warm flush filled Sienna's chest as he held her gaze, his brow wrinkled in a frown. It had been a long time since anyone had worried about her. Her stomach fluttered and she fidgeted beneath his touch.

"I'm fine. I've been working on my frogs." She stepped back and rubbed her arms with her hands, trying to ignore the sensation of his hands on her skin. She glanced over at the sofa. "I was thinking about sleeping here tonight."

"I was worried your car wouldn't start."

"Oh, damn." Sienna rolled her eyes. "I totally forgot about the car. I didn't call the mechanic."

"Have you eaten?"

"What are you, my keeper?" Sienna was sorry as soon as the words left her lips.

"I didn't mean to upset you. I was just trying to look out for you." He shrugged. "Besides, I had to come back in. There's some stuff here in the garage I need."

She'd forgotten all about the truck delivery this morning, and her curiosity was piqued. "Did everything arrive okay?"

"Yes. I just need to get myself organised now."

"Jack? Will you show me your work?" Her voice was hesitant. Maybe he didn't want her to see his work yet. Uncertainty filled her as he stared down at her.

He hesitated and she shrugged. "If you don't want to—"

"No." He walked over to the small loading area next to the door and put his helmet down. "It's fine. Employee confidentiality and all that. I'm sure you won't share what I show you with anyone."

Disappointment settled in Sienna's chest. He was worried
276

she'd take his ideas, and he'd found it necessary to remind her she was an employee. For a while tonight as she'd immersed herself in her work, she'd totally let the situation leave her thoughts.

"On second thought, don't worry about it." Sienna turned away and strode across to the door, her protective work boots making a satisfying clump as she walked. "I'm going back down to the kiln. I'll lock up when I leave here." She was almost to the door when warm fingers descended on her shoulder. She turned and looked up at Jack, knowing she was being snarky, but the unwanted feelings bubbled to the surface as the smell of his cologne surrounded her. "Thanks for checking on me anyway."

His fingers held her lightly and her shoulder almost sizzled from the warmth of his touch. She shrugged his fingers off. "What now?"

"I was going to wait for you to finish in case your car won't start." He held her gaze. "Would you mind if I came down and watched you work? When you're finished, I'll show you my pieces if you still want to see them."

Sienna stepped back and leaned against the doorframe. Her heartbeat was picking up, and her hands were trembling a little. A strange light feeling in her arms and legs matched the fluttery feeling in her chest. The hard wood of the doorframe pressed against her back and she focused on that as she slipped her hands into the pocket of the protective apron.

She hadn't eaten. She needed to eat. *That's why I'm all shaky. It's nothing else.*

Something shifted, just a little, and her resistance crumbed as all sensible thought took flight. She was tired of fighting it. Before she could stop herself, her hands came out from her pockets and she took a step toward him. Stepping up on her toes, she reached up, slid her hands up the front of his shirt, and held his face with both hands. His skin was warm beneath her fingers and the bristles of his unshaven chin rasped against her fingers.

"If we don't get this out of the way, I'm not going to be able to focus on my work," she whispered. She held his gaze and watched Jack's lips head toward hers. She closed her eyes in anticipation, and the soft puff of his breath warmed her lips.

Then nothing. Apart from the touch of his forehead resting on hers.

She opened her eyes and pulled back away from him a little.

"I thought you wanted to keep us on a business level." His voice was soft, but the husky note betrayed the way he was feeling.

Or she hoped it did. It wasn't fair if she was the only one fighting this.

"You said no dates, so I thought that would mean no messing around, too."

Laughter bubbled up through her chest, and Sienna didn't fight it as the giggle spilled over. "Messing around?"

"Well, isn't that what we were about to do?"

Sienna stepped back, relieved Jack had broken the tension building between them. "I guess it was. But you're right. We'll stick to what we agreed on."

She turned on her heel and pushed the door open and looked over her shoulder at him. "Come on, of course you can watch me work."

Chapter Thirteen

A blast of warm air hit them as Sienna pushed the door open. Jack was surprised at the size of the room beneath the gallery, and his interest was piqued immediately. With a kiln room this large at his disposal, he could work around the clock if necessary to meet his deadline.

Once they sorted out who was going to work where.

Three small kilns were placed along the back wall, and two large tables ran along the centre. Sculpting wax and containers of ground enamel filled a set of shelves beside the door. The tables were covered with a variety of small linear animal figures in various stages of the process. For a moment he forgot that Sienna was there as he wandered over to the table and picked up one of the small bronze figures. He held it up to the light and smiled as the colours merged into one another and deepened when he moved it around in his fingers.

"So?"

He glanced across at Sienna, and his smile grew. She was standing, hands on hips and a frown on her face.

"So what?"

"Do you think I'm kidding myself, or are they worthy of an exhibition?"

Jack held the small sculpture up to the light. It was a butterfly in the midst of flight, and its wings were enamelled in a variety of blues from the palest eggshell in the middle, to a deep cobalt on the wingtips. He twirled it around. It was small and delicate, very different from his work.

"It's beautiful. You're very talented. But I already knew that from the frogs in the gallery." He put it carefully back on the table and lifted his gaze to meet hers. "And I'm interested to hear about the process you use. The depth of colour you've achieved has escaped me so far with my glazing, but my sculptures are life-size and it's harder to get an even depth of colour over the metal."

Jack watched Sienna visibly relax beneath his gaze. She dropped her hands to her sides and rolled her shoulders. A small smile played about her lips, and the colour in her cheeks deepened as a soft rosy tinge stained her skin. "Hmph...well, thanks." If he didn't know better, a slight lack of confidence was coming out from beneath her usual sassy exterior.

She walked to one of the kilns and turned the temperature gauge up. "Pull up a stool and you can watch me for a while." She shot him a grin, and a jolt hit him in the solar plexus as her full lips curved upward. "Watch and learn."

My pleasure, thought Jack as he held her gaze. She was the first to look away as she turned to the kilns along the back wall.

Not sure about the learning, but the watching will be mighty enjoyable.

He slid onto the stool and leaned back against the counter when Sienna lifted the door of the kiln open with one fluid movement. She untied her apron and put it on the table before taking her long-sleeved shirt off and slipping the apron back on. Jack's breath caught in his throat when she turned to the shelves next to the door and stretched high on her tiptoes to reach for a container of ground enamel. She wore a pair of shiny black leggings, which he was beginning to recognise as her signature work pants. The pants hugged her like a second skin, and the bright red sleeveless cropped T-shirt clung to her back. The heat protective apron covered her from shoulder to knee in the front, and only the ties crossed behind her.

She turned and glanced across at him as she placed the enamel on the table and slid across a crate filled with pieces of copper and bronze. His gaze lingered on her long, narrow fingers, watching her lift the pieces carefully and place them in a row along the edge of the table. After she removed the coloured metal shapes waiting to be coloured, she lifted the crate back onto the shelves, and Jack dropped his gaze to the well-defined muscles flexing at the top of her arms. Her small biceps were sculpted, and her strength surprised him. Dozens of small frog figurines were soon laid out on the worktable.

Sienna might be petite, but she was strong, and he was beginning to realise how physically hard she worked running the gallery all day and then coming down to this hot cavern to work at night. His respect for her increased, and he wrinkled his brow in a frown. Hopefully the new assistant would lighten her workload. But she was busy now; they'd talk about her handing over more of the work later. In the meantime, he was going to enjoy watching her work. The temperature in the room increased as the kilns heated up to their baking temperature. Jack brushed away a trickle of perspiration from the back of his neck.

"When I add the water to the enamel powder, I pretend I'm making pancake batter." The tip of her tongue poked through her lips as she focused on stirring the liquid. Her brow wrinkled with concentration when she tipped the water into the enamel powder.

"Sometimes I get impatient." She shot him a look and laughed. "I know, that's me. I like to work fast, but this process has taught me to slow down. I used to think, 'I'll just add a bit more liquid this round,' and I'd inevitably end up with it too runny and it wouldn't stick. I lost one whole batch a couple of weeks ago. It's a wonder you didn't hear me ranting all the way down in Melbourne."

"So what did you find was the best way?" Jack was still experimenting with the coatings on his sculptures.

"Well, it depends on the metal, but it's a bit like cooking pancakes. It's good to rest the enamel before you start using it, and of course it settles between uses, so always stir it if it's been sitting for a while."

"I've never cooked pancakes."

She lifted her head and tipped it to the side as her dark gaze locked on him. "Never?"

"I don't cook much at all." Jack ran his hand through his hair, surprised to find it already damp from perspiration as the room heated up.

Sienna had a slight tinge of pink on her cheeks, but still looked fresh.

"Hmm. I forgot for a while you were the spoiled rich boy."

"That's a bit harsh." A rare fragment of temper tugged at him. She really knew how to push his buttons, and he fought it down. "I ate out most of the time because that's the way everyone lives in Melbourne."

"I thought you lived on your parents' estate. That's what Ana told me."

"I had an apartment near the city, but I moved back home after Dad had his heart attack."

"And I suppose you had servants to cook your pancakes?"

Jack stared at her. "Servants? We had people who were employed to help out." His eyes narrowed as a small giggle escaped her lips, and he realised she'd been teasing him all along and he'd fallen for it.

"Well, remind me to teach you how to make pancake batter, and then you'll have no trouble with the enamelling mix."

Her lips were full, and she had the prettiest mouth. Whenever she was brushing a difficult edge, the tip of her tongue appeared as she leaned closer to the frog in her hand and focused her attention on the gentle movement of the enamelling brush. Her black eyeliner was smudged from where she'd rubbed her eyes, and Jack couldn't be sure if the smudge of shadow on the delicate skin under her eyes was from the kohl she wore, or because she was tired. All he knew was that whenever she moved, he couldn't keep his eyes from her. He was aware of every inch of her. His gaze travelled from the short pixie haircut, down her long graceful neck, to her petite body. The snug-fitting T-shirt beneath the work apron outlined her small breasts. He deserved a medal for reminding her about their business relationship when she'd grabbed his shirt before. Looking down at her lips and not kissing her had been tough, but he didn't want to ruin things between them.

Sienna finished the piece she was working on, and with a soft grunt of satisfaction she held it up to the light, before turning to put it on the shelf farthest from the heat. Jack swallowed when she stood on her tiptoes to put it with the other finished pieces. The form-fitting pants and T-shirt hugged her curves, and his mouth was suddenly dry.

Damn shame they had this business agreement, because all he could think about was the feel of her leaning against him and her lips against his. Jack pushed the stool back and cleared his throat. It was time to get out of here before he did something he'd regret. They'd made a deal, and he'd keep his end of it.

"Are you finished now?" He glanced down at his watch. "It's almost midnight. You're not going to get much sleep."

"I'm going to sleep upstairs." She stood back and gestured to the door. "You go and do whatever you came here for, and I'll lock up down here." She rubbed her arms with those long slender fingers, and he fought the longing to have them running up his chest again.

"Fine. I just need to get a couple of things to take back to your place." He didn't move and kept his gaze on her. "Then I'll show you my pieces if you still want to see them."

"I do." She shrugged those delicate shoulders. "Are you going back upstairs?"

"Yes." He moved to the door and turned back to her. "But I won't go back to your place till you're in the studio."

"Thank you. That's nice of you, but there's no need to hang around. It's safe here."

"I'll wait for you upstairs." He let himself out without looking back at her and headed for the locked room to collect his gear.

***

When the door closed behind him, Sienna let her breath out with a whoosh and sat on the stool Jack had vacated. It sure was a change to have someone looking out for her, and it felt good. No matter how laid-back he was, and how much that annoyed her, Jack was a gentleman.

She'd been fully aware of his gaze fixed on her while she worked, and she'd enjoyed answering his questions. Teasing him was fun too, despite the warm shivers that skittered down her back every time he asked her something in that deep and sexy voice. She'd worked alone with her sculpting and enamelling for two years now. Georgie and Ana were skilled in carpentry, but they had no knowledge of the artistic processes she'd experimented with since she'd moved to the coast. Jack's interest had been gratifying. Knowing the process, he appreciated how hard it was to get it right.

So maybe she'd stretched a little higher and for longer than she would have if he hadn't been there. Her thoughts scattered, she moved across to the kilns and switched them off. He'd reminded her their relationship was about business. And that's the way it would stay, no matter what her traitorous body was trying to tell her. Listen to logic; her future depended on it.

"Shit." A sharp edge of one of the unfinished pieces pierced the palm of her hand when she picked up the last tray. She dropped it onto the shelf and held her fingers up. Blood was trickling down the side of her hand, and she moved across to the sink and rinsed it off. The cut wasn't deep, but it was long, and blood seeped out even after she washed it. She curled her fingers to put pressure on
284

the cut, and the blood stopped dripping. The first aid kit was upstairs in the kitchen. Sienna untied her apron with one hand and shrugged it off before uncurling her fingers.

Damn, the cut was still bleeding. *That's what happens when I daydream.*

She dabbed at the cut with her apron before wrapping it around her bleeding palm. Flicking the light off with her good hand, Sienna pulled the door of the kiln room shut, grateful for the light that spilled down out of the storage shed. It had rained while they were inside, and the wet cobblestones glistened in the moonlight. Ragged dark clouds scudded across the sky and the wind pushing them along brought a tang of salt air from the beach. She'd been so busy she hadn't been for a walk on the beach in days. Soon, she promised herself. It would help clear the cobwebs that seemed to be ensnaring the common sense that usually guided everything she did.

Getting tangled up with Jack was the least logical path she could take. She really had to brush him off. But she didn't want to…

Jack was banging around in the storage shed, and Sienna poked her head around the door. She looked around the boxes filling the small space, and her breath caught. She raised her hand to her mouth. "Oh, my goodness."

Two huge abstract sculptures stood on either side of the piled-up moving cartons. She walked over and ran her fingers down the fluid shape of the one closest to the door. "These are yours?"

Jack's face was shadowed, and she looked up at him, unable to read his expression.

"Yeah. The rest are still in the basement at my parents' place." His voice was tight, and she wondered if he was shy about his work.

She lifted her chin, caught his gaze, and challenged him to

hustle her from the room. "They're amazing. They make my pieces seem trivial." Then all of a sudden, her confidence disappeared as unexpected doubt rushed in. His pieces were spectacular. His artistic flair showed in every curve and angle of the pieces. For a moment it made her feel as though her pieces were insignificant.

Am I kidding myself thinking I'm good enough to show my work in an exhibition? In Noosa of all places?

Sienna stepped back and put one hand behind her, feeling for the door handle. "Wait." Her eyes met his, and all thoughts of sculptures, frogs, and shows fled and she caught her lip between her teeth as Jack followed her to the door. She could read the expression in his green eyes as clear as day. It mirrored the feelings racing through her.

He stood beside her and took her shoulders gently between his hands. Sensual intent filled his gaze, and a shiver started low in her stomach and travelled in every direction. She couldn't look away. She couldn't resist the feelings rampaging through her as he held her; accepting them came to her as naturally as breathing.

"What's wrong with your hand?" He looked down at her hand, which had the apron fisted against her chest.

"Just a little cut."

"Show me."

He pulled her closer and unwound the apron from around her hand. "Damn. That's a nasty gash there. What did you do?"

"I caught it on one of the rough edges when I was packing up." At least talking about her hand dispelled the mood that had ensnared them briefly. "It's nothing. I'll just go clean it and put a bandage on it." She pulled away from him. "I'll see you in the morning."

"Not so fast." A warm hand held her shoulder gently. "I'll do it for you. Working one-handed is a bit hard."

"It's all right, Jack. I said I'll do it." Sienna knew her voice

286

was testy, but being with him in the confined space, sharing her work with him, and then seeing his, had created an intimacy between them she didn't want. Okay, maybe she did want it, but it would complicate things way too much.

She moved away from him and wasn't surprised when he followed her into the studio.

"Where's your first aid kit?"

"In the cupboard under the sink in the kitchen."

Jack took her arm and pulled her over to the sofa before gently pushing her to sit down. "Sit there and don't move." He stared at her for a moment. "And there's no need to be sassy."

Sienna leaned against the soft back of the sofa, closed her eyes, and rested her head on the cushion. Her hand had started to throb, and her neck ached from working. As soon as Jack finished his first aid ministrations, she was going to sleep. It looked like there was no way she was going to get rid of him until she allowed him to look after her.

Which was kind of nice in a way.

"How often do you work here alone?"

She opened her eyes. She must have dozed off. He was crouched down in front of her and had placed a bowl of water on the floor.

"Most nights. Why?"

"It's not safe."

"I'm a big girl now, Jack."

"What if you'd cut yourself badly and passed out or something?" He unwound the apron from around her palm, and she drew a quick breath as the dried blood stuck to the fabric. "You could burn yourself…or start a fire."

"But I didn't."

"It's my gallery and my building, and I need to make sure that my staff are safe." His voice was firm.

A slow burn began in her stomach when Jack dipped a

cotton pad in the water and cleaned her hand.

My staff.

She'd been kidding herself about this intimacy between them. His comment brought her back to earth. It served as a good reminder of what their relationship really was. She bit back the words that were boiling inside, took a deep breath, and let the anger recede. He was her boss, and he owned the gallery. There was nothing she could do about it, and there was nothing to be gained by getting angry. She'd been there and done that already. She'd agreed to give it a month. Once her show was done, she would decide what to do next. Sienna bit her lip and frowned. The more she thought about it, the more she realised that working alongside Jack was problematic. But no matter what logic she used to convince herself she could get over this attraction to him, her body wouldn't cooperate.

"Any deeper and you would need stitches."

Sienna kept her eyes closed and her head back against the sofa. The sharp aroma of antiseptic liquid reached her before the warm pressure of a Band-Aid filled her palm.

"There you go. I don't think it needs more than that."

She opened her eyes when he let her hand go, and she gestured to the first aid stuff on the floor. "Leave all that. I'll clean it up in the morning."

"No. I'll do it. Do you want a glass of water or a coffee or something?" Jack gathered up the bowl and the ointment, and the box of bandages, and held his hand out for the apron that was still on her lap.

"For someone who's used to servants, you're pretty versatile." She shot him a grin. "Thanks for looking after me."

"So have a coffee with me before I go. I need a shot of caffeine for the ride back home." He stood up in front of the sofa and his deep green gaze pinned her. Her heartbeat skittered up a notch.

"Thank you, I will." She liked having him around and was reluctant to say good-bye to him. He was easy to spend time with, and if she could put the gallery ownership aside, they had a lot in common.

Art-wise, anyway.

It was strange to sit back on the sofa and listen to Jack rattling around with the coffeemaker. Eventually, the aroma of brewing coffee drifted out from the kitchen. A pleasant sleepiness began to overtake her, and she slipped her shoes off and pulled her legs up beneath her.

"Milk and sugar?" Jack called from the kitchen.

"Yes, please. Both."

Sienna watched as he crossed the studio grasping two coffee mugs. His dark T-shirt strained against his broad shoulders as he balanced the two cups trying not to spill the hot liquid. She grinned to herself. He'd picked the biggest mugs she had in the kitchen, so he'd be here for a while yet. She slid along the sofa to the end to make room for him. He put the cups on the small table at the other end of the sofa. The sofa cushion tipped when he sat next to her, and she grasped the cushion with her uninjured hand, so she didn't slide down on top of him.

"Thanks for letting me watch you work. I really enjoyed spending time with you tonight." Jack turned and slid his arm along the top of the sofa. His words mirrored her thoughts.

Uh-oh.

"I usually prefer to work alone." She crossed her arms in front of her chest and tried to keep her voice snappy. Having six feet plus of attractive male sitting so close to her when she was tired and feeling vulnerable was not her choice for sensible behaviour.

"Why are you so defensive, Sienna?" Jack held her gaze and his voice was low. "Who hurt you?"

"No one hurt me. I just prefer to be alone." She didn't like the little bit of need she could hear in her own voice, and she lifted her chin. "That's the way I am."

"Why? We all need people in our life, and around us. I've seen you with Ana and Georgie. That's not being alone."

"That's different. Georgie is my sister, and we've been friends with Ana all our lives." She stared at him. "And who's going to be around you once you get settled here, anyhow? It's a bit like the pot calling the kettle black. Unless you've got a heap of artist friends out here?"

She knew she was babbling, but his intense gaze fixed on her unnerved her. Sienna leaned forward to reach for her coffee mug, but Jack grabbed her hand. She held his gaze, and something elemental moved inside her when he put his arms around her. She tried to pull back from his hold, but he tightened it.

"Sienna?" His green eyes held a question as she looked up at him. He lifted his hand and brushed his thumb over her lip.

Her breath caught in her throat as a riot of unfamiliar feelings spiralled through her.

"Oh, what the hell." She pulled her hand away from his, rose to her knees, and grabbed his face with both hands. "I'll probably regret this in the morning, but we're going to have to get this out of the way."

Sienna leaned forward and pressed her lips against his…and it was heaven. He lifted his arms and slid her across to his lap without breaking the contact. She fit into the curve of his shoulder so naturally…a perfect fit.

"Are you sure?" His words vibrated against her lips as his arms tightened around her. She couldn't move away even if she changed her mind. She slid her hands down past his shoulders and gripped the tops of his arms, smiling as his muscles tightened beneath her fingers. Sienna lifted her head just long enough to answer, and Jack's lips moved across her cheek and down her neck.

"We need to do something about this attraction…and then we can move on," she said.

The feel of his hard chest against her, the slide of his lips down her throat, slammed into her, and the heat rushed in. Sienna closed her eyes and sank into the pleasure he was offering.

Chapter Fourteen

Sienna slipped Jack's T-shirt over her head and walked across the studio toward the sofa. Jack grinned up at her and held out his hand, but she ignored him.

"Where are the clothes you had on last night?" He shot her a lazy grin.

"You tell me and we'll both know."

"They must be here somewhere. Come back and we'll look together." He raised himself up on one elbow, but she shook her head and pursed her lips at him.

"As tempting as that may be, it's almost time to open the gallery. I've got an appointment with the newspaper at eleven a.m." She pointed to the clock above the door; it was almost ten thirty.

"So, mister, you need to get dressed and look like a gallery owner."

"Have we got time for breakfast? Pancakes, maybe?" The look on his face was comical and she shook her head.

"Someone has to run this gallery, so once I'm showered and dressed you can have the bathroom."

"And then we can go out for a quick breakfast?" He tried to put on a pleading expression, but it didn't work.

"When you decide to get up, can you make up the bed please?"

"Guess I'm not going to get lucky then?"

Sienna stood in the doorway away from the temptation of his reach. "Last night was fun, Jack. We've dealt with what was building between us, now we move on. Okay?"

The whole night had been…fun.

"Fun" was probably the best word to use. Two consenting adults giving in to a mutual attraction and doing something about it. They'd laughed and giggled and enjoyed each other's company. And given each other a great deal of pleasure…the soft teasing, the laughter and their banter had enhanced her night… and their lovemaking. Sienna hummed softly as she stripped down and stepped into the shower.

They'd move on, their relationship would go back to business; she'd have her exhibition, then decide if she was going to stay at the Sea View Gallery. All logical, and cut-and-dried, and she had a month to sort it out. So why did she feel so excited, and why was that silly grin plastered on her face?

Sienna managed to put Jack to the back of her mind when the reporter from the local paper arrived, and she approved the ads they were going to run for her show. After that, she focused on her email and the satisfying number of inquiries that were starting to arrive. The word about Sea View Gallery was getting out, and hopefully her debut show would cement that.

The morning flew by, but there was no sign of Jack in the gallery. He was either having a very long breakfast or he'd gone back out to Forest Lake. No matter how many times Sienna glanced at the door at the back of the gallery, he didn't make an appearance, and she pushed away the little tug of disappointment that insisted on staying with her. Maybe he'd gone back home; maybe he was unpacking some of his boxes in storage. Anyway, it was none of her business, and she wasn't going to go out to find him.

Move on. I've got a heap to do or my exhibition will never get off the ground.

Just after noon, when the gallery had cleared for the usual slow time during lunch, the front doorbell tinkled softly. Sienna looked up from the iPad where she was checking her afternoon appointments. A tall, elegantly dressed woman about her age stood in the doorway looking around the gallery as if for someone in particular. A designer-label dress, Sienna thought, if she knew her fashion, and the shoes were definitely Jimmy Choos. She'd salivated over the very same pair in a trendy shoe shop in Brisbane the last time she'd gone there on a shopping expedition with Georgie and Ana. She loved clothes and indulging her sense of fashion, but in her work, heels were impractical. She stared at the woman's feet—oh, she loved those shoes.

The woman turned to Sienna with a frown, but from her height she still managed to look her up and down. Sienna stood and straightened and plastered a smile on her face. All kinds came into the gallery, and they were all prospective customers.

"Hello. Welcome to Sea View Gallery." Sienna picked up an information brochure and held it out, but the woman ignored it, so she dropped it back on the table with a shrug. "If there's anything I can help you with, please ask." She gestured to the gallery and then turned back to her iPad.

"I'm here to see Jack Montgomery." The woman's voice was as impatient as her expression, and a frown marred her perfectly made-up face. Sienna got the impression that she'd done something to upset this visitor but didn't have a clue what it could be because she'd never seen this woman before.

"Do you have an appointment?" Sienna pretended to refer to the iPad. Jack had made it quite clear she was running the gallery and he would stay in the background, so maybe it was personal? "Who shall I say is calling?" Sienna smiled, trying to keep the interaction pleasant despite the woman's snooty behaviour.

"Arielle."

"And your last name…"

"Jack knows who I am." A perfectly manicured hand
294

reached up and smoothed the blonde hair, which was sprayed into place.

"If you say so, but I'm not even sure if he's in." Sienna was reluctant to go out the back and look for him, and this woman was pushing her buttons. "I'll take a message and make an appointment for you, Ms....?"

The woman stared at her and shook her head slowly. She put her bag on the floor and sauntered over to the love seat beside the glass desk. She draped herself over the seat and smiled at Sienna before trilling a little girlish laugh.

"There's no need for that. I'll wait here. I'm Jack's partner."

Chapter Fifteen

Jack revved the bike and hit the coast road. He'd needed some fresh air and some time to clear his head. Last night with Sienna had been magic, but then she'd put the walls back up this morning. Maybe she'd been focusing on having to open the gallery. Or that's what he was hoping. He wasn't used to being put in his place and told where a relationship could go. Last night had given him a lot to think about. Maybe seeing each other wouldn't complicate things too much; they were both adults and the night had been fun. They could separate business and pleasure. Surely, she could see that, too?

The relaxed Sienna was even more beautiful, and he hadn't been able to keep his eyes—or his hands—off her. There should be more of it. Life was for loving, and it was easy for him to become impatient with people who took things too seriously. His father was a prime example of that.

She'd declined to join him for breakfast, so now he'd take Sienna out for lunch and use his best persuasive techniques to convince her they could do business and...sex.

And be friends as well.

And it wouldn't impact anything. They were adults and could handle it as long as they were honest with each other. Jack had seen too much dishonesty back in Melbourne, both in business and in his personal life, and it had been one of the reasons for coming out west and starting afresh.

Honesty. That was the key.

The sweet salt-laden air rushed past and Jack took a deep breath as he turned the bike back toward Noosa. No matter what his reason had been, this move was the best damned thing he'd ever done in his life.

Five minutes later, Jack put his helmet on the sofa in the studio and smoothed his hand over his hair. He was quickly getting the impression that when he was in the gallery, he was supposed to look the part of the owner and not like a surfer bum. He pushed the door open and glanced around. The gallery was almost clear.

So, lunch it is.

Sienna was standing at the glass desk by the door. He walked up behind her quietly and put his arms around her waist and nuzzled her neck.

"Let's go have lunch. I missed out on breakfast."

"Jack Montgomery!"

His head flew up at the familiar voice, and Sienna stiffened beneath his hands as the shrill voice hit him.

Oh, damn. He thought he'd left all that behind him. "Arielle? What are you doing here?"

She lifted herself gracefully from the love seat where she'd been reclining, drew herself to her full height, and strode over to the table. She was almost six feet tall and towered over Sienna, who moved away behind the counter, a closed expression on her face.

"More to the point, what's going on here?" Arielle pointed to Sienna before she stepped up to him and put her arms around his neck. "But no matter, I'm here now. You can take me out to lunch." She pouted her little signature pout. "I've missed you, baby."

A snort came from behind the counter and Jack glanced over at Sienna at the same time as he disentangled Arielle's arms from around his neck. Arielle still wore the same cloying perfume that had always given him a headache, and he rubbed his hand across his eyes. Her timing couldn't have been any worse. By her stiff posture, he could sense Sienna withdrawing from him more by the second, and he needed to get Arielle out of here.

"What are you doing here?" He moved away from her and glanced at Sienna. She was looking at her iPad and focused on the screen. He'd sort this out right now and make it clear that Arielle was an unexpected visitor—and from his past.

"I came to see you. I thought it was time we sorted out that silly little matter you raised when you left."

"You flew all the way from Melbourne just to talk to me? Why on earth would you do that?"

Now Sienna was looking from one to the other, a small smile playing at her lips. The doorbell above the entry tinkled and she waved dismissively at Jack before she turned to greet the customer. "You pair of *lovebirds*"—despite the smile, her voice was sarcastic— "go out and have lunch. I'll look after the gallery."

"What? Wait a minute—" But Jack was interrupted by a customer who walked timidly to the counter. He turned to Sienna and watched the colour drain from her face as she saw the small, red-haired woman standing behind Arielle. Her face was thin and drawn, and she clutched her bag to her chest as though someone was about to take it from her.

"Now my day has gone to absolute and total crap," Sienna muttered.

The woman stepped forward and held her hand out. "Sienna, I really need to talk to you."

"So I've heard, Marjorie." The sarcasm was gone and replaced by an icy tone. "We can talk, but not here."

Sienna reached out and took Jack's arm between her fingers and he glanced down, surprised by her touch but instinctively sensing she was grounding herself.

"I'm sorry. Can you look after the gallery while I take a short break?" She held his gaze, and he watched curiously as she heaved a deep breath as though trying to dig deep to keep calm.

"I'll be quick and then you can go out with your *partner*."
298

Sienna flicked a gaze at Arielle, who had followed the whole exchange with interest.

Jack put his hand on top of Sienna's fingers to keep her hand there.

Who was this woman who had Sienna so rattled? A warm protective feeling suffused his chest and he wanted to put his arms around her and hold her close. Waves of distress were coming off her, and he knew this woman was more than a customer with a problem.

He lowered his head and spoke softly. "Are you okay?"

Sienna waved her hand dismissively as she stepped away from him. "I just need to have an hour, and I'll be back. Then you and *Arielle* can go have lunch."

"Of course, I can mind the gallery. Take as long as you like."

"I won't need long." She stared at the older woman and a shiver ran down Jack's back as she spoke.

"I'll meet you in the coffee shop next to the post office in fifteen minutes. Then I'll give you ten minutes, so make it good." Sienna disappeared through the door at the back of the gallery before he could speak. Arielle took his arm as the small woman left by the front door.

"Who are they, Jack?" The little-girl voice she put on was grating on him already.

***

Sienna went straight to the bathroom and splashed her face with cold water. She gripped the edges of the cold basin, her hands shaking. She took a deep breath, trying to gain a measure of calm before she left the gallery to meet Marjorie. She had stopped thinking of her as Mum years ago.

What a morning. Double whammy. First Jack's girlfriend appears and then Marjorie waltzes into Sea View Gallery. It was the first time she'd seen her in three years, and she'd aged considerably. And if she could be believed for once, she did look quite ill. She'd lost a lot of weight, and her skin had a yellowish tinge.

Picking up the towel, Sienna patted her face dry and applied another layer of kohl around her eyes. She stepped back and smoothed her top over her short skirt knowing she was only delaying the inevitable. She stared into the mirror and looked at her reflection.

"You can do this. Just find out what she wants and warn her off…for the last time." She picked up her bag and left through the back door to avoid the pair out front. She had one stop to make before she met the woman she refused to acknowledge as her mother. Jack and his girlfriend were the least of her worries.

By the time she'd left the post office and pushed the sealed envelope deep into her bag, Sienna's mood had moved to an icy calm. Once and for all she would ensure that Marjorie left them alone and didn't upset Georgie again. She was tough herself, but Georgie got hurt every time Marjorie came back into their lives. Georgie with her happily-ever-after outlook never gave up hoping that their mother would change and would one day want to be a real part of their lives. Having a mother who used people and had no love for her own children had taught Sienna a good lesson in life. Over the years she'd made sure she relied only on herself and needed no one else. Marjorie's arrival after she succumbed to Jack's charm was a timely reminder that she'd been heading to a place she didn't want to be.

Ever. With anyone

She walked down the three steps into the sunken courtyard of the coffee shop and looked around. She dug her huge dark glasses out of her bag and dropped them over her eyes as she walked over to the table at the edge of the garden where Marjorie was sitting.

At least she's by herself. A couple of times over the years she'd arrived with the current boyfriend in tow. The chair scraped on the rough cobblestones when Sienna pulled it away to the side and sat down.

"So how much this time?" She stared through her dark glasses at the woman she had never known as a mother. Marjorie had her head down and was shredding a tissue to bits with shaking fingers.

"I don't want any money."

"That's a change." Sienna kept her voice cold. She was not going to get emotional, and she was not going to show any reaction. The minutes ticked away in an uncomfortable silence and Sienna waited for the inevitable. She knew the pattern.

God, how many times have we sat through this same scenario? No matter how tough she was, Sienna knew she was a soft touch. Keeping their mother in money meant she'd never saved as much as she could have. She'd kept just enough aside for the gallery deposit and her exhibition.

Finally, Marjorie looked up and held her gaze. "I want to tell you something, and I want you to listen without interrupting." Her voice was quavering, and she cleared her throat as she dabbed the tissue to her lips.

Sienna sat back and folded her arms, ignoring the curiosity that tugged at her. "Make it quick. That's my boss who's minding the gallery."

"I thought it was your own business?"

"Ah. So that's the way the land lies." Sienna knew she was being an utter bitch, but she couldn't help it. She had learned how to protect herself from hurt growing up, and she'd do anything to make sure she kept Georgie that way too. There was too much history and too much hurt to be civil to this woman. As far as she was concerned, Marjorie was not her mother.

She looked down in surprise when Marjorie reached across

301

and grabbed her fingers in a death grip. Her thin hand held Sienna's tightly on the tabletop; her sharp nails pressed into Sienna's skin.

"Listen to me. Please? One last time and then I'll leave you in peace. For good." Marjorie's voice broke and Sienna pushed away the sympathy that began to well in her chest.

"I'm ill and I wanted you to hear the truth from me before…before it's too late. It's not right that Renzo has to tell you."

"Tell me what?"

Marjorie kept the tight grip on her hand as though she knew Sienna would get up and leave. It was tempting, but this time, she was going to finish with Marjorie once and for all.

"You're his daughter."

"What?" Sienna's world spun. "Are you crazy? He's my uncle, your brother. He can't be my father."

"It's true. I'm not your birth mother, but Renzo *is* your father."

"You're lying." Sienna reached into her bag with her free hand and pulled out the envelope before shoving it across the table. "I don't know what you're playing at, but I've had enough. There's money in here. I want you to take it and take your silly stories away and leave Georgie and me alone for good. That's it." She fought to keep her voice strong as the thoughts whirled around her head. "That's all I have, and it's worth giving to you to make you go away. I want nothing more to do with you and your crazy ramblings. Do you understand me?"

"Georgie is my child."

Sienna stared at her and let her hand and the envelope drop to the table as the significance of Marjorie's words hit her. For the first time, Marjorie had her attention.

"What are you saying?" Her voice came as a whisper and she pulled her hand out of Marjorie's grasp.

"What can I get you to drink?" The voice of the waitress was a welcome return to normality as she placed a bottle of water and two glasses on the table.

"Coffee, black." Sienna's voice was clipped. She pulled her hand from Marjorie's and poured herself a glass of water and wasn't surprised to see her hand shaking. What Marjorie said was a lie; it had to be.

But why?

Sienna drank deeply and looked up as the waitress turned to Marjorie with a curious glance, but the older woman shook her head and dabbed at the tears on her cheeks.

"Nothing, thank you." Marjorie waited until the waitress had walked to the next table.

"Over the holidays Renzo and I worked in the night harvest in the vineyards in the Hunter Valley. I met Georgie's father there." Her voice was quiet, and she lifted her head and held Sienna's gaze steadily. "I was friends with one of the other girls and she and Renzo had a fling before he came back home." She took a deep breath.

"And…" Sienna prompted her. "What are you trying to tell me?"

"Catherine discovered she was pregnant when she went back home to Tamworth, and she contacted me. When I told her that Renzo was about to get married to Lucia, she decided not to tell him she was having his child."

"I'm not following you. What are you telling me?" Sienna's world was crumbling, and she fought for control, gripping her hands together on her lap. "This sounds like something from a soap opera."

"My friend Catherine was your mother."

"Was? Where is she?" Her voice felt as though it was coming from someone else.

"She got sick when you were only a few weeks old."

303

Sienna watched as Marjorie shifted her eyes to the envelope on the table. "She came to see me when we were living in Sydney. It was the same week that Georgie's father was leaving to work in the mines. Catherine had put Renzo's name on the birth certificate and when she found out how sick she was, she wanted him to know he had a daughter." She lifted her head. "You."

"But what about Georgie? If this is the truth why did…Uncle Renzo…take us both in? Are you telling me we're not twins?"

Marjorie reached out again, but Sienna kept her hands gripped together. "You *are* cousins, and you share a birthday. You were born on the same day. When Catherine knew she was dying, she asked me to take you, but I wouldn't. I wasn't coping with Georgie, so Renzo and Lucia took you both. She gave them her blessing."

Sienna put her elbows on the table and dropped her head into her hands. It all made sense…sort of. All her life, she'd thought she and Georgie were so different because they were fraternal twins. A small bus pulled up outside and a group of tourists wandered into the courtyard, and their chatter washed over Sienna. She lifted her head and watched them choose a table.

"I followed Georgie's father to Western Australia. I was never very maternal. I knew if he went without me, I'd never see him again. He was the love of my life." Marjorie looked up when the waitress put Sienna's coffee on the table and filled her glass up. "Thank you."

"How do I know I can believe you?" A slow burn was beginning in her stomach, and she took a deep breath as the tears ached at the back of her eyes. She never cried and she wasn't about to start now. It was a sign of weakness, and she was always the strong one.

Marjorie opened her purse and pulled out a folded piece of paper and slid it across the table. "Your birth certificate." She smiled sadly. "I've watched both you and Georgie grow up and I knew you'd need proof. You are a very strong woman, just like Catherine was. She would have been proud of you."

Sienna looked at the paper sitting in front of her as though it would strike and bite her fingers if she touched it. Slowly she reached out, picked it up, and unfolded it. The lines began to waver as Marjorie's words were confirmed by the text in front of her. "What about Georgie? I don't understand. How could you have left her?"

"That's between Georgie and me."

"No." Sienna's control came rushing back. "You're not to tell her. I know my *sister*. She'll be devastated."

Chapter Sixteen

The cool sand squeaked beneath Sienna's bare feet. She walked toward the big tree stump at the top of the beach at the end of Hastings Street; it was surrounded by a few short trees and was private. She dropped her bag and her shoes to the sand and sat on the smooth timber, staring out over the crashing waves. Despite the cool wind, she could barely feel the chill on her arms; her skin was hot and burning. She sat there for a long time staring out to sea as the wind flicked her short hair into spikes around her face. Her whole life had just shifted, and she was numb inside and out.

She kicked at the sand with her toes.

Aunt Marjorie. Her life savings had extracted the promise that she wouldn't tell Georgie, and she hoped she could trust her. The time had sped by as Sienna had listened to her whole story, and now she glanced at her watch. She'd left the coffee shop and headed straight to the beach, the one place that always managed to soothe her. The way she felt at the moment, she didn't even care if she ever saw the gallery again. It was surreal, and she had to overcome this confusion filling her. She had to come to terms with the thought that Renzo was her father...and her own mother was dead.

The two unexpected visitors today had brought her to her senses. She'd been getting sucked in by her feelings for Jack. Okay, sleeping with him had been fun, but it wasn't going anywhere. Seeing Marjorie had firmed her resolve. Irrespective of the gallery—and the girlfriend—Marjorie reminded her why she didn't do relationships She needed no one in her life. The hollow feeling in her chest and the tears pricking at the backs of her eyelids had nothing to do with regret.

And I have to decide what to tell Georgie.

But first she had to go back to work and tell Jack her exhibition was canned. And she had to face him after last night and probably be in the company of his girlfriend. Giving everything to Marjorie to get rid of her had been worth it and Sienna didn't regret it. Even though it now meant she couldn't afford to pay the costs of holding her exhibition, and any thought of building a studio onto her house had disappeared with the money Marjorie slipped into her bag. She needed time and space to get her thoughts in order. And face Jack. The devastation that tugged at Sienna as her dreams crumbled around her was put away in a deep place where she wouldn't think about it until she had to.

***

Jack turned the closed sign over on the gallery door. He couldn't wait for Sienna to come back. She'd said an hour and she'd already been gone for more than two. He'd managed to convince Arielle that she'd wasted a trip—he ran his hand through his hair and shook his head. He couldn't believe she'd come all the way from Melbourne. He'd booked her on a flight from Brisbane tonight, despite her protests that he'd change his mind about their little misunderstanding.

The look on Sienna's face when he'd walked into the gallery this afternoon had been as cold as ice. Once he told Sienna that Arielle wasn't his girlfriend, maybe they could take up where they'd left off last night. But first he had to get Arielle back to Brisbane. He'd arranged for a bus, but he had to get her to the depot at Caloundra first, and they had to go on his bike.

"Are you ready?" He glanced at her sitting primly on the love seat by the door. "Your luggage will be sent from your hotel to the airport." All he wanted to do was get her on a plane…today.

The spoiled-girl pout was back. "Helen said you'd be pleased to see me." Arielle had always lived in a dream world. He

307

knew his mother would not have encouraged her.

"Helen was wrong. Come on, we've just got time to meet the bus."

###

An hour later, Arielle was safely deposited in the bus on the way to Brisbane Airport. She wasn't happy, but Jack was sure he'd managed to convince her she'd wasted her time. A pleasant tingle ran over his skin as he rode along the short street to the gallery. He'd expected to see the lights on in the gallery, but the building was locked and almost in darkness. Only the soft display lighting in the front was on. He gunned the motor and turned the bike toward home. It seemed like hours since Sienna had been in his arms this morning, and he needed to talk to her and convince her that they...that they could what?

Jack frowned to himself as he turned the bike toward Lake Weyba. They could have a relationship? Or they could just work and play together? He had a feeling Sienna was going to be hard to convince of anything. And the hardest part was he didn't really know what he was trying to convince her that they had between them. Look how Arielle had tried to complicate his life. Maybe he needed to think a bit more and pull back a little?

The house was in darkness too, and he let himself in quietly, heading to the apartment wondering where Sienna was. She'd probably been pissed off with him when she'd come back from her lunch with that woman and found the gallery closed up. But, damn it, it was his business and he could do what he liked with it. His stomach grumbled, adding to his feeling of being out of sorts with the world. He'd go for a run around the lake and then grab some dinner and hit the sack. Maybe she'd come home before then and they could talk.

He pulled on his running shorts and shoes and locked the door behind him as he took off at a slow pace toward the water. There was a distinct chill in the air and winter was not far away.

His thoughts ran around his mind and Jack wished he'd thought to grab his iPod so he could listen to music and clear his head.

When did things get so complicated?

Jack narrowed his eyes and peered through the dim light as he headed back toward the house after doing a circuit of the small lake. The light reflected on the small garage at the side of the house and he caught the flash of chrome. Sienna's car was there, but the house was dark. Maybe she'd been picked up? After all, he knew little about her life. But as he ran closer to the house, he saw the flicker of a candle on the back porch. He let out his breath in a sigh of relief, and anticipation filled him.

He grabbed both sides of the stair rail and pulled himself up the four steps leading to the porch as he levelled his breathing. Sienna was curled up in one of the rockers beneath the covered side of the porch, the flickering candle flame the only movement. For a moment he thought she was asleep, but as soon as his shoes hit the wooden decking, she unfolded herself from the chair, stood, and stretched, reaching for a pair of running shoes.

A tight black T-shirt almost reached the top of a pair of black leggings, and he caught a glimpse of bare skin as she raised her arms above her head.

"Great timing," she said. "I was just going to go for a run myself. Cool out there?"

Jack caught his breath, not so much from the exertion but from the cute picture filling his vision.

"Yeah, cool. But it's great by the water once you warm up."

Sienna tied her laces and stood. Jack's breath caught in his throat and he chose his words carefully. "Are we…are you okay?"

"Yes, why do you ask? I'm good. Are you?" Sienna's voice was soft and muffled.

"Whoa." Jack hurried across the porch to catch her, and gently took her arm before she could step down the stairs. "You sound like you're catching a cold. Maybe a run's not such a good idea?" Her skin was icy beneath his fingers. "How about I make you a hot drink? I make a mean lemon hot toddy if you've got a sore throat."

Sienna pulled away from him and bent, stretching her legs. "Thanks, I'm fine. I'm looking forward to a run. I need some fresh air."

"Want some company?" He didn't want to go inside alone. If it meant going for another run, so be it. He could pull the stamina from somewhere.

A slight smile crossed Sienna's face. "Are you up to it?"

The challenge gave Jack a burst of energy. "Of course I am. Are you?"

"Race you to the other side of the lake?" Before he could take another breath, Sienna shot past him, down the steps, and across the small patch of lawn. By the time Jack reached the bottom of the steps, she was opening the gate that led to the narrow path beside the lake. She shot a glance at him and her low chuckle pleased him.

By the time he was through the gate, she was ahead of him and had passed the next two houses along the lake. No way was he going to let her beat him, so Jack took a deep breath and stepped up his pace.

To his surprise, Sienna lengthened the distance between them, and he had to push himself to close the distance. The muscles in his calves burned and he smiled as he almost caught up to her.

"How far are we going?" he huffed as he drew closer to her.

As soon as he spoke, Sienna took off and the distance between them grew again.

"Eat my dust." Her laugh broke the silence of the night. Jack swallowed and gave it all he had.

By the time she'd reached the last house on the other side of the lake, he was right behind her. Her ragged breath as she pushed to the end showed him how determined she had been to beat him.

Sienna grabbed the rail of the jetty of the last house before the path ended in thick trees. She turned with a grin. Jack reached her, rested his arms on the rail, bent over, and tried to catch his breath. Finally, when he could talk, he straightened. Sienna was leaning nonchalantly against the fence, her breathing even and slow, her face slightly pink.

He shook his head with a wry grin. "You didn't even break a sweat."

"Out of shape, Jack?" She smiled back at him and then turned away. "Race you back?"

"Whoa, right there." He reached out and grabbed her arm. "You've made your point. You're fitter than me and you can run like the wind."

"And I feel so much better for it, too." It was great to see the smile on her face as she held his gaze. He pulled her closer and looked down into her eyes. "I'm sorry about today. It wasn't what it looked like."

"What wasn't?" Her eyes narrowed and he realised that even though he had been so worried about her take on Arielle, she seemed to not know that he was talking about it. She stood straight in the loose circle of his arms and looked up at him, her eyes shining in the soft moonlight.

"I want to explain to you…about Arielle."

She lifted her head, and he narrowed his eyes as his gaze settled on her face. At a closer look, her face was pale despite her exertion, and her eyes were slightly puffy. If he didn't know better, he'd swear she'd been crying.

Jack wanted to see her smile again. Frustration warred with wanting to pull her close and kiss her senseless. "Last night was wonderful, and Arielle's arrival was totally unexpected." He waited for her reaction.

A yawn escaped her lips and Jack let his shoulders relax.

"So, I'm boring you now?" he said.

"We didn't get much sleep last night," she said with a slight turning up of her lips.

He grinned, pleased the tension that was swirling between them was easing, and let his gaze settle on her. Dressed all in black, she looked even tinier than normal. She usually gave off an impression of strength, but despite the exertion of the race between them, an air of fragility hung around her tiny shoulders.

He closed his eyes for a moment, remembering the feel of her fine bones beneath his fingers last night. When he opened them, she was looking at him and he was sure she could read his mind.

"I didn't know Arielle was coming to see me, and I want to make one thing quite clear. She isn't my girlfriend, or my partner, or whatever she told you"

"It's all right, Jack." She stepped away, reached down and stretched one leg. "You don't owe me any explanations. Last night was fun and we got that out of our systems. Now we go back to the way we were. I don't care about Arielle, whatever she is...or was...to you."

"But you look—" He didn't want to say that she looked upset because it sounded as though he was an arrogant jerk, as though she cared enough to be upset by Arielle arriving. She'd made it quite clear from the outset that there was going to be nothing between them. Maybe something else was wrong? He'd give her some time and if she wanted to talk, he'd be there to listen.

"You look tired. And so am I." He pushed himself from the rail and held out his hand. "Okay, race you back."

Sienna grinned at him and stepped onto the path.

312

"Sienna?"

She stopped and looked back at him "Yes?"

"Your shoelace is undone."

She crouched down in the darkness and by the time she realised both her laces were intact Jack had taken off and was twenty yards ahead of her.

With a grin, he called back over his shoulder. "Gotcha."

The sound of her laughter behind him sent a warm feeling rushing through his chest.

Chapter Seventeen

Sienna slept deeply despite the crazy dreams of weddings where Renzo was giving her away. In her dreams, she walked down an aisle over and over, hanging on to his arm, but when she got to the front there was no one there. She was alone in the church and even Renzo had disappeared.

Runaway groom phobias. Something she'd never have to worry about. It must be the thought of her mother deciding not to tell Renzo about his child when she first fell pregnant—about *her*—and Arielle that had gotten her mind spinning.

Sienna stood beneath the shower and let the warm water run down her face and neck. She always did her best thinking in the shower, or by the beach, but today her thoughts whirled around, and she couldn't come to a decision. Closing her eyes, she leaned her head back and wished that the water could wash away all of her problems.

Marjorie had sworn that she wouldn't tell Georgie what she had told Sienna yesterday. Sienna knew that she couldn't trust her not to tell Georgie, so she was going to have to make time to see her tonight. Taking time out wasn't a problem anymore; her exhibition was going to be canned and there was no need to work on the enamelling every night. Her throat ached with the disappointment of her lost dream, and Sienna gave in to the tears and let them fall until she was drained. She had worked toward that dream for two years, and in one afternoon, it was all gone.

Along with my money. Maybe she'd been foolish, but she wanted to protect Georgie and ensure that she was the one to break the news. She knew that Georgie would be hit hard by the revelation that they weren't twins...or even sisters. Sienna tipped her head back and let the warm water wash away her tears. She couldn't cope with the knowledge either, but she knew she would have to learn to accept it.

She would have a busy day ahead, and she'd tell Jack he could have the studio as soon as he wanted it. Making the call to the newspaper to pull the ad, and cancelling the catering, would fill in some of the day.

###

Fifteen minutes later, she was dressed and sitting in her car—her dead car—as the damn motor refused to fire. Taking it to the mechanic had slipped her mind over the past couple of days.

"Problems?" Jack stood at the front of the bumper bar, his hands on his hips, his jeans slung low on his waist, and his chest bare as it seemed to be more often than not. Sienna's mouth dried and she tore her gaze away. Racing with Jack last night had done her good. He'd seemed genuinely worried about her being upset, and that had touched her, but she hadn't wanted to go into explanations of what was bothering her. They'd had fun and she had appreciated his thoughtfulness. Plus, she'd enjoyed beating him to the other side of the lake. If he hadn't tricked her, she would have beaten him back. She'd run that path so many times she could have done it in her sleep.

"Blasted car. I forgot to call the mechanic."

And I won't be able to for a while now that I've cleaned out my bank account.

She opened the door and eased herself out and avoided looking at Jack's bare chest as he moved closer to her. Turning the key in the door, she locked it and stepped back and began to count.

"One, two, three—"

"What are you doing? Trying to keep your temper intact?" Jack's roguish grin interrupted her counting and Sienna pursed her lips and waved her arm at him.

"Four, five, six, seven, eight, nine…ten!" She unlocked the

door and sat in the driver's seat. "I'm trying something."

Jack crossed his arms, watching her with an intent expression as he leaned against the side of the carport while she put the key in the ignition and turned it. The engine purred to life and she looked at him with a grin.

"It worked!"

"The counting? Was it overheated?" Jack stepped forward and crouched beside the car, and his face was close enough that she could see the gold flecks in his green eyes.

"No, I was experimenting." Sienna let the rush of pleasure flow though her as she looked at him. She was feeling very clever...and very relieved. "Before I had my iPad, I had a clunky old PC and every time it jammed, I used to shut it down, count to ten, and restart it. It always worked like a charm. I thought I'd test the theory on my BMW. After all, it has a computer system...I think?"

Jack burst out laughing and Sienna ignored the tremble that ran down to her fingertips. "I'd still take it to a mechanic and get it checked out."

"I will...when I get time," she said. "Are you coming into the gallery today?"

His gaze shifted from hers and he shook his head. "No, I thought I'd look around for a place to live. I'll move into the studio if I haven't found anything after your exhibition."

Sienna reached out and put her hand over his. "I was hoping you'd come in today because I wanted to discuss my plans with you."

"Your plans?"

"Yes, I've had a...er...a change of direction."

"And..." Jack raised his brows in question.

Might as well get it out of the way now.

"I'm postponing my exhibition." She couldn't bring herself to say cancelling. When he went to speak, she interrupted. "I don't

316

want to rush it. When I hold it, I want it all to be just right, and I've left it too late to give it my best work. So there's no hurry for me to finish my work. You can start using the studio as soon as you want to."

That sounded better than saying I gave all my money to my scheming aunt and I can't afford it now.

"No, you can't do that," Jack shook his head. "I'll come in today and we can talk about it. If you're running out of time, I'll help out. I'll hire someone else to work in the gallery while you get your pieces ready. And don't worry, I'll still pay you."

A sweet feeling of gratitude rushed through her and she squeezed his fingers. He really was a nice guy, but it was too late. "That's really kind of you, but I've made up my mind. I'm not ready. In a few months, I'll be in a better place."

"A better place? You're leaving the gallery?" Jack's brow wrinkled in a frown.

"No, I meant a better place personally." As soon as the words were out, Sienna bit her lip. *Shit*, she hadn't meant to say that. "I haven't decided about the gallery. Apart from deciding to postpone my exhibition."

"Personally? You *are* upset about the other night. Or was it Arielle turning up?" Jack's intent gaze was seeing way too much, and she lifted her fingers from his and put the car into gear.

"Nothing for you to worry about." She let off the handbrake and waited for him to stand up. "I'll see you later, then. Okay?"

"Okay. Have a good day. I'll call in later." Jack waved as she backed the car from the carport, and Sienna let out the breath she'd been holding. The sooner she sorted out her private life, and the sooner she decided what she was going to do about her job, the better it would be for all concerned. So much had happened in the last week, she needed to get away. As soon as Faith's birthday party was over...and she'd spoken to Georgie, she was going to take some time for herself.

Chapter Eighteen

After Sienna turned from the drive and the last flash of red sports car disappeared through the trees, Jack walked back inside. The place felt empty without her. He flicked on the coffeemaker and drew a deep breath as her perfume lingered in the kitchen.

I've got it bad.

And he felt bad. Despite what she said, he knew Sienna was upset because they'd spent the night together, and then Arielle flitted in the next morning.

Something else was bugging her.

One minute they'd been laughing and joking and sharing a great night in bed together. Now she'd canned her exhibition and was talking about moving on, when all he wanted to do was take her in his arms and try to make it up to her. He'd been in knots wondering how he was going to take over the studio and leave her without somewhere to work. He thought he'd wanted to date Sienna and have some fun, without living and working in the same place...now he couldn't bear to be away from her. When she was away from him, the light went out of his day. Hell, he'd even put in a day's work at the gallery if it meant spending more time with her.

What was wrong with him?

A few days away was what he needed. He'd committed to going to Faith's birthday party and was looking forward to catching up with them.

Especially Blake.

Maybe a game of golf and catching up with his mate would help him sort his head out. Blake and Ana and Sienna seemed to be great friends. Maybe it wasn't Arielle showing up that had turned her cold toward him. He shrugged; it wasn't any of his business. The week after the party, he'd jump on the bike and head down the coast and visit some of his mates down there. Then he'd come back, move into a new place, and get to work on his sculptures.

Here, in my *studio.* He didn't need to be around her.

It was so out of character for him to be worrying about things out of his control. He needed to chill and get his head back together.

He wandered through the apartment with his coffee and looked out the window over the lake. Despite being here such a short time, he felt right at home in this place, and it was going to be hard to move out. Maybe if he offered the right money, he could talk Sienna into selling it to him, especially if she decided to move on to another gallery or back up the coast. But if she did, he'd miss her, and he really hoped she'd choose to stay on at the Sea View Gallery.

He picked up his cell and dialled Blake's number. No time like the present.

"Jack! How's it going?" Blake's voice was upbeat as usual. Since he'd settled in the Sunshine Coast hinterland, Blake had unwound, and the uptight executive had changed into a laidback husband and father

"Hey, mate. I was wondering if you had time for a game of golf in your busy schedule?"

"Maybe. When were you planning to come up and play?"

"How about I stay up there and we get together the day after the birthday party?" Jack grinned.

"Sounds like a plan. How's the gallery going?" Blake's tone was bland.

"Hidden subtext? You mean how are Sienna and I getting along?"

"Yeah, I thought you might have some issues there." Blake laughed. "She's the toughest of the three girls. I wondered how things were going down there with you two. Ana hasn't spoken to her for a few days."

"We're getting on very well. She's a great person. She's a talented artist and she's done a great job with the gallery in the short time she's been here. And her house is amazing."

"Still smitten, then?"

"No, we have a business relationship, that's all. You know me, I don't mix business and pleasure." A little white lie, but it wasn't the right thing to share, even with a good mate.

"But you've been out to her place?"

"I'm actually living in her apartment—"

"You always were a fast mover."

"I'm taking it slow." That's as much as Jack was going to say.

"I've got some news for you, Jack. This golf game will be the last for a while. Ana and I are moving back to Melbourne for a year. I'm helping your dad out for a few months."

"How come? I thought you loved it up here?" A twinge of guilt was quickly pushed away. Dad knew he wasn't coming back, so getting Blake back to Melbourne was a good move. He was just surprised that Blake had agreed to go.

"Won't be for long. Ana was hoping you'd look out for Sienna a bit."

"I think she's pretty good at looking out for herself."

"That's the front she puts up, but she's as soft as butter beneath that." Blake's voice was protective. "But hey, listen. Don't hurt her, okay? She's a special lady."

Ah, maybe Ana moving away was what had upset Sienna? Jack wanted to get off the call so he could think things through a bit more. "Listen, I'm just on my way out. I'll see you at the party."

"Looking forward to it. Never thought I'd end up a doting dad and husband. Lot to be said for it, Jack."

"Not for me, mate. See you soon." He disconnected the call and headed for the shower. It was time to go and find a place to live before he got too settled in here.

***

By the middle of the morning, Sienna had cancelled all of the arrangements for the exhibition and taken down the posters from the window of the gallery. All she had to do was go for a walk and get the posters taken down in the post office and the few shops that had agreed to put them up for her around Noosa. And she'd taken a call from Katy, the new gallery assistant, saying she had a job in Brisbane and wouldn't be able to help out. She'd close at lunchtime, unless Jack came in to look after the gallery.

She swallowed hard and leaned back against her chair; regret spiked her chest. She'd have her show one day. For the first time since she'd moved to Noosa, Sienna looked around the gallery and thought of moving on. Maybe she would sell her house to Jack. Ever since Marjorie had dropped the truth on her, she'd found it hard to get motivated, and she even wondered for the first time if she was kidding herself thinking she could be a successful artist.

The pieces on the shelves glowed beneath the soft light, and she watched as a couple of tourists admired the display across the room. Her work here was done, and it was time to think about where she was going. In one way, Marjorie had done her a favour and pushed her to make the decision about the gallery—and Jack—more quickly. Sienna knew she had to get away, because he was altogether too damned sexy, and it would only be a matter of time before she gave in to what she wanted. Getting involved with him was too complicated. There were so many things she didn't like about him. He was too laidback and casual about this business, he'd lied to her about being an artist, and...

But if she was honest, she knew she was stretching it,

322

because she was so damned attracted to him. She wasn't going to get involved with anyone. She was keeping her heart intact from now on. Relationships were not for her. Not with anyone. Not with him.

Him. Jack.

And she intended to keep her life private and her emotions safe.

Sienna touched the screen of her iPad and opened a browser window. Her fingers hovered over the touch-screen keyboard, until she drew a deep breath and typed in the words "Catherine Elizabeth Stuart, Tamworth." She'd looked at the birth certificate so many times, it was almost falling to pieces.

Tears filled her eyes. Of course the first damn search result pulled up her mother's name and her dates of birth and death. Nothing was private these days. You could Google just about anything, but the last thing Sienna had expected to see was her mother's life dates on the screen in front of her. Her vision blurred as she ran her finger down the screen and read the funeral notice that had obviously been scanned in from a funeral home. She checked the website; it was archived newspaper issues scanned and indexed as a part of a local history project for an ancestry database. She emailed the page to the printer and put the iPad aside as a customer wandered over with a small vase in her hand.

Brushing her eyes with the back of her hand, Sienna greeted the lady with a smile. "You've chosen a lovely piece."

She still had a job to do.

Jack wandered in mid-afternoon. She'd closed the gallery at noon and visited the shops to take down the ads. The disappointment expressed by the locals that her show had been postponed had lifted her, one of the best things that happened to her this week.

Almost the best.

Her thoughts went straight back to the night with Jack in

323

the studio. Nothing could compare to that. She pushed away the thought, and because she was trying to block it out, her voice was short when she greeted him

"I'm about to close."

"That's fine. I came in to take you for dinner before you go home."

Sienna's head flew up. "Why?"

"Because you look like you need cheering up...and I wanted to convince you I'm a nice guy."

Tears pricked her eyes again. She'd been so damn emotional since Marjorie had dropped the news on her, she was tearing up at stupid things, and it wasn't the way she usually dealt with problems. Not by a long shot.

Turning away so he couldn't see her eyes fill, Sienna slid her iPad into its case. "There's no need for that. I told you last night what you do has nothing to do with me."

"Okay, how about we go to dinner and talk about why you've cancelled your show."

"No." Sienna put her iPad in the drawer beneath the desk and shut it with a firm push. The tiny desk rocked on its narrow legs, and Jack grabbed for the antique lamp that teetered on the corner at the same time she did. Their fingers brushed and she pulled back when her skin tingled.

"Whoa, that was close." He lifted the lamp and put it closer to the middle of the desk.

"Thank you."

"Okay, third and final try. One, I don't need to explain Arielle to you?"

"No."

"Two, you don't want to talk about your exhibition?"

"No." Sienna glanced up at him from beneath her lashes, and her breath caught in her throat. She bit down the beginning of a smile that was playing around her mouth as Jack got down on to his knees.

"Three." He put his hands together in front of his chest and Sienna let the smile spread.

"Three?" she asked.

"I want to go back to that fantastic Italian restaurant, and I hate eating alone, and I enjoy your company. Is that enough?"

For the first time since she'd raced him last night, a laugh bubbled up from Sienna's chest and she let it out past her lips. "You are one very persuasive man, Jack."

"And a hungry one. So, dinner?" He pushed to his feet and crooked his arm and held it out to her."

Sienna stared at his arm as a breathless feeling radiated throughout her chest. She had an inkling she was making a big mistake, but she guessed she had to eat. She would go and see Georgie tomorrow.

"How about a compromise? Instead of going all the way to Coolum, there's a nice little Italian restaurant around the corner." She pressed her lips tightly together, so she didn't look too enthusiastic, and ignored Jack's arm when she glanced at her watch. "And you do realise it's not dinnertime yet?"

"I can wait." He grinned at her. "I might have to grab a burger to see me through, but I'll look forward to Italian. Are you going home first?"

She shook her head. "No, I was going to close up here and do some accounts."

"Don't work too hard. I'll come back at six. Okay?"

Her gaze met his and held it for a long moment, and Sienna knew she'd made the wrong call. Spending more time in Jack's company than she had to was going to put her emotions in the way of logical—and safe—decision-making.

I don't need this. But the warmth filling her chest belied her thoughts.

She'd make certain they would have a quick meal, and then

she'd go home and get a good night's sleep.

By myself.

Things would look better in the morning.

They would.

Chapter Nineteen

"Sienna!" Giuseppe, the owner of the small Italian restaurant near the beach at Noosa, gathered her into a tight hug. "We haven't seen you here for a long time. How is your Uncle Renzo? I must go up to Maleny and beat him in a game of bocce. He owes me a game."

Sienna swallowed and tried to keep her composure when Giuseppe mentioned...her father. It brought the events of the last few days crashing back. She put her hand on the back of the chair to steady herself and forced a cheerful smile onto her face. "I haven't been to see him for a few weeks, but I'll let him know you're after a rematch when I'm"—she glanced at Jack— "we're up there next weekend."

She stepped to the side as Jack pulled her chair out for her, and Giuseppe opened the napkin with a dramatic flourish.

"Now, you must have the spaghetti marinara tonight." Once Sienna was seated and he'd laid the napkin on her lap, he put his fingers to his lips in a very Italian gesture. "*Delizioso.* The seafood is fresh off the boat this morning." His chest puffed out and he smiled before he walked back to the kitchen; a pang of nostalgia ran through Sienna. She missed her friends in Maleny. Apart from Ana and Georgie, they were all older folks, and many were Italians whose family had settled on the coastal fringe and worked in the sugar industry a couple of generations back. In one way she was looking forward to going back home to Faith's birthday party, but she was dreading seeing Renzo. She glanced up at Jack, who'd settled in the chair across from her. She knew the tongues would wag when he turned up at the party. Thelma and Mitzi would be in matchmaking heaven. They'd taken full credit for Blake and Ana's blissful state of matrimony, totally ignoring the fact that they'd

327

known each other since college.

"Penny for your thoughts?"

Sienna jumped as Jack's words broke through the happy background noise of the restaurant. "I was thinking about Montville. You're still coming to Faith's party?"

"Of course. I'm not going to let my Prince Charming tights go to waste." Jack grinned at her, and that ever-present warmth that filled her whenever she was near him spread a little further. "And I'm golfing with Blake on Monday."

"So you're not going to come back and open the gallery the day after the party. Did you get my message about taking time off?" She'd sent him an email about taking time off, and about Katy, but he hadn't replied.

"No, I haven't checked." Jack held her gaze as he picked up the water carafe and filled her glass.

Of course he hadn't.

"That's fine. Whatever suits you. You're the boss. I might just close the gallery for a few days."

"No, Jack. *You're* the boss. I'm the manager." His casual attitude really got under her skin at times. For the life of her she still couldn't understand why he'd bought the place. It would have been easier to buy a regular studio space. He said he wanted nothing to do with running a business and having any responsibility, but sometimes she sensed it was an act he put on. No one could be that relaxed and carefree all the time.

Could they?

"So you don't check your email either?"

He shrugged. "I got fed up with email when I was working for the company when Dad was sick. People expect you to jump immediately just because they can send you an email any time of the day or night."

Sienna held his gaze and watched him. He leaned back casually in his chair and looked at her, but it was hard to see what

328

he was thinking.

"I check it once a day." He sounded a little defensive. Great, she'd gotten under his skin. It felt good to get a reaction out of him. She decided to push a little harder.

It was as good a time as any to tell him she'd come to a decision. "I might as well tell you now. I've decided to leave at the end of the month, so if you're not interested in the gallery yourself, you'd better start looking for another manager." Sienna sipped her water and looked over the rim of the glass at him.

Jack steepled his fingers beneath his chin and stared back at her. The grin had left his face and his eyes were hooded. "You've made up your mind. I can't persuade you to stay?"

Sienna held his gaze and shook her head, still wondering if she'd made the wrong decision. Now that she'd put it into words, she'd have to stick with it.

"Where are you going?" His voice was soft, and she leaned forward to hear.

"I don't know. I've got some things I need to do. I might travel for a while."

"Shit, Sienna." Jack's voice held a rough edge. "You sure know how to make a guy feel bad. Where did all this come from? A few days ago, you were on a path to buying the gallery and having your first show." He reached across to take her hand, but she pulled it away and clenched it in her lap as he kept talking.

"Changing my mind about selling can't have had such an impact on your decision so quickly?"

For a fleeting moment the perplexed look on Jack's usually happy face, and the concern in his voice, rattled her, and she was tempted to tell him everything that had happened. She opened her mouth, and then she remembered what a laidback guy he was. Would he care? She wasn't going to risk it.

Keep your private business close to your heart. Don't depend on anyone else.

329

Taking a deep breath, she crossed her arms. "Don't concern yourself. I'm a flighty person, always changing my mind. You probably did me a favour. Just ask the girls next weekend. You can't rely on me."

Jack's eyes hadn't left her face, and she dropped her gaze to her lap, surprised to see her hands were white from clenching them so tightly. She relaxed them and looked back up at him as he leaned forward.

"Well, I hope you change it back again, because you're making the wrong decision based on very little reason."

The anger that shot through her was welcome. She was well and truly sick of feeling sorry for herself, and she lashed out at him. "Oh, do you? And what do you know about me? Do you think one night in my bed—actually it's your bed, isn't it, I keep forgetting—makes you an expert on how I feel and gives you the right to tell me you think I should change my mind back again?"

Jack held up his hand. "There's no need to be so angry."

Regret spiked through her chest. There was no need to take it out on Jack. Even though he drove her crazy with his casual attitude, he *was* too nice a guy to wear her temper. And way too nice for her peace of mind.

"Ignore me. I've been feeling sorry for myself and it's time to get over it." She swallowed and held his green-eyed gaze, trying to ignore the regret that was filling her. Maybe they could have had a relationship if he'd sold her the gallery. Just as well it had turned out the way it had, because she'd been sucked in by him. He'd almost gotten past her resolve of not investing emotionally in a relationship. Marjorie and Arielle had turned up in the nick of time. It would have been a huge mistake.

"I've got some news you might like. I'm selling my house, too. If you're still interested you can have first option on it. It'll save me a lot of time before I head off."

This time she couldn't help the tears that filled her eyes,

and she brushed them away angrily before they could spill onto her cheeks.

My job, my exhibition, and my cottage. And worst of all my sister. All from the telling of one truth by the woman she had thought was her mother. Sienna had lost so much in the last few days. She wasn't even going to think about losing what might have been with Jack. She steeled herself and swallowed back her despair

"Now let's order and get out of here as soon as we can. This was a bad idea."

***

Jack felt like a total and absolute heel. His move to Noosa and his decision to keep the gallery—the gallery that he'd had nothing to do with since he'd bought it—had brought a lot of turmoil into Sienna's life. He'd never been able to handle it when a woman cried. Arielle had picked that up mighty quick, and now Sienna was on the verge of tears. But she wasn't ready to fall into his arms to be comforted—she had her hard shell back up and in place.

The silence stretched uncomfortably as their meals were delivered; he ate without tasting anything. Finally, Sienna pushed her plate to the side and held his gaze.

Her eyes were huge and touched by shadows on the fine, transparent skin beneath them. Her cheeks were lightly flushed, and her full lips set in a straight line. A pang of sympathy shot through him, and his fingers itched to reach out and cup her face.

"I've had enough. Can you pay the bill? I'll see you tomorrow." The legs of the chair scraped on the tiled floor with a loud squeak when Sienna pushed it back and rose gracefully to her feet. Her shoulders were stiff, and he sensed she was only just holding herself together.

"I'm sorry. I'm not very good company tonight." Sienna's voice was soft, and she avoided his gaze.

"Wait for me. I'll walk you back." He kept his voice firm. "We need to talk."

Sienna ignored him and strode to the door, giving Giuseppe a wave in the kitchen as she hurried past. Jack pulled out his wallet and threw a hundred-dollar bill to the waitress. "Keep the change." He pushed open the door and looked up the street. She must have run, because she was almost to the corner of the street where the gallery was.

"Wait," he called after her as he took off in a jog. Even without running shoes, she had the key to the front door in her hand by the time he caught up.

"I asked you to wait for me."

"I heard you, and I didn't want to."

Jack took her arm gently. "Sienna, listen to me. We're going to sit down and talk this out."

"I don't want to."

Jack ran his fingers through his hair. "Well, I do." He took the key from her and opened the door with one hand without letting her go with the other. Sienna tried to pull away as he gently led her through the gallery to the studio.

"I'm not going to let you go, or you'll take off."

She glared at him without speaking. At least the tears had gone. They reached the sofa bed, and he sat her down on it before he let go of her arm. He stood in front of the sofa and crossed his arms.

"I've changed my mind." Jack waited for her to look at him after he spoke.

She lifted her head. "About what?" Her face was closed, but at least she was listening to him.

"About the gallery. About the studio." He crouched down in front of her, and the whiff of perfume that reached him pulled him back two nights to when they'd been laughing together in this bed. Jack held her gaze with his. "I've watched you work here, and I know how well you do it. I'm going to contact Dad's secretary and tell her to redo the contract and we'll go ahead with the sale."

She gazed up at him. "You can't do that. What about your commission?"

He waved his hand and grinned. "I'll sort something out. It's not the end of the world if it's a bit late." Surprise shot through him as his words hung in the air. He realised it didn't matter. Sienna's happiness was more important than anything he had to prove to himself...or his father. Or had thought he did. Yeah, he had a deadline, and he wanted to show Dad he wasn't a loser, but none of that mattered. Sienna's happiness was more important to him. His priorities had switched, and he hadn't even been aware of it happening. Money wasn't going to rule his life; if he lost this commission, there would be more.

Her sharp floral perfume washed over him as her eyes lit up, and then her face closed again as she drew her lips together. "I don't want it anymore."

"Sienna, do you know what you want?" As soon as the words left his lips, he regretted them.

Her mouth dropped open as she took a deep breath, and he couldn't keep his eyes off her lips. "Oh, yes, Jack. I do. But what I want, and what's right for me, are not necessarily the same thing."

Goddamn it, he couldn't help himself. His arms seemed to go around her of their own accord and he crushed her against his chest. He dropped his chin to the top of her head as she leaned into him and relaxed. "I'm sorry I've made you so unhappy by coming to Noosa."

He felt her take another deep breath before she pulled away and tipped her head back. "It's okay." Her eyes held his steadily, and a flash of desire shot through him. "It's not you."

"I made the wrong decision in the first place. You've just helped me move forward with some personal issues I have to consider now."

Jack shook his head slowly. "Has it got anything to do with Arielle?"

Sienna stared at him for a moment longer before she reached up and patted his cheek in an almost motherly touch. "No, it hasn't. You're a good man, Jack. You're very kind and thoughtful, but it's too late. You're not as casual and carefree as you try to make out you are."

She moved away from him and stood. "Now, I'm going home. I'll see you tomorrow if you come into the gallery."

Jack rocked back on his heels and watched as she picked up her bag and pulled her car keys out. He didn't follow when she let herself out of the back door. He waited till the throaty purr of her car reached him as she backed out of the parking space. At least it had started.

He stood and dropped onto the soft cushions and inhaled her floral perfume which lingered in the air. The sofa bed was looking good. He couldn't trust himself to stay away from Sienna if he followed her home.

***

Sienna walked into the cold, empty bedroom and threw her bag onto the bed. It landed with a soft *thump* and she crossed to the window. The moon was hidden behind heavy clouds and the night was dark. It suited her mood. Leaving Jack had been hard; when he'd held her, she'd enjoyed the comfort of his arms and tried to ignore the excitement that his touch brought. But the last few days had reinforced her conviction not to let anyone too close—not even Jack, though it was so very tempting to lean on him.

Georgie had hit the nail on the head. "It'll just complicate matters if you have to work for him," she'd said. But neither of them had any idea that Sienna would fall for him. Or what this week would bring.

Admitting to herself that she was falling for him was in a strange way, cathartic, and Sienna felt a bit happier. She turned away from the window and her gaze settled on her cell phone, which must have fallen to the floor when she threw her bag onto the bed. She groaned as she picked it up. She scrolled though over twenty missed texts and calls from Georgie. All thoughts of Jack fled from her mind as her protective instinct kicked in.

"Damn it. Marjorie, if you've told her and broken your word, I'll have my money back." Sienna muttered under her breath as she scrolled though message by message trying to see if Georgie knew the truth.

When Jack said he'd still sell her the gallery, hope had filled her for an instant, before she remembered she'd given Marjorie her life savings. The bank wouldn't approve the business loan without a substantial deposit. Now her bank account was empty, and it looked like giving the money to Marjorie to buy her silence had been a waste of time.

How could I have been so gullible?

She held the phone in her hand and looked at the screen as she tried to decide what to do. There was no decision to be made. She took a deep breath and pressed speed dial for Georgie. She should have gone up to Maleny tonight and not given in to the temptation of being with Jack.

Georgie's voice broke as soon as she answered the call. "No matter what she's done, she can't destroy our relationship. We're still sisters."

"She told you." Sienna fought back the dismay that flooded through her. "What about...have you seen Uncle...Renzo?" she asked. She was still having difficulty coming to terms with him being her father and not her uncle.

"No, but Marjorie said she told him she was going to tell both of us."

"She promised me she wouldn't tell you. I wanted to tell you."

"You don't always have to be the strong one, you know. I'm not as weak as you seem to think."

Tears ached behind Sienna's eyes. "I'm sorry. I just wanted

to be there when you found out. After all"—she tried to inject some mirth into her voice to lighten the mood— "I am the oldest.

"You are. But I'm okay. It makes sense, doesn't it?"

Sienna wiped her eyes with the back of her hand. "Yes, it does."

"Are you coming up to see Uncle Renzo?"

"No, and I'm not going to call. I'll see him at Faith's party."

"Love ya, sis. Remember I worry about you, too. You don't have to do all the worry for both of us."

Sienna swallowed. Georgie would be so upset when she heard she'd paid off Marjorie.

They ended the call and Sienna gave way to the tears. She didn't feel very strong at the moment. She wiped her face with the back of her hands; it was time to pull herself together and get on with her life. How could things have changed so much since their birthdays such a short time ago?

The rest of the week passed quickly. Sienna avoided Jack on the odd occasion he came into the gallery. Luckily the gallery was busy, and she'd been with customers each time he walked in. He must have been staying in the studio because there'd been no sign of him at the house each night.

Sienna started to clear out the studio; she packed up the frogs and took them home. Her car hadn't let her down again, and she decided it was a glitch she'd ignore. Hopefully it was all right, because she couldn't afford to get it fixed. She straightened her shoulders with a grim smile; she couldn't afford anything, but she was not going to give in to tears.

The gallery was quiet this morning, and there had been no sign of Jack since yesterday. She stared at the display on the shelves in front of her, flicking a duster without really seeing what was in front of her. The conversation with Georgie the other night had

336

been emotional, and she was pleased Jack had given her some space since then. Maybe the situation wasn't going to be too bad. The next hurdle was seeing Renzo—her father. Once she'd done that, she could figure out what was next.

As much as she tried, she couldn't put Jack out of her thoughts. The worst part about the week had been his absence. Even though it had been merely a week, she'd seen him only from a distance and she missed him around the gallery and the house. He was obviously avoiding her, and that was something she was going to have to get over. She'd booked a flight south for the night of Faith's party and she needed to make sure Jack had found someone to look after the place. He couldn't shut it, no matter what he said. That would be bad for business. She typed him an email. They could work out the details on the weekend at the birthday party.

A reluctant smile tugged at her lips. But would he check it?

Chapter Twenty

Sienna leaned closer to the mirror and drew a perfect circle on each cheek before filling it in with bright pink lip gloss. Being an artist and having a steady hand helped with getting into costume. Hopefully, she'd remember to keep her hands away from her face while she was driving up to Maleny. She'd figured it was easier to get dressed in the fairy costume and wear it and carry a change of clothes for the plane in the backpack she packed for her trip. She'd already asked Georgie to take her to the airport.

Smoothing down the stiff tulle of the short skirt, she pirouetted and grinned at herself in the mirror. She could just see little Faith clapping her hands when the three fairies arrived in costume for her party. The low throb of a motorcycle engine caught her attention and her hands stilled on the skirt of the costume and her heart sped up. She tried to ignore the excited anticipation that curled in her stomach.

I wonder why he's here.

She'd been hoping to see Jack before the party, because she wanted to apologise to him for her moodiness the other night. Now that she was beginning to get used to the bombshell that Marjorie had dropped, her mood had improved, and she was more settled—or had been until she'd heard the deep roar of the motorbike.

She waited for Jack to come through the house, biting her lip as she stood there. She hoped he still felt comfortable enough to come in. A couple of taps at the front door sounded rather than the expected turn of a key she'd waited to hear.

Holding her breath, and with her hands clenched together in front of her, Sienna took one last look in the mirror before she crossed the hall to open the door.

At least the fairy clothes might lighten the situation.

"Wow, a fairy princess."

Sienna held the sides of the tulle skirt and dropped into a little curtsy. Jack's face lit up in a wide grin and a pleasant shiver trembled down her back. If anything, he was more tanned and relaxed than he'd been earlier in the week when he'd last been in the gallery. It was impossible to upset the man. He was always so damned *happy.*

"That's me. What can I do for you, Jack?"

"I'm on my way to the birthday party, but my Prince Charming costume is here."

She stepped back to let him inside.

"I was going to get in my costume when I got there. Maybe I should get changed before I go?"

A little devil poked her as she thought of Jack riding up the highway as Prince Charming. "Definitely. Ana made it quite clear on the invitation that we all arrive in costume."

"Hmm. I'm going to look ridiculous riding up the mountain." His nonchalant grin sent a tremble down her back.

"You are." Sienna smiled at him. She felt so much better now that he'd stopped by. "I'm going straight to the airport after the party." She wasn't going to tell him where she was going. Or why she was going there. He unsettled her enough without adding feeling sorry for her to the mix. She *had* to get over him.

"Okay. The holiday will do you a lot of good. You work too hard." He grinned and her heart went triple time as the sexy crinkles around his eyes deepened.

"Why didn't you use your key?" She followed him down the hall. "You didn't have to knock."

"I thought it was more polite."

"Have you been sleeping in the studio?" If he had, he'd been gone every morning when she'd got there.

"No, I've been staying at a hotel."

Guilt ran through her, and she frowned. "You didn't have to do that."

"No problem. Once you finish up at the gallery, I'll stay in the studio." He stared at her. "You know yourself how convenient it is to work and sleep there."

"Yes, I do." Heat filled her cheeks as she thought of the last time she'd spent the night there. "It's a great space. It's got everything you could need."

The last couple of days had passed in a blur, but the time she'd spent finalising the bookings and the accounts had been hard, especially not knowing where she was going to go after she left here. Every time the phone had rung about her cancelled exhibition, Sienna's confusion deepened, and she was almost—only almost—beginning to regret her quick decision to leave. As far as cancelling the exhibition went, she'd had no choice; she couldn't afford to pay for it now. Once she visited her mother's grave, she was going to find closure and think about her future.

"Sienna?" Jack's voice interrupted her thoughts. "I've parked behind your car. Can you wait until I get changed?"

"Sure, I still have to pack the cakes up."

Jack disappeared into the apartment. "I'll be quick."

Sienna went to the kitchen and transferred the fairy cakes from the fridge to a large container. She hummed a nursery rhyme as she worked; Mitzi and Thelma would be proud of her—a domestic goddess and cook she was not. She stepped back and surveyed her creation. As much detailed work had gone into decorating each cake as she put into her sculptures. Each cake was topped with a couple of little fairy-tale characters in a profusion of bright primary colours.

"They're not for eating, are they?" Jack must have been standing close behind her, because she could feel his breath on her neck. "They're fantastic. Make sure you get a photo of them."

Sienna stepped sideways away from the warmth of his arm when he pointed to the cakes. She walked around to the other side of the table and reached for the lid of the container before leaning across and snapping it shut. "Will you carry…oh my goodness!"

Her hand flew to her mouth to stifle the giggle that threatened to spill over.

With his sun-lightened hair and his tanned face, not to mention the skin-tight costume, Jack made a stunning Prince Charming.

"You like?" He grinned and dropped into a bow. Hot–pink tights encased his long muscular thighs, and a deep green slimline satin top was tucked into the waistband of his tights

"You look like the guy in *Shrek*." She stumbled over the words when heat reached her cheeks; she was grateful for the pink makeup. Every inch of him was outlined by the tights.

"Which one? Not the Mummy's boy one?"

She let the giggle spill out. "Yes, *that* one. I think that's the costume they've sold you."

"But is it okay?"

"Yes, I love it." She lifted her gaze to meet his as her giggle broke into a laugh. "You're not really going to ride your bike like that?" She looked down at the heavy motorcycle boots he held in one hand. "I guess you are."

"It's good to see you smile again, Sienna." He held her gaze. "There's something I want to talk to you about."

No, he sounded way too serious. She ignored his words and the tremble that ran down her back. "You'll certainly attract some attention on the road."

"I've done worse," he said with a sexy grin, and the tremble hit her legs.

It was good to have him back around. She liked the happy way he made her feel but wasn't so sure about the shaky feeling that went with it. "I don't think I need to know."

"Come on. Time to go to the party." He held his free hand out for the cake box. "And we are going to find time for a talk sometime this afternoon before you leave."

**

Jack waited beside Sienna's car as she lifted a red backpack into the trunk. He hated the thought of her leaving and wondered where she was going on her trip—she was travelling light—but he didn't want to pry. He'd done a lot of thinking over the past few days and he'd decided he was going to back off, but one look at her in that fairy dress and he was smitten again. He had fallen for her, and he didn't know what to do about it. All he knew was that he didn't want her to leave. She seemed a lot happier today, and it had been great to hear her laugh ring out. But he was going to tell her how he felt before the day was over.

Once her bag was stowed, he handed her the cake box and she opened the door and placed it carefully on the backseat. "I'll follow you," he said. "I don't quite remember where Blake and Ana live."

"Okay." She slipped into her car and Jack walked across to his bike. He pulled his boots on, swung his tights-clad leg over the seat, and waited for Sienna to start her car. After a couple of minutes, she opened the door and stood by the car.

"One, two, three," she muttered under her breath as he got closer.

"You haven't had your car fixed yet, have you?" he asked.

"No, I didn't have time." She frowned. "Bugger, I didn't need this today of all days." "Four...five..." She finished counting to ten. "It must have something to do with the battery, because if I get out and wait it always starts when I get back in."

Jack shrugged and waited for her to get back in. "That's not very logical. Make sure you have it serviced as soon as you get back from your holiday."

Sienna tried the engine again, but the only sound was a loud

342

click. He waited while she tried again. As she climbed from the car, she shot him a regretful smile.

"I guess I'm going to miss the party after all."

Jack looked at her. Her brightly painted pink lips were clamped together tightly and her forehead was still wrinkled in a frown.

"Have you got a couple of smaller containers?" He grinned as the solution hit him.

"What for?"

"The cakes. If you've got some smaller containers they'll fit." He pointed to the panniers on each side of the bike.

"That's thoughtful of you," she said. "At least Faith won't miss out on the cakes. Show them to Thelma and Mitzi before they get eaten. And make sure they know I made them. Oh, I forgot, do you know them?"

Jack grinned at her. "No, I don't. But you can tell them yourself."

"I can?"

"Open your trunk." With a curious look, she did as he asked. He walked over and lifted out her backpack. "You've only got the cakes and that bag?"

"You think I'm going to go there on your motorbike?"

"Yes. You can wear the backpack and we'll put the cakes in there." He hoped like hell that she'd agree. "And then you won't miss out on the party. I'm sure someone will give you a lift to the airport later. And if not, I can take you on the bike."

His breath caught in his throat as her face broke into a wide grin.

"Serves me right for laughing at the thought of you riding up the highway in your costume. I guess you'd call it poetic justice. But I'll do it for Faith. I won't miss her birthday." She shook her head. "You know what? We'll both look ridiculous. But maybe that's just what I need."

343

Her laugh tinkled around him and he watched in appreciation as she grabbed the cake container from the car and hurried up the stairs. She wore pink tights beneath the short skirt, and her feet were encased in dainty silver slippers.

"You'll have to change your shoes," he called after her, trying to ignore the anticipation that was curling in his gut. Things were going his way.

A couple of minutes later, Sienna pulled the front door shut and ran lightly down the stairs. He waited at the bottom and took the two containers she passed him.

He looked down approvingly at her feet. She'd shed her sparkly slippers, and the pink tights were tucked into a pair of purple Doc Martens boots.

"Nice," he said. He couldn't take his eyes from her as she stared at him with a smile.

God, she is so beautiful.

"Take me to the party, Prince Charming."

Trying to keep his attention on the winding mountain curves was one of the hardest things Jack had ever done. Sienna's soft breasts pressed into his back and her hands clung to his waist. Every time a car tooted at them, she leaned forward and laughed in his ear, pressing even closer. It got to the point that he prayed no one else honked at them and she'd move back, because he'd be in no state to get off the bike wearing his pink Prince Charming tights. He knew now why they were called tights.

Sienna leaned forward and called out. "Two more driveways and then turn left into the third one. It's the driveway with the yellow mailbox."

Thank God, we're almost there.

Jack focused on the road, the bike, the sky, the trees, and the occasional glimpse of the silvery ocean at the bottom of the mountain—anything to forget the soft swells pressed up against his

344

back. Up until he'd met Sienna, he'd been happy to be a loner. Life by himself had satisfied him. In fact, he'd needed the space. The thought of her leaving wrenched at his heart. If it meant keeping her by his side, he'd give up the gallery, his commissions, and if it was what she wanted of him, hell, he'd even go back into business and take life more seriously. Since he'd been out on the Sunny Coast, and since he'd fallen, yes, fallen in love with Sienna, he was prepared to change his ways.

Now was he able to convince her that he could?

Chapter Twenty-One

Jack steered the bike slowly to the end of a row of cars parked on the grass in front of Blake and Ana's cottage. The trip up from the coast had been exhilarating, and despite knowing what was waiting for her at the destination, Sienna had enjoyed every mile.

Sitting behind Jack, with her arms around his muscular frame, she'd wished the trip could go forever. But reality intruded as he drove the bike slowly through the gate. A tall, thin man with a craggy face and black hair stood leaning against the fence. He dropped his cigarette and buried it in the soft ground with the toe of his boot. Jack cut the motor and Sienna slid off the back of the bike. She stood beside him as he reached down and unclipped the helmet before lifting it from her head. She dropped her gaze from his and turned away without speaking. Her life was about to change, and she wasn't sure how she was going to handle this meeting. Conscious that Jack was watching curiously, she gave him a hesitant smile before walking over to the man who was waiting for her.

Uncle Renzo. My father.

He stepped toward her and held out his arms. Sienna caught a glimpse of Georgie standing on the porch watching, before the tears blurred her vision.

"*Mia figlia.*" My daughter. His voice was ragged, and she forgot all about Jack as her father held her close.

"I'm so sorry." His words hitched as she leaned into him and inhaled the familiar fragrance of this man who'd raised her. Tobacco and Old Spice aftershave mixed together in a familiar fragrance that brought back memories of sitting on his knee when he'd read her stories.

My father.

"I made a promise to Marjorie when she gave you to us, and Lucia made me keep it. So many times, I wished to tell you, but we could see how attached you and Georgie were. I knew if I broke it, Marjorie would come back and take Georgie."

"It's all right." Sienna stepped back and looked at her father. "I'm all right. I understand."

"And so do I." Sienna moved her gaze from Renzo to Georgie, who was standing beside Aunt Lucia on the porch, and happiness washed through her. Dressed in a similar outfit to Sienna, the pink of the fairy costume clashed ferociously with her tumbling red curls. Renzo held Sienna's hand tightly as they crossed the small patch of lawn and waited at the bottom of the steps. Aunt Lucia smiled down at them and Sienna could see the sheen of tears in her eyes. Georgie hurried down and jumped off the last step and stood beside her. Despite the tears in her eyes, she grinned and reached out to hug Sienna.

"Hey, sis."

Sienna hugged her back. "Hey to you too, sis."

"Let's go find the birthday girl," Sienna said, turning and looking around. "Ooh, I forgot about Jack."

Georgie squeezed her fingers. "He went around the back way. Love his costume. So what gives there?"

"I'll tell you later. You go find Ana and Faith, and I'll catch you up."

Jack was standing next to Blake at the edge of the lawn.

"Jack, did you remember the cakes?"

"No, I didn't. Sorry. I put your bag on the front porch, but I forgot the cakes."

"They might be a bit icky by now." Sienna followed Jack around to the front where the bike was parked. "You and Blake make a fine pair. Did you synchronise your costumes?"

A ripple ran through her at his sexy chuckle.

"No, coincidental." He looked down at his legs with a grimace. "He was the lucky one. He didn't have to wear tights. If I'd known he was dressing as Shrek, I could have come as Donkey."

"Or Princess Fiona." Sienna couldn't resist teasing him. "Seriously, Jack. You look gorgeous...and you know it."

She looked at him, letting her gaze sweep up from his boots. His long, muscular legs looked even bigger in the hot-pink tights, and when her gaze reached the tops of his thighs, she lifted it quickly to his face. He ran his hand through his hair, a gesture she was beginning to recognise when he was unsure of how to read her. She glanced around; no one was following them, and she put her hand on his arm. She couldn't help herself; she had to touch him.

"Thanks for the ride up. I enjoyed it very much."

"So did I." His gaze locked with hers and they shared a long look before Sienna dropped her eyes.

She cleared her throat and reached to the clip on the side of the pannier. "It was important that I come today. There was some family stuff I had to deal with. So, thank you."

He put his hand on top of hers as she undid the clip, and a warm tingle ran up her arm.

"No need to thank me. It's good to see a smile back on your face and..."

Sienna waited for him to continue, but he hesitated. He dropped his hand and waited while she unclipped the cover on the top of the compartment and reached in for the container.

"Great driving. All intact."

"Sienna?" The emotion in his voice sent panic spiralling through her, and she lifted her gaze. His green eyes captured hers and her breath caught.

No. She didn't want to hear it. She could read his mind before he even spoke.

God, she was acting like a teenager. She'd never let a man affect her like that before, and she wasn't about to start now. Men had been put in their right place from the minute she'd discovered them in her teens. She swallowed and straightened her shoulders.

"What?"

Jack took the cake container from her. "Once we go around the back and join in the party, you're going to get lost in the crowd. I want to tell you how I feel before the day ends, and right now is as good as ever." He reached out and took her shoulders with gentle fingers and Sienna's breath caught.

No.

"I've fallen for you, Sienna." Jack held her gaze, and the panic swelled in her chest. "I love being with you. I love watching you move. You're beautiful, you're talented. Forget the gallery, forget our work relationship…just trust how we feel."

Her throat closed as he slid his hands down her arms and held her elbows, pulling her closer.

"You do know what I am saying, don't you?"

She clung to him and his muscles flexed beneath the green Lycra of his shirt. She'd never seen him in anything but jeans and T-shirts, and she didn't want to think about how devastating he would look in a suit.

"I'm sorry." Her voice broke as she shook her head, and she saw the instant his face closed to her. "Jack, we might look like we believe in fairy tales, but there's no such thing as happy ever after."

No matter what he believed or how he thought he felt, Sienna wasn't going to be a part of it. She couldn't trust—even though her heart was screaming at her to listen to him. Marjorie had ensured enough hurt to last them all a lifetime, and Sienna didn't intend to add to it by listening to Jack. She pulled away from his grip and fought the tears that were threatening to fall.

"I'm sorry. I just can't. It's got nothing to do with you."

She could give him that much. "It's not the gallery, it's not you, it's me."

She left him standing there. A beautiful man in a Prince Charming suit. A man she knew she loved but couldn't risk listening to.

###

As far as parties went, it turned into a huge celebration. Faith clapped her little hands with delight as her mother, Georgie, and Sienna formed a fairy ring around her and sang "Happy Birthday."

"Goodness, you look more like your daddy every day." Sienna swung her high and kissed the little girl's cheek as they finished singing.

"She sure does." Ana looked on proudly. "How are you, Sienna? Georgie came to me as soon as Marjorie left her." Ana's voice was quiet as she looped one arm around Sienna's shoulder. "I didn't call since it wasn't something that we could talk about on the phone, and I knew it was something you and Georgie needed to talk about together."

They moved toward the table where brightly-coloured presents were piled high. Faith's little friends ran around the table looking at the presents, squealing with excitement.

"I'm fine. Really, I am. The last few days have answered a lot of questions about my life and where I'm heading." Sienna glanced up and heat ran through her as she caught Jack's intent gaze fixed on her. He was standing on the other side of Blake. She elbowed Ana and giggled. "Look at them...whoever would have thought that? Remember the first day the pair of them came into the shop and the wheelbarrows fell on you?"

Ana smiled. "I do. So, what's happened between you and Jack?"

"You and Georgie are nosy. Remember, I'm the private one who doesn't share." She softened her words as she tapped Ana with her fairy wand. "There's nothing between us. I'll tell all when

I get back."

But what was there to tell? she wondered. The feelings she had for Jack had overwhelmed her. They were unfamiliar to her and she wasn't sure she could handle rejecting him. Every time she caught his eye, her heart felt as though it was going to burst out of her chest, and her legs trembled.

They stood together as friends came over to give Faith a birthday kiss. Aldo and Maria, Joe and Magda, and many of the people she'd known all her life. She knew Jack was watching her. She couldn't stop looking over there—his gaze was fixed on her, and a tremble ran down her back. Renzo stood beside her and kept his arm around her shoulders, and a small measure of happiness filled the empty place in her chest. Knowing the truth had settled her and seemed to have taken away the distance she had always sensed that Renzo kept between them.

What Marjorie had done was a good thing. A sharp pang of sadness shot through her; it might have been good if she'd been here and there was forgiveness all around, but Georgie hadn't heard from her mother again after she'd told her the truth and disappeared with Sienna's cash. They just had to accept that Marjorie had her own problems and they couldn't do anything about it. She'd have to watch Georgie and make sure she was okay with it.

Mitzi and Thelma came over to say hello, and she was enveloped in a cloud of lavender perfume and happy laughter. They were surrounded by children. Blake's nephews and niece had come to the party and were dressed as fairy-tale characters.

"Is there cakes?" Billy, the second youngest of the five tugged at her leg. "Ana said you had the cakes."

"Yes Billy, there are lots of cakes. Did you see them?" Sienna turned to the elderly sisters and kissed each of their soft, papery cheeks. "They're over near the table with the presents."

Billy ran off and Mitzi grabbed Sienna's arm. "Yes, and we

351

saw your Prince Charming, too. Are you going to introduce us to your man?"

"My man?" Her stomach dropped. She had to nip this in the bud before Thelma and Mitzi got their hands on Jack and gave him the third degree and told him every detail of her life.

Mitzi pointed to Jack. "Prince Charming."

"Not *my* man. Jack's simply a friend who gave me a ride up here when my car wouldn't start." The two elderly women exchanged a glance, and she knew they didn't believe a word she was saying.

She escaped before they could ask more.

She was broke, thanks to Marjorie, and she'd quit her job. All she had was her house and a few boxes of frogs. And she'd offered her house to Jack...if he accepted her offer, she wouldn't have that either.

But before she left, Sienna wanted to share the news with the whole family...and their close friends. A lot of the guests had left and there was mainly family left. Sienna looked around for Jack. She wanted him to be close by. She walked over to Renzo and stood on her toes and whispered in her father's ear. "Ready?"

Renzo nodded before he called for quiet. Their family and close friends gathered around. Lucia stood beside them and held his hand. A small group of interested faces looked at her and for a moment, her vision blurred as tears filled her eyes. But they were happy tears.

"This week I found my father." Sienna's breath hitched as she caught Jack's eye. A frown wrinkled his brow.

Sienna turned to Georgie with a smile. "And Georgie and I finally discovered this week why we are so different. It's a complicated story, but I'll tell you all about that later. Today is for Faith's birthday." She turned to Renzo. "All I need to say is I have found my father and even though Georgie and I have found out we're not blood sisters...to each other we always will be true sisters."

As the party wound up, Sienna looked around for Jack, but he was nowhere to be seen. A hollow feeling settled in her stomach when she wondered if he'd left without saying good-bye. Maybe all this family stuff had been too much for him? Maybe it wasn't his scene? It had been something she needed to be a part of, and she was sorry if it had bothered him. Maybe it was too much for his laidback attitude. When she thought about it, he hadn't told her much about his family, but she'd sensed there was a problem there.

"Are you going to get changed before you leave for the airport?" Blake reached for Faith, and Sienna glanced at her watch.

"We'd better get a move on."

"Before you do, Jack was wondering if you'd see him before he leaves. He's out by his bike." Blake hoisted Faith up onto his shoulders. "Come on, young lady, let's go check out your new toys."

Georgie and Ana followed him inside and Sienna slowly made her way over to where Jack had parked. He'd changed out of his costume and into a pair of jeans and a snug black T-shirt. Standing beside the bike, he looked as sexy as hell. Deep down, Sienna was afraid. Her emotions had been on a rollercoaster for the past week, and she had to dig deep for strength. She couldn't hook up with Jack for a lot of reasons, no matter how much she wanted to.

"I thought you'd left."

"Blake invited me to stay, but I've got some business I have to attend to. I've postponed the golf game. I wanted to wish you a good trip…and say no hard feelings. I guess I read too much into things."

He took a step closer to her and a shiver ran down her back. "I'll look after the gallery while you're gone."

She shook her head. "It's your gallery, Jack."

He ignored her. She backed away as his intent became
353

clear, but she wasn't quick enough. His warm fingers glided up to her face and cupped her gently as his mouth settled on hers. Sienna stretched up onto her toes and kissed him right back.

It was a sweet kiss. A kiss made for lovers, and she couldn't resist his mouth, losing herself in the sweetness that she didn't want to succumb to. Warmth flooded through her.

By the time Jack lifted his head, Sienna had managed to get a grip on her emotions. She dropped her hands; she hadn't even been conscious of holding on to him as his lips had explored hers.

"It would have been so much easier if you hadn't done that," she said.

He stared at her for several heartbeats before his soft reply. "Probably, but I wanted to say good-bye...properly."

He swung his leg over the bike, turned the key, and the engine fired with a throaty roar. Before he could put his helmet on, Sienna grabbed his arm.

"Jack?"

Those beautiful green eyes held hers and she swallowed.

"Good-bye." It broke her heart, but Sienna tried to put conviction into her words. She wanted him to know she was really saying good-bye.

"For now." Jack stared at her for a moment longer before he lifted his helmet on.

Sienna stood for a long time until the bike and its rider were a small black speck in the distance. For the first time in her life, her heart yearned for another. A little niggle of regret snaked its way through her thoughts.

For now?

Chapter Twenty-Two

The flight from Maroochydore to Tamworth was delayed, and Ana and Georgie made the most of the time, hitting Sienna with a barrage of questions. Finally, they realised they weren't going to get the answers they wanted from her. Sienna stared off into space as Ana and Georgie chattered away beside her. Change was in the wind, just like it had been when they'd sold their business to Blake, and Ana and Blake got together. Ana had just told them that she and Blake were moving to Melbourne for a while to help out Jack's father while he wound down his business interests.

"But it's only temporary? Right?" Sienna hated the thought of them moving so far away.

"Yes, it is…and just think of the galleries you can visit when you come to see us." Ana squeezed her arm. "You will visit, won't   you?"

"Of course I will." Sienna laughed. "I need to find a job first." A little voice niggled at her. *You could always stay at the gallery and work for Jack.*

"What about you, Georgie? What are you going to do?" Sienna asked.

A new manager was coming in to oversee the Maleny store while Blake was away, and she wondered whether Georgie would stay.

"I've booked an around-the-world air ticket. As soon as the new guy is settled in, I'm off. I may see Machu Picchu for my next birthday yet." Georgie squeezed her hand. "It's about time I learned to stand on my own two feet."

Despite all the change and her own uncertainty of what the future held for her after she finished up at Jack's gallery, Sienna felt settled—almost. If only she could keep Jack's face out of her thoughts. She put her hand up to her lips. After he kissed her this afternoon, he'd smiled at her, and her toes curled now as she remembered the feelings that had run through her.

Georgie tipped her head to the side. "Now what about you? Maybe the sale fell through and you say you're going to leave, but I know when there's something going on."

"I'll tell you about it when I come home next week."

Georgie narrowed her eyes. "You're still having your exhibition before you leave, aren't you?"

Sienna shook her head. "No, I cancelled it. I gave some money to Marjorie, and now I can't afford it. I wasn't ready for it anyway. Too much of a rush to get it finished." She didn't like the thoughtful look that Georgie shot her as she picked up her bag.

"Don't you go meddling in anything that doesn't concern you, okay?" She hugged her cousin first, and then Ana. "Thelma and Mitzi are bad enough. Just let me sort my own life out. Remember, I'm more than happy being alone." She looked at Georgie. "I am."

***

Jack leaned back against the front door of the gallery, his legs stretched out in front of him. The cold marble tiles pressed against the backs of his legs and he shivered. All the way back from the party on Sunday night, Sienna's good-bye had echoed through his head. He'd known she meant more than a casual good-bye and was trying to tell him something more. He'd come straight back to the gallery, planning to stay there until he found something more permanent. He'd spent the first night castigating himself for telling Sienna how he felt too soon. He should have given her more time, but he'd been scared of letting her go without telling her how he felt. And he'd blown it.

No matter how it turned out, he'd been honest. Her words of a couple of weeks ago stuck in his mind.

"Your family is loaded, and you have a playboy

356

reputation."

She said she'd had no idea why he saw her as a challenge, because he knew now the challenge was getting her to love him back. But would his honesty give them both happiness? After a sleepless night, he unlocked the storage area and pulled his biggest sculpture into the studio. He managed to lose himself as the creative muse kicked in and thoughts of Sienna fled—almost. It was as though she was there with him as he shaped and moulded the metal. He'd smiled to himself as he made his perfect 'pancake' mix of enamel.

He pushed himself to his feet and pulled out his phone and snapped a series of pictures of his creature from all angles. A creature it was—certainly different from any of Sienna's small creatures. His had the shape of a phoenix rising from the ashes, but from the front view it appeared to be a dragon, the small pieces of scarlet enamel looking like fire surrounding its long jaw.

He messaged his parents and attached one of the photographs. A short message that he knew would please his father.

Beat the deadline by three days, Dad.

His phone beeped almost immediately, and a surge of satisfaction rushed through him.

Proud of you, son.

He stared down at the phone. No. He was going to give her space while she was away. As he held the phone, it rang and he looked down at the unfamiliar number for a moment before taking the call.

"Jack?"

"Yes?"

"It's Georgie. I was hoping you were around." Disappointment hit him; for a moment he thought maybe Sienna had gotten hold of him. He wasn't going to push her. He'd decided what he wanted; she had to come to him of her own accord.

Jack ran a hand across his face. Since he'd been immersed in the enamelling, he hadn't showered or changed. His stomach grumbled and he realised he hadn't eaten since yesterday.

"I'm coming to town and I was hoping I could meet with you?"

"Sure, what time will you be in town?"

They made arrangements to meet at the coffee shop where he'd eaten with Sienna on his first day in town. He was about to end the call when Georgie continued.

"And Jack? I hope you don't mind me stepping in. I hope I was reading you right when I saw the way you looked at my sister?"

Jack ordered the biggest plate of pancakes and bacon from the menu and was on his third coffee by the time Georgie arrived. She slid into the chair opposite him and smiled.

"You look like you haven't slept."

"I've been working."

"Missing Sienna?"

"You are spot-on there." Jack frowned as he forked the last piece of bacon from his plate. "The place isn't the same without her."

"Sienna will kill me when she finds out what I'm going to tell you." Georgie settled back into her chair and looked at him as the waitress poured her a coffee. "But I want her to be happy. She's kidding herself that she can ignore the way she feels about you."

Jack's fork clattered to the table as he stared back at her. "Are you sure?"

"Yes, I know my sister. You have to know a bit about our background to understand why she protects herself so much."

Jack's world filled with colour. For the first time he noticed the bright flowers spilling from the half wine casks scattered

358

around the terrace they were sitting on. Even though he'd been working with colours for the past two days, everything apart from his sculpture had looked grey and bleak.

"I know she cares about you—otherwise I wouldn't be here." Georgie stared at him and her words filled him with happiness. "Sienna's always been the tough one and so independent, but I've seen the way she looks at you."

For the next half hour, Georgie told him of their family and how she was sure that the only reason Sienna was pushing Jack away was to protect herself from being hurt. Knowing that it was Sienna's personal circumstances that had caused her so much angst relieved the burden that pressed on Jack. He carried a lot of guilt because he'd changed his mind about selling the gallery, and then Arielle's arrival had topped it all off.

"Once she's been to Tamworth and accepted what she finds there, she'll be ready to listen to you. I promise. I know her almost as well as I know myself." Georgie had filled in a lot of the gaps for him about why Sienna kept herself so private. "She doesn't share her emotions easily, but I know how she feels about you. Trust me."

Even though Sienna had said good-bye, the way she had kissed him before he left the party had filled him with a smidgeon of hope. Knowing that his actions had nothing to do with why Sienna had cancelled her show was a relief. A glimmer of an idea began to form as he thought of a way to make her happy.

"Georgie, have you got a day or two to spare before Sienna comes home?"

It had taken a long time to get things organised. Jack knew what he wanted to do, and the conversation with Georgie had nailed it.

Now all he had to do was persuade Sienna to trust him. When he heard about the payoff she'd made to Georgie's mother, the final piece had fallen into place. Even if Sienna couldn't buy the gallery, he'd give her a half-share on the condition that she'd manage it for him. Hell, he'd even share the studio with her. And he'd share his life with her.

If she'd have him.

Maybe he was kidding himself, but he really hoped that the welcome he and Georgie had planned would convince Sienna where his heart lay. His future—their future—depended on the next couple of hours. Now all he was waiting for was the text from Georgie to say they were on their way.

Jack flicked the collar of his white shirt and straightened his tie as he looked around the gallery with satisfaction.

Chapter Twenty-Three

The week in Tamworth reaffirmed Sienna's belief in herself as an artist. She'd wandered around art galleries, taken in a few exhibitions, and learned to relax. She'd stayed in bed late and eaten in a different restaurant every night. But she hadn't slept. Despite being there to find closure about her family and say good-bye to her mother, her mind had been filled with thoughts of Jack, wondering what he was doing and how he was coping with the gallery.

By Wednesday, when she'd picked up the phone for the tenth time to call, she finally admitted to herself that if he'd have her back, she'd keep working for him. She could accept his casual interest in the gallery. And he had a work ethic, no matter how much he pretended he was laidback and didn't care. The argument went back and forth in her head until she sighed and cleared her thoughts. If she didn't get some sleep, she'd be no good working for anyone.

And he'd said he loved her. That had to count for something.

She was filled with uncertainty, and it didn't sit well with her. Sienna, who always knew what she wanted and went for it; Sienna, who had been secure and comfortable where she was in life was struggling with the knowledge that she'd finally fallen for someone and fallen hard.

The half hour she had spent in the small cemetery beside the plaque with her mother's name on it finally brought her closure. This woman was someone she'd never known. She had no regrets and bore no malice. She'd done her research; there was no other family to look up. Her grandparents were dead, and her mother had been an only child. There was nothing for her in Tamworth apart from a lonely grave.

Back on the Sunshine Coast was a man who had kissed her and told her to think about that kiss. A man who loved her. She had thought about him constantly, and a feeling of lightness filled her as she came to a decision. Her true family was back at Maleny. Her heart—she finally admitted to herself—was with a green-eyed Prince Charming in Noosa.

Sienna's flight arrived late Friday night, too late to text Georgie to pick her up, so she stayed in a hotel and called the next morning.

"Can you pick me up and take me to Maleny?" Sienna stared out over the bay from her hotel window. It was good to be back on the coast.

"I'll do better than that. I'll drive you all the way to Noosa. I'll be there in an hour." Georgie disconnected before Sienna could say she'd planned on spending the weekend catching up with Blake and Ana before they moved to Melbourne. It had nothing to do with her nervousness about seeing Jack again.

She checked out and headed down to the restaurant to have a coffee while she waited.

"Blake and Ana are away for the weekend," Georgie said as she drove past the exit to Maleny..

"I'll spend some time with Renzo and Lucia instead."

"They're away, too."

"Who's running the restaurant?" Sienna had never known Renzo to take a day off when they were growing up.

"One of the chefs, apparently." Georgie shrugged.

"Take the next exit. I'll go and see Thelma and Mitzi."

"They're away, too."

Sienna narrowed her eyes. "They never go away."

"They are. They got invited to a…party."

Sienna was curious, but Georgie didn't say any more for a

while, focusing on the road ahead.

"So, you had a good trip?" Georgie shot her a glance.

"Yes, went to lots of galleries and had a good break."

"You look relaxed. What are your plans now?"

"I'm still not sure." Sienna didn't want to share just yet in case things didn't work out.

Georgie took the exit into Coolum from the motorway and Sienna looked across at her.

"Time for a coffee before I take you to the lake," Georgie said with a grin.

"It's only five minutes to my house." Now that she was almost home, Sienna was keen to get there. "I'll make you a coffee there. Or better still we can go into Noosa and I can…"

"Can what?"

"Nothing." She'd been going to say call in at the gallery. "I'm not sure if my car will start. That's why Jack gave me a ride to the party. She's been a bit temperamental."

"A bit like her owner." Georgie shot her a grin.

"Thanks, sis." Sienna waited as Georgie found a parking spot. "I guess we're having coffee here."

They found a coffee shop in the surf club and Sienna examined the art on the walls while they waited for their order and Georgie sent some texts. She was up to something. Sienna knew her all too well.

"Not a new man?" She gestured to the phone.

"What? Ah, no. Just some texts for the…er…store."

"Just be careful, Georgie. No more Cals, promise?"

"No more *Coles*, that's for sure." Georgie laughed. "Hurry up, finish your coffee and I'll drop you at home."

"We just got here." Sienna narrowed her eyes. "Please tell me you haven't done something I'm going to hate."

"*I've* done nothing. And that's all I have to say on the matter. Now come on." Georgie picked up her phone and purse and waited for Sienna to finish her coffee.

Sienna knew Georgie was up to something. She folded her arms and didn't say a word as Georgie went past her turn off and drove into Noosa and turned into Hastings Street.

She parked the car and turned to Sienna. "Have you got your lipstick handy? And fluff up your hair. Someone's got a little surprise for you."

"Who?"

"You'll see. Now stop asking questions, make yourself pretty, and follow me."

Bemused, and slightly nervous because she knew Jack was involved, she let Georgie lead her along the street until they turned back onto the main street and headed toward Sea View Gallery. The tourists were out in force this morning and a large crowd was gathered outside the gallery looking at the window display. Sienna thought back, trying to remember what she'd put on display before she'd left last week.

A group of white bowls certainly did nothing to get that much attention.

"I like the red one with the dangly leg." The woman's voice carried across as they finally cleared the crowd and stood at the door. Sienna looked up and her ears began to buzz. She put her hand up to her chest.

"Oh my God."

"Don't you go fainting on me, Sienna."

Her heart almost stopped as she saw the man who was waiting beside the door. Jack was dressed in a dark suit and white shirt.

Oh God, he is so gorgeous.

The look in his eyes banished the last uncertainty that lingered in Sienna's mind. He reached out for her and ran the pad of his thumb over her bottom lip just as he had a few days ago.

"Close your mouth and stop gaping, Sienna, so I can kiss

you hello."

She stepped toward him and moved her hand up to his smooth-shaven cheek.

"I missed you." Jack's deep green eyes were fixed on hers, and the noise of the street and the chattering tourists faded into the background as he filled her vision.

"Before you kiss me hello, I want to tell you what I found." She kept her voice low and Jack lowered his head closer to hers to listen to her words. "I fought this so much. Not because of you, but because of where I came from. I knew I was falling in love with you and it terrified me. I couldn't trust those feelings that I could be happy and that it would last."

Jack's cheek was against hers and she closed her eyes as she revelled in the feel of his skin against hers.

"But you taught me how to feel happy again, and I know I can trust you. You made me laugh when things were tough even though I didn't share them with you." She turned her face, and his lips were almost touching hers.

His warm breath caressed her skin.

"I was going to wait no matter how long it took. I fell in love with you all over again when you glared at me the first night in Fish Divine." Jack's voice sent a shiver down Sienna's back and she opened her eyes and tipped her head back to look at him.

"Again?"

"It was the same feeling I had when I saw you the first time a couple of years back. I just didn't know what it was then. We're meant to be together. Have I convinced you of that yet or do I have to lock you away in my Prince Charming castle to convince you?"

"Maybe you'd like to try a little harder to convince me right now?" It was as though they were in a fairy-tale world of their own making. She closed her eyes while Jack held her face gently and his lips finally slid onto hers. Warmth stole over her and spread through her. Only their lips and hands were touching, but a wealth of feeling poured through Sienna when the pressure of Jack's lips increased on hers. She sank into the pleasure until he murmured against her mouth. "We have to go inside."

"To the sofa bed in the studio?" She looked up at him and let a saucy grin spread across her face.

"Er…I don't think it's quite the right moment for that, but please hold that thought for later."

Her gaze stayed on him as he took her hand and tucked it in the corner of his arm.

"Follow me."

Jack led her inside as Georgie held the door open.

***

The banner stretched across the gallery spelled out **A VISIT WITH CREATURES, with SIENNA SACCHI** written in scrolling letters along the bottom. A table laden with finger food and champagne glasses was along the back of the gallery, and the shelves she could see through the mass of people were filled with her frogs and tiny creatures. Not as many as she'd planned for, but still enough to look good.

A small cheer went up as Sienna paused in the doorway. Jack's hand was against her back and she reached behind and held it tightly as she looked around. Renzo and Lucia, Thelma and Mitzi, Aldo and Maria, Joe and Magda, and Blake and Ana stood at the front of the large group of people filling the gallery.

"The guest of honour is here." Renzo stepped forward and kissed her cheek. "I'm very proud of my daughter. Her work is amazing."

Sienna shook her head, unable to believe what she was seeing. She turned to Jack and grinned again as she took in the uncharacteristic white shirt, and tie and suit trousers. Her heart was thudding, and the familiar tremble was back in her legs, and it didn't have as much to do with the shock of seeing her exhibition set up as much as this sexy man holding her as though he'd never

366

let her go,

"Where's my Jack gone?" she whispered with a smile.

Joy spread across his face and another small cheer went up as Sienna lifted her arms up around his neck and pressed her lips to his in front of everyone who mattered to her.

"Your Jack's right here and he's not going anywhere," he murmured.

Sienna dropped her head and buried it in his neck for a moment until she regained her composure. When she turned, she caught Georgie giving Jack a thumbs-up gesture.

"So, I guess Georgie spilled the beans about why I cancelled the show?" She held his gaze and Jack nodded.

"She did, but that was only part of it. I wanted to have Sienna Sacchi, amazing artist, and her frogs, to be the first exhibition at *our* gallery."

"Our gallery?"

"Oh, there's lots more I have to tell you." Jack held her hand tightly as she looked around in amazement. Jack—she assumed he'd set up the show—had done a wonderful job of spacing her pieces, and the lighting was incredible. "Everything else can wait except for one thing."

"What's that? What else can you possibly have for me?" She gestured around the room. "Apart from all of this." She let out a small cry as she noticed the large sculpture just inside the foyer. "Oh, you finished. You met your deadline."

Jack shook his head with a cheeky grin that almost curled her toes. "I finished one. I can't get too organised. Just one more thing…I have to tell the artist how much I love her again before the guests take all her attention."

"I love you too." She stretched up to her toes and kissed him again. "While ever you're here, Prince Charming, no one else will get more of my attention than you."

Jack's eyes widened as he looked over her head, almost lost

for words. "Oh my God."

"You make me so happy." Sienna smiled up at him. He was always happy and smiling; that was one of the things she loved about him. Now his eyes were alight with pleasure even as he looked over her head.

Yes, I love him. It was a wonderful feeling that coursed through her veins.

"Oh. My God," he said again.

"I love the way nothing ever fazes you," she said.

"Oh yes it does," he said. He stared over her shoulder and Sienna followed his gaze.

"Chris Hemsworth just walked through the door. *Our* gallery's hit the big time."

Epilogue

"Hurry up, Jack."

"I'm almost ready." His voice was muffled and Sienna grinned. It sounded like he was still in the bathroom towelling his hair.

She stood at the door of the Park Hyatt Hotel bathroom as she waited for Jack to come out. Three months of sharing the management of the gallery, as well as sharing her house, and her bedroom, with him had taught her some of his quirks.

He hated being late. As much as he denied that he was working and co-managing with her, and that he hated deadlines, Sienna had seen a different side to Jack over the past few months. Scheduling shows and liaising with artists, while she did the day-to-day running of the gallery, he had demonstrated the business skills he'd kept hidden and still wouldn't admit to having. He'd met his deadline and today they were in Melbourne for the unveiling of his sculptures in the entry of the building in Federation Square.

"Jack, your parents are waiting in the foyer. Are you almost ready?"

"I'm coming. Where's my shirt?"

"I don't know. It's your shirt." Sienna still preserved her prickly side, but Jack saw through it every time. She loved sharing her life with him and was looking forward to this special day with him.

Finally, he appeared in the doorway in casual chinos and a T-shirt.

"You can't go dressed like that." She frowned at him and he grinned his sexy grin that always melted her resistance. His hair was mussed, and he looked like he was going to the beach, and she said as much.

"It's my day and I'll wear what I'm comfortable in." He tapped her on the behind as they walked toward the door. "I didn't tell you what to wear to yours, did I?"

"That's because I didn't know I was having one." Sienna stopped and turned to Jack as he reached for the door. She slipped her arms around his waist as she looked up at him.

"Before we go and you get lost in the adoring masses, I want to tell you how much I love you. "She stood on her tiptoes and pressed her lips against his, revelling in the feel of this man she loved so much. "And to wish you an amazing day." She kissed him again. "That's for luck."

"If you keep that up, we are going to be late." Jack swooped her into his arms and sat down in the fancy antique chair by the door. "But keep going, I think I need more luck."

Sienna giggled as Jack settled her comfortably in his lap and trailed his lips down the side of her neck.

"You are incorrigible. I didn't think you wanted to be late," she said.

"I'm the guest of honour. A few minutes won't hurt."

His lips reached hers and Sienna closed her eyes. She'd laughed so much over the past three months. Being with Jack filled her with a joy she'd never experienced before, and he amazed her every day with the ways he could make her laugh. His hands lingered on her skin, and she swallowed a smile as the phone rang on the antique table beside the chair they were perched in. She slipped off his lap and stood in front of him. "Come on, your parents are waiting."

Jack rose reluctantly and looped his arm around her shoulders as they walked down to the corridor to the elevator.

"Do you think Chris might come?"

"

Healing His Heart

Annie Seaton

Sunshine Coast: Book 3

Second Edition: Healing His Heart, June 2021

Chapter One

Liam Wyndham rested the paddle on the front of the kayak while he caught his breath. The small waves at the beach break rocked the small craft gently in the light breeze. He'd been paddling for an hour and had managed to clear his mind—almost. He looked up to the top of the cliff and examined the sprawling old house that looked to be teetering on the edge of the rocky cliff.

The view of the house was completely different from the sea. Located ten kilometres south of Noosa, it suited him very well. There was only one other house close by and it had been in darkness, with no sign of life in the week since he'd moved in.

Apparently, according to the local real estate agent, the owners had moved interstate for work, and that made the location even more attractive. He wanted no interruptions and desired no neighbourly company. All he wanted was a place where he could lick his wounds and think about his future. With online communication and a huge stash of groceries, he'd be able to bury himself with little disruption and get his damned book to his publisher. The only issue would be the workmen who were coming to build bookshelves for him, but once he let them in and showed them where to go, he'd stay out of their way.

Liam needed to find himself and his place in life after the hellish six months he'd just endured. If he was honest, he'd admit he needed more than a place to finish *Guardian of the Village*, his latest adventure book set in Nepal. He also needed space and solitude to regain some stability in his life after the shock of Vanessa's death. He'd been researching his book in the Himalayas and the media had had a field day, portraying him as the jet-setting author who always left his wife behind when he travelled. Vanessa had come up with that story for a trashy gossip magazine interview and it had spread like wildfire. Truth be known, she was the one who hadn't wanted to go with him.

"Why the hell would I want to go with you to a third world country?" She had stared at him, her heavily made-up eyes open wide. "No restaurants, no shops, and we've just been invited to three premieres—and the after-parties!"

Then, right before he'd left, she'd told him she was seeing someone else and was going to move out while he was in Nepal. So he'd gone off alone to research his latest book and hadn't cared one bit about missing the Sydney social scene. While in the Himalayas, he'd realised that he didn't miss Vanessa and being dragged around to the parties that his fame had given them entry to. He'd worked hard to make the money to keep her happy, but it hadn't been enough for her, so he had decided that he'd be happier alone, so he'd give her a divorce—and a settlement, whatever it took.

The pileup on the motorway that had resulted in Vanessa's death had left him numb, and a little guilty. Maybe if he'd tried harder to understand her, she would have stayed with him and not been out on that fateful night.

Then the vultures had come in for the kill, blaming him for leaving her alone. Liam had gotten sick of seeing his face plastered on all the entertainment sites and blogs. Sarah, his agent, had advised him to sue, but he had hoped the whole set of lies would die a natural death and they'd move on to their next victim. All Liam wanted was shut himself away from the world and write. It was all he'd ever wanted to do, and he wasn't going to get caught again. He intended to become a recluse. Uncle Joe had done just that in this house, and he would do it, too. Liam had never been comfortable in the false world of Sydney; attending celebrity events, the fancy restaurants and book signings had been at Vanessa's request. His wife had thrived on the publicity, until she'd found a more famous celebrity to hang on to. Ironic, really—she'd accused him of being unfaithful almost every time he'd signed a book for a female reader. Vanessa had been needy, and he hadn't been able to give her what she wanted. It was too hard. Liam knew he didn't have it in him to pander to the demands of a clingy woman. Most of the time he was lost in his own thoughts and planning a scene, or setting up a plot, and he missed the cues that other guys just seemed to pick up on.

So he was here to bunker down and write. He didn't need people in his life. He had his books and enough travel memories and stories in his head to keep him writing for years. His days of travelling the world were over. He had a home, and he wasn't going anywhere.

For the life of him, he couldn't understand the macabre interest in his being widowed and what it had to do with entertaining the masses. The sales of his books had skyrocketed after the articles were published, but he didn't care. What he needed now was some privacy and peace. Then maybe the muse who had deserted him would return. He had been given three months to find it, or his deal with a top New York publisher was toast. No matter how well his previous books had sold, if he didn't deliver this book by Christmas, they were going to terminate the contract. He had four weeks left to write it. Even as he thought about it, dread rose into his throat and his mind went blank.

The wind picked up and the chill of late autumn settled on his bare shoulders as he lifted the paddle and headed for the shore. There was a trail at the base of the cliff leading up to the house. When he'd set out, the waves breaking on the beach had been tiny, but now he had to focus on paddling through the small swells that lapped at the kayak. He glanced behind him as a strong gust of wind pushed him closer to the shore and the kayak slewed around side-on to the waves. Liam knew he was going over and braced himself for the shock of the cold water.

"It's not you, it's me."

What a cop-out. The words ran like a mantra through Georgie Sacchi's head as she followed the trail to the beach. What was it about guys? Did they all gather around the bar together and come up with stock phrases to end a relationship with? Did they really believe any woman in her right mind would fall for it?

"Mutt, I swear, if you pull on your lead one more time, I'll...I'll..." A litany of swear words hovered on Georgie's lips and she grinned. She was known as one of the kindest, most even-tempered products of Maleny where she had grown up, and her friends would be horrified to hear a swear word cross her lips. They'd be even more surprised to read her dark thoughts this bleak afternoon.

Everyone saw her as a good sport. Happy, easy-going Georgie. Practical joker Georgie. Life-and-soul-of-the-party Georgie.

She'd toughened up in the weeks since her mother, Marietta, had died, only a couple of weeks after spilling the truth to Georgie and her "sister", Sienna that their lives had been a sham. For twenty-nine years, she and Sienna had believed they were fraternal twins. Not only had her mother told them they were actually cousins born on the same day, but she had also told them her cancer was terminal. Georgie had spent most of her mother's last days by her bedside, but they had never spoken of the deception again.

Sienna was her best friend in the whole world and Georgie's sounding board when things went wrong. Georgie didn't think it mattered if they were sisters or cousins. But Georgie had not told Sienna about the spectacular breakup with her latest man. "It's not you, it's me." When Brent had used the same line as Cole, and Harrison before him, Georgie had foolishly pressed him for details and his words had turned around to cut her.

"Not marriage material," he'd said. "You, not me."

In the weeks since then, Georgie had put on a brave face and carried on in her usual happy way. In front of her friends, anyway. The friends who were the problem, according to Brent.

"You hang around with old people." The look on his face had been full of disdain. In that moment, she had been happy to let him go.

Georgie's best friends—her age—were no longer around. Sienna was happy in her new life with Jack, living down in Noosa, and Ana had moved to Melbourne with her partner, Blake, and their baby, Faith.

Okay, so I'm happy for Sienna and Ana. They were in love but deep down Georgie carried a belief that she would never admit to her friends. Not in a million years: she was never going to find a partner and it was time to accept that.

Especially after Brent…and Cole…and Harrison…and—

Oh, shite. She wasn't going to waste any more time thinking about them. So she picked losers. Either that, or Brent's reason for breaking up with her was true. She just wasn't marriage or permanent relationship material. Maybe she did take after her mother.

It didn't matter anyway. Once she finished this rush job for Blake's hardware store, Georgie was heading out. She was going overseas and staying away from men…for good. Before Blake and Ana had left for Melbourne, Blake, her boss, had begged her to do this one small building job before she left on her big adventure. All of the other local builders were too busy, and the client wanted the work done immediately. It was convenient for her because the house was next door to the cottage where she was house-sitting until she left on her trip. She had agreed to delay her trip by a month to get it finished. She could put in long days. Georgie had pretended it was a big deal to change her ticket, but in reality, it had given her time to delay the trip. Yet now that Ana and Blake

377

were in Melbourne and Sienna was at Noosa, she could drop the brave front she'd put up.

Georgie wasn't even sure she wanted to go away on this trip. It was going to take a lot of courage to leave behind all that was familiar, and a place she'd lived for twenty-nine years. A place where she'd been settled and content until Brent's final comment had made her take a long hard look at her life. But the trip was booked now, and her departure day was set in stone. Georgie was leaving from Brisbane on Christmas Eve. First stop, Honolulu. She had agreed to help out an old school friend and her husband and look after their animals over Christmas while they visited family, and she was living in tier cottage in Hideaway Bay, down the coast from her hometown of Maleny. After that, she had an open round-the-world ticket…and the world was hers to discover.

Mutt leaped ahead as something moved on the trail in front of them and the leash pulled from her fingers. He disappeared over the sand dune onto the beach and Georgie hurried after him. By the time she'd reached the base of the dune and clambered over the piles of driftwood, he was in the water and was barking and jumping about in the shallows.

The sun was almost to the horizon in the west and Georgie put her hand up to her eyes to shield the silver glare reflecting on the water. She squinted as she spotted a small kayak floating upside down in the break. Mutt barked and took off toward a large log lying on the wet sand.

"Oh God." It wasn't a log, it was a person lying face down on the sand, and Georgie took off at a run. "Not a body, oh please, not a body."

The sun broke through the low cloud and bathed the beach in front of her in late-afternoon sunshine. As she ran toward the unmoving shape on the now-glistening sand, she dug in her pocket for her phone and a swear word did escape her lips this time. Her phone was on the counter in the kitchen where she'd thrown it before she'd picked up Mutt's leash.

"A...B...C..." Her breath caught as she ran toward the person. "Or is it C...A...B?"

All she could remember from the first aid course that Blake had insisted that the staff complete each year was the first two words...circulation and breathing. Or was it airway and breathing? Even as she tried to remember the sequence, a memory flashed through her mind. Damn, she couldn't even remember the funny song she'd made up at the course. She'd changed "shake and shout" into "twist and shout" and had performed an impromptu dance with the mannequin. All she could remember was the rest of the staff rolling around with laughter at her little performance. Blake had glared at her before his lips had twitched, too, and he'd given in to laughter. Now Georgie racked her brain for the rest of the words. She'd never had to administer first aid. The guy—she was now close enough to see it was a man—was lying on his stomach with his arms stretched above his head and his face turned away from her. Georgie reached him, knelt down, and grabbed his shoulders to put him in the recovery position. She could remember that much at least—hopefully the rest of the first aid knowledge would follow.

"What the hell do you think you're doing?"

Georgie rocked back on her heels as the guy pushed himself up onto his forearms and turned his head to face her. A pair of ice-blue eyes stared into hers and a shiver ran down Georgie's spine as she sat back on the wet sand, and the shiver didn't have anything to do with the cold water that was seeping through her shorts.

Oh...my God. He's gorgeous. She exhaled a huge breath of relief and put her hand to her chest. "Oh, thank goodness. I thought you were drowned."

"Well, I'm not." His voice was short, and Georgie

379

narrowed her eyes. A trickle of blood was running down his cheek.

"But you're hurt."

He rolled over, sat up, and looked away from her. "No, I was just catching my breath." She sensed that every word he spoke to her was done so reluctantly. "So thank you, you can go now. Your dog's waiting for you."

Mutt had bounded over to see what was happening and stood next to Georgie as he shook the water from his coat, spraying her with drops of cold water.

"Your head's bleeding. What happened?" She reached out to touch his face, but he leaned away from her reach.

"I told you, I'm fine." His voice was rude, and he scowled at her, his expression grim.

"Well, get up and show me you're okay." Georgie pushed herself to her feet, put her hands on her hips, and stared down at him. He had longish hair plastered to his head, and despite being pale and gaunt, his face was beautifully proportioned. His clothes were soaked and stuck to his body; a pair of black shorts clung to long muscular legs and a sleeveless white T-shirt showed off a set of well-toned biceps.

"What about your kayak? If you're all right, are you going to get it before it floats away?" She wasn't convinced that the guy was okay, and even if he was angry at her for some reason, she wasn't going to leave him until she was sure. He frowned at her before looking out to where the kayak was now bobbing in the small swell.

"Damn." He tried to stand but grabbed his head and sat back down.

Georgie gestured for him to stay sitting. The blood was trickling down his neck now. She called to Mutt and the dog walked over quietly, as if sensing there was something wrong.

"Sit." She pointed to the sand next to the man. "Stay."

Heading into the break, she gasped as the cold water hit her bare thighs and she waited for the wave to recede. The kayak was floating in waist-deep water, and when the surge pulled back, Georgie grabbed the end of the small craft and dragged it to the shore. It slid up the wet sand with a harsh grinding sound, and she pulled it up as far as she could, away from the rising tide.

"Leave it." The voice was peevish.

Georgie turned and glared at its owner as she dropped the kayak. She put her hands on her hips and stood over him. "I don't know who you are, mister, but here in Hideaway Beach, we do the neighbourly thing and look out for someone who needs a hand."

By the time she'd finished speaking, he'd pushed himself to his feet and she took a step back to look up at him. She was tall, but he towered over her and stared at her before she dropped her gaze and turned away.

"Come on, Mutt. It's time for us to go home."

She shot him a final look to make sure he was still standing before she headed toward the path, through the orange grove, and back to the cottage, Mutt close at her heels.

##

House-sitting the cottage for her friends until she left for Hawaii was opportune, as Georgie had given up the lease on her small apartment in Maleny. She had also offered to look after Ana's pets, Mutt and Sooky, the cat, while she was there, and the owners of the cottage had had no problem with that. Mutt was supposed to be going into town to stay at Uncle Renzo's house until Blake and Ana came back from Melbourne in the spring, but until Georgie left he could stay by the beach and Sooky could also stay with someone she knew. Now Sooky wrapped herself around Georgie's legs, meowing for her dinner. Georgie threw Mutt's leash onto the table on the porch. By the time she'd walked up from the beach the sun had set, and she flicked the light on after she opened the door.

She couldn't get the guy on the beach out of her head. Maybe she should have stayed with him, no matter how rude he'd been. There was no sign of a car anywhere along the road. He could have paddled for miles before he'd come ashore.

With a shrug, she tried to put him from her mind. That was the old Georgie; always the worrier, always the caretaker of everyone's feelings and well-being. The new Georgie, with strong resolve and thick skin, would forget all about him and let him look after himself. She'd always hated confrontation, but her soft side would have given in and she would have stayed to see if he was okay, no matter what he'd said.

Yes, that's a big step forward. Turning my back on him and leaving him to look after himself.

Brent's comments had toughened her up. Knowing that he had used her sealed Georgie's determination to change. Supposedly, what didn't kill you made you stronger, so now she was a new, stronger Georgie. No more looking after guys in need. Mr. Kayak Paddler was her first test. Okay, she'd sort of rescued him—but now he could go it alone.

No longer was she going to try to make everything right for everyone.

And I passed with flying colours.

Now for an early night, to get ready for an early start at the house next door, while she worked up the courage to take on her trip around the world.

I can do it. But the last thing to flit through her mind as sleep claimed her was a gaunt, unshaven face with ice-blue eyes.

Chapter Two

Liam sneezed and put his hand up to his forehead as he felt the pull on his skin. His hand came away smeared with a streak of blood.

The small wound had begun to bleed again. He'd managed to staunch the slow bleeding last night once he'd climbed the hill, stripped off his wet clothes, and showered, but he'd ended up with a raging headache. Now he swung his bare legs over the side of the bed and sat for a moment until the throbbing eased. Then he pulled on his jeans and padded barefoot down to the kitchen.

He rummaged in the medicine cabinet above the stove and found some of the Panadol he'd unpacked a couple of days ago. He swallowed two and chased them down with a large glass of water. Standing there for a moment, he debated whether to put the coffeemaker on or go back to bed. A shiver ran through him as he registered the chill of the cold tiles beneath his bare feet. He glanced up at the clock and sighed. It was close to seven o'clock and it wouldn't be long before the restoration company arrived to start work on his bookshelves. He had to get to the computer today. He couldn't afford to let another day slip by without putting some words on paper—or screen.

After he put the coffee on, Liam crossed to the window and looked out over the ocean. There was not a breath of wind, and the silver sheen of the calm water soothed him. Nothing moved; the trees were still in the quiet before sunrise, and there was no birdsong. He'd been relieved to only occasionally hear the dull roar of traffic when the wind blew from the west, but he had been dismayed last night to see lights on at the house next door. It looked like there was someone in it. He'd avoid them and keep to himself.

The last thing he felt like doing was being neighbourly. This house was perfect for him. He grinned to himself. Okay, he might be too young, but he saw this cliff top house as his place to settle and be happy as a recluse. He'd had enough of travelling and the experiences that went with it. He was here on the Sunshine Coast to stay. If the neighbours thought he was a hermit, that would suit him just fine.

That thought reminded him of the woman down on the beach last night. He knew he'd been rude, but overturning his kayak had been a stupid, careless thing to do, and he'd been angry at himself. When she'd tried to help, it had been the last straw, and she'd borne the brunt of his ill temper. It was bad enough that she'd retrieved the kayak while he'd lain on the sand. He hadn't needed her to administer first aid to him. God, he was lucky she hadn't tried mouth-to-mouth on him. Even though he'd told her he was okay, the headache this morning was bad enough to make him suspect he had a touch of concussion.

A flash of bright colour along his fence caught his attention and he leaned forward and peered through the glass. Damn, it was almost as though he'd conjured the woman up. He stepped back into the shadows as the woman from the beach followed the dog along the back of his fence line. He'd discovered who lived in the house next door. She was dressed in jeans today, with a long-sleeved red-and-white-checked shirt hanging loose over them, and a small bag slung over her shoulder. The red in her shirt clashed with the deep auburn hair he'd noticed yesterday. He waited for her to turn onto the beach trail, but she headed for his back gate. The clang of the metal latch told him she was coming onto his property, and he groaned.

What the hell is she doing here and why so early in the morning?

He definitely was not feeling neighbourly this morning.

***

As Georgie opened the gate to the house next door to the cottage, an unfamiliar ripple of fear ran through her.

Alone. It had been almost two years since she'd last been out on a building job, and back then she'd always had Sienna and Ana with her. Since the three girls had sold their restoration business and gone their separate ways, she'd worked in the office of Blake's hardware store. Ana had settled down to look after her new baby and Sienna had immersed herself in her sculpting and her gallery in Noosa.

Now Georgie stood inside the gate and took a deep breath as she curled her hand in Mutt's fur. He put his head against her leg and looked up at her with his deep brown eyes.

Alone, completely alone. And she knew it wasn't just the experience of being alone on a job that was making her legs tremble. It was accepting that being alone in life was what she wanted. It was the decision she'd made. What she'd pushed herself into in the last two months finally hit her as she stood outside this dark, forbidding house. She was similar to her mother. Marietta had pretty much died alone, and it looked like her own life was going in the same direction. Her mother had been unhappy, but that wasn't going to be Georgie's way.

I am going to be positive about my life alone. It wasn't about being alone; it was about independence, and she would embrace it. No more mooning about for her. No more men to make her life complete.

It was certainly not a prediction any of them would have made a few years ago. The standing joke among the three friends had been Georgie's determination to get married and live the suburban dream.

Who would have imagined their current situations? Ana had Blake and their gorgeous little baby, Faith. Sienna was madly in love, settled into domestic bliss and running the gallery with Jack, her artist partner.

And here am I. Not alone…just independent.

"You are such a coward, Georgie Sacchi." She fought back the tremble in her legs and took a deep breath as she gripped the gate with shaky fingers and pulled it shut behind her with a firm click. "Get over it. That is your new mantra. Forget 'it's not you, it's me.' From now on it's going to be, 'I value my independence.'"

385

As she looked around, her muscles slowly relaxed and the panic began to subside. The sun cleared the silver ocean to the east, and a glimmer of confidence filtered through her as the early-morning sunlight hit the water of the Pacific Ocean. The water was a mirror of unruffled silver this morning, and it calmed her. She swallowed and headed around the house to the front door of the old mansion. She and the girls would have loved to have gotten their hands on this place when they were in the restoration business, but old Mr. Humphries had hung on to it until he'd died. When the house had finally gone on the market, it had sold within a week. No one even knew who'd bought it.

All Georgie knew was that it belonged to some author who now wanted two whole rooms of bookshelves built. She'd dropped the contract off for Blake in Maleny a few weeks back.

She had no doubt she could do the job. She'd brought her tape to measure up this morning. After she did the measuring, she'd take Mutt back to the cottage and head into the hardware store to pick up the supplies to get started. Georgie let a grin cross her face; the new owner would soon find out there were a lot more jobs needed in the old house. It could keep her cousins, Tony and Johnny, the new owners of the restoration business, in work for years, if the man could afford it.

"Are you lost?" The deep voice pulled her out of her reverie, and she looked up at the open door and stifled a gasp. It was the guy from the beach. She hadn't even considered that he might be her new neighbour.

"You're still bleeding," Georgie said stupidly as the smile left her face.

She stared at him as he brushed his hand through his longish hair and pressed the pad of his thumb against the small cut. With his hair dry and some colour back in his face, he was even better looking than yesterday. The angles of his face, which had appeared gaunt and harsh in his pallor yesterday when his hair had

386

been wet and plastered to his skull, now settled into high cheekbones that were accentuated by the dark stubble on his jaw. His light brown hair curled slightly and reached past the base of his neck, brushing his bare shoulders. Pale blue irises in almond-shaped eyes were fanned by long dark lashes, but his eyes were still as cold and unfriendly as they'd been yesterday. He had the most beautiful lips she had ever seen on a man, but they were set in a straight line.

"What do you want?" His voice was terse.

Georgie pulled herself together and closed her mouth as he stared at her. "I'm here for the, er…the job."

He ran one hand through his hair at the same time he eased the door closed. "Look, I've got no idea what you're talking about. And yes, I'm bleeding, and I have the mother of a headache. Good-bye."

The door shut in her face and she looked down at Mutt. At least her sad thoughts and panic had fled. She grinned and rapped on the door. Showing the rude man up was going to be enjoyable.

"Go away." Even when he was being rude, his husky voice sounded sexy.

She lifted her hand and knocked again and waited. The door opened slowly, and he stared at her without speaking.

"Knock, knock," Georgie said.

"What?" Mr. Kayak Paddler frowned and put his hand up to his forehead.

Maybe the guy had a concussion?

"You're supposed to say 'who's there?'"

"Who's there?" Gritted teeth and not even a glimmer of a smile.

"The bookshelf."

"The bookshelf who?" There was a tiny twitch at the corner of his gorgeous mouth.

"The bookshelf builder. I am here"—Georgie enunciated

387

each word clearly—"to build your bookshelves."

"What?" The look on his face was priceless, and any sympathy she had for his injury had disappeared.

"I'm from BB Hardware. You ordered two rooms of bookshelves to be built?" She grinned down at Mutt when he supported her with a loud bark.

"Yes. Yes, I did." The hunk holding the door looked from her to Mutt and frowned. "You're the handyman?"

"Yes, I'm the tradesperson. That's correct." Georgie held out her hand as she bit back the nasty retort that had sprung to her lips. Brent had had a problem with her doing a "man's job," as he'd called it

"Now let's start again. I'm Georgie Sacchi and I'm here to measure for your bookshelves."

He looked at her through the open door and scratched his head, ignoring her outstretched hand. Georgie kept her eyes away from his bare chest.

"So? Are you going to let me in…or don't you want the job done anymore?"

"Yes, of course I do." He opened the door a little and she took a step forward. "Where's your car?" The frown was deepening the furrows at the top of his nose. "And why did you bring the dog?"

"My car is at the cottage and I knew if Mutt saw me come over here without him, he'd howl all day."

"The cottage?"

"Look, are you sure you don't have a concussion from your accident yesterday?" It was time to take control. "Hold that door open. I'll be back in a minute." She grabbed Mutt's collar, led him around to the back of the house and opened the gate to the small garden. There was a bowl beneath the garden tap, and she filled it with water. She took a quick look around to make sure nothing had changed and that the garden was still secure before she closed the gate behind Mutt and hurried back around to the front door.

The door was wide open but there was no sign of Kayak Man. Georgie took a hesitant step inside and called out. "Can I come in?"

She waited, but all was quiet. Taking a tentative step toward the hall, she looked around and shook her head; the place was in even worse condition than she remembered from her last visit here.

The sound of running water drew her to the kitchen. She'd visited here with Ana when they used to drop meals off for Mr. Humphries when he'd been homebound, and she knew her way around the place. Kayak Man stood at the sink holding a small cloth to his head.

"The blasted cut won't stop bleeding." He threw her a look, but she couldn't read his expression.

"Sit down." She pointed to the stool at the breakfast bar. "Where's your first aid kit?" She might have forgotten how to do CPR, but she was more than capable of putting a Band-Aid on a wound. He lifted his head and those piercing blue eyes held hers for a moment before he inclined his head to the left and winced. "There's a small plastic basket in the cupboard above the fridge."

Georgie walked across the kitchen and opened the cupboard he'd indicated. The basket was at the front of the shelf, and overflowed with boxes of bandages, tubes of lotion, and packets of medication. She dug through until she found a box of small circular bandages. "One of these should do the trick."

He sat on the stool as she'd directed, but if the look on his face was any indication, he wasn't at all comfortable with the *handyman* administering first aid.

She picked up the Band-Aid and walked slowly around the counter. "The quicker you let me do this, the sooner I can get to work and leave you in peace."

Georgie ripped the Band-Aid open. The snap of the plastic

filled the uncomfortable silence in the room. She looked down at the bandage as she peeled the adhesive cover from the back, without once looking directly at him. "What's your name? The guys at the store didn't tell me, and I haven't collected the job sheet yet."

She grinned. *I'm not going to tell him I call him Mr. Kayak Man.* The expression on his face gave little hint of a sense of humour.

"Liam. Liam Wyndham." At least he answered her. The name was familiar, but she couldn't place it.

Deftly, she reached out and lifted away the small towel he had pressed to the wound. The cut was small and surrounded by a deep blue bruise. Georgie's legs went to jelly. As much as she was acting as though she could do this, she looked away from the jagged sides of the cut, which was still slowly seeping blood.

"You did a good job on yourself there. That's a nasty cut and you have a spectacular bruise. Do you think you should go to the hospital?"

"No." He reached his hand out. "If you can't do it, give me the Band-Aid and I'll put it on."

"I can do it." She leaned forward and tried to concentrate on placing the bandage carefully across the wound without getting the adhesive edges on the broken skin. She ignored the warmth from his bare shoulders as she leaned over him.

"There, that's it." She looked at his forehead and waited for a minute. The uncomfortable silence stretched between them and he kept his gaze averted. "There's no sign of fresh bleeding."

Liam pushed himself up to his feet and turned toward the door on the far wall. "Follow me."

And that's all he said, not even a thank-you. She followed him down the hallway, up two flights of stairs, and across another small hall before he stopped outside a set of solid carved double doors.

"This is going to be my office."

He flung open the door and stepped into the room without checking to see if she was behind him. Despite his injury, he'd taken the stairs two at a time and she'd had to hurry to keep up. The room was huge, and she spun around slowly, looking at the bare plastered walls.

"So where do you want the shelves?"

"All around." He gestured with a sweep of his arm.

"On every wall?" She knew she sounded sceptical. It was a huge room that Joe had used as a spare bedroom. The room was bigger than the apartment in Maleny she'd just vacated.

"Yes, and butting right up to the side of both the windows." The windows were large and pushed out and there was a magnificent view of the ocean from this side of the old house.

"How high?" She waited for his answer, knowing what he was going to say before he answered.

"To the ceiling."

"It's a very big job."

"If it's too much for your firm, I'll get someone to come down from the city." He went back to the entrance and stood in the doorway with his arms folded, leaning on the doorframe.

"No, there's no need to do that. It's quite within the scope of the store." Georgie pulled out her tape and walked across to the far side of the room. "Some of the walls may need reinforcing to carry the weight of shelves to the ceiling."

A look of astonishment crossed his face, as if he was surprised that she knew what she was talking about. "So you do the measuring, and the builders come in and do the job?"

"No, Blake—the owner—asked me to do this job."

"Why? Because you live next door? You are a builder?"

"Yes, despite being a woman, I am a builder, and Blake asked me because this sort of job was—is—my specialty." Irritation at his obtuseness burned in Georgie's gut and she stared

391

at him, waiting for him to come up with some sexist remark. "Living next door is purely coincidental—and temporary. So don't worry, I won't be bothering you."

Why the heck she'd said that she didn't know. Georgie slipped a professional mask over her face, tucked her tape into her jeans pocket, and turned to him. "Working with wood and creating features that match the age of the house is part of the restoration work that I've done for the past few years. I was in partnership with two others in our own company, and I'm very good at what I do. If you want to see my work, I can give you some addresses to check out." She pulled out her notebook and her pencil. "Now, while I measure up, I want you to think about what you want."

"I want bookshelves."

"What sort of bookshelves?"

"Ones that hold books." If he hadn't been scowling at her, the conversation would have been comical. Like something from a comedy sketch.

"Heavy books? Light books? Big books? Little books? Encyclopedias? Paperbacks?" Georgie refused to let him bother her and she grinned. "They certainly won't hold e-books."

"Ah, a comedian. Just what I need." He scowled at her. "Just book books."

He is so rude. She hoped he would stay out of her way while she was working here. It was such a big job; it would certainly fill up the whole month before she left on her trip.

"Fancy edges? Deep shelves? Different heights? And isn't there a second room on the order, too?" She stared at him and tapped her pencil against her notebook.

God forbid. This room alone was going to take a few weeks' work. There wouldn't be time for her to do both rooms, but she'd call Blake and sort that out later.

"Just this one will do, for the time being." He was obviously going to check her work out before he got her to do the second room. Georgie shrugged and turned away from him. Didn't matter, she wouldn't be around to do it, anyway.

Distant, aloof, and totally full of himself. It was a shame Blake and Ana would have to put up with him for a neighbour when they came home from Melbourne. He was very different from sweet old Joe Humphries.

Georgie wondered what sort of books this Liam Wyndham wrote and why he'd moved to the coast to write them; his name had rung a bell, but she couldn't place him.

The only thing she knew about him was his propensity for falling off kayaks in the ocean. He was in for a shock if he thought he could get away with keeping to himself in this community. She swallowed a grin. Maybe she would drop a hint to Thelma and Mitzi that there was a new person in town…well, almost in town. It wasn't that far to Maleny from the bay.

Focus. She turned her attention to the job in front of her.

"Okay, now I want you to think about what you'd like. You've hired a restoration firm through the store, so I'm assuming you want to keep it in line with the style of the house." She straightened her shoulders and looked at him. "You don't want me to go and buy a set of ready-made IKEA bookshelves, right?"

He waved his hand, and his disinterest was clear. "Do whatever you think will suit the house. As long as it holds my books—of all shapes and sizes—I'll leave it up to you. I don't want to be disturbed. I'll leave the front door unlocked each morning. There's a bathroom at the end of this corridor." His voice was short as he turned away from her. His final words reached her as he disappeared through the door. "Send me the bill when it's finished."

Georgie snapped her mouth shut. The ruder he was, the happier she would be. His amazing good looks were at such odds with his personality that the attraction that had initially tugged at her was doused with cold water. And to completely kill it, all she

393

had to do was remember her new mantra.

I value my independence. Georgie grinned. It was getting easier every time she thought the words.

It was of no concern to her that this guy looked like a film star. She needed no man...and this rude guy who wanted bookshelves would get just that and no second thought or consideration from her. If she could let herself in and out each day and pretend he wasn't around, that would suit her just fine. She would do the job and prepare herself for her big adventure. The size of the job would help. She'd have no time to worry about Mr. Kayak Man, and get the shelves done before she set off.

Hmmm. Liam. Nice name. Suits the good looks.

Georgie shook herself and pulled out her measuring tape.

Chapter Three

Liam leaned back in his chair and looked around the small room he'd set up as his temporary office. The desk was clear, apart from the laptop computer; his essential reference books were in a box on the floor within reach; and the bulletin board was covered with glossy photos from Nepal. The floor in this room had a slight slope to it, and there was an ominous crack in the moulded arch above the door.

He'd known when he'd bought the place that it was in need of repair, but the location had appealed to him. Knowing it from his childhood had also brought a measure of security with it. Private and perched on top of the cliff overlooking the bay, it reminded him of some of the houses from Alfred Hitchcock movies. He'd hoped the mysterious atmosphere would feed his muse.

What he hadn't factored in was that if the house was to be restored—and repaired—there would be a constant stream of workmen—or women, God forbid—through the place. So much for living the life of a recluse. This morning he was blaming the presence of his redheaded rescuer for the desertion of the muse. No matter that he hadn't been able to write for months. Today, he knew that someone else was in the house, and she would likely come around when she'd finished measuring up, even though he'd told her not to bother him. Waiting for the inevitable interruption was wreaking havoc with his *concentration.*

It was. That's all it was. Once the redhead was gone for the day, he'd get some words down. He looked at the blank document on the monitor in front of him and it caught his reflection, and his eyes stared back accusingly at him.

I give up.

Liam pushed himself to his feet with a grunt and blocked all other thoughts from his mind as he crossed to the window and looked down at the untidy backyard.

Another job that needs doing. He'd deliberately set up this room as his study because it had no view over the sea. No distraction. The last thing he needed was to stare out over the water when he should be getting his word count up.

Ha. That's a joke. It was impossible to count words that were not written. As if on cue, his phone buzzed and he debated whether to answer it or not, especially when he picked it up and his agent's number flashed on the screen accusingly.

"Hello, Sarah." Liam stared down at the overgrown lawn below.

"Liam, where have you been? I tried to reach you all day yesterday."

"I was kayaking."

The silence on the other end of the phone relayed Sarah's displeasure. He knew he was letting her down, but somehow he'd get this book written as soon as he was settled in the house. He had to.

"So you've got some words down then? You're feeling better…the block is gone?"

Last month, he'd stupidly shared with her that he'd been suffering from a great dose of writer's block—ever since he'd come back from Nepal. It wouldn't hurt to stretch the truth a little to get her off his back. "Yeah, I have…and I am."

Liam straightened and brushed his hair back, accidentally knocking his head, and a deep throb winged across his brow.

"That's good then. Your new editor wants to meet you in Brisbane next Tuesday and have a look at the first few chapters." Sarah sounded a bit happier after hearing his white lie. He did have some words down. He'd thought of a title for this adventure story and typed it at the top of the first page. And he'd typed "Chapter One" below that.

Mustn't forget that. He ran his hand over the back of his neck as panic lodged in his throat.

"A new editor? Why do we have to meet? It takes time away from my writing." Liam frowned and the bandage pulled again. "And I'll have to hire a car. I haven't bought one yet."

"Yes, I know." Sarah's tone was patient, and he knew she was trying to placate him. But he also knew she was as hard as nails and would ride him until he finished the blasted book. Sarah had been with him since he'd shopped his first book around to publishers. She'd seen the worth in his story, taken a chance on him, and had sold it in a bidding war that had surprised both of them. Then she had celebrated with him when *Guardian of the Soul* had made *The New York Times* bestseller list two weeks after release. When he'd needed pushing, she'd been the one to do it.

And by God, he needed it now.

Sarah had also been a rock when Vanessa had died, and with Mike, her lawyer husband, had dealt with all the paperwork. Even though Liam and Vanessa had already separated, Liam had still felt as though he should look after the formalities of her death. Sarah and Mike had pulled strings and gotten him home from Nepal as quickly as they could. So he felt guilty about letting Sarah down now. He was her biggest client, and if this three-book contract went west, she stood to lose a lot of money, too. That thought had nagged at him for the past few days. Sarah and Mike were good people, and he was honoured to count them among his friends.

Ha. Probably my only friends. It was amazing who had disappeared after they'd read the crap about his marriage in the papers. None of his so-called friends had called him since he'd been back in Queensland. Not that he really cared. A private life with no socialising suited him and meant that he had more time to write.

"Do you want me to fly up from Sydney and come to the meeting with you?" Sarah's voice was soft and he hated lying to her. "You have been out since you moved up there, I hope? You're not turning into a recluse, are you?"

Sarah knew him too well. Liam chewed the side of his cheek as he stared down at the garden. The redhead's dog was stretched out in the warmth of the morning sun. A feeling of nostalgia ran through him. Big clumsy dogs had been a large part of his growing up on the farm. He probably should get a dog, now that he was settled. Vanessa had had one of those fluffy toy dogs and he'd hated the yapping thing. It was one of the many things they'd fought about before things had gone really bad. Crazily enough, when she'd finally left him and taken off with that other guy, he'd missed the dog more than he'd missed her.

"Liam? Are you there?"

"Sorry. No, there's no need to come." He turned away from the window and focused on the conversation. "I'll be fine. Just email me the details of the meeting and I'll be there."

"With your chapters?"

"Yes, with my chapters. Look, I have to go. I've got someone here measuring the house for some work for me." He used that as an excuse before Sarah could ask more specific questions about his progress. "Say hello to Mike for me. I'll let you know how the meeting goes. Bye."

He disconnected and put the phone in his pocket before Sarah could reply. With an impatient glance at the desk—any desire to write had completely disappeared now—he opened the door and headed outside for some fresh air.

***

Georgie frowned as she tucked the pencil into the back pocket of her jeans. The walls were out of alignment and she was going to have to find Mr. Kayak Man and talk to him about the design. She couldn't think of him as Liam—it was too soft a name for someone with his hard and implacable demeanour.

Liam—the name—should belong to someone kind and creative. An artist, although Sienna's Jack was an artist and Jack wasn't a name they would have picked for one. Georgie grinned as she stepped into the hall. She and Sienna had always thought up characters for guy's names when they were in their teens. Liam had been one of her favourites…and now it just proved her poor judgment. This guy was a sullen and rude jerk, not the soft and dreamy Liam of her teenage imagination.

Before she sought him out, she'd go down and check on Mutt. It had taken longer than she'd thought to measure, and she hadn't left him much water. At least he wasn't howling; that would really set the guy off. Apart from the creak of the stairs beneath her heavy boots, the house was quiet as she hurried down to the bottom level. There was no sign of Liam, and she put her notepad and pencil on the table beside the front door before she went out quietly, leaving the door half open so she could come back inside after she checked on Mutt. Her footsteps were quiet on the grass, and Georgie breathed deeply as she walked along the side of the house. A stiff breeze blew in from the sea, and the salt gave the air a sharp tang. She'd always loved it out here. The fragrance of the orange blossoms on the breeze was amazing.

If she did come back to the Sunshine Coast after her year away, she'd look for a place on the cliffs along this beach. Even after she paid for her air ticket, she still had a tidy sum put away from the sale of their restoration business, and the generous salary from Blake for working in the store office had added to it over the past couple of years. Her trip was going to be economical; she was planning a backpacking tour, much to her travel agent's dismay. The round-the-world ticket alone had cost her enough as it was, without going the five-star-hotels route. That way she'd save her money and have more options when the year was up. Nerves jangled in Georgie's stomach and she pushed away the thought of her planned trip.

Plenty of time to think about that.

As she neared the corner of the house, the muted tones of a soft voice reached her. She paused with her head tilted to the side and listened. It was coming from the backyard. She stepped forward quietly, put her arms on the gate, and looked across the unkempt lawn. Liam was sitting on the ground beneath the hanging branches of a large tree and had his arms around Mutt. His face was in Mutt's fur, and his voice was sad as he spoke to the dog.

"Just like you, boy." His words were muffled, but Georgie could make them out. She stepped back, feeling as though she was intruding on his privacy—and he'd made it quite clear he wanted privacy, no matter what.

"He was a good dog, my best mate, and he died." Before she could step back far enough, Liam lifted his head and looked out to the ocean, and the naked grief on his face slammed into her chest like a physical pain. She put her hand up to her mouth and took another step back before he could see her. Her foot rolled over on the edge of the path and Georgie gasped as her legs went out from under her. Her butt hit the ground with a solid thud, and her elbow hit an empty pot, which tipped over onto the path with a loud crash.

By the time she caught her breath and righted the pot, she was looking up into eyes that were dancing with amusement. The sadness on Liam's face had gone and she wondered if she'd imagined it.

He opened the gate and Mutt bounded past him and licked her as she tried to push herself to her feet.

"Are you okay?" His voice was *almost* kind as he held his hand out to her. She was pleased to see he'd put on a T-shirt and she didn't have to look at his bare chest any more. Georgie reached up for his hand and pulled herself up, dropping it as soon as she was on her feet. She brushed the back of her jeans and tried to ignore the heat that filled her cheeks.

What a klutz.

"Yes, I'm fine." She tried to keep her voice businesslike and brisk as her eyes met his. A warm, familiar feeling curled in her stomach as he stared at her. It had been dim in the kitchen, and she hadn't noticed the tiny smile wrinkles that fanned out beside his eyes, despite putting the bandage on his head. He was older than she'd first thought, and altogether too good-looking for her peace of mind. He was much easier to deal with when he was being rude to her.

"I was just coming to check whether Mutt had water before I came to find you. I didn't plan on making such a graceful arrival." Georgie chuckled.

One dark eyebrow quirked in a question and she rushed on. "I know you didn't want to be disturbed but I need to ask you about the design. There's a problem with the room."

Mutt slunk away from her toward the track to the beach, and she wagged a finger at him. "Uh-uh, no beach today, Mutt." She reached out and grabbed his collar. "I'll just check he has water and I'll meet you up there. Okay?"

"It's okay. He can come inside with us. I'll get him a bowl of water on the way through the kitchen." Liam reached down and patted Mutt's head. "He's a friendly dog. How old is he?"

"I'm not sure. I'm only minding him for a friend before I—"

Liam looked at her curiously as he walked beside her along the path to the front door. "Before you what?"

"Before I go away."

"Where are you going?"

Where had the taciturn man from this morning gone?

"I'm going on a holiday." She wasn't going to share all her personal business with him.

401

"And so what happens to Mutt then?" Liam stood back and gestured her through the door in front of him. Mutt pushed past as though he belonged inside. "Where will he go?"

"He goes to my uncle's house until my friends come home. I'm minding the house—and Mutt for my other friend—while I do your job. And Sooky the cat." She swallowed and followed him to the kitchen. Chatterbox, wear-her-heart-on-her-sleeve Georgie was back and telling the world her business. God, she could feel the blush stealing over her cheeks.

Now close your mouth and stop blabbing.

Liam opened a cupboard and pulled out a plastic container. She watched as he crossed to the sink and filled it with water before placing it on the tiled floor for Mutt, who took a big slurping drink and flopped down.

Georgie frowned at the dog and muttered beneath her breath. "Make yourself at home, why don't you."

"He's fine."

"Thank you." She turned to the door. "Now are you interested in listening to me this time?" Again, she pulled out her brisk, businesslike voice. Being in Liam's company was starting to unnerve her, especially now that he was being a bit more hospitable. She wanted to appear calm, and not gab all her private business just because he was acting like a reasonable human being. She deliberately pulled an image of Brent's face into her head to remind herself of her determination to stay distant, and not allow herself to be attracted to any man, and especially not this one, just because he'd been pleasant to her friend's dog.

He levelled a cool gaze on her. "If I have to."

Good, the difficult Liam had returned.

Chapter Four

Liam stood back and allowed Georgie to precede him up the staircase. He'd noticed the moment when she had gone quiet on him. Her whole demeanour had changed and it had been strange to watch. Uncertainty had crossed her face while she'd told him about going away, and the brisk tradesperson had disappeared. Now, a woman with a distinct lack of confidence walked ahead of him.

He pushed away the surge of interest. That was the writer in him, always interested in people and their lives and their personalities, and in one way, he welcomed the feeling. It was the first sign of his muse that had appeared in weeks. On the other hand, he didn't like the response his body was having to the sight of her shapely derriere moulded by snug-fitting jeans as he followed her up the staircase.

She'd knotted the long work shirt at the front of her waist, and her red hair was scraped back into a high ponytail that swished in front of him. The colour of her hair fascinated him. He'd never seen anything like it. It wasn't auburn and it wasn't red, it was more like a deep golden copper, and he wondered what it would feel like if he reached out and undid the ponytail and ran his fingers through it. Tucking his hands in his pockets, he followed her along the hall that ran the length of the top floor. They didn't speak until they reached the room at the end. Georgie opened the door and led the way in.

"So, what's the problem?" Liam glanced down at his watch and she compressed her lips, obviously getting the message he was trying to convey. The sooner she got out of here, the better for his peace of mind. He leaned against the door and waited for her to speak.

"I left my notebook downstairs by the door, but I don't need it. I'll be quick." She walked to the long wall at the back of the room and tapped her knuckles near the corner. A chunk of grey and white plaster fell and landed on the floor next to a few other pieces of similar size. "This bit will have to be knocked out and replaced before any shelving can be built onto it. It won't support the weight of the shelves, let alone when they are loaded with books."

"So do it." Impatience took over. He should be writing. Most of the morning had flown by and he hadn't written a single word. His desk was tidy, his pencils sharpened, and his email filed into folders. Another morning gone with nothing added to his story. This block had to crumble soon, but it certainly wasn't going to happen while he stood and listened to this far-too-attractive woman talking about knocking walls down in his house.

"And the—"

"Look. I appreciate that you want to share all this with me, but I don't really care how you go about it and what you have to do." Liam crossed his arms and kept his eyes on hers. "I want bookshelves. Just do whatever it takes." He flicked a dismissive hand, and he knew he was being rude, but the sooner he could go into the small room with his computer and lock himself away, the better. He was uncomfortable with his reaction to her. It had been a long time since he had taken pleasure in looking at a woman. Despite her old jeans and red work shirt, she had a sweet vulnerability that tugged at him.

He'd always been a sucker for a woman in need and look where that had gotten him.

But he did smother a grin as her voice followed him when he turned away and headed for the door.

"I'm sorry I bothered you. You'll get your bookshelves. Eventually."

A woman who always had to have the last word.

Mutt tugged on the leash, eager to get home when Georgie finished measuring up. Honestly, Georgie didn't know if she wanted to do this job or not. Maybe she should just forget it—leave for her trip and hand it back to the store.

But she'd promised Blake she'd do it, and she knew he was worried enough about leaving the business in the hands of a manager while he and Ana were in Melbourne helping his old boss wind up his hardware business interests.

The wind had picked up and Georgie looked up at the scudding clouds. The weather was closing in and the temperature was dropping quickly. The look on his face as he'd buried his face in Mutt's fur came to mind and she hoped Liam wasn't planning on going out in the kayak today…and she was totally forgetting the tremble that had worked its way down her spine as he'd followed her up the stairs.

All men are off-limits. Even a sad-eyed rude guy who was drop-dead gorgeous. If he wanted to go out in his kayak, it was absolutely none of her business. She was not going to worry about him.

The sooner she got this job finished, the better. As soon as her vacation began, this uncertainty about leaving home behind would disappear and she'd have a wonderful time while she explored the world.

Who knows? Maybe she'd settle somewhere else and never come back to Hideaway Bay. There was a great wide world to discover and she was going to do it.

I am. Soon.

Backing out of the driveway in Ana's old work ute was tricky. One of the side mirrors was hanging loose, and Georgie had to reach out and hold it steady as she steered with one hand. Georgie had sold her car before Blake asked her to do this job.

Now she glanced across the seat and grinned. She'd thrown her notebook and tape on the seat and it had landed on a pile of papers. Ana's untidiness had driven Sienna crazy because she preferred everything in its right place. Georgie had teased her mercilessly when they were growing up. One sure-fire way to get Sienna hopping mad was to rearrange her shoes...or even better, hide one of a pair.

It had taken Georgie a couple of days to settle into the cottage and find everything she'd needed. But it was lonely—even with Mutt and Sooky to talk to. She fought back the surge of want that filled her throat, and the tears that pricked at her eyes. It was not to be for her, but she could still be happy that both Ana and Sienna had fallen in love and found their life partners.

The sun broke through the clouds as she parked the truck at the back of Blake's hardware store. The timber yard was empty and there was no sign of life. Her stomach grumbled and she realised she hadn't eaten since last night. This morning, she'd been keen to get next door to Liam's place and get the measuring done. Her coffee had kept her going for a while. Then she'd been too busy trying to ignore her reaction to the owner of the house to think of food.

Georgie sighed and headed out to the back street and walked along the small alley that brought her to Main Street. Since Blake had been the president of the local business organization, a few new shops had opened, and the tourist trade had picked up. She headed south toward Uncle Renzo's café and grinned as she spotted her surrogate aunt's pink Fireflite parked outside the new sweet shop. When old Joe Humphries had passed on, they'd all been amazed when he'd left the car to Mitzi. It had been locked away in his shed for years, and no one had even known it was in there. Everyone had been used to taking turns driving Mitzi and her sister, Thelma, around. It had been a surprise to learn that Mitzi was the holder of a driver's license that she had actually kept current.

Mitzi wouldn't divulge exactly why Joe had left it to her but hinted at a story. Now she was fast becoming a character as she drove the 1960 Fireflite to town each morning with her elderly sister sitting in the passenger seat beside her.

"Georgie!" Mitzi spotted her as soon as she stepped onto Main Street. The old lady was standing outside the sweet shop, dressed in her best clothes. A floral hat was perched on top of her soft white curls and an overflowing basket was balanced on her arm.

Georgie crossed the road and stepped up onto the high curb. She loved this town with its old-fashioned quirks, and she adored her elderly friends. It was going to be very hard to leave it behind when she set off on her adventure. A cloud of lavender enveloped her as she kissed the woman's soft cheek and took the heavy basket from Mitzi's arm.

"What on earth have you got in there? Have you been buying sweets?" Georgie lifted the red-checked cloth and peeked beneath. Bottles of lemon butter and small packets of fudge in clear cellophane tied with red ribbon filled the basket.

"We're going into business." Mitzi tapped her nose as she smiled at Georgie. "Now that we have wheels."

Georgie narrowed her eyes. "Business?" As well as not missing a trick, and being the district's busiest matchmakers, Thelma and Mitzi were full of moneymaking schemes that always seemed to fail.

"Yes. Thelma is inside negotiating now."

"Where?" Just as Georgie answered the question, the sweet shop door opened, and Thelma stepped out. Her smile spread even more as she saw Georgie standing beside her sister.

"What a lovely surprise and excellent timing." Tiny hands latched onto Georgie's arm and before she knew it she was being dragged into the shop. "Come on, Mitz, I've got us a sale."

Before she knew what was happening, Georgie had been introduced to the new owners of the sweet shop, Thelma had unloaded her basket onto the counter, and they were back out the door.

"Now we are going to have a celebration lunch." Mitzi held on to Georgie's arm. "And isn't he a nice young man?"

Georgie shook her head, not sure who Mitzi was referring to. "Who?"

"The owner of the sweet shop." Mitzi lowered her voice to a conspiratorial whisper. "That's his sister, not his wife."

Georgie rolled her eyes and grinned. "Ah, but you forget. I am leaving for my round-the-world trip on Christmas Eve. By myself. No time for a new man this week." She played along with them. They were well used to her succession of boyfriends and didn't need to know that part of her life was over. She'd done a great job of hiding the pain of Brent's breakup, and she was still cheerful and helpful Georgie to the world.

Thelma and Mitzi both frowned as they stared at her.

"We know, dear. That's what we're worried about. What if you meet someone on the top of one of these South American mountains? Why, we may never see you again." Mitzi's high-pitched voice trembled.

"I'll be quite safe."

"Oh, we're not worried about that. Well, don't get us wrong, we are, but what if you fall in love and never come home?" Thelma added her two cents.

"Of course I'll come home and visit you. And besides, I'm not going to fall in love."

Georgie let their chatter wash over her and gave the appropriate nods as Thelma put the empty basket in the boot of the car before they walked the short distance to Uncle Renzo's restaurant. She looked around, pleased to see the busy lunch trade. She missed Sienna and Ana so much. The three of them had often lunched here together when they'd been between restoration jobs and working in the hardware store before Blake had bought it.

Why did life have to change?

Renzo blew her a kiss as he put a plate of rolls in the middle of their table, and Georgie grinned back at him. He had been like a true father to her, when he and Lucia took her and Sienna into their family after Marietta had taken off.

"I have to be quick, girls." Georgie reached for the bread. The old dears loved to be treated as one of the gang. "I only came into town to get some timber for a job I'm doing for Blake."

Mitzi had a sad, dreamy look on her face and let out a little sigh.

"We heard you were working at Joe's old place." Thelma stared at her intently.

Georgie rolled her eyes.

Did nothing escape this pair?

But she did love them. They were like family to her.

"What's the new owner like? We must welcome him to town." Thelma's face brightened. "We could visit this afternoon and take him a cake!"

Mitzi clapped her old, gnarled hands. "Yes, we have plenty left from our market stall."

Should I be nice?

Georgie's better nature won out and she cleared her throat. "Mr. Wyndham, the new owner, seems to want to be left alone." How could she put it kindly? "I think he values his privacy and wants to keep to himself, so maybe give him a while to settle in."

"Of course he does, the poor man."

Georgie looked up from the roll she was buttering and frowned. "The poor man?"

"Yes, the poor man. Don't you know?" Thelma and Mitzi looked at each other and they both shook their heads. "Georgie dear, you do live in a little world of your own."

"Maybe I just don't listen to gossip." She knew her voice was sharp, and she immediately regretted it when Thelma's eyes clouded. "I'm sorry. I just like to keep to myself."

Mitzi reached out and took her hand. "Oh, darling, we know how much you're hurting, no matter how much you smile. If I was brave enough to drive on that highway, I would chase that horrible Brent all the way to Brisbane and give him a kick in the bum"

Georgie couldn't help the peal of laughter that bubbled up from her chest at the thought of Mitzi kicking anyone in the bum. "Oh, I do so love you gals."

"You have to get over him," Thelma added.

Georgie swallowed and plastered a smile on her face. "I'm fine. You're worrying about nothing. I'm well and truly over Brent." She leaned forward and stared at Mitzi. "Okay, I know I'm going to regret this, but why is Liam a poor man?"

"His wife was killed when he was in the Himalayas."

"His wife? In a climbing accident?" No wonder Liam looked so sad.

"No, no, no." Thelma and Mitzi spoke together, and Georgie looked from one to the other. They were back in their element.

"*He* was in the Himalayas. She was killed in a car accident in Sydney," Mitzi said.

"The magazines said she was with her lover." Thelma shook her head from side to side. "That poor man. It's so hard to believe what they said, that he made her stay at home while he travelled around the world."

"Why would the magazines write about her? And him?" Slowly it dawned on Georgie that she'd thought his name was familiar. "I know he writes books, but I've never heard of him."

Mitzi sighed and gently shook her head. "Georgie, Liam Wyndham is a *famous* author. He was researching his next book

410

when his wife died…with her *lover*."

Thelma leaned forward. "And the magazines said he'd stopped her from accessing their bank account before he went away. And changed the locks on their house. Of course, I don't believe a word of it. He looks like too nice a young man to do such a terrible thing to his wife."

"Oh, how sad." She closed her eyes and remembered the look on his face as he'd been with Mutt. "But you know what those magazines are like. They make most of the stories up just to sell more copies. I'm sure none of it's true."

"Well, she was killed, and we will go down to the coast and visit him tomorrow."

Georgie propped her chin in her hand and smiled at them, trying to divert the old ladies from their "welcome" quest. "I think that's very sweet but honestly, he's still unpacking. He barely had time to show me the room I'm building the shelves in. There are packing boxes piled up everywhere and he's obviously very busy." There was no need to tell them that he had found time to go kayaking in the ocean. "I know he doesn't want to be disturbed."

"Very well. Whatever you say, Georgie." They smiled sweetly at her.

It was mid-afternoon by the time Georgie had loaded the truck with buckets of plaster, a stepladder, and her tools, as well as a small amount of lumber. She asked the store to deliver the rest of the wood to Liam's house tomorrow.

Mr. Wyndham. Think of him as a client. Not the man with the sad life that Thelma and Mitzi had spilled the beans about. Now that she knew all that, she would keep them away from him. Not that her life was anything spectacular or worthy of gossip magazines, but she knew the pair of them would love to fill Liam in on her recent man trouble. And visit him they would, she had no doubt of that. She was really starting to regret confiding Brent's

411

nasty words to Thelma and Mitzi. She should have known better, but Ana and Sienna weren't around anymore, and she'd needed a couple of soft shoulders to cry on. It was going to come back to bite her, for sure.

And all the more reason for her to keep her distance from Liam. He was ripe for the picking by the old, soft-hearted Georgie.

She was pretty sure she'd persuaded them to stay away, but knowing the pair of them so well, they were capable of anything to help a soul in need, especially now that they had *wheels*. A giggle bubbled up in Georgie's throat.

Oh, if only the world worked under their rules. A slice of cake and a cup of tea would solve any problem.

Georgie smiled as she drove Ana's ute up the drive to the old house. It was a good feeling to be back out and about to start a job. As much as she had enjoyed working in the store and doing administrative stuff, it was not the same as the hands-on work she loved doing—and was good at. Building, creating, and restoring old houses to their former glory was the best job ever.

This place was still Joe's old house to her, and it would be hard to start thinking of it as Liam's. She was hoping to slip in and unload the truck without being seen. He'd said he'd leave the door open for her, and he'd made it quite clear he didn't want to be disturbed. Georgie winced as she missed a gear with a loud crunch on the final bend before the truck rattled to a stop outside the front door.

Chapter Five

Liam shut down the computer, leaned back in his chair, and rubbed his eyes with the heels of his hands. At least the ferocious headache had gone. He'd spent a few hours clearing his email and changing the address for some of his bills. Then he'd read through his research notes and waited for inspiration to hit.

But nothing. Not one word, not one thought crossed his mind. The creative well was dry. He picked up a pencil and opened a fresh notebook. Maybe if he turned away from the computer the words would come. Concentrating, he gripped the pencil so tightly that it snapped in his fingers, and in disgust, he dropped it into the garbage pail next to the desk.

His heart skittered a beat as the crunching of gears sounded through the window. The interruption was welcome.

Georgie was back. The house had seemed empty since she'd left late this morning. Liam had not been able to help himself when she'd left. He'd stood at the window and watched her as she followed the dog down the hill to the cottage. She interested him and he wondered why she was living alone in someone else's house.

None of my business. But he still couldn't stop himself from pushing the chair back and crossing the room to the window. An old, battered ute was parked in the driveway. The truck bed was loaded with buckets, a ladder, a few lengths of timber, and a large toolbox. As he watched, Georgie opened the door and stood next to the truck. She looked up and he leaned out the open window.

"Would you like a hand?" He might as well help; there was nothing productive happening here. It was the polite thing to do and it had nothing to do with the warmth that ran through him when she smiled up at him.

"Yes, please. I won't refuse that offer." She waved and disappeared out of sight between the house and the truck.

Liam buttoned up his shirt and ran his fingers through his hair as he walked downstairs. By the time he opened the door, she'd unloaded half of the gear from the back of the truck onto the pebbled driveway.

"That was quick." He picked up two of the buckets and turned back to her. "You unload what's left while I carry it up. I assume it's going upstairs where you've been measuring up?"

"Yes, please, but you don't have to help me. I'm quite used to working by myself." Georgie held his gaze and a frisson of something ran down his back. He welcomed it; it was so good to feel. He knew he'd been in a state of numb disbelief since he'd come back from Nepal.

The buckets were heavy and the muscles in his arms were burning by the time he got to the top of the stairs. Despite telling Georgie he'd take everything up, she was right behind him, with a bucket in each hand. Liam put down the buckets he was carrying to open the door, and then stood back to let her past him into the office. Her shirt was still unbuttoned over her T-shirt, and he looked away from the soft swells beneath the close-fitting fabric. A lazy kick of something swirled through him as the fragrance of orange blossom drifted from her, and he pushed it away.

"I said I'd carry them up for you." His voice was short.

"You're the client. I'm the builder." She grinned at him as she put the buckets in the far corner and waited for him to carry his load through.

He should pick them up and stop standing there appreciating her curves, but it was almost impossible. He couldn't take his eyes from her, and he couldn't stop thinking about how gentle her fingers had been when she'd looked after his wound.

Liam clenched his hands around the bucket handle as

414

determination filled him. *Push these feelings away; they are crazy.* He'd made a vow when Vanessa betrayed him. He'd fallen in love with her when he'd met her at a book signing and these same feelings had filled him when he'd first seen her standing in front of him, waiting to have her copy signed. Any pretty woman in a close-fitting T-shirt would elicit the same response.

Get over it.

"Put them over here in the corner. I'll go and get the tools." She passed him as he crossed the room, and he made a noise of assent in his throat.

They made four trips from the truck up to the office, but Liam made sure he took his time and that he was upstairs each time Georgie was down at the truck. He was already regretting helping and the feeling intensified when she came up with the final load.

"Thanks heaps for the help. You've saved me quite a few trips. Your stairs are killers."

Reluctantly, Liam turned from the window and looked at her. Her arms were full of assorted small packets of nails and screws that she clutched to her chest with one hand, and she had a medium-size piece of wood held beneath the other arm. He crossed the room and slid the lumber out, and his arm brushed her hand. When she dropped her head and her fair skin pinked up, he knew he was in trouble. What was it about Georgie that made her so easy to read?

Because whatever he was feeling, the feeling was obviously mutual. She was feeling it as well.

Holy hell. He had to get out of here before he did something he'd regret.

He stepped away from her and put the wood down next to the buckets. The packs slid from her arms to the floor, and she crouched down, picked them up and pushed them into a small pile.

"So what's next?" He had to say something to break the

tension in the room. He knew it wasn't just him, because something had flared in her eyes as she glanced up at him. He hadn't seen anyone look at him like that in a long time.

And I don't want to.

Georgie stood and smoothed her hands down over her thighs.

"Once my muscles stop screaming at me, I'm going to knock out the back wall." She put her hands up and twirled her ponytail into a knot on the top of her head before she reached into her pocket for a clip. Liam swore he could feel his blood pressure spike as her T-shirt strained against her soft curves.

"That'll be enough for today, and then when the truck brings the rest of the lumber tomorrow, I can start putting in the reinforcements for the shelves. They're cutting the timber to the right lengths for me since I've done all the measuring." She walked away from him and he stared at the back of her head and not at her shapely butt. "Then I'm going to—"

Georgie sat on the windowsill and kicked her boot at the floor. "I'm sorry. I forgot you didn't want to know what's happening." She lifted her head and met his eyes squarely; her face pinked up even more. "Thanks for the help. I'll be fine now."

He waved his hand at her. "That's okay. I asked. I just wondered what was next."

"It's going to be very noisy while I knock that wall out. I hope it won't interrupt your work?" She chewed on her bottom lip, and he could tell she was ill at ease with him. She hadn't been like that before.

"My work?"

"I'll be honest with you. If you're going to live in this district, you'll soon find out nothing's private. I heard today in town that you're quite the celebrity and I put two and two together. But please don't think I was listening to gossip about you. With all these bookshelves"—his heartbeat kicked up a notch as a grin crossed her face—"I assume this is going to be your workspace and you're working somewhere else while you wait for this room to be ready?"

Liam was taken aback by her honesty, and he stared at her. Her eyes were clear as she held his with her steady gaze, and he could tell she was being open with him. In the world he'd become used to, no one ever came out and told the truth. There was no coquetry or game-playing in the way she spoke to him. And despite saying she hadn't been listening to gossip, she'd obviously heard all the stories about him. He looked away but he could still feel her stare fixed squarely on him.

"I thought you seemed sad, and now I know what happened, but it's none of my business, and if I can help or if you ever want to talk, just—" A strange expression crossed her face and she stopped talking and closed her eyes. "Shoot. Total rewind." She screwed her face up and clenched her hands in front of her eyes. "Please ignore every word I just said."

Liam opened his mouth, but before he could speak, she shook her head and pushed herself up from the windowsill.

"Look, I'm sorry." She brushed past him and for a moment he was tempted to reach out and pull her back. "I've changed my mind. I mean I've just remembered something I must do. I'll come back in the morning, and don't worry, I won't bother you again."

The sound of her work boots hitting the wooden stairs was followed by the slamming of the front door. Liam crossed to the window and watched as she drove off down the hill a lot faster than she'd driven up just a short time ago. He waited for her to turn onto her driveway, but the truck kept going, and she turned it onto the highway and headed south.

Maybe she had thought of something she had to do, and he'd read too much into the atmosphere between them. But it had been tense and for some reason he couldn't fathom why she'd taken off so quickly. And he hadn't even been rude to her. She'd

417

been upset and that bothered him.

He tried to forget the way his body had responded to Georgie as she'd brushed past him, but more than that, the way he had reacted to the sadness in her expression when she'd babbled on about changing her mind. His heart had lodged in his throat as her eyes had widened and she'd stared at him.

Something was bothering her, and it was a good feeling to worry about someone else for a change.

***

For the first time since Brent had told her she was not marriage material and then had hightailed it to Brisbane with his new girlfriend, Georgie let her feelings out. She'd barely made it up the highway to the small beach where Uncle Renzo and Aunt Lucia had brought them to swim when they were small. Turning the ute into the small parking area, she was pleased to see there were no other cars there. The hot tears spilled down her cheeks as she killed the engine and it stopped with a noisy rattle.

God, she was so embarrassed and so stupid. One look at a man, and here she was offering to help him through his personal crisis. Mortification filled her as she remembered the words, she'd said to him. *If I can help…or if you ever want to talk.*

A client. And not only a client, a famous author, at that. He must think she was an absolute idiot. He probably had a heap of friends and family, and here was the small-town builder offering to listen to his woes. She dropped her head into her hands and groaned.

It was so very tempting just to go back home, pack her bags, and leave. Georgie didn't want to face him again. In fact, she didn't want to see anyone she knew anymore. She needed to go away and try and find this independence she'd promised herself.

She pushed open the car door and stepped out into the cold wind. The chill was welcome because it took her mind off her problems for a brief moment as she crossed the parking lot to the wooden steps that led down to the beach.

The afternoon shadows lengthened as she walked along the wet sand. She had to get over this. It wasn't that she'd made a fool of herself and offered to listen to him that was the real problem.

Yeah, she was embarrassed, but being upset had more to do with the fact that she couldn't help herself.

Why? Why did she have to be so concerned about other people's problems? Every time she got involved with someone, it turned out badly. Sienna had always had her own theory about it. She said Georgie was trying to be the mother she'd never had, and so she tried to mother everyone else in her life.

But that was rubbish. They'd had two mothers. The woman who'd given birth to her, and then Lucia who'd done a great job bringing them up after Marietta had run off and Uncle Renzo had taken them in.

So it had nothing to do with the way she'd grown up. There must be something lacking in her and she had to face up to that. She was just not meant to be in a relationship. Maybe it was because she tried too hard? Maybe it was because there was something missing in her character? More tears threatened as Georgie muttered, "Maybe I'm just unlovable?"

Maybe I should disappear and go and work in one of those African orphanages or something? But the thought of leaving the safety of the Sunshine Coast and all her friends in Maleny, and her family scared her half to death. Georgie knew she was firmly entrenched in her comfort zone and she didn't really want to leave it, no matter how excited she was pretending to be about this once-in-a-lifetime trip. It would probably be better to put the money it was going to cost for the trip into a house here at Hideaway Beach.

And forget about men, marriage, and the white-picket-fence dream the girls tease me about.

There was something about her that turned men away as soon as they got to know her, and Georgie knew she tried too hard

419

to compensate for whatever it was. She looked up as a gust of cold wind came around the rocky point at the end of the bay, and realised it was getting dark. She turned around and walked slowly along the shore until the parking lot was in view again.

She let her thoughts settle on Liam and what she'd blurted out. Was it because of the attraction that had kicked in between them? She'd been aware of him watching her as she'd unloaded the truck. He was such a good-looking man and on top of that, his sadness had pulled at her heartstrings.

Why can't I just get on with my life, do the job that has to be done, and stay aloof? Independent.

She needed to take lessons from Sienna. No one could ever tell what she was thinking, and she pretended she didn't care about anyone. And she didn't spill her heart at the first opportunity, blab her business, and scare everyone off.

Now that she'd made a fool of herself, maybe he'd disappear, and she could put her head down and work as fast as she could. Get his shelves finished and get out of there.

Maybe she'd call Blake and see if he could find someone else to do the job. But she knew things had been tight since he'd taken over the store, and she didn't want to see the job go to a city firm because her cousins were booked up for months. So she'd honour her commitment.

Her mobile was ringing when she got back to the ute. Georgie reached for it and a wry grin lifted her lips when she glanced at the screen.

We might not be twins, but there is a connection between us.

"Hi, Sienna."

"Hey, sis."

A warm feeling settled in Georgie's chest and she laughed. "Don't you mean, hey, cuz?"

"No, we're sisters at heart. That's why I'm calling. I just

had a feeling that something was wrong. You haven't called and I was worried about you. Is everything okay?"

Georgie hesitated. She and Sienna had always been completely truthful with each other...but now Sienna had Jack and she was finally happy.

Really happy. She doesn't need my problems.

"Georgie?"

"Yes?"

"What's wrong? I knew something wasn't right when you put your trip off for a month."

"No, everything's fine." Georgie hastened to reassure Sienna. "I've delayed my holiday as a favour for Blake."

"But you're still going?"

"Yes, I leave Christmas Eve." It looked like she'd managed to divert Sienna from the "are you okay" talk. "I'm going down to Brisbane to the travel agent on Tuesday to make the final plans on my itinerary."

"So what's so important about this job for Blake?"

"The guy who bought Joe Humphries's place is an author and he needs his office fitted out quickly. Tony and Johnny are on a big job at the moment and Blake asked me to take it on. He didn't want to lose the job to a city firm."

"Anyone we know?"

"No, I'd never heard of him. It's Liam Wyndham."

"Liam Wyndham! Are you kidding me? The same Liam Wyndham who wrote the Guardian series?"

"Yeah, I guess so."

"Georgie, have you been living under a rock? My God, he's huge. And he's living next door to you? I've got all his books."

Georgie knew something was coming by the tone in Sienna's voice. They might as well be twins. They could read each other like a book.

Very appropriate. She giggled softly...Sienna could always

421

cheer her up.

"Do you think you could get him to autograph them for me?"

"No." Georgie could think of nothing worse than facing Liam again. "No way. I hardly see him. He's made it quite clear he wants his privacy and he'll be closeted in his study while I work." A hit of warmth ran up her neck as she remembered how she'd breached that privacy. "I tell you what you could do though, and you *might* get to see him. Mind you, only a very small *might*."

"What?"

"Are you busy this weekend? I could use some help. How would you and Jack like to come up to visit and you could do some fancy edges on a set of bookshelves for me?" If Sienna helped her out, she'd be able cut the job by a few days. And Sienna's work with wood was amazing. It would give the shelves that special touch to suit the old place. "I could do with some company, too."

"Suits me just fine. Jack's going back to Melbourne to sign for a commission in a building down there." The pride was evident in Sienna's voice and Georgie loved hearing it.

"I was thinking about a visit. And we can catch up and you can tell me what's wrong with you."

Georgie rolled her eyes. She thought she'd gotten away from that inquisition.

"I've got to take Jack to the Maroochy airport on Friday. I'll come to you after that."

"Girls' night in. Sounds good. Shame Ana's in Melbourne." Georgie was feeling happier by the minute. A gossip session with Sienna was just what she needed…as long as her cousin didn't pry too much into Georgie's feelings.

"Chill the wine," Sienna said.

"If you cook." Georgie laughed as they finalised their plans, and she threw her mobile onto the seat after they disconnected. The afternoon light was fading quickly by the time she backed the ute out of the small parking lot and turned onto the highway. Winter was taking a hold on the coast, but she'd soon be in a warmer climate. After that, who knew? In a way, it was exciting not knowing where she was going to go after Hawaii.

The walk on the beach and the conversation with Sienna had done her a world of good. Georgie took a deep breath. Tomorrow, she'd go back to Liam's and act like the professional tradesperson she was and pretend she hadn't been on the verge of tears and run out on him this afternoon.

She *would* be professional, and she *could* remain aloof.

Chapter Six

The best-laid plans flew out the window when Georgie shut the door of Ana's house behind her the next morning. She'd slept soundly, but late, and had deliberately left her starting time until midmorning so Liam would be settled into his study. She hoped that he'd left the front door unlocked as he'd promised, and she wouldn't have to face him. She'd have to see him sometime, but the later it was, the better prepared she'd be.

The delivery truck with the lumber for the shelves was due at eleven so she timed her arrival for then. He probably hadn't even noticed she wasn't there.

She walked up the hill, ignoring Mutt's mournful cries at being left behind. That was one less thing to be concerned about today. She didn't want to have to worry about leaving him in Liam's backyard.

One less opportunity for bumping into Liam.

She crested the small hill and groaned. Mitzi and Thelma's pink Fireflite was parked in the driveway outside Liam's front door and there was no sign of the truck from the store. The pebbled drive crunched beneath Georgie's feet as she debated whether to sneak upstairs and start work or acknowledge Thelma and Mitzi.

She'd kill them, she really would. Or she'd give them a good talking to about respecting people's privacy and turning up unannounced. Taking the cowardly option, she pushed the door open quietly and ignored the voices from the large living room as she tried to tiptoe across to the staircase. She frowned, trying to remember which step creaked.

"Georgie. Come in and say good morning to your *friends.*"

Busted.

Liam stood at the door and she turned around slowly.

424

"They wouldn't leave until you arrived. Thelma and Mitzi wanted to say hello to you." His voice was cold and the implication that she was late for work hung in his words.

Georgie pulled herself up straight and tried to stare him down. She was her own boss, and he had no say in her working hours. A little spurt of anger stiffened her spine as she held onto the banister.

Good, embarrassment zero. Anger, one. Keep it together.

She raked a cool glance down his body and ignored the little jolt of her heart. He had knee-length chinos on this morning and his feet were bare. A loose white shirt completed the casual look and as she lifted her eyes to his face her heart thudded uncomfortably in her chest. It was just like the shirt Colin Firth had worn in the famous lake scene that she and Sienna used to swoon over. His face was unshaven, and those sexy cheekbones were highlighted by the dark stubble. His ice-blue eyes held hers, but she fought the feeling that crept through her bones.

"All right. And then I have to get to work. The truck with the wood is due to arrive any minute."

"So that's why you're late?"

She stepped off the bottom stair and walked across the entry hall toward him, knowing there was a flush on her cheek. "Late?" She reached him and looked up into an amused gaze. God, I wish the man would shave, she thought irrationally. The stubble just makes him better-looking.

"I'm not late."

"I thought you had to knock the wall out?" His voice was low and there was dead silence from the living room. A grin pulled at the sides of Georgie's mouth as she imagined Thelma and Mitzi straining to hear their hushed conversation. Not hearing what she and Liam were saying would be killing them.

"I do." She let the grin take over and shot him a smile as she reached up and patted his shoulder. "You worry about your

425

work and your guests, and I'll look after my work. Deal?"

Liam's arm stiffened beneath her fingers and she knew he'd picked up the censure in her voice despite her sweet smile. She dropped her hand from his shoulder and pushed past him. Unfortunately, he was standing in the doorway, so she had to squeeze by to get to the living room. Every nerve ending stood at attention and her heartbeat picked up.

"Georgie." Thelma patted the sofa beside her. "We were worried about you, and so was Liam."

Liam? Already?

"You're very flushed, dear. You're not getting ill, are you?" Mitzi fluttered her little hands around.

"No, I hurried up the hill. I've got a delivery truck due at eleven. Now, don't you two have somewhere else you have to be? I'm sure Mr. Wyndham has some work waiting for him."

"It's all right. Liam knows you told us he was busy and that he didn't want to be disturbed. But he's such a sweet man. He said he was very happy to have us visit."

Georgie closed her eyes and took a breath. And she was sure they'd left nothing out about her, too.

"We had to come. There was a part from our car still in the garage here and we've been waiting for the new owner to arrive so we could come and get it."

"What part?" Georgie asked suspiciously. She knew them too well. Apart from their craftwork and going to the markets, their day was filled with good-natured meddling and matchmaking.

"Oh, just a pink thing." Mitzi waved her dainty little hands again. "Liam is going to look for it on our way out."

Thelma smiled at her and Georgie bit back the sarcastic reply that was hovering on her lips. She looked up and was surprised to see a grin on Liam's face. Of course he'd picked up on what was going on. He could see right through this devious pair. She would be having stern words with them later.

"I'll go to the garage and see if I can find the pink 'thing.'" He walked over to the elderly pair and offered a hand to each of them to help them up. "And then I'll come back and give you a hand to unload the timber truck." He turned to Georgie as the elderly women picked up their bags.

"Oh, don't worry about the part now," said Thelma. "It wasn't urgent. We'll leave you and Georgie to wait for the truck. We'll come back and get it another day."

"Yes, it will give us a reason to come and visit again. We do love being neighbourly," Mitzi chimed in. "It's so important to make new residents of the coast feel welcome."

Georgie turned to Liam with a genuine grin this time. "And since Joe left Mitzi his car, they've been neighbourly everywhere."

Georgie watched Liam as he escorted her two friends to the door. A tray with teacups and leftover cake sat on the coffee table and she grimaced. By the look of things they'd been here all morning.

Love it!

It didn't matter. She'd made up her mind about how to handle Liam. She would ignore the nervous jolts and warm feelings that ran through her and get to work as soon as the truck was unloaded. Mitzi and Thelma's being here when she'd arrived had broken the ice with Liam a little, although she still resented his comment about her being late.

"Oh, Georgie dear?" Georgie waited for what was coming as Thelma turned to her. "We've organised a little welcome reception for Liam at our place on Sunday."

Mitzi piped up. "We're having a garden party. You know how we love them."

Georgie shook her head. "Sorry, gals, I can't make it. I'll be busy working here. And I've already welcomed Mr. Wyndham." Her eyes met Liam's and she could see the mirth in them.

What happened to the guy who wanted total privacy?

A welcome reception? He seemed pleased about it, by the grin on his face. Maybe she'd read him wrong. Maybe it was just her he didn't like?

And unfortunately for her, he exuded even more hotness when there was a hint of a smile on his face. God help her if he actually smiled at her. She went weak at the knees just imagining it.

"Oh, but you have to come. Liam doesn't have a car yet and we've organised for you to drive him to our place."

Why did they always do this to me? She swore that Mitzi and Thelma had completed People Manipulation 101 right before they'd taken up Matchmaking 101. She tried to stare them down but they both quickly looked away from her and back to Liam.

"Come on, Liam. Help us into our car like the true gentleman you are, and we'll go back to town. If we leave now, we won't block the driveway for the timber truck. We'll come over and see your new office when it's finished. Georgie's work is magnificent."

"It's only a set of bookshelves; I'm not doing a full restoration." As soon as the words left her mouth and she watched Mitzi's face light up, Georgie wished she could pull them back.

"Oh, but you could. Joe's…I mean Liam's house is crying out for a touch like yours. You could do it instead of going—"

"Mitzi, I think Mr. Wyndham is waiting for you." Georgie clenched her fists by her side as she glared at her sweet old friend and kept her voice firm.

Mitzi walked to the car where Liam held open the driver's door. She turned her little wrinkled face up to him and a surge of guilt hit Georgie for thinking badly of them. They were just trying to be kind.

"Perhaps we could make you some frilly curtains," Mitzi said.

Thelma winked at her over the top of the car. Georgie snorted, and Liam closed the door, seemingly oblivious to the silent messages being passed around him.

***

Liam turned around to speak to Georgie as the huge old pink car drove sedately down the driveway, but she'd disappeared. He walked thoughtfully through the door and closed it quietly behind him as the sound of hammering began on the top floor.

So much for being a recluse.

He valued his privacy, and he'd come here just for that reason, but those dear old souls had managed to break through his barriers before he'd even had a chance to think. They'd bundled him into his kitchen, made a pot of tea, and produced a cake from a basket. He still didn't know which one was Thelma and which one was Mitzi. He'd barely managed to get a word in while they'd taken great delight in filling him in on all the locals around Maleny. There was enough new material filed away in his head to create a whole imaginary town populated with the colourful characters they'd described to him as they'd brewed tea and fed him cake. A little creative spurt niggled, and he welcomed it.

And they'd talked about Georgie. They'd hinted at a big secret but were loyal enough not to tell him anything private about her. It had whetted his curiosity. Maybe it would explain why he found her fascinating and so easy to read. He'd lost sleep last night worrying about what he'd done to upset her. It seemed as if she'd gotten embarrassed after she'd offered to listen to him if he wanted to talk. Then she'd run out and he'd let her go.

Kind. As well as interesting and beautiful. And a hard worker. He'd only known her a couple of days. She'd rescued him—or so she thought—retrieved his kayak, ministered first aid to him, and then turned up in dungarees and work boots. One of the most independent and self-contained women he'd ever met. Very different from Vanessa and her needy personality.

Before he went into his small study, he detoured via the kitchen and cut a huge slab of cake to take upstairs with him. He grinned; a spark of enthusiasm fired in his blood and it was unfamiliar. Ideas were turning into words in his head and he needed to get them down. He'd go up and see Georgie after he was done.

A long while later, Liam stretched at his computer desk and looked around. The afternoon sunlight was pouring through the window and he was thirsty. He glanced down at the time on the bottom corner of his laptop screen.

"Damnation." He pushed the chair back and strode toward the door before cursing and turning back to his computer to save his work. The words had flowed, and he'd written the first three chapters of a new book.

Not the book his publisher was waiting for, but the story that had come into his head when he'd been listening to his visitors. Now he felt guilty that he'd locked himself away, and he'd completely forgotten about Georgie and the delivery truck. She would think he was the biggest louse around. He just hoped she hadn't carted the timber upstairs herself. After he saved his file, he headed for the door. The house was quiet. There was no banging, no sound of any work—he tipped his head to the side and listened. There was no sense of anyone in the house but him.

He strode along the top hall, listening as he made his way to the study. The door was closed, and he stood outside and tapped lightly on the heavy wood.

"Georgie? Are you in there?"

All was quiet as he pushed the door open. She'd gone but she'd obviously worked hard, and he'd heard none of it while he'd been in his creative zone. The back wall had been pulled down and piles of old plasterboard were sitting neatly in the corner. A new frame had been built, ready to support the shelves. Liam swivelled around and groaned. Four high piles of wood were stacked neatly beneath the window.

God, I hope she had some help to carry that up. Surely the truck driver would have helped. He'd apologise to her tomorrow.

For a moment, he debated whether he should wander down to her cottage now, but common sense won out. He wasn't going to go visit her for any old excuse just because he found her— Liam frowned. Why did he find her so fascinating? She was confident and independent and interesting. But that didn't mean he had to bother her.

Despite enjoying his visitors today, he still intended to keep to himself. He'd get Thelma and Mitzi's number from Georgie tomorrow, and take a rain check on the welcome. They'd sucked him in, and he'd agreed to come to their party but it was totally not his scene.

Too cosy for me. He valued his privacy too much to get involved with the townspeople.

They were sweet old ladies and although he'd seen right through the reason for their visit, it had been kind of nice having company in his new house. Once he'd gotten on top of his book— the other one—he'd invite Sarah and Mike up for a weekend. Not a total recluse; just when it suited him.

It was time to start living again. *But slowly. Take it slowly.*

Liam crossed to the window and looked at the cottage down the hill.

Chapter Seven

It was Friday morning and Georgie cursed as she tried to lift the last length of wood into place. It was heavier than the rest and she had to get it up before she could start building the frame on the wall that joined this corner. She put the solid piece of lumber down, dropped to her knees, and caught her breath. It wasn't worth throwing her back out.

Looking around, she tried to figure out whether she could start at the other end of the window wall and wait till tomorrow, when Sienna would be here to help her lift the heavy piece of timber. In the meantime, she could set the joints at the corners where the two shelves would intersect.

She'd worked all week and hadn't laid eyes on Liam since Thelma and Mitzi had left on Tuesday. On the second day, she'd had a dreadful thought, worrying that he'd gone out in his kayak and tipped over again. Creeping quietly downstairs and through to the kitchen, a pile of dishes in the sink caught her eye. She put her hand to the coffeepot and breathed a sigh of relief as the warmth touched her skin. He wasn't far away. She could stop worrying.

Another day had passed, and Georgie had made great progress on the shelves. Occasionally, she would hear a door open and shut downstairs while she was working, reassuring her that he was around. Each morning when she arrived, the front door was unlocked, and she let herself in. She walked home for lunch each day, and Liam was nowhere to be seen as she came and went. She left Mutt down the hill and after the first day when he'd realised that he wasn't going with her, he had stopped howling.

Liam was either totally angry with her that Thelma and Mitzi had invaded his space, or he was simply indulging in that privacy that he'd indicated was so important to him.

Georgie stood and stretched. Whatever it was, it was none of her business, and her equilibrium had been restored because she hadn't had to deal with him all week. It had been very easy to stick to her plan of being professional and remaining aloof. She pulled a face.

It was pretty easy to remain aloof when I don't even run into the person I'm being aloof to.

But now she needed a hand, and she would ask in a professional manner, unless she could get away with leaving it. One last look at the wall convinced her that she had to keep working at that end. It was the first time she'd needed any help since she'd started this job.

Georgie slipped into the small bathroom next to the study and filled the old-fashioned pink porcelain basin with water. She scrubbed her hands clean and then patted cool water onto her cheeks. As she pulled her hair back into a high ponytail, she stared at her reflection in the antique mirror above the basin. Her cheeks were pink, and she knew it had nothing to do with the exertion. The curse of fair skin and red hair. She was nervous about seeking Liam out and it showed in her complexion.

Smoothing her T-shirt down over her work shorts as she walked down the hall toward the stairs, Georgie glanced into the open doors. It really was a beautiful old house—run-down, but beautiful. It had been one of the first mansions built along the cliffs when Hideaway Beach was developing into a commercial centre back in the twenties. She loved this area and its history fascinated her. The local region from Maleny to the beach had been settled in the early twentieth century by Italian immigrants who had planted acres of vegetables to supply the Brisbane market, and it still had a distinctly Italian feel. The old mansions that had been built along the coast road before the Depression had provided most of their restoration jobs when she'd been in business with Ana and Sienna.

433

Georgie stood at the top of the staircase and let her hand sweep the beautiful wood. It still had a high gloss and was worn smooth from years of hands running down it. The sound of a door opening beneath her jolted her out of her thoughts. She knew exactly what she was doing—putting the moment off.

Liam walked along the hall below, heading for the kitchen without looking up, and before she could change her mind, Georgie took a deep breath and walked slowly down the stairs. When she reached the kitchen door, he was at the sink filling the coffeepot and she stood in the doorway, watching him for a moment. Faded denim jeans hugged his legs and—God help her—he was shirtless again. Didn't the man feel the cold? His shoulders were smooth and tanned, and broader than she'd noticed before. Her mouth dried as she let her eyes wander freely up the length of his muscled back. His hair was pulled loosely into a piece of leather at the nape of his neck, and a few loose tendrils brushed his shoulders.

"Ah…" Just as she went to speak, he turned, so she stepped into the kitchen.

"Hello." He held the kettle up and tilted his head to the side. Oh man, he hadn't shaved again, and the angles and planes of his face were as sexy as the baby blues looking at her. "Coffee?"

It was as though she'd only just been talking to him and there hadn't been four days of being in the same house without a word spoken between them.

"I'm fine, thanks."

"Cold drink?"

She shook her head. "I'm sorry to bother you, but I just need a bit of help upstairs. It will only take a minute."

"I'll make you a deal. Keep me company while I have my coffee and then I'll come and help you." As he waited for her to answer, his blue eyes assessed her, and Georgie held her breath.

"I haven't seen a soul or spoken to anyone since Thelma

and Mitzi left the other day." Liam gave a rueful laugh. "Privacy is a bit overrated."

She smiled at the woebegone face he put on before she slid a chair out from the table. "Okay. I could do with a break. If you're sure you want company?" Usually she was confident in the company of others, but there was something about him that made her nervous. It wasn't because he was ridiculously good-looking. Maybe it was because she now knew he was a celebrity author. "Anyway, I wanted to apologise to you for the other day." Georgie ignored the fluttery feeling in her stomach and casually rested her elbows on the table, at odds with the words rushing from her lips.

"The other day?" Liam's brow wrinkled as he wandered over to the table with his coffee.

"Thelma and Mitzi turning up uninvited."

"But they were looking for the pink thing." Liam's face broke into a wide grin and Georgie's legs went to jelly, even though they were tucked beneath her on the wooden chair.

No, no, no.

She folded her arms in front of her on the old table and nodded mutely as his bare chest filled her gaze. She had known what a full-blown smile directed at her would do to her composure.

Pull yourself together.

"They were adorable. And the stories they told me"— Georgie rolled her eyes as the grin stayed on his face—"kicked off a spark for a new book and I've been writing ever since they left."

Georgie swallowed and tried to ignore the warmth filling her as he leaned close. This was an entirely different Liam from the one she'd been dealing with.

"I wasn't sure you were okay about them." She cleared her throat. "I'll have a cold drink, after all." Anything to take her attention away from the bare chest that filled her vision.

"Are you all right?" Liam reached out and put his hand on her arm and more heat surged into her cheeks. God, she'd be as red

435

as a fire engine soon.

"Yes," she said slowly.

"I'm sorry I didn't help you unload the truck the other day." His fingers stayed on her arm as he looked at her. "Oh, no, I didn't expect you to. Troy, the driver from the store, carried most of it up for me while I was working." She moved away a little and Liam lifted his hand from her arm.

"I was worried that you were angry with me because Thelma and Mitzi had turned up unannounced," she said.

"Even if I had been upset by getting interrupted, it wouldn't have been your fault. You didn't invite them." Liam narrowed his eyes thoughtfully and she felt like a butterfly pinned to a board. "And besides, they are a delightful pair."

Georgie slipped the tip of her tongue out and licked her dry lips, immediately regretting it as his gaze dropped to her mouth.

"Someone's done a real number on you, haven't they?"

"What?" The word came out as a squeak.

Liam ran a hand through his hair and tucked the loose bits behind his ear. "When you're not blushing, you're apologising, and I noticed the other day when the old dears were here, you were trying to make everything right."

He leaned back in the chair and sipped his coffee. Georgie stood and crossed to the sink and threw a glance over her shoulder as she filled a glass with water from the tap.

"So what makes you the expert?" He'd hit way too close to the bone, and she swallowed hard. "Do you write psychology books, too?"

"No, I'm a writer. I observe people and I've become pretty good at figuring out what makes them tick."

Georgie drained her glass and put it in the sink. "Well, what makes me tick is the job that's waiting upstairs and the time clock that's ticking away." The sudden hurt that lodged in her chest took her breath away. She knew what was wrong with her.

She didn't have to have some too-good-looking, pseudo-psychoanalyst writer look at her with his sexy eyes and put it into words. "My time goes on your bill and the sooner I get this job finished, the better."

His was still looking at her intently and she shifted from one booted foot to the other, uncomfortable beneath his stare.

"For both you…and me," she added.

"Look, I'm sorry if I overstepped the mark. I didn't mean to hurt your feelings."

"You've got me wrong, Liam. I've been trying to stay out of your way to preserve your precious privacy." Georgie waved a dismissive hand. She could act with the best of them. "And yes, I do have fair skin and I can't help it if I blush a lot. It's my complexion…nothing to do with my feelings." She strode to the door and casually flicked her ponytail with her fingers. "Matches the hair.

Her legs were shaking as she walked up the stairs. Just when she was enjoying the work and getting her head together, he had to remind her of how she always tried to smooth the way for everybody.

Okay, so I used to try to make everyone happy, but that's the old Georgie.

Get this job finished and then she'd be out of here. She'd take off into the big wide world and worry about no one but herself. The new, confident, look-after-herself Georgie would face life head-on and enjoy every minute of it.

I will.

She picked up the hammer and began knocking down the only wall left intact. A few minutes belting at the plaster had a soothing effect and she put the hammer down and wiped the perspiration from her brow. A light breeze was blowing in from the sea and she walked across to the window and let the cool air play on her damp skin.

When Sienna arrived tonight, she was going to unload on her. If she talked the whole Brent thing out, maybe she'd get over it quicker. That's what sisters were for. Though now they weren't real sisters—she'd never get used to that—they were still sisters in spirit. God, here she was on a trade job, building bookshelves for a man—okay a really, really good-looking man—and she was turning it into an emotion-fest.

Georgie knew she was overreacting. And the feelings brought to the surface by overthinking the guys who'd dumped her had made her more vulnerable to yet another good-looking man. And now the usual sequence of events was starting all over again.

Fall for a man.

He leaves.

Broken heart.

Move on.

Okay, maybe she was exaggerating. They hadn't all dumped her. She'd broken a few of the relationships off herself. But with Brent, she just hadn't seen the end coming.

A good dose of Sienna reality was just what she needed to jolt some sense into her. She picked up the hammer again but before she could start swinging it a light tap at the door alerted her to Liam's arrival.

"Still need a hand or did my big mouth make you mad enough to give you superhero powers?" He looked at her sheepishly as he pushed the door wide open.

Georgie ignored his attempt at humour and pointed to the corner, where the piece of wood was propped against the wall. "That's the one I need help to lift."

Liam walked over to the wall and she indicated the supports up near the ceiling. "I'll need to get up on the ladder to get one end up there, if you can just take the weight at the other end?"

Much to her relief, he'd put a T-shirt on before he'd come

up, and he hefted the piece of wood up to his chest while she dragged the small stepladder across the room. "I'm not used to working by myself. I'm sorry I had to—" She cut herself off as he looked at her. Climbing the first two rungs of the ladder brought her just above the top of his head and she looked down at him. "Okay." She put her hands up. "No more apologies. Cross my heart." She climbed up another rung and reached down for the lumber. "Ready?"

Liam lifted it up to her and Georgie gripped the wood firmly before she positioned it into the support in the corner.

"Keep a hold on your end, please. I just need to move the ladder over a bit more." She climbed down and because Liam was holding the wood in place, she had to duck beneath his arm to pull the small ladder across to reach the other support. She ignored the jolt as his arm brushed against her shoulder and she quickly climbed back up the stepladder and reached out for the wood. Her hands grasped the end and she slotted it into place.

Georgie leaned back to survey the wall, conscious of Liam's proximity. She forgot she was on the top step of the small ladder and stepped into mid-air. She let out a gasp as her arms flailed for a second. With a nimble turn, she twisted and jumped onto the floor, her heavy boots just missing Liam's bare feet. Unfortunately for Georgie, she teetered forward as she landed, coming up hard against his chest. His arms went around her and her head banged against his shoulder.

"Oomph." Closing her eyes, she stood there for a moment catching her breath. Finally, she lifted her head and looked up at him. "Sorry," she whispered.

"Are you okay?" Liam's voice was husky, and a shiver spiralled down her spine. Georgie stiffened in his arms so that he wouldn't feel the effect he was having on her body. She had turned to mush, not to mention that her resolve to remain unaffected by him had gone flying out the window. Her heart was thudding and as she looked up at him, she could see a pulse flickering in his cheek.

Why is he looking at me like that? His eyes were fixed on hers, and he had the strangest expression on his face. Georgie tried to pull back, but he tightened his hold around her. Chest to chest and thigh to thigh, she felt the tremble that rippled through him. She stopped pulling away as another exquisite shiver ran down her back.

"Do you mind if I just hold you?" His words were soft and his voice ragged, as though he'd been the one exerting himself. "It's been a long time since I've held anyone this close."

Georgie looked back at him and when she saw her own need reflected in his eyes, her arms lifted, almost of their own accord. She stood on her toes, reached around his neck, linking her fingers beneath his long hair, and lifted her face to rest against his cheek.

His face was cool against her heated skin. Liam's lips gently slid across her cheek in a soft kiss that was full of yearning. He paused before his lips reached hers. It was like coming home; different from any other kiss she'd ever experienced before. After a moment, he moved his head back a little before he rested his cheek against hers again. His lashes brushed her skin as soft as a butterfly and the rasp of his unshaven chin rubbed against her cheek. They stood locked together, no words, no movement, and Georgie revelled in the comfort of his closeness.

Finally, Liam pulled away and she frowned as the cool air replaced the warmth of his skin against hers. She looked up and he was staring into the distance above her head, and she looked down knowing she wasn't going to like what he was about to say.

She put her hand up before he could speak. "That was very sweet but it was a mistake and we both know it."

He lowered his head and stared at her for a moment before shoving his hands in his pockets.

440

"Yeah, it was. I'm sorry."

Georgie's phone trilled in her pocket as Liam turned on his heel and left her alone.

Chapter Eight

"Would it be okay with you if Jack drops me off on the way to Brisbane?" Sienna launched straight into her conversation as Georgie tried to compose herself. She gripped the phone tightly against her ear and tried to concentrate on what Sienna was saying.

"Yes...that's fine...no problem. Are you still coming tonight?" She lifted her hand and touched her cheek, trying to hold on to the feeling of Liam's lips on her skin.

"Yes, we're about to leave Noosa now. We realised it was crazy for me to go all the way to Brisbane and come back down to Hideaway Bay, so Jack's going to leave the car at the airport. Are you at home now?"

"No." Loose tendrils of Georgie's hair had come adrift from her ponytail. She lifted her hand from her cheek to push it back from her face and was surprised to see her fingers trembling. What had passed between her and Liam in those few minutes had rocked her to the core. When he had stepped back from her and let her go, it was like being cast adrift. It was a feeling she had never experienced before. She was aware of her heart thudding, and she drew in a deep breath trying to stop the lightness in her chest. "But I'm almost done here. I'll head home soon."

"Can't wait to see you."

"You, too. Bye." Georgie disconnected the call and slipped the phone back into her pocket. Now she had an excuse to leave and go home. She needed to escape from the house before she went looking for Liam to take up where they'd left off, even though she knew that was the last thing she should do.

Taking a final look, Georgie scanned the room, making sure all the electrical tools were switched off and unplugged before she closed the window. She didn't want to start a fire in this beautiful old house. As well as needing a restoration, she was sure the wiring wasn't up to code. The whole house needed work, and her fingers itched to be a part of bringing it back to life.

The afternoon sun was streaming through the window, bathing the half-built shelves in the strong light reflected by the large expanse of glass in the walls. Liam would have to put some sort of window covering up before he filled the shelves, or his books would fade quickly. Maybe he'd need Mitzi's frilly curtains, after all. The glimmer of a smile tugged at her lips, and Georgie knew she needed to lighten up. As she packed up her tools, she looked around, imagining what a beautiful room this would be once the shelves were finished and lined with books. Polished floorboards covered with a rich traditional rug, a desk sitting beneath the window... She shook her head and focused on tidying up. Not her house, and she wouldn't be here to see it finished, anyway. Closing the door behind her, she focused on the night ahead with Sienna.

Mutt looked at her mournfully as she pushed opened the gate to Ana's cottage. There'd been no sign of Liam when she'd let herself out of his house. Tomorrow, Sienna would be working with her, and hopefully that would put the end to any more almost-kisses from Liam. Georgie grabbed Mutt's lead and whistled for him. A walk on the beach would clear her head.

The walk on the firm wet sand at the edge of the small waves did do her a power of good, despite getting soaked from Mutt frolicking in the shallow water. She threw driftwood for him and he chased it and dropped it at her feet. He made the walk more enjoyable. She'd have to get herself a dog.

Shoot. She couldn't. Why did she keep forgetting she was going overseas? How could she forget about the around-the-world trip looming ahead of her? She had plenty of money in the bank

443

and an amazing adventure planned. What was the big deal about leaving home?

She was almost thirty, for goodness' sake.

Leaving for Hawaii on Christmas Eve? First stop at a luxurious beachfront house on Niu Beach, ten miles out of Honolulu. Most people would give anything to be in the position she was. Why, then, was she less than enthusiastic? Wandering upstairs, Georgie pulled off her T-shirt and turned on the taps of the deep bath in the small bathroom. Once she sat down with Sienna and a glass of wine, she'd get some excitement happening about this trip. Maybe Sienna could meet her in Machu Picchu for their birthday like they'd talked about at their last birthday dinner. She needed to cheer herself up and stop mulling over what couldn't be changed. Whatever had happened in the past had to stay there and now she must move on.

Life goes on, no matter what is thrown at me. She had her health, great friends and family, a job that would be there when she came back from her trip, and enough money to have a good life, if she was careful. She'd gotten over the need to have a significant other in her life.

So why do I feel so unsettled? Liam's face flashed into her thoughts. She'd known the man less than a week, and it was time to push this unwelcome attraction aside.

Ana's bathroom was filled with an array of bath oils, soaps, and salts. Georgie chose a bottle of amber and musk salts, and let the powder trickle between her fingers into the steaming water, taking a deep breath as the Oriental fragrance filled the small room. She slipped her shorts and panties off and stepped into the water, sighing as the heat warmed her chilled skin. She lay in there for half an hour, deliberately pushing Liam from her mind, despite the number of times his sexy eyes filled her thoughts.

Ice-blue eyes that stayed with you, filled with sadness and secrets.

444

We are a fine pair.

The water cooled and she climbed out of the bath and picked up one of the fluffy pink towels from the shelf beneath the window. Ana had an eye for pretty things and this bathroom was a lovely room. When she bought her own place—when she came home from overseas—she'd do something similar in her own bathroom. Georgie hummed and grinned to herself as she wrapped the soft towel around her.

But without the pink. Definitely without the pink. The tune from *Pretty in Pink* filled her mind and she hummed as she patted herself dry.

She didn't hear the car come up the drive but a soft tap at the front door heralded Sienna's arrival. Georgie twisted her wet hair into a knot on the top of her head and knotted the towel above her breasts before she ran lightly down the stairs. The carpet was soft and deep beneath her bare feet. It was a relief to have her heavy work boots off.

"You're early!" She pulled open the door and gasped as Liam's face filled her vision. Not in her thoughts this time, but standing in the doorway with his mouth hanging open and his eyes wide with appreciation

***

Liam couldn't help himself. All thoughts of spare parts and welcome parties fled from his mind as the door was flung open. He'd come down to see Georgie to get the old dears' number so he could take a rain check on the welcome party on Sunday. He'd totally forgotten about the invitation. He'd been out in the garage when he'd come across some Fireflite parts, and he remembered he was supposed to be going there on Sunday. The parts he'd found certainly weren't pink, but they were indeed Fireflite spares. He'd had a bit of a chuckle and put them aside in a small box. The old girls had been telling the truth. Now the box was tucked beneath his arm as he rapped on Georgie's door.

He'd done his best to put Georgie out of his mind since he'd held and almost kissed her, even though he knew he was kidding himself. Cancelling Sunday was an excuse. He'd wanted to see Georgie again. When she'd left early, he'd resisted the urge to come out of his study in case she'd thought he was having a go at her about her hours again.

"You're early!" The words were followed by a gasp as a prettily wrapped parcel of pure woman, encased in a pink towel, stared at him. Liam dropped his eyes to the bare legs at the bottom of the towel and then lifted his gaze to the hands that were covering the knotted towel above her breasts. A heavy musky fragrance enveloped him and he closed his mouth. He was gaping like an adolescent.

"Liam! What are you doing here?" Georgie's face was flushed and tendrils of wet hair stuck to her neck and cheeks. "I thought you were my sis…my cousin."

Her eyes were wide as she raised her hand to push back the wet hair, and the towel slipped a fraction lower. Liam didn't fight the grin he knew was spreading over his face. He'd been uncomfortable about facing Georgie after their "hug," but now he was pleased he'd chosen this particular time to come and see her. The ice was broken. Well and truly—in shards.

"Stop looking at me like that." Her voice was stern. Her green eyes fairly glowed.

"Like what?" he asked innocently, doing exactly what she asked him not to do. Hell, she made too pretty a picture to look away.

"You know what." She slipped him a tentative smile and his eyes fixed on her lips as she half closed the door to block his view, and peered around it. He'd never noticed the full curve of her bottom lip before; she'd usually been concentrating on banging a piece of wood or sticking a bandage on his head or dealing with two recalcitrant old ladies. Come to think of it, he'd never seen her

446

standing so still before, apart from when he'd kissed her this afternoon. She was always moving around doing something.

"Wait there. I'll be back in five minutes. Don't go away." Her irritation with him was now mixed with faint amusement at the look he knew was on his face. If it was anything like he was feeling, he must look like a stupefied adolescent with his mouth hanging open in a silly grin.

She was beautiful. *Drop. Dead. Gorgeous.*

Even in her work clothes and heavy boots with her hair pulled back from her face, she'd made a lasting impression on him. But now wrapped in that pink towel, all flushed and rosy with tendrils of wet hair trailing down her shoulders and stuck to that alabaster white skin…well…she was bewitching. Words failed Liam. His mouth dried at the thought of running his hands over her soft curves.

But it was way past time to gather himself together and stop acting like a fool. He put the box on the floor next to the door and walked along the porch. There was an old cane chair near the steps and he flopped down into it, and leaned his head back against the wall. A cat lying along the table beside the chair lifted its head and opened one eye before deciding he wasn't worth the effort of moving. It stretched and then curled itself back up into a ball.

Liam refused to let himself think. But he had to. His brain was going in the direction his body was telling it to. The sooner he told Georgie why he was here and hightail it back up the hill, the better for all concerned. He knew she was aware of the spark between them, but he wasn't ready to do anything about it.

He'd never be ready for it.

Not with her.

For a fling or a one-night stand, okay, he might be interested. But Georgie was a neighbour, and too close to his new home to get involved with on a casual basis. If he was going to settle into his new house and this community, she was the last

447

person he'd choose to get involved with.

Not because he didn't want her but despite her confidence, there was an air of fragility about her. In spite of her heavy boots, and her skill with a hammer and nails, he knew she was vulnerable beneath the tough exterior she presented to the world, and he could tell she'd been hurt badly somewhere along the line. And the last thing he wanted was another needy woman in his life.

Whoever the guy was, he had obviously been a fool. The few moments this afternoon when Georgie had clung to him before he'd pulled back had been pure heaven. Liam had to fight the temptation to go there again. Her pale skin and her green eyes had stayed in his mind. He hadn't noticed the deep green depths of them until they'd widened when she had opened the door.

Man, he had it bad. He looked across at the door, tempted to just leave the parts on the porch and head home before she came out. But he couldn't leave; he had to tell Georgie he wasn't going to make the welcome party at Thelma and Mitzi's.

As he looked along the porch toward his escape route up the hill, a little red sports car turned off the highway and slowed to a stop on the grass just inside the gate.

Great, now she's got visitors. It must be her cousin she was expecting. Liam pushed himself to his feet and watched as a tall, solid man climbed out of the driver's side. A pang of jealousy hit Liam in the gut. He was a fool. It looked like Georgie already had a boyfriend. His overactive imagination had kicked in, and he'd dreamed up a sad past for her. That same imagination had sucked him into dreaming up a future with Vanessa, and fool that he still was, he'd been about to go down the same path with Georgie. Okay, maybe not planning a future, but he'd been more attracted to her than he should have been. From now on, he'd use his imagination for his stories.

Liam headed for the steps, ready to leave, but paused when the guy went around and opened the passenger door. A petite woman with black hair cut in a bob climbed out and looked over at the house before she linked her arm through the guy's. They walked over to the steps together.

"Hi, I'm Sienna." The tiny woman let go of the man's arm and several gold bangles jangled on her arm as she held her hand out to him. "And this is Jack. You must be Liam?"

He took her hand briefly before nodding at her and then shaking the hand of the tall guy standing beside her. "Yes, that's right. I'm Liam from up the hill. Pleased to meet you both."

"Georgie told us you were living next door. How do you like living in Joe's old place?" Jack shook his hand firmly while Sienna stared up at him. Her eyes were circled by dark black pencil, and her skin was as fair as Georgie's.

"I haven't been here long, but it seems like a nice quiet place, so far. Great house."

"I won't pretend we don't know who you are, but you probably do get sick of people telling you they love your books?" Sienna crossed her arms and smiled at him.

Liam laughed. She was brash and up-front, and he liked the vibes he was getting from her. "No, an author never gets sick of hearing that. If we didn't want to please our readers, there'd be no point writing the stories in the first place."

"Good. Well, I can tell you I loved them all. Hey, Sooky." She reached down and patted the cat as it wound around her legs before switching a curious gaze back to him. "Is Georgie home?"

"Er, yes. She's just getting dressed. Look, I'll go back to my place and leave you to your visit. I can see her later."

"No, please don't leave on our account." Jack slung his arm around Sienna's shoulder. "I'm only here for a minute to say hello to Georgie before I head off to the airport. I'm catching the late flight to Melbourne."

"Yes, please stay. I'd love to chat with you some more." Sienna grinned wickedly. "I know Georgie wouldn't have talked to you about your books. She'd never heard of you."

"I know. I imagine she's too busy working to read. She's always on the go."

"You've got her number and you've only known her a few days." Sienna shot him an intent look. "Yes, our Georgie has kept herself very busy lately. That's one of the reasons I've come to visit," she added enigmatically.

Liam sensed there was more behind her words, but before he could comment, the door opened. Georgie stepped out and her face lit up in a sweet smile.

"You're here." She hurried over to greet the couple.

Liam's heart took off. She wore a floaty pale green dress, and she'd dried her hair and left it loose in a cloud around her face. A touch of pale pink lipstick highlighted her lips and the same sweet fragrance reached him as she moved past him to Sienna. As the light caught her from behind, the curves of her body were silhouetted through the thin fabric. Every sensible thought disappeared from his mind.

"Hey, sis." The two women shared a warm hug before Georgie turned to Jack with a broad smile. "How's my favourite sculptor?"

Jack leaned down and kissed Georgie's cheek as he took her hand. "You're looking particularly gorgeous this afternoon." Another shaft of jealousy lodged in Liam's chest.

Georgie coloured bright red and put her hands to her cheeks. "Thank you. I figured if we were having a girls' night, I might as well dress like a girl."

Liam watched without speaking as Sienna narrowed her eyes and then looked back at him. "Very dolled up for a night at home, Georgie." Her voice was droll.

If it was possible, Georgie's cheeks flushed even more as she waved a hand at Sienna. "I've been in work clothes and boots all week. I felt like a change."

Liam let his gaze follow her hands, and then kept going down to her feet. He was used to seeing her in heavy work boots, but now her feet were bare, and her toenails were painted a soft shell pink. He could tell she was uncomfortable, and he decided to make himself scarce. Although he would have preferred to stay here on the porch drinking in the sight of her for a little while longer. His arms itched to reach out and pull her close, even with the two people who were watching him with interest. Sienna's stare was particularly sharp—and protective, if he was reading her right.

"I've left a box of car parts by the door." He held Georgie's gaze as he schooled his expression into a casual look.

"Car parts?" She cocked her head to the side and her brow wrinkled in a frown.

"Yes, parts for an old Fireflite, but they're not pink." He grinned at her as she realised what he was talking about. She burst out laughing and put her hands over her mouth.

"Are you telling me those two naughty women were actually telling the truth?" She held his eyes steadily.

"Seems like they were."

"Don't tell me…Mitzi and Thelma?" Sienna looked from one to the other with a grin before she settled her gaze on Liam. "I've already had the call and been invited to your welcome reception. You do know half the town is coming to meet you on Sunday? I hope you're ready for the old folk of Maleny."

"I hope you didn't come up here especially for that, did you?" he asked. Damn, maybe it was too late to get out of it.

Sienna shook her head. "I'm here to help Georgie, but I did say I'd love to come. I wouldn't miss one of Thelma and Mitzi's dos."

Liam turned to Georgie. "That's why I came over to your place, apart from dropping in the spare parts. I was going to cancel on Sunday but I didn't know how to get in touch with them.

451

Georgie shook her head. "That would be a real shame. They'll be so disappointed. Do you have something else going on?"

Liam shook his head slowly and tried to focus. He was having trouble taking his eyes off Georgie's pretty mouth. "Not really, just a writing deadline. I have to go to Brisbane on Tuesday and I must get some chapters done before I go." He stared across the top of the porch railing out to the ocean. "I've been a bit preoccupied and I'm way behind with this book."

"It's up to you." Georgie put her hand out and touched his hand and the zing went skittering all the way to his shoulder. "They can still have a party…they often have a Sunday get-together—"

He cut her off before she could finish. "No, it's too short notice. It would be rude. I should have cancelled it earlier. Are you still okay to give me a ride? I don't have a car yet."

"I guess so. Now that Sienna's here to help me, we'll get a lot more done on your bookshelves tomorrow than I would have by myself."

Liam was surprised and turned to Sienna. "You've come down to help with the job at my place?"

Sienna shot him a lazy grin. "Yep, you get a double dose of Sacchi tomorrow."

He looked from one to the other. "So you're sisters?"

"We were for twenty-nine years. In fact, we were twins."

He looked from to the other in confusion and caught Georgie frowning at Sienna. "Were?"

"It's a long story, but we don't have time for it now." Sienna glanced down at her watch. "And it's time for you to hit the road, Jack."

Jack shook Liam's hand. "I'll look forward to catching up with you on Sunday, Liam."

He hugged Georgie and looped his arm around Sienna's

452

shoulder. "Come on, woman. Give me a fitting farewell."

Liam stood next to Georgie as the couple walked back toward the sports car. Sienna looked up at Jack and the love in her face hit Liam in the gut. No one had ever looked at him like that, not even his wife. He glanced across at Georgie. She was blinking away a tear.

"They look good together, don't they?" She sniffed and smiled at him. "They've only been together a few months. And they're so happy."

"Do they live close by?" He was curious about Georgie's background.

"No, down the coast in Lake Weyba. Sienna bought one of the houses we restored." She looked at him and Liam's stomach did a double flip as he tried to keep his eyes off her lips. The glossy pink stuff on them glistened in the afternoon light. "We used to be in business together but now Sienna and Jack have an art gallery in Noosa…and Ana has gone to Melbourne with her partner, Blake, for a while."

They stood side by side on the porch and watched as Jack lifted Sienna onto the hood of the car and stood in front of her with his hands on her shoulders. She grabbed the back of his head and pulled his face to her with a joyful laugh.

Liam turned to Georgie, as the moment between Jack and Sienna was a private one for lovers and he felt uncomfortable intruding on it. "I'll head on home now. I guess I'll see you both tomorrow?"

"If you're not busy. We'll probably come over early." She looked up at him with a smile. "I'd like to make the most of Sienna being here. Your bookshelves will truly be unique once she puts her touch on them."

Liam felt like a teenage boy on his first date. He knew he should go but he was finding it hard to leave. The thought of returning to the empty house up the hill was unappealing, especially when Georgie was standing here with a welcoming smile.

A smile directed solely at him. A smile wide enough to make his toes curl.

"Don't go yet. Sienna will be really upset if she doesn't get to talk to you. She's probably brought a load of her books with her for you to sign." The expression on Georgie's face weakened his resolve. She wanted him to stay, too, and then she confirmed it. "In fact, why don't stay you stay for dinner? I can give you our neighbourly welcome."

She looked horrified as soon as the words left her lips. Those shiny, kissable lips.

He intended to decline but he accepted before his brain kicked into gear. "Sure. I'd love to." What the heck was wrong with his mouth? It was apparently disconnected from his brain.

Sienna and Jack were still in a clinch by the car, and Liam shot them a glance before turning back to Georgie. "I'll go back up the hill and get some wine after Jack leaves." He didn't want to intrude on their privacy even if it was in the middle of the driveway.

"No, come on in. We don't need anything. Jack and Sienna will be ages yet." Her embarrassment had disappeared and she smoothed her hand down the skirt of her floaty dress. His whole body began to buzz with arousal, and the need to put his arms around her and hold her close took over once more.

Thank goodness Mutt chose that very moment to come bounding around the side of the porch and careered to a stop beside them, dropping a wet slobbery ball onto Georgie's bare feet.

"Eww, Mutt! I wondered where you'd gotten to." She reached down and rubbed her hands through his damp fur. "You're wet! You've been down on the beach haven't you, you naughty dog?"

Liam managed to push away the feelings that threatened to

take control of him as the dog pushed between them. Maybe staying here any longer was not such a good idea.

"He gets out through a gap in the fence. I'll have to fix it...or leave him inside for the night." Georgie frowned. "I worry about him going in the water. He loves it."

"Yeah, and you've already done one rescue down on the beach this week."

She gave him a little smile. "Don't remind me. That was embarrassing. I thought you'd drowned and you didn't need any help at all."

Liam lowered his voice and reached out and took her hand. "I'm sorry for being rude to you that afternoon. I was in such a cranky mood...and I was embarrassed that I'd fallen out of the kayak." He let a smile play about his lips. "If I'm honest, I was a bit sorry you didn't try mouth-to-mouth on me."

Georgie coloured brick red and laughed. "I was going through the first aid steps in my mind when I first saw you lying there."

He looked down. Her hand was still in his. Even though her fingernails were short and he could feel a slight callus on one palm, her nails were painted the same soft pink as her toenails. She worked so hard, and it was good to see her relaxed and joking with him.

"How about I give you a hand to fix the fence? Not that I'm much good with tools and things."

The memory of helping her today when she'd fallen off the ladder came flooding back, and Liam let go of her hand, trying to focus his attention on something other than Georgie. The throaty roar of the car saved him, and he reached down to retrieve the ball from beside her feet. He was getting way too sucked in here by a beautiful barefoot woman in a pretty dress.

"I'll have a look at the fence while Sienna decides what's for dinner. Have you seen the orchard behind the house yet?"

455

Georgie picked up a towel and began to wipe the dog down as Sienna walked up the steps.

Sienna leaned against the steps. "I'm doing dinner?"

Georgie caught his eye and despite his brain telling him to pull back, his insides swirled as her lips parted in a huge smile. She'd smiled more in fifteen minutes than he'd seen in a week and it was doing his head—and the rest of his body—in.

"Yep, it was a girls' night in, I told you that."

"Was?" Sienna tipped her head to the side.

"I've invited Liam to stay, so now it's a dinner party." Liam was fascinated by the unfamiliar teasing tone in Georgie's voice.

The swirling dress, the loose hair, and the smile on her face turned her into one altogether tempting package.

"So what are we eating, Sienna?" Georgie asked innocently.

A look that could lure a man to his doom. *Ugh, maybe I should write poetry instead*

Chapter Nine

Georgie's heart was doing crazy things. When she looked at Liam it was almost skipping a beat. And when his sexy blue eyes held hers, it beat so hard it thudded in her chest. She didn't have a clue what had possessed her to invite him to stay for dinner, and she was already regretting the invitation. An independent woman would know better than to get involved with her next-door neighbour. But try telling that to her nerve endings. They were skittering all over the place. Logic said *no*, this was not the way to independence. Her body said *yes,* go for it. Georgie wanted him to be here, and close to her, even with Sienna there. It was the strangest feeling.

Georgie had tried to cover her confusion by teasing Sienna about cooking dinner. Her pantry was well stocked. She'd driven into Maleny earlier and had plenty of food, but Sienna always bit back when she was teased.

She was also looking at Georgie and Liam now with a speculative gleam in her eye. "Well, in that case, it's just as well I got a huge order of Indian takeout on the way over. Raj is delivering it at seven o'clock." Sienna grinned at Liam. "Neither of us cooks very well. It certainly doesn't reflect our Italian upbringing."

Sienna held Georgie's eye and there was a question on her face. Georgie knew she was going to get the third degree when they were alone later, but her relationship with Liam was as a neighbour and a client only, and she would make that quite clear to her cousin. Despite these unfamiliar feelings surging through her, she was only being neighbourly. It had nothing to do with feeling sorry for him being alone, or that she couldn't get the feel of his mouth against her cheek out of her thoughts. She turned to Sienna.

457

"Mutt got out again. Do you want to come for a walk? Liam's going to help me fix the fence."

"No. I'll unpack and maybe read a bit by the window." Sienna waved a lazy hand and turned to Liam. "I know Georgie's going to work me to death tomorrow, so I need to rest up."

Mutt ran ahead of Georgie and Liam as they walked through the backyard. They walked close together, side by side, almost touching, but not quite. Liam chuckled as the dog ran past the gate that opened into the orchard and pushed his nose against a loose piece of fencing. The plank lifted and with a happy *woof* he ran into the orchard and onto the path that led down to the beach.

"There's the escape hole." Liam pointed to the hole in the fence. "It doesn't look big enough for him to get through, though.

"He's determined. I know Ana's had a lot of trouble keeping him in. He adores the water. Mutt! Come back here." Georgie pushed open the gate and stepped into the orchard as the dog ignored her call. "Mutt. Now!" She hadn't stopped to slip on her shoes, and the grass was cold and damp beneath her bare feet as the afternoon drew to a close and the sea mist settled onto the ground.

The large dog slowed down, turned, and slunk back to them with his tail between his legs.

"He loves to run on the beach and I haven't had a chance to take him down there much this week." Georgie drew in a deep breath. Small buds were beginning to form on the trees despite some of them still being loaded with ripe oranges. A couple of late blooms lingered and a whiff of sweet fragrance drifted on the late-afternoon breeze.

"I love this house. One day I'd like to live along the water and have my own place that looks out to the sea." She was babbling, but there was tension hanging in the air between them and she willed it to go away.

Liam walked over to the fence and turned around to stare at

458

her. Her feet seemed to be stuck to the ground and she dropped her gaze, while trying to stop her legs from trembling. Mutt walked along beside her and she curled her fingers in his soft fur.

"Your perfume smells like the orange blossoms," Liam said quietly as she reached him. Being close to him made her heartbeat pick up again and Georgie swallowed, trying to ground herself. She was in trouble here. No matter how much she told herself she wasn't going to fall for her sexy neighbour, her insides were like jelly as his soft words washed over her. Inviting Liam to stay for dinner had been foolish. Bringing him out into the orchard, doubly so. She should have just taken the car part or whatever was in the box he'd left on the porch and let him go home. She had to stay away from him and spend as little time in his company as she could, despite the job. This trembling feeling and uncertainty, the wanting to be with him, were new to her; she'd never experienced them with any guy before, even when they'd gotten to the sleeping-with-each-other stage. Sure, she'd enjoyed their company and she'd had a few relationships that had lasted for a while, but this all-encompassing wanting-to-be-next-to-him feeling was throwing her for a loop.

It must be his good looks and fame. That's all it was.

"It's my shampoo," she said, and as she spoke the wind picked up her hair and whipped it across her eyes. Liam lifted one hand and brushed her hair gently away from her face.

"I like your hair down." He stared at her with those sexy blue eyes. Each of his dark lashes was clearly outlined and the pupils in the centre of his eyes were dark. It wasn't fair that a man could have such beautiful eyes. Georgie couldn't look away. His hand was still on her face and as she stared back at him, he slid it gently back through the loose curls, and placed his fingers on the back of her neck. "You look really different without it pulled back off your face."

Georgie swallowed and attempted some self-deprecating

humour. "Yeah, the red is more obvious when it's out and loose."

"It's not red. It's a beautiful golden copper." Liam still hadn't taken his eyes from hers. His intent stare was turning her insides to mush.

"Well, I suppose being an author, you can always find the nicer words." She stepped away from his hold, willing her heart to settle, and gave herself a little internal shake.

For some reason he's flirting with me. "It's red to me. I've put up with plenty of teasing because of it." Georgie kept her voice matter-of-fact.

She was reading way too much into the way he was looking at her and the way his fingers were gently caressing the back of her neck. But when Liam put out his other hand, took her arm, and pulled her against him again, she knew she wasn't imagining the intent in his expression. She stared back at him as he moved both hands to cradle her face. He held her gaze as he lowered his head and she lifted her face just like she had the other day. She couldn't help herself, any more than she could stop her heart from thumping madly. Their lips met and clung, sweetly and gently, and as he increased the warm pressure, a shiver ran right down to her toes. She leaned into him and Liam moved one hand to the back of her head to hold her close.

Not that she wanted to move away. Georgie lifted her hand to his face and brushed her fingers against the rough stubble on his cheeks. It felt as sexy as it looked, and she let out a contented, soft sigh against his lips. Closing her eyes, she opened her mouth to him as he deepened the kiss and let his tongue slide over her bottom lip. Georgie didn't know how long they stood there in the late-afternoon sunshine with the breeze blowing her hair around them. It was how she'd always dreamed a kiss should be. The physical sensations, the emotion filling her, and the euphoria of being held so gently in Liam's arms as his lips explored hers left her stunned. She couldn't gather her thoughts together while she was in this dreamlike state, but she knew they shouldn't be doing this.

When Mutt finally pushed his wet nose between them and whimpered, Georgie opened her eyes and pulled her head back slowly. She swallowed and closed her eyes, licking her lips nervously as she took a moment to compose herself. Finally, she found her voice and managed to speak firmly...almost.

"We shouldn't be doing this." She dropped her arms to her sides and stepped back, almost falling over Mutt in her anxiety to put some distance between her and Liam.

"Probably not." Liam didn't move away as she expected. "But I couldn't help myself."

"Let's get this fence fixed." Her voice was husky but steady.

Georgie turned away to the fence, trying to shove her trembling hands in her pockets before she realised she was wearing a dress and not her usual work shorts with their deep pockets. Nervously, she clenched her hands in front of her until they steadied.

"There's a piece of wood beneath the middle row of the oranges trees." She pointed across the orchard. "If you can get it for me, we can leverage it to stop this loose piece of fence. Mutt won't be able to get out again if we wedge something against the bottom." She was desperately trying to return to normality. Her heart was beating so fast she was sure she would fall into a dead faint or a swoon at his feet if it didn't settle. Taking a deep breath, she closed her eyes for a moment and focused on breathing in and out.

By the time Liam had dragged the large slab of old wood across to the fence, Georgie almost had herself under control. Physically anyway, but all the fears that had been plaguing her about falling for the next man who came along had resurfaced.

I'm overreacting. It was a simple kiss between a man and a woman in a romantic setting. Don't read too much into it.

Treat it lightly and don't act like a love-struck fool. But when she was done talking to herself, she brushed her fingers across her lips to capture the remnants of the kiss that lingered.

"Here you go." Liam let go of the slab of wood and frowned, concentrating on the loose plank in the fence. Georgie dropped her hand away from her mouth.

"Which side do you think would be best?" he asked.

Georgie was pleased to have something concrete to focus on, and she walked through the gate and looked at the fence from both sides. "Definitely the outside. I'll hold this down while you shove it underneath."

Liam crouched down beside her, wedged the wood beneath the plank, and gave a satisfied grunt when it held. "Now all you need is a small rock to fill in the hole where he's been digging and it should be blocked."

Georgie looked around the garden. There was a small pile of rocks in the garden by the children's play equipment. "Over there." They were both apparently going to pretend that the kiss hadn't happened. Liam followed her over and she bent to pick up the rock.

"That's too heavy. Let me help you." He stepped past her.

The piece of rock was long and narrow and as he reached to take one end, his fingers brushed against hers and Georgie almost dropped it. She lowered her eyes as they lifted it together, and they walked sideways across the garden and through the gate. Georgie concentrated on watching where she was walking so she didn't have to make eye contact with Liam. They manoeuvred the piece of stone near the hole at the bottom of the loose plank and as she bent to secure her end, Liam's shadow fell across her. His jeans-clad thigh brushed against her leg and she jumped as a hot jolt ran down to her toes. She stumbled and the rock slipped from her grasp and narrowly missed her bare feet. Luckily, it landed in the space it was meant for and she let out a sigh of relief.

"That was close. Sorry I let go too soon." Even to her ears, her voice was breathless, and she risked a glance up at him through her lashes. She couldn't remember ever wanting anyone to hold her the way she wanted Liam to hold her. No one had ever had this effect on her. Just as well; it was wreaking havoc with her breathing and her composure.

He didn't move. "I think I'd better pass on the dinner invite. If I'm going to spend Sunday away from my desk, I really should get back to my writing tonight."

"That's probably a good idea. I'm sorry I've taken up so much of your afternoon." She bit her lip as she realised she was apologising again.

"Saying sorry again?" Liam lifted his hand and brushed his knuckles across her cheek as the heat rushed up her neck to her face. "You sure get a great blush going."

"Sorry, it's my fair skin." She shrugged with a little laugh. "Oh, you know what I mean." His fingers lingered on her face and Georgie closed her eyes fighting the urge to lift her hand and hold Liam's fingers against her cheek. He was standing so close she could drop her head onto his shoulder and lean on him.

"Oh, what the heck." Liam's other arm came around her and he pulled her close. "I was going to leave because I knew if I didn't I'd kiss you again."

Her head flew up and warmth rushed through her. The afternoon light had faded while they'd worked, and his face was shadowed, making the angles of his face sharper. But his eyes were soft and his mouth…she let her gaze linger on the lips that had given her so much pleasure just a little while ago. Nervously she flicked her tongue out over her lips and Liam groaned.

Georgie closed her eyes and reached her arms up around his neck. She forced away all of the reasons why she shouldn't be kissing him and lost herself in his kiss. She hoped Sienna wasn't

463

sitting at the window.
That's all I need.

Chapter Ten

Liam had reluctantly headed up the hill after he'd kissed her senseless and Georgie knew she had a smile on her face when he waved to her.

"I'll see you tomorrow," he called back as he went through the gate. "Tell Sienna I'll catch up with her then."

Georgie pushed open the door to the house. Her legs were still trembling and her bare feet felt as though they were walking on air. Sienna was leaning back in the chair, by the window—*of course*—waiting for her to come in.

"Where's lover boy gone?" Sienna grinned at her. "Wow, Georgie. You've sure moved fast this time. And what a honey! He, my dear, is drop-dead gorgeous."

"I haven't moved at all," Georgie snapped. "And there's nothing going on."

Sienna tapped a finger against her lips. "There was from where I was watching. You know if I hadn't been here, I'm pretty sure the two of you would be heading for your bedroom about now."

Georgie shrugged, trying to stay nonchalant. "Maybe." The thought of having Liam in her bedroom sent the fire racing to her cheeks and she lifted her hands to her face. Her self-control slipped and she finally shook her head and dropped onto the sofa next to Sienna's chair.

"It was a silly thing to do."

"Why? Didn't look too silly to me; in fact, it looked pretty good from here." Sienna's eyes were dancing. "You're a dark horse. How long's this been going on? He's only just moved in, hasn't he?"

465

"There's nothing happening. I fell off the ladder the other day and we had a bit of a…moment and then that…that kiss just came from nowhere and it…it…blew my socks off." She leaned back and covered her eyes. "Holy hell, I can't stop shaking."

Sienna burst out laughing. "You should see the look on your face. I've never seen you look like that. *Ever.*"

Georgie put her fingers on her mouth. The problem was she shouldn't have let the kiss affect her like that, and she shouldn't have kissed him back. "But it's not going anywhere."

"Why? He seems like a really nice guy and he's obviously got the hots for you." Sienna tipped her head to the side with a frown. "There's been something wrong with you for a couple of weeks. I knew you had something on your mind. Is it Liam?"

"No. Yes. Sort of." Georgie jumped to her feet and crossed to the kitchen. "How about wine while we wait for dinner?"

Sienna followed her slowly across the room. "And then you can tell me what's going on inside that head of yours."

Georgie reached into the cupboard and pulled out two wineglasses while Sienna hunted up some crackers and cheese. She poured a glass of wine for each of them and carried it back to the chairs in front of the window overlooking the orchard and the ocean. The sun had dropped below the horizon, and a shaft of pink and golden light shattered the low clouds. She looked down at the fence where they had repaired the hole. Where Liam had taken her ever so gently into his arms and given her the kiss of a lifetime. Sienna had been sitting by the window and had seen them. Georgie's face heated again and she placed the cool glass against her cheek as Sienna wandered over and put the plate of snacks on the small table beside them. Georgie was having a hard time understanding what Liam was thinking and why he'd kissed her like that.

"So spill." Sienna looked at her over the top of her glass. "I want to hear all about it. And then you can tell me what's got you so unsettled, if it's not the sexy author up the hill."

Georgie swallowed. It was time to be honest with herself and with Sienna. *Past time.*

"Okay. There are a few things bugging me." Georgie looked over at Sienna, who narrowed her eyes.

"A few?"

"One. When my mother…when Marietta…dropped the news on us a few weeks ago, it explained a lot of things to me."

"What sort of things?" Sienna's eyes were still fixed firmly on her.

"I've never had much luck in love, apparently because it's in my genes." Georgie swallowed. "I just don't have what it takes to commit to a relationship, no matter how much I think I want it. Look how many partners Marietta had in her life, and I haven't even told you about the fiasco with Brent."

"Oh, that's such a load of rubbish and you know it. And who's Brent?"

Georgie waved her hand. "No matter. He's gone now. How many guys have I gone out with over the past ten years? And what's happened with every one of them? They've taken off before we ever got serious."

"It's not about the relationship. It's about the *man*. Finding the right one. How many of those guys did you really want to get serious with? How many times was it that *you* called it quits?" Sienna put her wineglass down and reached over and took Georgie's hand between hers. "Come on, sis. Be honest here. It might sound clichéd but were any of them really Mr. Right?"

"No." Georgie thought back to all the dates she'd had over the past few years. She'd met some great guys, but not one of them had ever lit a spark within her. "None of them, I suppose."

"You and Ana and I were pretty happy working together with our little business. We were all content with our lives, and then Blake came along and you saw what happened there. *Wham.*

467

Ana was lost." Sienna's lips curved in a smile. "If you'd asked me six months ago whether I believed in love and happily ever after, you know what I would have said, don't you? I would have said that what Blake and Ana have is very rare."

Georgie nodded. Sienna had vowed she would never depend on a man.

"And then Jack came along and I fell hard. He was the man for me. And I've never been so happy." Sienna let go of Georgie's hand and cupped her chin in her hand as she rested her elbow on the table. She stared at Georgie. "How can I convince you that you've been trying too hard to find that happiness? You can't search it out. It will happen when the time...and the man...is right."

Georgie shook her head and grinned. "Where's cynical Sienna gone?" She looked around the room. "There's an imposter in her place. Help me find her!"

"Okay, I'll forgive you for that." Sienna grinned back at her. "So that's one reason why you've been mooning around. What else is wrong?"

Georgie sighed. She'd been feeling a little happier for a moment, but she knew she had to be honest. "This trip I'm taking."

"What about it?"

"I don't know what to do. The thought of going away scares me, and being scared scares me, if that makes sense. I'm so settled and secure here on the coast.'

"It will do you good. You spend way too much time worrying about everyone else and solving their problems. You need to get away and take some time for yourself...for the first time in your life." Sienna leaned back in the chair and waved at the view. "This is a beautiful place, but it will be great for you to get away and spread your wings. Let everyone here take care of themselves for a change."

Sienna was right; Georgie thought of her faux pas the other

afternoon when she'd offered to be there for Liam. It obviously hadn't scared him away, even though she'd taken off out of his house like a madwoman. For the life of her, she still couldn't understand why he would want to kiss her. Not that there was anything wrong with the kisses. She put her fingers to her lips again.

"Okay, what else? How much does the gorgeous Liam have to do with how flustered you are?" Sienna's voice interrupted her daydreaming.

"Just a little. I've made a fool of myself in front of him a couple of times."

"So, is that the end of the world? It sure hasn't scared him away, if that's what you were trying to do. It's obvious that he likes you. A lot. Are you going to sleep with him?"

Georgie choked on the wine she was sipping and Sienna leaned forward.

"Well?"

The noise of a car turning into the driveway saved her from answering Sienna's gleeful question. She jumped up and put her glass on the table as she went to take delivery of their Indian food.

Georgie turned to Sienna before she opened the door.

"Promise me one thing? You'll behave while we're working over at Liam's house tomorrow?"

"Of course I'll behave." The wide-eyed innocence on Sienna's face did nothing to reassure Georgie. Why did Thelma and Mitzi and their matchmaking spring to her mind?

Chapter Eleven

Liam's front door was open the next morning when they arrived at the house up on the hill. George had extracted three promises from Sienna while they'd eaten breakfast. One, okay, she wouldn't tease Georgie about Liam. Two, she wouldn't hound him about his books, and three, yes, she would remember that this was a job for a client and not a social visit.

Despite Sienna's reassurances, Georgie's nerves were jumping. Anticipation at seeing Liam curled through her. She'd been tempted for a while to tell Sienna to sleep in, and come up to the house later so she could see Liam alone. But Sienna had bounded out of bed at first light and by the time Georgie had stumbled out of her own bedroom, Sienna was dressed in her work clothes and had their coffee brewing.

"Have you seen my boots, sis?" Sienna was dressed in her work pants but was barefoot.

Despite having spent a restless night, Georgie managed a chuckle and spread her arms innocently. "You've only been here five minutes and you've misplaced your shoes already?"

"Okay, smarty-pants. Where did you hide them?" Sienna punched Georgie lightly on the shoulder as she walked toward the door.

"Me? Do I look like someone who'd steal your shoes?"

Sienna pursed her lips. "The longer it takes me to find them, the longer it will be before we get to lover boy's place."

Georgie grinned and pointed to the door. "You're getting warmer."

"Thank you." Sienna shot her a grin. "It's good to see the old Georgie is still in there somewhere."

Talking to Sienna about her worries had allayed a lot of Georgie's uncertainty, but as the night had gone on, she'd remained firm in her decision that she was not going to get tangled up with Liam. It was only because he was so good-looking and had that vulnerable air about him that she was interested.

Just someone else for me to look after. That's all the appeal was. Nothing else.

Come Tuesday, she would go to Brisbane as she'd planned and organise the rest of her trip. She'd finish the job, stay well out of Liam's way, and remain professional. No more chatting or socialising...or kissing.

She headed through the open door with Sienna close behind, but there was no sign of Liam.

"Shame we didn't get our hands on this place when we were restoring houses." Sienna's voice followed her up the stairs.

"*Ssh.* Liam might be asleep still." Georgie put her fingers to her lips. "He might have stayed up writing till all hours."

Sienna grinned and dropped her voice to a whisper. "Coward. You just don't want him to know we're here."

Georgie glared at her and scurried up the steps, taking care not to tread on the creaking stair. She'd memorised that one the other day. "We may not even see him. Last week, he stayed in his study and I didn't lay eyes on him for days."

Okay, Sienna was right. The warmth pooling in her stomach, the shaking legs, and the increased heartbeat were new to her. Until she got a hold on how she was feeling, and restored her composure, she didn't want to come face-to-face with Liam.

One look at those sexy blue eyes, the shadowed planes of his face, and all her resolve would go out the window. She just knew it. At least Sienna's being here would protect her from any silly behaviour that she was sure to regret.

They worked all morning and Georgie's jangled nerves finally relaxed as they settled into a familiar routine.

471

"All we need is Ana back here and it would be like old times," Sienna said. Georgie nodded with a smile and went back to marking the lumber for the next cut. She wanted to get as much of the heavy work done while Sienna was here with her today. Then the next time she needed help, she'd call the store and have one of the workers come over to help her lift the shelves into place. Then she wouldn't have to interrupt Liam.

The house was quiet apart from the noise they made hammering and sawing. They were just about to take a break and head back down the hill to Ana's cottage for lunch when the door pushed open.

"Morning." Liam poked his head around the door and Georgie's heart gave a little blip. She dropped the hammer she was holding and went to speak, forgetting she had two nails between her lips.

"M...m...morning." Georgie spat the nails out of her mouth and the usual heat crept up her neck.

Great, red cheeks with a blush staining my skin and he's not even in the room yet.

"I just put a couple of pizzas in the oven. I thought you might like to share lunch with me?" Relief filled Georgie as Liam looked from her to Sienna. She picked the nails up and busied herself with the hammer, willing the colour to leave her face as Sienna answered for them,

"Sounds good to me. I'm starving." She turned to Liam with a smile. "Great timing. We were just about to head down the hill for a break."

Georgie hesitated. "I really need to check on Mutt first. Make sure he hasn't gotten out again."

"I have to go down and get my phone. I'll check on him for you." Sienna winked at her and Georgie frowned. Where had the sister—or rather cousin—gone who didn't believe in love and who'd loathed matchmaking when it had impacted *her* life?

Liam waited while they finished up, and then held the door open as they walked past him into the corridor.

"Thanks, Liam." Sienna followed Georgie toward the steps. Georgie focused on her breathing and tried to keep the heat from her cheeks. She was pleased when Sienna chatted to Liam and kept the conversation going as they walked down to the kitchen. Liam gestured to the table, which was set for three, and they sat down as he pulled some plates from the cupboard.

"I was going to bring my books up for you to sign, but Georgie wouldn't let me."

Liam and Georgie laughed at Sienna as she pouted. Their eyes met and held, and their laughter died away. Georgie pushed her chair back to fill the sudden, awkward silence. "I really need to wash my hands. I've got glue stuck on my fingers."

Sienna's chatter to Liam followed Georgie as she went into the small utility room next to the kitchen. She ran the cold water and patted her cheeks with her wet fingers before she scrubbed her hands. Liam was uncomfortable around her, too. It was obvious. Embarrassment flooded her as she realised he probably regretted kissing her.

Professional and cool. Keep my wits about me and I'll get through this.

She was actually looking forward to getting on that plane and flying to Honolulu on Christmas Eve.

* * *

Liam tried hard not to look at Georgie as she slipped out to the utility room. Sienna's cool and assessing gaze was fixed firmly on him, and he sensed that beneath the light banter was a mother hen who was looking out for Georgie. He'd spent a restless night trying to figure out what was so fascinating about her, and he regretted kissing her. In the end, he'd gotten out of bed in the early hours and written many new words of the book the publisher was waiting for. The muse had returned in fits and starts. He needed to capture it and hold it.

But he should keep his distance from Georgie. The last thing he needed was to get involved with someone. Someone who would take much-needed focus from his work. He'd come here intending to keep his life private. He hadn't minded being alone before, and there was a big difference between being alone and being lonely. But when he'd been writing in the early hours before dawn, his thoughts had kept going back to a beautiful face surrounded by golden copper-coloured hair, and he could have sworn he could smell that orange blossom fragrance. He'd wondered what it would be like to watch her sleep. Her bottom lip was full and lush, and even when she wasn't smiling he couldn't keep his eyes from her mouth.

At least he'd made a start on the contracted book, and the words were flowing more than they had since he'd come home from Nepal. They were coming in slowly, but at least the story was shaping up. If he spent most of the time writing, apart from this garden party thing tomorrow, he should have a decent number of chapters done to take with him to meet with his new editor on Tuesday. Thinking about the meeting reminded him he still had to find a way of getting to Brisbane. It was the last thing he wanted to do.

As Georgie sat back down, Liam walked across from the oven and placed a tray of pizza slices in the middle of the table. "Is there somewhere close by where I can rent a car?"

Georgie shook her head. "No. The closest car rental place is up at Noosa. At the Ritz-Carlton hotel."

"What about a taxi service? Is there one of those?" Liam frowned. He'd spent all night convincing himself he wasn't going to let her get under his skin, but even in her work clothes with her hair pulled back, she was beautiful, and he couldn't keep his eyes off her.

"Aldo, one of the retired locals, runs a service in Maleny,"

Georgie said.

"I have to go to Brisbane on Tuesday to meet with my editor."

"Aldo will be at the party tomorrow. I'll introduce you—"

Sienna interrupted her before she'd finished speaking. "You won't have to do that. Georgie's going down to the city on Tuesday to organise—"

Georgie cut her off. "Yes, I'd forgotten I have to go up to the city. I can drop you off at the car rental place."

"Thanks. I'd appreciate the ride." Liam's gaze stayed on Georgie and she held it steadily. Her expression was closed and he wondered whether she really wanted to run him up the coast. "But if it's a problem for you, I can see the taxi man tomorrow. Aldo?"

"No, no. I'd be happy to take you." She shook her head with a smile and his chest clenched. All he wanted to do was reach over and slip his hand through her hair, cup the back of her neck, and breathe in her sweet scent.

God, he had it bad. He reached for a slice of pizza to occupy his hands. Georgie had the same idea, and their fingers brushed as they both reached for the same slice.

She pulled her hand back as though she'd been burned. "I'd appreciate the company. So long as you can put up with the rattle of Ana's old truck."

"Thanks. I'm going to owe you for ferrying me around. I'd forgotten how far this house was from town." He put a slice of pizza on his plate before lifting the tray and holding it out to Georgie. "I'm going to buy a car after I meet with my editor on Tuesday."

Sienna looked at him with interest and he turned to her. "You knew the area around here before you bought the house, then?"

"Yes, I used to visit here with my grandmother when I was a child. I always loved the house, and when Uncle Joe died, I decided to buy it."

"*Uncle* Joe?" Georgie's voice was almost a squawk as her head flew up and her eyes locked with his. "Joe Humphries was your uncle?"

"A sort of uncle. He was my grandmother's cousin, and we came out to visit a couple of times when I was a kid. I don't know what it was, but something had happened in his life. Gran and I stayed with him one summer when I was about twelve."

Sienna laughed. "God, wait till Mitzi and Thelma hear that. You'll make their day."

"You know what?" Liam frowned. "Now that I think about it, I'm sure I remember that pink Fireflite parked in the garage when I was a kid."

Sienna frowned. "I wonder why he left it to Mitzi and not to your family?" Georgie took the opportunity to study Liam's face as he turned away from her to face Sienna. He must have shaved last night, as only a hint of stubble shadowed his chin today. His eyes were alight with curiosity, and she took a deep breath as that hollow pang, the same one that had been there all night, came back and lodged in her stomach.

"He was in the war in Vietnam. His will stipulated that he wanted the house sold and the proceeds to go to a returned soldier's home. I was looking for somewhere to buy at the time, and it was perfect for what I wanted." Liam frowned. "I remembered that the car was to go to someone in town. I didn't make the connection till the two dears turned up here in the Fireflite in case they thought I should have it."

"Ooh, I do love a mystery. We'll have to dig, hey, Georgie?" Sienna elbowed her and Georgie glanced at her watch.

"What we have to do is get back to work." Georgie lightened her words with a smile. "I want you to get on to those fancy edges this afternoon and teach me how to do it so I can finish the rest when you're gone." She stood and pushed her chair back and began to clear the table. "I'll go home and check on Mutt."

"Leave the dishes. I'll clean up. Why don't you bring Mutt back up here, if it's easier? He was fine the other day." Liam took the dishes from her and she was careful not to touch his fingers.

Sienna pushed her chair back. "You stay here. I want to go and get my phone. I left it in my room. Jack's probably been trying to call me all morning. I'll check on Mutt for you while I'm down there, too. If it looks like he's tried to escape I'll bring him back up with me." She disappeared through the door before either of them could answer.

A prickle of discomfort flitted across the back of Georgie's neck now that they were alone, and she looked down at her boots. "Ah, I'll go up and get to work then. Lots to do." She was terrified Liam would come over and hold her, and she was equally terrified he wouldn't. Confusion filled her and she willed her feet to move, but they seemed to be stuck to the old-fashioned black-and-white checked tiles on the kitchen floor. "Thanks for lunch. I'll get out of your way."

Her words ran together in a rush and finally her feet came unstuck and she took off for the door. She almost made it when a warm hand touched her elbow. Liam must have moved quickly and quietly; she hadn't been aware of him following her.

"Georgie, wait." His voice sent a shiver down her back to join the butterflies in her stomach.

She turned slowly and looked down at his long fingers now gently wrapped around her wrist.

"Yes." She lifted her gaze to his face. "Was there something you wanted?" *Stupid, stupid question.*

"No, I just wanted to ask what time you wanted to leave tomorrow." Crushing disappointment roared through her as he dropped his hand, and she raised her glance to his face. A small smile played about his lips, and she was scared he could read her mind.

477

"Tomorrow?"

"Yes, tomorrow for the…er…garden party thing." He laughed. "I've never been to a garden party before, let alone one that's being held in my honour. You'll have to tell me what the dress code is."

"The dress code?" *God, I must sound like a parrot, repeating everything he says.* She took a deep, calming breath and smiled at him. "Oh, you mean what to wear? Thelma and Mitzi will expect us all to dress up. They lean toward the side of formality. Not quite a tux"—a nervous laugh escaped her lips—"but certainly not too casual. Especially for the guest of honour. "Just wear whatever you wear to a book signing and come over to the cottage about noon." She shot him a smile, slipped through the doorway, and ran upstairs as quickly as she could.

To her relief, he didn't follow her, and a short while later she heard the study door close.

Chapter Twelve

By the time Sienna had put the decorative edges on the completed shelves and shown Georgie how to do it, the sun was hovering above the horizon and they had to turn the lights on as the room got darker.

"Why don't you close in the bottom and make cupboards for the base?" Sienna stood back and tipped her head to the side. "If you did the whole back wall as a cupboard base, it would balance the room. How about I go down and get Liam and see what he says?"

"No." Georgie shook her head. "He didn't want to be bothered. He just said to build whatever I want."

"He's been conspicuous by his absence this afternoon." Sienna pointed to the bag she'd brought back with her after lunch with a sheepish look on her face. "I thought he might sign my books for me."

Georgie put her hands on her hips and frowned. "Nuh-uh. Remember, he's the client. We're here to do a job. You can't be bothering him. It wouldn't be right."

"For goodness' sake, Georgie, the *client* cooked us lunch, and he *was* coming for dinner last night. And you were in a clinch with him in the backyard! Are you saying that because you're trying to avoid him? That speaks to me of an attraction."

Georgie ignored Sienna's question and began packing up her tools. Sienna knew her too well, and she was way too close to the truth.

Sienna huffed impatiently and walked across to pull the windows closed. "Come on. I won't mention him again."

"Good."

There was no sign of Liam when they left the house apart

from a strip of light beneath the study door, and Georgie led Sienna quietly through the front door and closed it behind them. They looked at each other as the mournful howls of Mutt greeted them as they walked down the hill in the fading light.

"I should have taken Liam up on his offer."

Georgie grinned as the howls got louder. "That dog's so naughty."

The resulting giggles broke the uneasiness between them and they had a relaxing night talking and catching up, but studiously avoiding any further mention of Liam. Georgie was grateful that Sienna knew when to pull back. All she had to do was survive the garden party, where the matchmakers were sure to pool their resources, but she would be on her guard.

***

But Georgie wasn't quick enough the next day. Sienna deployed her first tactical move before they even left. Georgie glared at her cousin as Sienna slid from the bench seat of the car just as Liam was about to get in.

"Oh, silly me." Sienna put her hand to her cheek. "I left my phone inside. You slide across next to Georgie, Liam, and I'll sit by the window after I get it."

Sienna had already packed her bag and placed it in the back of the truck. Jack was picking her up from the party on his way back from the airport. Georgie shook her head. She was sure Sienna was using her phone as an excuse to get Liam in the middle of the seat and sitting next to her. It was as though they were teenagers again, trying to manoeuvre things so that they could sit beside the current hot guy on the school bus. As soon as she got Sienna alone, she'd tell her to back off. The last thing Georgie wanted was anyone interfering, even if they thought they were helping her out. It was bad enough that the day was going to be spent avoiding the matchmaking efforts of Thelma and Mitzi. Though since she knew exactly what to expect from them, she was prepared.

Sienna hurried purposefully toward the house and Liam slid in next to Georgie. She waved her hand around and gestured to the floor. "Watch out where you put your feet. I wiped the seat down for you but there's still a mess on the floor. Sorry."

"Sorry again?" He grinned at her, and this time she was ready for the warmth that radiated through her chest.

"Yep. Sorry." She turned the key and the truck's old motor rattled to life. They sat for a moment without speaking and waited for Sienna to come back. The silence lengthened until it was uncomfortable. Georgie drummed her fingers on the steering wheel and cleared her throat as she peered through the windshield. "Sorry about the noise. Even though Ana doesn't use it much these days, it is a ute."

Finally, Sienna came out of the cottage and locked the door, but her hands were empty. Georgie shifted the truck into reverse and glanced into the rear view mirror before turning to Sienna. "Find your phone?"

"It must be in my bag in the back," Sienna said, smiling innocently.

Liam moved along the seat. It was only a small cabin with one bench seat, and by the time the truck began to move, his thigh was pressed hard against hers.

Thank goodness I wore long pants. Georgie had taken extra care with her appearance today. After all, one had to look the part to welcome a famous author into their small community. It didn't have anything to do with wanting to look her best because it was Liam.

As for him, Georgie's breath had caught in her throat when he'd walked through the gate. He was dressed in light-coloured pants with a long white shirt hanging loosely over them. Forget Mr. Darcy, he could have been a model for a fashion magazine. His hair was caught back behind his neck with a leather tie and he hadn't shaved. He had a dark blue sweater thrown casually over his shoulders, and Georgie had had to close her mouth when he came through the gate. Sienna had let out a soft sigh and murmured, "Yum. I might have Jack to go home to, but that sure doesn't stop me from looking." She'd fanned herself. "Ooh, he comes close to the best-looking man I've ever seen. The picture on the back of his books doesn't do him justice."

"All we need is a wet shirt and our dreams would come true," Georgie had muttered with a reluctant grin.

Now Liam's leg was pressed up against Georgie's loose silk trousers and her mouth dried. The warmth travelled upward from her thigh, and her skin tingled.

Thank goodness it's not too far to go.

She concentrated on driving while Sienna engaged Liam in conversation as they drove up the mountain. Cliff Cottage Thelma and Mitzi lived on the edge of town, so it was only a short while before she turned the truck onto Main Street, past the hardware store, to where Main Street turned into an unpaved road and meandered through the vegetable farms.

"It's like being out in the country," Liam commented, as Georgie parked the car on the road outside the old farmhouse.

She pulled on the hand brake and turned to him with a smile, determined to keep her cool. "You are in the country. Even though we're not far from the Sunshine Coast, the Maleny Chamber of Commerce does all it can to preserve the old feel of this town."

Liam smiled at her as she opened the door. "I like it. It has a nice vibe."

Georgie laughed as she slid from the car. "Let's see if you still feel that way after an afternoon in Thelma and Mitzi's clutches."

***

Liam sauntered along with Sienna as Georgie charged
482

ahead of then. He was fast getting the impression that Georgie really wanted to hand him over to someone else. That would suit him fine. Being around her was not a good idea. As usual, he was having trouble focusing on anything else when she was in his sight. Her long legs were covered with some sort of soft green fabric and a cropped lace top beneath a shawl showed an occasional glimpse of bare skin at her waist. Her loose copper curls cascaded down her back and as he lowered his gaze, he didn't intend it to linger quite so long on the soft curves of her bottom displayed by the slinky fabric.

"Will you?" Sienna was looking at him and he realised he'd been totally immersed in looking at Georgie and hadn't heard her question.

"Will I what? Sorry, I was miles away." He stopped as Sienna took his arm.

"I said, Georgie is pretty fragile at the moment, and I asked you not to hurt her." Her face was serious and she looked back at him steadily.

"I don't intend to." Liam's body tensed defensively.

"Look, Georgie would kill me if she knew what I was saying, but you'd have to be blind not to see the sizzle sparking between the pair of you. She's had a few rough weeks and she's vulnerable, so if you are just looking for a quick roll in the hay, back off."

Her lips were pursed and her eyes were dark as she stared at him.

"I won't hurt her. I can promise you that." Liam didn't know where he was going with these feelings that seemed to take over whenever she was within his sight, but he certainly didn't intend to hurt her. God knows, he didn't want to put himself or anyone else through more emotional turmoil. He'd had enough of that to last him a lifetime. And if he was sensible, that should be warning enough for him to fight this crazy attraction that seemed

483

to be consuming him. "I'm here to work, but I am also here to stay."

"Good, so we know where we all stand." She flashed him a grin, as though they hadn't just had such a serious conversation. "Now brace yourself."

Liam looked ahead as Sienna led him through a high arch covered with the yellow roses. A large garden, full of people, opened up in front of them. Even though it was almost winter, touches of colour still tinged the trees hanging along the fence line and a riot of bright flowers filled the garden beds. The familiar fragrance of orange blossoms drifted over to him and he looked for Georgie, but she'd already made her way across to a large group of people sitting near the house. He realised there was a small fruit orchard outside the fence and the orange blossom fragrance was drifting in on the soft breeze. A dozen large tables were covered with snow-white cloths, and a table along the back wall of the quaint little cottage was filled with food. Two elderly women, dressed in old-fashioned black-and-white outfits, moved through the crowd with a tray of drinks.

"Welcome to a Thelma and Mitzi 'do.'" Sienna grinned impishly at him. "You're in for a treat."

Liam shook his head as she led him past a couple of tables filled with various craft objects. Coloured rugs, crocheted doilies, and an assortment of knickknacks he had never seen before, and had no idea of their purpose, were crammed onto the table.

"It's like a country fair." He watched as an elderly woman behind a table laden with bottles wrapped up a bottle of fruit preserves and put the money in the pocket of her voluminous apron.

"It's like nothing else you'll ever see again." Sienna's face was alight with laughter but Liam was looking for Georgie. He caught a glimpse of her bright hair through the crowd and after muttering a quick excuse to Sienna, he followed her. He assumed

Georgie had gone to the hostesses and he should thank them for inviting him. By the time he caught up to her, she was standing beside a tall thin man. Liam hung back, watching her smile as she chatted with the older man, who was beaming down at her. She caught sight of Liam and he noticed the moment she lost her composure. Satisfaction filled him with a warm glow. So, no matter what she said, she was certainly unsettled by his presence.

And that pleased him.

"Uncle Renzo. This is our guest of honour, Liam Wyndham." She turned toward the man with a look of pride. "Liam. This is my uncle."

"Ah. I have heard much about you. Welcome to our community." Renzo pumped his hand vigorously and before Liam could speak, Georgie flitted off to another group.

Liam shrugged an apology to Renzo and followed her. "Excuse me."

Thelma and Mitzi were sitting at the table Georgie was heading toward, and when they spotted him, they both jumped to their feet. Before Georgie could take off again, he put his hand on her wrist and whispered to her with a grin.

"Don't leave me. Please?"

"Why? You're the guest of honour. Don't spoil their fun. They're going to want to take you around and introduce you to everybody. You're the celebrity in town." When she looked up at him, her eyes were dancing. "In fact, I think you're the first celebrity we've ever had.

"Though we did have the national champion pumpkin grower from the Gympie Pumpkin Festival here last year. He was here to tell us about the great pumpkin roll up at the Ecca." She tipped her head to the side with a little giggle. "But I don't think that compares with your adventures in Nepal. Everyone's so looking forward to hearing about them."

"Oh. God. Please don't tell me they're expecting me to give

a talk." Dismay filled him as Georgie looked at him and then burst into laughter.

"I hate public speaking. Can't I just wave hello to everyone from afar?" he said.

"No, that wouldn't be fair. Half the folk here are deaf and the other half would have trouble seeing you."

"Really? How long will we have to stay?"

He hadn't been too thrilled about coming, and now it seemed that the occasion was going to be just as bad as he'd imagined.

A final giggle escaped her and Georgie put her hand on top of his on her arm. "I'm just teasing you. You don't have to give a talk."

He groaned. Thelma and Mitzi were marching toward them with purpose in their step.

"But there will be a book signing." Liam loved the teasing glint that came into Georgie's eyes, even though he knew it was directed at him.

"A book signing?" He looked down at her and his eyes fixed on her lips as she smiled and nodded.

"Yes, a book signing. And now here come Thelma and Mitzi to whisk you away." She gave him a gentle shove in their direction, but before Georgie could step away, he reached back and grabbed her hand and gripped it tightly.

"Oh, no, you don't." He leaned over and whispered into her ear, gratified by the shiver that rippled through her. "I need company. I'm not doing this by myself."

"But I have to help with the food." She stared back at him wide-eyed.

"I'll help you do whatever it is you have to do. That way I can meet more people." He kept a firm grip on her hand until she stopped trying to pull away. It was nice having her fingers curled in his. This country atmosphere must be rubbing off on him.

Thelma and Mitzi descended on them; there was no other way to put it. The sisters bustled across the lawn, both dressed in long dresses and woollen shawls, and sporting large sunhats that were trimmed with lace and tied beneath their chins with coloured ribbon. Liam noticed the significant look the two women exchanged as they spied Georgie's hand firmly clutched in his.

"Welcome, dear boy." He was enveloped in a cloud of overpowering rose perfume as each of them kissed his cheek, both taking care not to step between him and Georgie. Looks like he had some support there, although he wasn't sure what he wanted to do about it. He was also aware of her uncle watching them from across the garden with an intent expression on his face.

Thelma and Mitzi each blew a kiss in Georgie's direction, and her hand moved in his grip as she went to greet them.

"How do you want me to help, ladies?" She wriggled her fingers again but he was not letting her go, squeezing them tighter as she shot him a glare. "How about in the kitchen? Looks like there are a few here for lunch?"

"No, no." The shorter of the two, who he now knew was Mitzi, shook her head. "You're in charge of the guest of honour this afternoon. We've got plenty of help."

"You show him around and we'll call you when it's time to eat." Thelma glanced down at their hands and winked at Georgie. Liam could almost feel the heat radiating off her face and neck as the blush stained her cheeks.

"I hope you don't mind, but we told everyone to bring their copy of your books and you might be happy to sign them?" Thelma pointed to the tables and he noticed there was one with a pile of books in the middle and a small queue forming already. "And we also bought some more for those who didn't have a copy already."

This time it was Georgie's turn to gloat, and she nudged him in the ribs as the two women headed back toward the house.

Liam took the opportunity of slipping his arm around her waist as she leaned toward him.

"What are you doing?" she whispered.

"Making sure you don't leave me to face all of these strangers alone."

She frowned at him and he looked down at her as she spoke. "I hope you understand you are setting us up for every gossip in town."

"Sticks and stones, and all that." It was all he could do not to kiss her, no matter who was watching. That would really keep the town talking. But he saw the look of distress on Georgie's face as she pressed her lips together before he could give in to the temptation, and he pulled back.

"Sorry, you deserved to be teased after you've had your fun. Come on. Do what you're supposed to do and introduce me to my new neighbours."

Five minutes later she'd introduced him to a bevy of folk and Liam had his free hand pumped a dozen times, not to mention the number of kisses bestowed on his cheek from women who were old enough to be his grandmother. Come to think of it—he looked around—Sienna and Georgie were the youngest here, by many years. It was almost as though they'd entered an aged care home.

He finally let her hand go and he settled at the table, signing his name for more readers than he ever imagined he'd find in such a small town.

When he said as much to Georgie, who had agreed to stay at the table, introduce him, and help with the books, she'd stared back at him and grinned. "We're not that far from civilisation."

He smiled at the next woman in the queue, and wrote "To Dorothy" with a flourish when Georgie introduced her. Before the next book was placed in front of him, he murmured to her, "I wasn't having a go at you about the town. I'm just surprised so many of them actually have a copy of this book."

Georgie just smiled. After the next reader was introduced, had her book signed, and wafted away in a cloud of yet another floral perfume, he leaned back in the chair.

"Enjoying yourself?" Georgie looked back at him and her smile was still in place. Her fair skin was tipped with a soft pink blush on her cheekbones and her eyes were alight with something. Whatever it was, he'd like to keep that look on her face forever.

Liam realised he was enjoying himself. For the first time in many months, the heavy fog of sadness that had been with him since his marriage ended and Vanessa died had lifted, and he was feeling good. Even at the beginning of their relationship, he'd never been this relaxed in Vanessa's company. From the early days of their marriage, it had been very clear that she was not going to be happy with his company alone. They always had to be somewhere they would be *seen.*

Liam grinned. Vanessa would not have appreciated a garden party miles from the social scene in Sydney—let alone one where his face was the only famous one in sight. His contentment had more to do with being in Georgie's company than being out with a nice group of people on a glorious winter afternoon. He'd never let his guard down so quickly with anyone before. Her green eyes held his and her eyebrows rose as he nodded.

"Yes. Yes, I am."

"Why do you sound so surprised?" She tipped her head to the side and put down the book she was about to push across to him.

Liam was silent. There was a break in the book-signing line, and he and Georgie were by themselves. He wasn't going to screw this up, and he spoke slowly. "Are you?"

"Am I what? Surprised?" He watched as the tip of Georgie's tongue licked her bottom lip.

Slowly. Go slowly. Don't kill this mood.

"No, are you enjoying yourself?" She didn't answer, and Liam reached over and lifted her hand, looking at her pink-painted fingernails as he sought the right words. Chatter buzzed around them but they were alone at the table.

"Yes, I am. For the first time in quite a while, actually." Georgie looked back at him. "But don't read too much into that."

The words hung in the air between them. "What should I read into it?"

Georgie smiled sadly. "I guess you're just someone else who needed a little bit of pushing to feel a bit happier and maybe I've helped you…with this." She gestured around to her friends as laughter and happy conversations washed over them, though it seemed as if they were cocooned in a world of their own. "I'm good at that," she said and her voice was sad.

Never before had he felt this connected to another person as her eyes locked with his. "You know it's more than that. Admit it." Liam kept his voice low, and he reached up and brushed his fingers gently over the soft skin of her cheek. "Will you come to my place tonight for dinner and we can talk about it some more?"

Before Georgie could answer, Liam looked up as a woman stood behind Georgie and put her finger to her mouth in a shushing motion. A short man with a shiny bald head stood beside her and beamed as she put her hands over Georgie's eyes from behind.

"Guess who's home?" The woman leaned down and Georgie turned with a shriek.

"Magda!"

Any chance of further conversation disappeared as Georgie jumped up from her chair and embraced the couple. Liam watched as she grinned and introduced them to him.

"Liam, this is Joe and Magda. They used to own the hardware store, but now they spend most of their time cruising in the Pacific, or the Bahamas, or the Hawaiian Islands." Her face was alight, and unfamiliar warmth took him unawares.

"And I hear it's your turn next?" Magda held Georgie close and Liam's interest was piqued as she spoke softly. "We heard all about that silly stuff with Marietta. Are you and Sienna okay?" He moved away; whatever they were talking about was none of his business.

Her turn? Gossip had gotten around quickly. Magda appeared to assume they were a couple already.

"Everything's good. I'll come and visit you next week and fill you in. Okay?" Georgie turned to Liam. "Now I'm sure Joe would love to take one of your books on their next vacation." Liam frowned as Georgie reached beneath the table and pulled up another copy of one of his books.

She grinned at him with a sheepish expression. "Thelma bought all of the copies of your books she could find at the Maleny bookshop and told everyone they had to buy one. She said it was the best welcome the town could give you."

Liam rolled his eyes. "She didn't have to do that."

"They wanted you to feel at home." A little smile played about those gorgeous lips. "And besides, they tell me it's not a bad story."

She pushed the book to Liam and passed him the pen.

"Later," he mouthed to her before he picked the pen up, and was gratified to see the blush that stained her cheeks.

Chapter Thirteen

Georgie made good her escape while Joe engaged Liam in conversation. Apparently, Joe was already a fan of Liam's and had read all of his books. He questioned him about some of the places he'd been while he was researching his stories. It sounded like he was very well travelled. As she would be soon. She slipped her arm though Magda's and walked inside with her, and tried not to feel Liam's eyes on her back the whole way.

Later? Later what? Could she cope with later? The banter between them at the book-signing table had been fun, but every time Liam had turned his attention—and his charm—to one of her old friends, Georgie's heart had beat a little faster. Every time he'd picked up the pen and his long slender fingers had signed the page, she'd recalled the feel of them caressing her neck, or brushing her cheek…or just touching her.

He'd rolled his sleeves up and she hadn't been able to take her eyes from his smooth, muscular forearms as he'd talked to the person who was waiting for him to sign her book. The quiet sullen man had disappeared and she was sure it wasn't just an act for his new readers. Liam had looked at her with the same expression that Jack looked at Sienna, and Blake looked at Ana. No man had *ever* looked at her like that.

She had to get away. Not just away from him, or the party this afternoon, but away from here, before she fell in—fell into a big hole of feelings she didn't need or want.

She wasn't going to go near the L-word. She'd been hurt too often when she'd thought a relationship might be heading that way.

A relationship? Get real, we don't have a relationship. No matter what Liam said about having dinner and talking some more.

492

No matter how he looked at her.

No way. Not going there. She was not leaving herself open for anything. Besides, he hadn't realised they'd still be here for dinner. Thelma and Mitzi's parties went all day and into the night.

Georgie hadn't even noticed that Magda had left her alone until she heard her chattering away to Thelma by the old stove in the kitchen. She walked over to the window above the sink and watched as Liam charmed another person waiting in line.

No more kisses. The first time they'd kissed in the study she'd been uneasy with the way she'd felt. The second time in the orchard, it had scared the living daylights out of her. The third time—if she let a third time happen—she'd probably melt into a useless puddle at his feet.

No way. It was not going to happen. No dinner, no talk, no more kissing…nothing else, no matter how good it might be.

"Penny for your thoughts?" She jumped as Sienna leaned against the sink beside her.

"Just taking a break while Liam signs some more books." She forced a false gaiety into her voice. "The old gals have outdone themselves today. Lots of guests."

"Don't change the subject." Sienna sighed as she put her hand on Georgie's arm. "Liam's a good man. I hope you're not going to mess this up. It's a chance for you to be happy…finally."

"Happy? I'm going away, remember?" Georgie straightened, reached for a dish towel, and passed it to her cousin. "Help me with the dishes."

For a few moments she scrubbed vigorously at a pot that was soaking in the sink. "Just because you've fallen for Jack doesn't mean I have to do the same thing."

Sienna stared at her without speaking.

"Have you seen the way Liam looks at you? He can't take his eyes off you. And I saw the state you were in after he kissed you on Friday night." Sienna took the pot from her. "It's me you're

493

talking to, sis. You can't kid me." A little grin crossed her face. "Not since Billy Stephenson kissed you in the back of the school bus and I knew it before you were even down the steps and off the bus."

"Okay, so you might be a teensy…just a teensy bit right, but I'm a coward. Maybe a few months ago I would have risked it…but not now. I've decided that independence is my mantra. No more dreams of wedding dresses and houses with little white fences." Georgie clenched her jaw and shook her head. "But he wants me to go for dinner and I've decided I will. That's all it is."

"Good." Sienna put the dish towel on the bench and smiled at her.

"No, not good. I'm going to make it clear to Liam, once and for all, that I'm not available." Georgie folded her arms across her chest. "I've only got a few weeks before I go away and then I'll find out how to be happy on my own, without a man in my life. I cannot risk being dumped one more time. If I don't get together with him, he can't leave me, can he?"

***

Jack arrived late in the afternoon and Liam hung with him for a while. They helped carry platters of roast meat and baked vegetables out to the garden, and then Mitzi appeared with a bottle of homemade elderberry wine. Jack raised his eyebrows and sniffed it once it was uncorked.

"Not bad." He poured a glass for Liam and lifted his own glass in a toast. "Welcome to the Sunshine Coast. I hope you find it as wonderful here as I have."

Liam sipped the wine and was pleasantly surprised. There'd been a lot of surprises today. He nodded at Jack and lifted his own glass. "Thank you. So far the move has been pretty good."

For most of the afternoon, Liam had watched Georgie flutter around and look after the elderly folk. She'd brought them cups of tea and settled blankets over their legs as the chill of the late afternoon had settled in, and she hadn't stood still for one moment. She'd managed to avoid him for most of the time, despite the curious looks a couple of the women had thrown her way as she'd scurried past him. As for him, he'd had to concentrate on not looking at her the whole time. It was like being back at high school with the heart palpitations and the eye contact, focusing on the pretty girl who'd caught your attention.

He'd been pleased when Jack had sought him out and they'd spent some time getting to know each other during dinner.

Dinner. Not quite what he'd planned, but Georgie still had to run him home at the end of the night, and he intended to have a good talk to her before he let her go. He pushed away the thought that kept creeping into his head. *Slow down.*

"Sienna says you're buying a car this week?" Jack slipped his arm around Sienna's waist as she came up and stood by his chair. Liam looked around for Georgie. She was back in the kitchen helping clean up, and as he watched through the window she lifted her hair from her neck and wound it into a topknot on her head. The soft, silky fabric she was wearing slid up her arms and the light caught her bare skin as she stretched. His knees felt weak suddenly, and he switched his attention back to Jack.

"Yeah, I've been making some enquiries, but I won't be able to pick it up for a couple of weeks." Jack launched into a discussion of motor sizes and fuel consumption, but Liam kept one eye on the door, waiting for Georgie to come and join them. Finally, she wandered out and looked around the garden. He beckoned to her, before she could head off in another direction to help someone else, or clear a table, or just generally avoid his company.

She stood beside him as she greeted Jack.

Liam stood and leaned over to her, speaking quietly so he didn't appear rude. "What time do you want to leave?"

This whole afternoon with the Maleny community had been

fun, and he'd enjoyed himself much more than he'd expected. They'd also stayed hours longer than he'd anticipated and he was beginning to get anxious about getting back to his study.

The sun had gone down and the flickering lights shining over the garden burnished the copper colour of Georgie's hair. She'd removed the clip and her long auburn curls fell over the shawl she'd put around her shoulders before she'd come outside. The wind had picked up and there was a hint of rain in the air as the clouds swirled in.

"Soon." She yawned and covered her mouth with her hand. "Oops, sorry. It's past my bedtime."

"Mine, too," he said softly and grinned as she coloured up.

Good, keep her guessing.

There was a flurry to pack up the garden, and he and Jack helped carry the furniture into an old shed behind the house as the last of the food was carried inside. Finally, they made their farewells and as he thanked Thelma and Mitzi for inviting him, they presented him with a pumpkin pie. Georgie was quiet as they walked out to the street with Jack and Sienna to get Sienna's bag from the ute, and she didn't speak even as Sienna hugged her good-bye.

Georgie opened the car door and slipped onto the bench seat and waited for him as Liam shook Jack's hand and kissed Sienna's cheek before getting into the truck. He was looking forward to getting to know them more. As he climbed in, she was rubbing her hands up her arms and shivering.

So much for my plan to be a recluse. The community had made him feel welcome, and as far as Georgie went, his desire for privacy had flown out the window. It suited him and it seemed like he'd chosen the right place to put roots down.

"Too breezy?" He waved as Sienna's red sports car passed them but kept his gaze on Georgie.

"A little."

Liam wound the window up and looked at the dashboard in front of him as she started the car. "Would you like me to put the air on?"

"It's broken." Finally, a glimmer of life appeared on her face as she shot him a smile. "Don't worry, home's not far."

The first raindrops splattered on the windshield as she turned off the motorway onto the shared road that led to both of their houses.

"Don't worry about going up to my place. Park at your house and then I know you're inside safely. This weather is closing in quickly." Liam leaned forward as a flash of something caught his attention on the top of the cliff. "I'll walk up the hill."

Georgie groaned as there was another movement ahead of them. "Oh, no. That was Mutt. He's gotten out again." She accelerated and turned into her drive at the bottom of the hill. The engine stopped with a shudder as she turned the key, but she left the headlights on.

"I'll help you find him." Liam opened his door. The rain had started to fall in earnest now and cold needles of ice hit his bare neck. "I'll call him while you get an umbrella."

He didn't wait for her to answer as he slid from the truck and ran to the path at the top of the cliff where he'd last seen the dog.

"Be careful. Don't go too close to the edge. It's soft." Georgie was right behind him and he reached back and held out his hand.

"What about the umbrella?" he asked.

"No time. If that blasted dog gets down onto the beach, he'll run for miles."

Liam smiled to himself as Georgie slipped her hand into his, and they followed the sandy path lit by the headlights.

"Mutt! Get back here."

Liam whistled as Georgie called out and they were

497

rewarded with a scuffling noise a short distance ahead of them. She stopped and put her hand up. "Wait up. If we keep walking, he'll think we are going down to the beach."

"In the dark?" Liam peered ahead but couldn't see the dog, nor could he hear it any more.

"He's not real smart." He could hear the grin in Georgie's voice, despite the rain that was getting heavier by the minute. Water was beginning to trickle down beneath the collar of his shirt, but he didn't care.

He squeezed her hand as they kept walking. He was beginning to love this dog.

Chapter Fourteen

A litany of swear words was running through Georgie's head and she bit her lip to stop them from coming out of her mouth.

Blasted dog.

"Mutt, come here!" Her voice cracked as she attempted to call the dog back to them. They stood at the top of the cliff where the path ran down to the beach. She shivered as a trickle of cold water ran down the side of her face, and then she trembled again as Liam's arm went around her waist to pull her close to him.

"You should have gotten that umbrella," he said.

"I didn't have time."

The rain pelted them more heavily as he spoke; it was as though the heavens were having a laugh at their expense. As she peered into the dark at the end of the path, a very wet dog slunk toward them, his tail firmly between his legs. Georgie reached down and looped her fingers through his collar. The smell of wet dog drifted up to her as he shook himself and water droplets went flying around them.

Liam laughed. "Well, at least we're already wet." His arm was still firmly around her waist and he reached down with the other to hold Mutt's collar. "I've got him. Where do you want to put him?"

Georgie let go of the dog and straightened, blinking the water from her eyes as she looked up at Liam. The light from the car was shining directly onto his face and his eyelashes were clumped together in spikes as he stared back at her.

"He'll have to come inside because I can't risk him getting out again tonight. You take him onto the porch and I'll turn the car lights off." Liam let his arm drop and ran across to the porch with the dog as Georgie headed to the car. She grabbed her bag and Liam's sweater off the seat, and locked the door.

By the time she'd followed them onto the porch, deep rivulets from the heavy rain were running across the lawn. Her feet sloshed through ankle-deep water and she regretted the ruin of her favourite pair of shoes. Liam was waiting at the top of the steps.

"I'm glad the rain held off for the afternoon. I hope everyone got home safely," she said.

Liam grabbed for her as her wet shoes slipped on the top step and she almost fell. Mutt barked as she regained her balance and she frowned at him.

"It's your fault, you naughty dog." She reached up and brushed the wet bangs from her eyes with the back of her hand, and wrinkled her nose as the cloying aroma of wet dog hair hit her. "Come inside and bring him, too. He can go in the utility room and I'll dry him off."

The task of looking for Mutt had kept her mind focused, but as Georgie unlocked the door and turned the lights on, all the warm and trembling feelings came rushing back as Liam pushed the dog gently into the laundry room. Despite the moisture in the air, and her dripping hair and sodden clothes, her mouth dried at the sight of Liam bathed in the bright light.

Oh, Sienna! Who needed Mr. Darcy on the big screen when she had Liam Wyndham standing here in front of her?

Damn wet shirt. From the first moment she'd come across him lying on the wet sand, she'd known how good-looking he was. On top of the great looks, the sexy eyes, the muscular chest encased in the wet shirt that was filling her vision, she also knew what a nice guy he was.

Thoughtful, funny, and kind. And a great kisser.

Don't go there.

Gradually it dawned on Georgie that Liam was standing there grinning at her as she gaped up at him. The heat rushed up

500

her neck and it was a wonder it didn't sizzle the water on her face as her cheeks burned.

"Have you got an old towel? I'll rub him dry for you," Liam asked.

She took a step back and scrabbled through the cupboard, not knowing what was in there. Finally she pulled out an old drop cloth that they'd used to cover the furniture when they'd painted Ana's cottage a couple of years back, and she handed it to Liam. "This will have to do. I don't fancy using any of Ana's good pink towels to dry him off."

She leaned back on the doorframe and watched as Liam's hands rubbed the dog's wet coat with the stiff piece of fabric. The cloth softened as he stroked him up and down gently, and if it was possible for a dog to have an expression of ecstasy in its face, Mutt was wearing one. She'd have one on her face, too, if Liam's hand were moving on her body like that.

Don't think about it. She swallowed again.

The rain was still drumming down onto the shingled roof and Georgie could barely hear Liam's words as he turned to her. She leaned closer and heard him say something about getting warm, before he folded the drop cloth and placed it in the corner of the small room. Mutt flopped down onto it, curled into a ball, and promptly closed his eyes.

Liam gestured to the door and she stepped out onto the porch and he followed her, pulling the door of the laundry room shut behind him. The wind had picked up and the rain was driving almost horizontally in from the sea, and the tang of salt came from the droplets that settled on Georgie's face. She unlocked the front door and a gust of wind blew it open and it crashed into the wall.

"Quickly," she called to Liam to follow her and he pushed the door shut against the wind.

"I guess you're stuck with my company for a while." He lifted both his hands and pushed his hair back from his face, and

Georgie slowly became aware of how bedraggled she must look. Her hair was in wet tangles and her fringe was stuck to her forehead. She looked down. Her lace top was sodden and stuck to her chest, moulding the curve of her breasts. Her silk pants stuck to her legs and her shoes were a pulpy mess of wet leather.

"This was one of my favourite outfits." She lifted her hands in the air and grinned at Liam. "But you don't look much better."

Actually he does, but there is no way I'm telling him that.

"You're soaked. Go up and dry off."

Georgie had a quick shower and dried her hair with the hair dryer before dressing in a pair of jeans and a cotton jumper. The wind and the rain were still beating against the upstairs windows, so it was clear Liam wouldn't be going back to his house any time soon. She grabbed a fresh towel and riffled though the spare room where she'd noticed some of Blake's clothes on a shelf when she'd been making the room up for Sienna. A pair of faded but neatly pressed Levis and a soft sweatshirt filled her arms as she walked slowly downstairs.

Tonight would be the perfect opportunity to make it quite clear to Liam that this attraction between them wasn't going to go anywhere. Her breath caught in her throat as she reached the bottom step. He was standing in front of a crackling fire holding his wet shirt up to the heat. As he raised his arms, the muscles in his back flexed and rippled, and Georgie's mouth dried. His long pants were still damp and moulded to his legs.

Even though it was almost summer, he'd lit a fire. The firelight flickered and patterns of light danced across the walls and she knew as soon as he turned to her, the shadowed room would only enhance those high cheekbones and the planes of his face that were becoming very familiar to her. Straightening her shoulders, Georgie flicked on the light switch on the wall at the bottom of the stairs and the room was bathed in bright light, dispelling any romantic scene he may have tried to set.

Liam turned slowly and a smile spread across his face as he spied the clothes and the towel in her arms. "For me?"

Georgie nodded, still not willing to trust her voice. She walked over and stood beside him in front of the flames and cleared her throat. "If you'd like to use the bathroom upstairs, there's plenty of hot water."

Liam shook his head. "It's okay. I'll just dry off and get changed. As soon as the rain lets up I'll go home. I really must do some writing tonight."

"There's a small room over there where you can change." Georgie pointed to the door beside the kitchen, avoiding looking at his bare chest. "I'll make us some coffee while you get dried off. Would you like some pie to go with it?"

"No, thanks." Liam shook his head as he headed for the door. "I feel as though I've been eating all day."

"It's Thelma's pumpkin pie." She smiled at him. "Trust me, it's to die for."

"Okay, maybe just a small piece."

Great. So far so good. A normal conversation.

When he came back out dressed in a pair of jeans that hung loosely around his legs, and the old stained sweatshirt, Georgie busied herself in the kitchen. Liam walked back over to the fireplace and spread his wet clothes on the fire guard.

"Did you know that you can get a pumpkin beer at Maleny?' She placed the sugar and cream on a tray before she added one slice of pie to a plate. "And there's pumpkin wine and pumpkin rum, too."

She glanced across at him as she carried the tray over and placed it on the low table next to the sofa. "You've got a good fire going there," she said briskly. "I might go out and get Mutt. He'd enjoy it in here. Sit down, make yourself at home." She plumped up the cushions. "So did you enjoy yourself today?"

503

A normal one-sided conversation. She was babbling, but she wanted to fill the room with everyday conversation. All she could think of was the "later" that he'd mouthed earlier. As she turned to go and fetch Mutt, Liam's warm hand gently touched her on the shoulder.

"Georgie?"

"Mmm?" She looked down at his bare feet.

"Forget Mutt…and stop talking."

Slowly she raised her eyes as he gently tucked a stray tendril of hair behind her ear. Her brain was slow to respond as her blood heated her faster than any fire could. "Stop talking?"

Liam dropped his hands and took both of hers between his. She looked down at her small hands enclosed between his slender white fingers. She loved his hands; she couldn't begin to imagine how much she'd love to feel them on her skin.

"Yes." He murmured as he lifted her hand to his mouth. "Just feel."

His warm lips touched the inside of her palm and Georgie closed her eyes as he spoke softly. "I told you I wanted to talk to you."

"Because I was teasing you?" She swallowed and opened her eyes and immediately regretted it. Liam's sexy blue eyes were fixed on her face.

"No. Because I want to sort out this…this thing between us." He uncurled his fingers from around hers and raised his hand to cup her cheek. His thumb brushed her skin ever so gently. "I'm not ready for this, but I can't get you out of my head. I want you to know how I feel but I want to be honest. I don't want to give you the wrong idea."

A little voice in her head was telling her to take this one night, enjoy being with him, and then she could worry about it later. *What was the wrong idea?*

No. Georgie knew she had to be strong, but as she opened

her lips to speak, he moved his fingers from her cheek and brushed them against the sensitive skin at the nape of her neck before he gently cradled the back of head. Her resolve disappeared like the smoke that was puffing up the chimney.

One night. She could have one night. With a soft sigh she leaned forward and pressed her lips against his, and their breath mingled as he whispered against her mouth.

"You are so beautiful. You've bewitched me, Georgie." She loved the way he rolled her name on his tongue. His whisper ran through her body as he pulled her close and his firm chest pressed against her breasts. Liam slid his lips across her cheek, his hand still cupping the back of her head. "Your green eyes, your gorgeous hair, your lips. I can't take my eyes off of you."

For the first time in her life, Georgie felt truly beautiful. Liam was worshipping her body with gentle hands. She closed her eyes as he ran those hands down her shoulders and caressed lazy circles on her back as his mouth moved on hers. This time the pressure was firmer and she opened her lips to welcome him. She arched her body into his as the sensuality of the moment consumed her.

They stood there for a long time, lost in a pleasure that was filled with soft breaths and deep sighs, until a log snapped with a loud *crack* in the fireplace. Georgie drew back slowly and reached her hand up to Liam's cheek. He turned his lips and kissed her palm again as she spoke. "I want to talk to you tonight. I want to tell you about me. I want to be honest with you." Her throat filled with emotion as he looked back at her with a gentle smile. No man had ever looked at her as though she was the most beautiful woman in the world, but she sighed. It was too late.

She turned away from him, trying to put a brake on the feelings racing though her. "Our coffee will be cold."

Liam sat on the sofa and didn't take his eyes from her as she picked up the coffeepot. "What do you want to tell me?" He patted the sofa, and she sat next to him after she poured the coffee. Both cups sat untouched as he looked at her.

"It's all right, Georgie. I'm not going to make you go anywhere you don't want to." She lifted her eyes to meet his. "But I want you to know—"

"No, you don't need to tell me anything." Her voice caught on a breath and she cleared her throat. "I'm not good at relationships, and I've failed at them so many times I'm not going to risk it again. No matter how tempted I might be."

Liam picked up her hand and smoothed his thumb across the back of it. The jolt from his touch went straight to her heart. She had taken care of herself for long enough now to be able to resist a simple touch, and she closed her eyes as she fought the temptation to lean against him.

His soft voice interrupted her thoughts. "That makes two of us. I'm not good at relationships, either. In fact, I've recently had a mammoth failure. So what do you say? Can you have a casual relationship? Can we do this?"

No man had ever been so honest with her. And it was the first time in Georgie's life she'd gone in with her eyes open, expecting nothing. Expecting no permanent outcome; having no dreams of dresses and wedding cakes. She slid across the sofa to him, and the coffee was forgotten as she opened his arms to her.

"This?" she asked. "What is this?"

"I'll try to show you," Liam murmured as he lowered his lips to hers once more.

Chapter Fifteen

A mournful howl woke Georgie the next morning and she opened her eyes slowly, wondering what the heavy weight on her leg was. She tried to roll but she was pinned to the bed with two firm arms wrapped around her.

"I think Mutt wants to go out." Liam's lips were warm as he nuzzled them against her cheek. Georgie arched her neck and stretched her body as she sought the right words. She'd never been any good at the morning-after stuff.

"I'd better go and let him out." Self-consciousness flooded though her as she rolled over and reached for her jeans, which were in a pile of clothes on the floor. She waited for Liam to look away.

He grinned at her. "You're shy?"

She nodded but he didn't look away.

"You're beautiful." His eyes moved slowly down from her face to her shoulders as she stood and grabbed the sheet to cover herself.

This was crazy. How the heck did she ever get herself into this situation with Liam Wyndham—the famous Liam Wyndham—in her bed in her friends' cottage?

Grabbing her jeans and her sweatshirt, Georgie took off into the bathroom. She let the sheet drop and stared at herself in the mirror as she ran the faucets. Her cheeks were flushed and her eyes were heavy. They hadn't had much sleep. Slowly, she let the smile that was tugging at her lips spread over her face and she nodded as she pulled her clothes on.

A very satisfied woman looked back at her. Tapping into her newfound self-assurance, she sauntered back into the bedroom, her confidence buoyed now that she was fully clothed.

Which was more than she could say for the sexy man still lying in her bed.

Liam was on his back, hands tucked casually behind his head, which was resting on *her* lacy pillow cover.

"Get up, lazybones. I have a job to go to up the hill." She grinned down at him as he rolled over and reached for his watch on her bedside cupboard.

He groaned. "And I've got to go write. If I don't get those chapters written today, I won't have a house for you to build bookshelves in."

Before she could walk away, he grabbed her hand and pulled her down to the bed. "How about a good-morning kiss from you before you go see to that dog?"

Georgie's hand shook in his as she leaned down to meet his lips. This man was like a drug. No matter what her mind was telling her, her body was not listening.

She giggled as another mournful howl reverberated from below. "At least Mutt isn't disturbing the neighbours."

***

Liam looked around the small bathroom as he washed and dressed. There were little signs of Georgie everywhere, and that filled him with a warm glow. He had it bad. Never before had he grinned at a pair of women's work boots on the floor and a pair of dirty socks hanging over the bath.

By the time he'd dressed in the borrowed clothes and sauntered down the stairs, the smell of brewing coffee greeted him. Georgie was standing at the window looking over the ocean as she nibbled on a piece of toast. The sky was a brilliant blue and the sea was smooth after the storm. The world was washed clean and Liam watched as Mutt raced around the yard below with a piece of wood. Did everything look as bright as he thought, or was it the way he felt?

He stood behind Georgie and put his hands on her

shoulders. "Morning."

"Gorgeous day." She leaned back into him.

"It is," he said as he lowered his head and nuzzled into the soft skin of her neck, disappointed when she moved away slightly.

"Do you mind if we go now? I'll pour you a coffee and you can bring it with you so you can unlock for me. I really need to get started."

"Can I have some pumpkin pie to go with it?"

"*Ugh.* For breakfast?" Georgie glanced down at her watch with a smile. "Come on, I have to get to work."

Liam laughed. "I'm the one with the deadline. I don't mind how long it takes you to build my shelves." He turned her around and looped his arms around her waist as an idea struck him. "In fact, when you finish them, how would you like to start work on the rest of the house?"

Her smile faded as she stared back at him. "It would be a fabulous job, but I won't be able to. I'm leaving on Christmas Eve."

"You can do it when you come back from your vacation?"

Disappointment filled him as Georgie's brow wrinkled and she shook her head.

"But I'm not coming back. I'm leaving Hideaway Bay."

Her words surprised her, but Georgie knew it was the only way to guard her heart.

***

Liam unlocked his front door and Georgie nodded her thanks to him. He'd offered to bring Mutt up with them and she thought it was more for him to have something to focus on so they didn't have to talk. When she'd mentioned moving on, he hadn't commented. He'd dropped his arms and gone into the kitchen, and she heard the gurgle of the coffeemaker as he poured himself a coffee. She'd gone upstairs and changed into her work clothes and boots and shoved her mobile phone into her pocket.

The walk up to the house had been quiet, with each of them making desultory comments about the weather and the beautiful sapphire blue of the ocean. Mutt eased the tension by bounding from one to the other, but Georgie sensed that Liam's thoughts were elsewhere as he headed for his study and she went upstairs to work.

Probably on his book.

"Damn!" She swore as she hit her thumb with the hammer for the fifth time in three hours. Like Liam, her thoughts were elsewhere, but they weren't on his book or even on her upcoming trip. His face filled her mind. The night they'd shared had been magic. He was kind, considerate, loving, teasing, and damn beautiful to look at. Last night he'd opened up and let her into his soul, and she'd seen the creative side of him flow as he'd whispered softly to her. Words that brought them so close to each other, and words she would remember for the rest of her life.

If only... Georgie shook herself and willed herself to move on. She'd killed it all by telling him she was leaving.

I am leaving. Get the job done. Finish up and move on. Independence.

She picked up a length of wood and pulled out her tape, measured it, and cut it to size. It was only when she carried it over to the wall and tried to fit it that she realised she'd cut it too short and too wide. She moved across to the window and sat on the ledge, letting the breeze cool her.

Had last night been a mistake? They both carried baggage and they both had things they wanted to achieve, plus she had places to go. They would have to come to terms with it and break it off before one of them—or both—got hurt. And God knew, neither of them could handle any more hurt. She'd just read about Liam and his ex-wife in a magazine that she was sure Sienna had left lying around deliberately.

While Sienna had been trying to matchmake, maybe she'd

also wanted to make sure Georgie went in with her eyes wide open. Well, she had, but it was beginning to hurt already. The fear of leaving the Sunshine Coast was now real. She could almost taste the uncertainty building in her chest, and the thought of leaving Liam when she'd just met him was one she didn't like.

She closed her eyes but his face wouldn't go away.

His gentle smile, his blue eyes, and the angles of his face. She raised her hand to her own cheek—it was still tender from the rasp of his rough stubble against her skin. The memory of how little sleep they'd gotten brought a smile to her face, and she opened her eyes as resolve flooded through her.

She was overthinking this…as usual. Georgie could almost hear Sienna's voice in her head. *"Stop analysing everything. Just enjoy the moment."*

Over the past few months, she'd forgotten how to have fun, how to enjoy life. She'd always been the one who had played the practical jokes and thought up the harebrained schemes when they'd been growing up. It was time to lighten up and retrieve her old sense of fun. She'd been the mistress of sending funny texts. Sienna had even threatened to print them out and publish them in a book.

There was no reason why she couldn't spend some time with Liam before she went away. Ana had Blake, Sienna had Jack, why couldn't she hook up with Liam and have some fun with him before she went away? Memories to hold on to while she was off learning how to be independent. Georgie grinned as she remembered some of the memories that had been made last night. Okay, if she'd been looking for the real thing, it might have worked out. He might have been the One… Now that she had planned out her life, though, she didn't need Liam.

But there was nothing to stop her from seizing the moment, was there?

Three more weeks. She might as well make the most of it.

They'd have a good time and if they spent the odd night together, well, that would add some more amazing memories to take away with her. It was time to take what life offered her before she headed off into the big wide world.

And she was going to start right this minute.

Georgie stopped outside the door of the downstairs study and balanced the tray she was carrying on one arm. With the other hand she pulled the band from her hair, shook her hair loose, and licked her lips, trying to ignore the sudden lack of moisture in her mouth. Taking a deep breath for courage, she tapped lightly on the door before pushing it open.

As she walked across the room, Liam turned and his eyes crinkled at the edges.

Phew. First hurdle overcome.

"It's way past lunchtime." She kept her voice bright and busied herself finding a clear spot to put the tray down. "I made us some sandwiches." She grinned as she looked around at the piles of books on the floor. "You sure do need those bookshelves."

Liam jumped up, took the tray from her, and put it on his desk. He looked distracted, and for a moment she was worried that she'd intruded on his privacy. That worry disappeared when he reached out and pulled her to him. His hair was mussed as though he'd been running his hands through it, but his smile was sweet as he looked down at her.

"I was just thinking about coming up and telling you it was time for a break. You work too hard." He pulled her closer.

"Really? I thought—" But she didn't get to tell him what she thought because he was kissing her. Softly and gently, and Georgie slid her hands up beneath his shirt and splayed her fingers on the smooth skin of his back. Liam's mouth moved from her lips to her cheek and then to that ticklish spot on her neck beneath her ear. He'd discovered that last night and now he headed straight for it.

She couldn't help the giggle that bubbled through her lips.

"So you find my lovemaking amusing?" He pulled back and looked at her for a long moment. "Hmm. I must be out of practice. Maybe I'd better do something about that?"

"What about lunch?"

"Lunch?" His eyes were half closed, and the way he was looking at her sent a thrill shooting all the way to Georgie's toes. "Seeing as you've gone to all that trouble, we'd better eat...first."

The thrill turned into a shiver and Georgie swore that her entire body was covered in goose bumps.

***

The afternoon flew by in a very pleasurable manner, but Liam didn't spend it writing new chapters, and Georgie didn't build any new bookshelves. He propped himself up on one elbow and watched her as she stood looking out the window of his bedroom. She was wearing one of his white shirts and it just covered her bare thighs.

"I'd better go downstairs and check on Mutt. It's almost dark." She picked up her shorts and slid them up over those long legs with his shirt hanging out loose over them

"You made lunch, so I guess it's my turn to cook dinner?" Liam slid off the bed and reached for his jeans. "You will stay?"

"For dinner?" Georgie's beautiful green eyes held the hint of a smile.

"I was hoping for the night?" As she walked toward the door, he grabbed her hand and held it against his chest. Her cheeks were rosy and her skin was still damp with perspiration. Liam inhaled the sweet smell of her hair as she rested her head against his shoulder.

"Shouldn't you be writing?" Georgie asked. She was a perfect fit against him, and he slid his hand through her silky hair.

"I should be, but I've written enough to make my editor

happy." The muse had come back with a vengeance, and the more time he spent with Georgie, the more the words flowed. "Very happy."

"Shoot, I forgot we were going to the city tomorrow." She pulled back with a frown. "I've hardly done any work today. What time is your appointment?"

"A lunchtime meeting at the Ritz. If it's a problem for you to take me there, I can call Aldo and get him to drive me down to Brisbane." He smiled when the tell-tale blush stained her cheeks and her frown disappeared. "But it would be nice to have your company."

"No, it's all good. I have to go up there, too. I just worry about getting your job finished. No matter what"—she looked at him coyly from beneath her lashes—"you are paying the store for me to build you a room full of bookshelves. I've made very little progress today."

"But it has been a good day?"

"You know it has. And I don't think you need any more practice for a while." Georgie's eyes held a mischievous glint as she moved away from him. "Now I'm going down to see to that poor neglected dog while you cook."

Liam sat down on the bed after she went downstairs. The sense of contentment that flowed through him was unfamiliar. He hadn't felt this at ease in a long time. He took a deep breath and basked in the warmth that was flowing through him. His book was coming along brilliantly, and he knew that Georgie was responsible for the way he was feeling and the way the words were appearing. She'd gotten beneath his skin and brought his emotions spiralling back to the surface.

The good ones.

If he kept writing like this, he'd have this book finished well before the Christmas Eve deadline. Georgie had brought a fresh outlook and joy into his life in the short time he'd known her.

Even when he'd been with Vanessa, her neediness had stifled him.

The social life she had made for them had been time-consuming and had bored Liam. The joy that his writing had given him had disappeared as he realised the mistake he had made in marrying Vanessa—along with his muse. That had been the problem with his writing over the past few months. Events since her death had overwhelmed him, and it had continued to block his creativity. He'd buried his feelings and not let himself feel the emotions that were bubbling under the surface—the facade he showed to the world. The person he'd become in the artificial world she'd created for them.

But he still had work to do. *If I can drag myself away from Georgie and back to the computer.* And he had to sort out exactly what these feelings were. He'd only just met her, but in ten days she'd made him feel more alive than he'd felt in the last two years.

Liam frowned and made his way down to the kitchen, deep in thought.

Chapter Sixteen

Sex between two consenting adults.

That's all it was.

Nothing else.

Georgie cursed as her hair band snapped and her neatly coiled hair tumbled down. Good times before she went away.

They were going to be late. Even though she didn't have an appointment, she knew Liam had to be at the Fairmont hotel at noon to meet with his editor. It wasn't far from there to the travel agency on Queen Street, and it was a beautiful day for a walk.

Even though Liam had wanted her to stay the night, she'd insisted on coming home after dinner, telling him she had things to do, but she'd come home mainly because she'd needed some space. She did have to organise some dates and papers to take to the travel agency and she should have done it last night, but when Liam had insisted on walking her home, he'd come in and ended up staying and they'd talked until after midnight.

Georgie couldn't help grinning as she fixed her hair. She'd taken extra care with her appearance today. A touch of makeup, an elegant hairstyle—if only she could get it to stay up—and a long-sleeved silk top over black jeans. A pair of flat but strappy sandals completed the look. If she was spending at least part of the day in Liam's company, she wanted to look nice.

"Oh. Damn." A tap at the door announced his arrival and she opened her window and called down to him. "I'm coming." She gave up on her hair and gave it a quick brush, leaving it loose, checked her lipstick, and picked up her bag and travel itinerary.

Liam was waiting on the porch, stroking Ana's cat, Sooky, and Georgie's mouth dropped open as she pulled the door shut behind her.

"We...ell, Mr. Author, don't you look right pretty." She tipped her head to the side and looked him up and down. From the tip of his polished shoes to the neatly knotted tie at the collar of his pale blue business shirt.

"Not as pretty as you do." His smile sent a pleasant buzz through her and she smoothed her hair back from her face.

"It's a shame we have to climb into that old truck," she said.

Liam looked over at the truck and then glanced down at his watch. "I have an idea. We have plenty of time. My editor called just as I was leaving. Her flight's been delayed so my meeting's been put back till two o'clock. I hope that doesn't mess with your day?"

Georgie shook her head and waited to hear his idea, but he smiled enigmatically without telling her what it was. She shrugged and called out to Mutt as she opened the door of the old ute. "You guard the house, boy, and don't even think about getting out."

"Will he be okay home by himself?" Liam frowned as he slid in beside her and a shot of warmth filled her. He really was a great guy, and she was getting more sucked in each time he did or said something sweet—and there had been more than a few of those times over the past couple of days.

"He should be okay. I got up early and checked the fence where he's been getting out and it looks sturdy. He might howl a bit but he'll be fine." She looked up with a grin at Liam's house perched on top of the cliff. "At least he won't bother the neighbours."

The Bruce Highway was busy, and Georgie concentrated on driving as they headed south. They were just past Caloundra when Liam's phone rang. Georgie turned off the motorway at the next exit while he answered. The ute was so damn noisy it was almost impossible to hold a conversation when it was speeding along the road, let alone hear someone on the other end of a mobile phone when the motor was revving away.

Liam shot her a smile as he took the call. They were parked on a bluff just before the golf club and the view of the sea opened out in front of them. The birds were diving for fish close to the shore, and when Georgie opened her window, their shrill cries floated in on the sea breeze. It was a glorious day—no clouds and very little wind. Despite being early summer, the forecast was for the high twenties. The smell of the salt air was refreshing as it drifted up from the sea.

"Thank you, I'll wait for your email." Liam's words were formal and Georgie glanced over at him. A frown wrinkled his brow as he stared out through the windshield and he was unaware of her looking at him. Georgie made the most of the opportunity. He was clean-shaven this morning, and the angles of his face were less pronounced without the shadow of his usual dark stubble. His shirt was the same ice blue as his eyes and his hair curled softly onto the collar.

Georgie knew she was falling for him and that it was a crazy thing to do. She had to put a halt to it before she got hurt. And she knew that hurt would come as sure as morning followed night. It would be worse, much worse than any other time, because she'd never fallen so deeply for any other man. She sighed and turned back to the view over the ocean.

"No problem, it's not your fault. Talk soon." Liam disconnected and put the phone back on the seat between them.

"Change of plans," he said. "Larissa's flight has been cancelled and she's postponed the meeting till next week."

"Oh." Georgie bit her lip. "So what do you want to do?" Did he want to go back home? They were only half an hour away and she'd have time to drive him back and still go down to Brisbane.

"Can you take a left here and go back to Caloundra?" Liam grinned at her and her stomach did a double backflip. If he'd asked

518

her to fly to the moon with a smile like that, she would have done her damnedest to do it.

"Sure…where to?"

"Do you know where the Ritz-Carlton is?" He looked very pleased about something as Georgie started the car.

"Yes, it's the next left, overlooking the top of the island."

She followed the curving road until they reached the hotel. The yellow brick building perched on the sweeping lawns glowed in the morning sun. It was a beautiful place and Georgie had always had a yen to stay here. Liam grabbed his jacket and climbed out.

"I won't be too long, I hope."

Georgie shrugged and settled in to wait. Ana's old ute looked out of place next to all the flashy cars parked along the manicured hedge. She pulled out the folder holding her travel documents and began to think of the questions she had for Sandy, the travel consultant. She hadn't had a chance to think about her trip for a while. Either that or she was blocking it from her mind. The tentative itinerary was Hawaii to Rio de Janeiro after Christmas and in March she'd fly to California. She had to decide how long she would stay in San Francisco and then choose her next destination so Sandy could book her flights. Georgie flicked through some of the brochures the travel agent had sent her, but nothing appealed. She sighed and put her head back on the headrest. It was too late to change her mind; she'd paid for half of the trip already and changing her mind because she was a coward—or for some other reason she was not even going to think about—was not enough for the travel insurance company to refund her money.

The noise of her door opening had her eyes flying open and Liam stood there jangling a set of keys.

"Your chariot awaits, madam."

This time her stomach did a triple somersault. His face was

alight with laughter and his hair had gotten mussed in the light wind. He'd loosened his tie and unbuttoned the top button of his shirt. He looked like a movie star.

"What?" Her mind was no longer focused on her trip. When he looked at her like that, she couldn't focus on anything apart from how good he looked.

"Grab your gear." A whiff of his cologne added to her bemused state as he reached across her and picked up her jacket. "It's my turn to drive you."

Liam took the keys from her and locked the truck, before he led her around to the back of the hotel. The concierge stood next to a low-slung silver Porsche and Liam handed him the ute keys, before opening the door for Georgie to climb in.

"I'll drive you to the travel agent and Queen Street.'

"Oh wow! In a Porsche, no less. Just as well I dressed up." Georgie shot him a grin. She was going to enjoy the day.

***

Georgie had been quiet when Liam had met up with her near the State Library. He'd dropped her off at her travel agency and parked the Porsche in a garage near Southbank before walking back down across the bridge. He'd filled up the hour by browsing in an antique bookstore near where he was supposed to meet her at noon. She'd been waiting on a bench on a patch of lawn near the river and had slid a blue travel wallet into her bag when he strolled across to her.

She'd looked up at him with a smile but he could have sworn her eyes were sad.

"So where to now?" he'd asked. He'd never visited Brisbane apart from the airport. Georgie had told him he was in for a treat. Since then he'd had the whole tourist experience and he'd enjoyed letting her show him the Brisbane she knew and obviously loved. She'd laughed with delight as they'd caught the River Cat down the river and back to Southbank.

They'd strolled along the waterfront through the tourist crowds, and the smell of the river surrounded them. When she'd heard that Liam had never experienced Brisbane as a tourist, she'd insisted that he hadn't lived until he'd eaten ice cream from the Southbank Ice Cream and Chocolate Shop.

As they sat outside, it seemed as if whatever had been on her mind had disappeared and she was smiling at him as he put the napkin down.

Liam grinned when the ice cream creation began to topple.

"Quick, catch it," Georgie squealed.

Now he grabbed for his spoon as the Earthquake they were sharing teetered precariously. Eight scoops of ice cream and eight different toppings including fresh bananas, whipped cream, chopped almonds, decadent chocolate chips, cherries, and more were tilting as he tried to hold them.

"Give me your spoon, too." He glanced up at Georgie as she handed over her spoon and he placed it strategically to balance the melting ice cream. "Now what?"

"We keep eating it. I'll go get another spoon...or two." Georgie had a smudge of ice cream on her lips and he stared at it. She headed for the counter and came back with two long-handled spoons and a handful of napkins. He smoothed the pile of ice cream down and slowly lowered his two spoons as she picked up one of the others.

"You've got strawberry ice cream on your mouth." Liam reached for a napkin, dabbed at her top lip, and grinned as the colour shot into her cheeks. "Are you really going to eat all that ice cream before it melts?" They were sitting out in the courtyard in Southbank and the midday sun was warm on their heads. Georgie's sunglasses were holding her hair back from her face and she reached up, dropping them down over her eyes.

"You'll have to help me." She filled a spoon with banana

and whipped cream and placed the last cherry on top before lifting it to his lips. Liam opened his mouth and she slid the spoon between his lips and stared at him, but he couldn't see the expression in her eyes.

"Your turn." Before he picked up the spoon, he lifted her sunglasses back onto her head. He wanted to see her face. Her green eyes held his as he filled the spoon with more ice cream and held it to her lips. The noise of the crowds faded around them and it was as though they were in their own private world.

Georgie licked the ice cream from the spoon and looked away as she reached for a clean napkin. "No more. I'll burst."

Liam leaned back and folded his arms waiting for his heartbeat to go back to normal. "So what have you got for me next?"

Georgie glanced at her watch. "You're not in a hurry to go home?"

Liam laughed. "After the amount I had to pay to rent the Porsche, I'm not taking it back till midnight, so you'd better find something to entertain me for another twelve hours."

Georgie's fair skin coloured and his heart skipped a beat. She was obviously thinking the same thing he was.

"We could go for a drive or we could take another cruise up the river?'

"How about we do both?" He pushed the plate with the mess of ice cream to the middle of the table and stood. Georgie picked up her bag and walked along beside him. Liam reached for her hand and smiled as her fingers curled in his.

They filled in the afternoon by walking around the wharves and taking another Rivercat cruise ride before coming back and joining the sunset cruise that went underneath the Storey Bridge. Liam laughed as she dragged him into a magnet shop in the Valley and they pored over the thousands of varieties of magnets on display.

"You're full of surprises. All the women I've ever taken shopping wanted to go to clothes and shoe stores."

She sent him a glance from beneath her long lashes. "And I suppose there were lots of women? All in the name of research, I'd guess."

It was the closest she'd gotten to asking him about his past. They'd both steered clear of personal questions.

"Hundreds," he said. He put his hand on Georgie's arm and dropped his voice. "I'd like to sit down and tell you about my…about me…one day."

"If you want," she said slowly, but she looked uneasy. He wanted to open his heart to her, to tell her about the grief and the disappointment of not being able to make his marriage work and the shock of Vanessa's death after they'd split up and how hard it had been to deal with the lies the media had told. The heaviness that had filled him until the last couple of weeks and the reason he had been so rude to her on the beach when he'd fallen from his kayak. Why he'd thought he wanted to be alone.

Liam picked up a magnet depicting a Viking woman with long red hair holding a hammer. "This reminds me of you."

"Thanks, not." She looked at the wall in front of them and giggled and the panic faded from her expression. He wouldn't go there again.

"So if that's me, this is you." She held out a little man with a long beard hunched over a pen with a pile of books surrounding him.

After purchasing their souvenirs, Liam handed her one of the small bags as they crossed the square to the wharf where they were to pick up the cruise.

Georgie stopped walking as she took it and held his gaze steadily. "You can put yours on your desk and it will remind you of the redhead who built your bookshelves, since I'll be gone." He opened his mouth to speak, but Georgie put her fingers against his

523

lips.

"Don't say anything. When you tell me all about you later, I'll tell you all about my trip and why I'm going away. Deal?" Her voice was soft and he reached up and held her hand against his face.

"Deal."

***

The sun set in a flash of colour as the yellow and black tourist boat cruised beneath Brisbane river bridges. The breeze had dropped and the night was still, as the sky filled with streaks of purple- and gold-edged clouds. It was one of the most amazing skies Georgie had ever seen and most of the passengers on board were all rushing to the upper deck to get a clear shot with their cameras, phones, or iPads. She stood at the side of the deck and sighed softly as a guitarist strummed his Spanish guitar from the centre of the boat. Liam was behind her with his arms loosely draped around her waist and he rested his cheek on her hair.

"Tired?"

"Mmm. A little." She leaned back against him and closed her eyes as the warmth of his body pressed into her back.

"I am. You've worn me out with your knowledge of this city." Liam's voice was quiet and his breath brushed her cheek gently as he spoke. "I've seen most of the attractions in one fell swoop. But I've had a great day."

"Me, too."

"There's only one more thing that will make it perfect."

Georgie straightened and she wondered what he was going to say. She knew what would make the day perfect, but she wasn't going to go there.

"How about we have dinner at the Ritz-Carlton at Caloundra when we take the Porsche back?" Liam smiled down at her.

"Now that *would* be a perfect end to a wonderful day."

Georgie almost jumped into his arms with excitement. "I've wanted to go there for years, but staying there is definitely out of my league. When I was a teenager I used to dream of having my wedding there in a marquee on the lawn on top of the cliff." Her face clouded as she looked away, but she kept talking. "Going back home in Ana's truck is going to be a bit of a change after driving around in that fancy car all afternoon."

###

The drive back to Caloundra was quiet. Liam closed the soft top and the luxurious car cruised the miles silently. Georgie closed her eyes and listened to the classical music coming from the stereo, trying not to think of this perfect day coming to an end. She knew when she got home that she needed to study the itinerary that Sandy had printed off for her. Her bank account was also several thousand dollars poorer, but if the truth be known, she was more excited about having dinner at the Ritz-Carlton than about her planned trip.

"Georgie?" A light touch on her arm roused her from sleep. "We're here."

She opened her eyes slowly and smoothed her hair back.

Great, I was probably drooling.

Georgie headed to the ladies' powder room off the foyer as Liam handed the Porsche keys over. She stood in front of the huge mirror and brushed her hair until all of the tangles were gone before she swept it up into a French plait on the back of her head and secured it firmly with a clip she'd found in the bottom of her bag. Washing her face with warm water, she patted it dry with one of the soft warm towels put out for patrons' use and then reapplied her makeup. A final glance at the mirror to straighten her clothes and Georgie was satisfied she looked ready to dine in one of the most upscale restaurants on the coast. Her eyes were sparkling and there was a rosy flush on her cheeks. It wasn't from anticipation; it was a touch of the sun from today.

She looked good and she stepped into the foyer with assurance as Liam smiled appreciatively and took her arm. He'd done his shirt buttons back up and knotted his tie. She handed him his jacket and when he slipped it back on, he was the epitome of elegance.

Georgie's mouth dried. Was she really about to have dinner at the Beach Restaurant at the Ritz-Carlton with Liam Wyndham, famous author? She shook her head and Liam looked down at her.

"Is something wrong?" His voice was concerned and she loved him for it.

Oh please, don't say the L-word. Don't even think it.

"No, I was just pinching myself. This is like a dream come true for me. Maybe I'll wake up in a minute." She shot him a grin as the maître d' led them to a table by the window, and when Georgie was seated, he flicked a snow-white napkin over her lap.

"I've been a bit presumptuous." Liam watched her as she lifted her water glass and sipped.

"Yes?" She tipped her head to the side. He had a flush on his cheeks and she wasn't sure if it was from the sun or if something was bothering him.

"I thought by the time we had dinner it would be late…and maybe we would share a bottle of wine to celebrate the end of a perfect day…"

"And?"

"And I've asked if there are any rooms available." His words came out in a rush, as though he were a nervous teen on his first date. "If you'd rather go home, we can."

Excitement coiled low in Georgie's belly, but she kept her face bland as she answered him. "Rooms or room?"

She bit back a laugh as the colour deepened beneath Liam's gorgeous cheekbones. It was usually *her* face that coloured up, and it was the first time she had seen him lose his cool.

"Ah…one room?" He held her gaze steadily, and as the

waitress came over to hand them the menu, Georgie let a small smile tilt her lips.

"I think that would be a perfect end to the day. But there's only one problem." She glanced down at her bag.

Liam frowned. "A problem?"

"I don't have any night things with me."

A huge grin spread across his face and when he winked at her, the nervous jolt shot through her whole body. "I don't think that will be a problem at all."

Chapter Seventeen

"As good as you expected?"

Liam's eyes were closed and his expression was one of pure bliss. He opened his eyes and put his fork down on his plate. "I think I can safely say that this steak is even better than that ice cream delight you made me eat for lunch."

"The purest flavours of the country for the discerning palate." Georgie read from the card on the middle of the table to keep her attention from straying to Liam's lips. They had shared a plate of plump, succulent oysters before their main course was brought to the table, and Liam had kept his eyes on her lips as he'd fed them to her. Georgie leaned the card on the ice bucket in the centre of the table before looking around the restaurant. No matter how much she was looking forward to spending the night here in *one* room, she wanted to enjoy every minute of their meal.

The restaurant was elegant and the hushed conversation of a small group across the room combined with the classical music to provide a pleasant background ambience. Georgie glanced across to the window. The lawns on the edge of the cliff were floodlit and the ocean spray was highlighted by the bright light as the waves crashed against the rocks below. She gave a little sigh of pleasure and picked up her glass. "You know, I feel like I'm in a Hollywood movie."

"So long as it's not an Alfred Hitchcock movie. Uncle Joe's house sort of reminds me of one of his thrillers." Liam nodded to the waitress as she took his plate. He looked back at Georgie and his smile faded. "So if we *were* in a movie, I guess this would be the time when the two main characters gazed into each other's eyes and talked about their past?"

Georgie hid a smile. The only restaurant movie that came to mind was that famous scene with Meg Ryan and Billy Crystal, but she sure wasn't going to mention that. Embarrassment filled her as she thought of Liam's reaction if she *were* to bring that up. Although she didn't want the happy mood of the day to disappear, if they started talking too seriously. Their surroundings were full of romance, the soft light, the low music in the background, and the private alcove they'd been seated in. It would be a perfect night for a couple in love, but she pushed that thought away. They were a long way from that.

We're simply two adults enjoying each other's company. A day spent together, a pleasant dinner in an elegant restaurant. Casual conversation followed by a night of casual… Well…that's what it was…casual sex.

Or maybe friends with benefits? That sounded better. No big deal.

Act like a grown-up, not a teenager mooning over a movie star. She fought the tremble that consumed her as she thought of the night ahead. Was she being foolish? Was she setting herself up for serious heartbreak?

"Tell me about you. What it's like to be famous?" She tried to keep her words light and Liam reached over and lifted her hand, staring at her fingers. He seemed to be searching for the right words. Finally, he broke the silence and she tried to ignore the nervous flutters running along her fingers.

"I've been happier these last couple of weeks than I have for a long time," he said softly. Liam was still staring at their joined hands. "Am I being egotistical to assume you've read some of the crap written about my life and my marriage?"

"I know you were married and your wife died while you were overseas." Georgie waited for him to look at her, and when he did, she looked back at him steadily. "The old dears devour all the gossip magazines and they hinted there was some scandal, but I

529

didn't read it myself." She squeezed his hand. "Look, Liam. It's your business and I'm sure it was tough, but you don't have to tell me anything."

His eyes were dark as he looked back at her, and Georgie's stomach began doing double flips.

"I want to. I want you to know what you're taking on."

"Whoa." Georgie pulled her fingers from his grasp and held up her hand. "Just slow down. I'm not 'taking anything on.'" She kept her voice even, but her mind was spinning.

Too late. It was way too late. These were the words she'd yearned to hear from a man, but not now. Ahead of her was the trip where the new Georgie would find her independence. There was no longer any need for a man in her life to complete the old girlish dream.

And how foolish would I be to think that someone as gorgeous and famous as Liam would want me?

"You're kidding yourself, Liam." Her heart was thudding and Georgie took a deep breath, but the waitress came to take the rest of their order before she could finish speaking. She took the menu from the waitress and read off the first thing she could see. "Pineapple cheesecake. I might as well try the cuisine. I'll be in Hawaii soon." She stared at him as he gave the menu a cursory glance before ordering apple pie.

He waited for the waitress to leave before he spoke. Georgie's heart set up a dance beat in her chest as he looked at her. His blue eyes held hers and he reached for her hand again and she let him take it.

"Who hurt you so badly, Georgie?" His voice was husky, and his thumb caressed the back of her hand. Tears pricked the back of her eyelids but Georgie was determined not to show him that she was a quivering mess inside. Lifting her glass, she took a huge gulp of wine. She could have listed them but instead, her answer was flippant.

"We can have fun together"—she deliberately looked at him in what she hoped was a coquettish way—"and I'm looking forward to tonight. But Liam, I come from a long line of non-committers. So no involvement with *anyone* for me. Ever. I need my independence."

Huh. One of the biggest lies I've ever told.

She willed away the ache in her throat as Liam stared at her. "So we can stay friends—friends with benefits, even, but I'll be out of here in a week or two. I finalised my trip today." She put on a sexy chuckle. "And I've paid for it, so you can't even tempt me to stay. No matter how much fun we have tonight."

"I don't believe you. You sound bitter." The expression on Liam's face was doing her no good. She didn't want to talk about why she felt the way she did. "Talk to me, Georgie. I mightn't be able to help, but I am a good listener."

Not now. Not ever. But he kept looking at her, waiting for her to answer and she heaved a small sigh.

"There's nothing to talk about. The bottom line is, I've decided to take off and see the world." Georgie swallowed and tried to make her words dismissive as she lifted her hand from his. "It's time for adventure and there's nothing for me here anymore…" No matter how long she had waited for a man like him, it still didn't feel real. She would give in and then he wouldn't want her the way she wanted him. It always happened, and this time she would not be the one falling first.

***

The glib exterior that Georgie was hiding behind didn't fool Liam for one minute, and he could sense she was trying to cover up something. What it was, he couldn't pinpoint exactly. The day had been fun, and he'd been looking forward to the night ahead. He hadn't told her, but he'd booked the suite overlooking the ocean.

Maybe it's not the right time?

531

They ate their desserts quietly, the soft music filling the silence between them. Liam raised the wine bottle and waited for Georgie to look at him. She'd spent a lot of time with her head turned to the window, watching the spray of the ocean dancing in the spotlight outside the restaurant.

"More wine?"

"No, thank you." Her lips tilted in a smile and the rush that tore through him almost took his breath away. "I couldn't eat or drink another thing. It was beautiful. Thank you for bringing me here."

Liam reached across and took her hand. "You're beautiful." The feeling that filled his chest when her fingers curled in his was like nothing he'd ever experienced before.

Maybe he should pull back now, or it was going to be very hard for him when she went away. And she seemed determined to go. When she'd said there was nothing left for her in Maleny, her eyes had been sad. He'd seen her with her friends at his welcome party and he knew that it wasn't true. She was loved by everyone there that afternoon, but now there was hesitancy in her expression that showed him that she didn't realise how important she was to those people. There had been so much hurt in her voice, even though she'd tried to cover it. All he wanted to do was to take her in his arms and make everything better for her. He looked down at her small hand entwined in his and brushed his thumb over the soft skin. She looked up at him and her eyes were dark.

Should they go home to their respective houses? Was he taking advantage of her vulnerability?

Georgie pulled her hand from his and rose, pushing her chair back. "I don't know about you, but I'm tired. It's been a busy day."

Liam cleared his throat. "So?"

"So take me upstairs and show me...show me this wonderful room you've booked."

"You're sure?"

Georgie smiled and nodded.

Liam called for the bill and signed the check and tipped the waitress while Georgie waited by the window, watching the waves smash against the rocks. He walked over and slipped his arm around her waist and closed his eyes as she leaned back against his chest.

"I love the water. Whenever I'm upset, I walk on the beach and watch the waves and it soothes me here." She raised her hand to her chest and Liam placed his hand against hers, brushing against the softness of her breast.

Georgie drew a quick breath and Liam dropped his head, brushing his lips against her cheek.

"Come on, I've already picked up our room key."

They walked together to the elevator, and anticipation curled in Liam's belly as they waited for the door to open. He stood back and waited for an older couple to enter before them, when all he wanted to do was rush in there and get to their room. Georgie stared back at him as the elevator rose quietly and smoothly to the top floor.

"Have a good evening." The elderly gentleman nodded at them as they walked along the hall, and Liam could have sworn he had a gleam in his eye.

Surprised to feel his hands trembling as he swiped the room key, he pushed the door open.

"Oh. My. Goodness." Georgie's voice was hushed as she stood beside him and looked around. "The ocean suite?"

Liam nodded, feeling like a teenager on his first date. His mouth was dry and his breath caught as he watched Georgie hold her arms wide and spin in a circle.

Fighting back the need that was pulsing through him, Liam followed her across to the window and stood beside her as they took in the majesty of the rolling swells pushing into the cliffs.

Finally Georgie turned and splayed her hands on his chest. He was sure she could feel his heart thudding beneath his shirt.

"The view is amazing. Thank you for booking the suite," she whispered. "Are you sure you can afford this?"

"At least you've stopped saying sorry all the time." He grinned at her as her eyes widened, and he was touched by her concern. "And yes, I can afford it."

Liam moved slowly, watching Georgie's green eyes as he took her face between his hands and dipped his head to taste her. Her breath sighed out through sweet lips and her eyes closed as he felt her hands move from his chest to grip the top of his arms. His legs were unsteady as a surge of panic rushed through him.

I love this woman. Certainty filled him. Liam was as sure of that as he was that the sun would rise in the morning. He didn't want to. He wasn't ready to go anywhere near there, and besides, she was leaving.

Never again, he'd vowed when his marriage had died.

But the feelings that coursed through him were new and unfamiliar. Liam closed his eyes and gave in to them. He needed to think it through, but with Georgie's fingers loosening his tie and moving to the buttons of his shirt, he was captivated, and his confused thoughts disappeared as Georgie pushed the shirt from his shoulders and her warm hands settled on his bare chest.

Chapter Eighteen

"So what's for breakfast?"

Liam opened his eyes slowly. Georgie was sitting in the chair by the window, looking out over the glistening water. It was like a millpond this morning; the long lazy swells of the Pacific Ocean had settled to a calm surface and there was no sound of waves crashing below them. She'd obviously showered; her hair was damp and she was dressed in her clothes from yesterday.

"Me?" he asked hopefully.

Georgie laughed and pointed to the clock beside the bed. "I've got work to do. A certain author is in need of some bookshelves, and I also suspect he may have some writing to do." She tipped her head to the side and Liam reluctantly pushed himself up against the soft pillows at the head of the bed.

"True. We do need to get back to work. Or at least I do." He held her gaze steadily. "I'm really impressed with my builder's…er…skills and it wouldn't worry me if she took a year or so to finish the job."

Georgie was the first to break eye contact.

"But yes, breakfast downstairs first. I've noticed how much you love your food. And then we'll find your old ute." Liam swung his legs over the side of the bed.

Georgie's hand flew to her mouth. "Oh, no."

"What's wrong?" For a moment Liam thought he'd said the wrong thing about her enjoying food. Maybe she was like Vanessa, who'd thought it was not feminine to enjoy eating, but he didn't think so. Especially not after that Earthquake ice cream she'd devoured yesterday.

"Your new car," she exclaimed. "You were going to go to

the car dealership yesterday but I dragged you around the tourist traps and we totally forgot all about it."

Liam shook his head. "I didn't." His kept his voice rather smug. "I ordered one when you were at the travel agency."

"Ordered one? Without even taking it for a test drive?" Georgie wrinkled her nose and a surge of warmth shot through him. Her face was full of joy and he enjoyed being with her. Last night had been magic and he'd woken a few times through the night and just enjoyed feeling her pressed against him, breathing softly as she slept. He'd run his fingers gently through her hair and she'd stirred slightly but hadn't woken.

He'd pushed away the doubts that niggled at the edge of his mind. He'd think it through when they got home. Or rather when he was home at his house.

"We did take a test drive."

"What?" Confusion was written all over her face. "When?"

"The Porsche," he said. "I ordered one. All I had to do was pick the colour and I went for the silver. They're trucking a new one up from Sydney later this week. I'll pick it up here."

"Oh, wow. You won't want to get in the old noisy truck with me anymore, will you?" Georgie grinned at him as she stood and crossed to the door. "I'll go down and wait in the breakfast room while you shower and dress. Okay?"

***

Georgie sat beside the window in the restaurant and stared out over the water. The morning sunlight glistened on the breaking waves and the soft shush of the surf echoed her pensive mood. After Liam had gone to sleep in the early hours, she had lain there beside him. His hand had been resting on her hip and she'd closed her eyes and listened to his breathing. A smidgeon of hope had slowly filled her in the still of the dawn, and she began to think that maybe this time, just maybe, things might be different.

Yesterday had been perfect. The only downside had been

spending the time and her money at the travel agency. For a brief moment last night, Georgie had wondered what would happen if she just put the trip on hold for a while and hung around.

Hung around Liam and waited to see what developed.

No. She was going on her trip; she was not going to leave herself open to more hurt.

"Coffee, madam?"

She smiled up at the waiter as he held the coffee pot up. "Black, please." He filled her cup and stepped away and Georgie's breath caught in her throat, all her conviction fading. Liam stood in the doorway looking around the tables and she fought for composure as his eyes settled on her. His hair was damp, and he hadn't shaved. She smiled as she watched him cross the room to her.

To me. All the women in the room turned and watched as he walked past their tables. Georgie knew Liam was totally unaware of how sexy he was, and that just added to his attraction.

And she had spent the night in his bed. A little bud of warmth unfurled in her chest.

Maybe?

***

Liam pulled the chair out and sat opposite Georgie. "I'm starving."

As she lifted her eyes to meet his, a smile lit up her face and an unfamiliar rush of need flooded through him.

"You've worn me out, woman. I need food." He tried to cover up his confusion by being flippant.

"Good, it will give you energy to write all day."

"I can think of better ways to spend the day." Liam reached out and took her hand, but Georgie shook her head.

"I have work to do, and so do you."

Liam looked down at her fingers laced with his. "Georgie?"

"Yes?" She tipped her head to the side.

"Would you consider putting your trip off for a while?"

"Why? So I can do the second room of shelves for you?" A frown crossed her face and Liam held her fingers more firmly.

"No, of course not. I don't care about the shelves. I mean, I do. I want them, and you are doing a great job, but that's not what I meant." Liam stared at her and her green eyes widened. "I mean let's spend some more time together. Can you change your itinerary?"

"No." Georgie stared back at him but it was hard to read her expression. He was hoping that he would be able to tempt her to stay.

"I'm doing a favour for a friend in Hawaii over Christmas." She pulled her hand back from his and rested her elbows on the table, with her chin cupped in her hand.

Before he could reply, the waiter appeared with the menu and their conversation turned to food.

***

On the way back up the Bruce Highway, Georgie was grateful for the rattling of the old ute. Liam seemed to be in a world of his own and stared through the window as the coast flashed past them.

Her independence was taking flight. It seemed to have a mind of its own. She needed to get that new mantra tattooed on her arm to stop her from staying here—for a guy.

I value my independence. What the heck had she been thinking of to spend the day—and the night—with him? She was falling in love with Liam, and who was going to get hurt? Just like every other time—her. Georgie straightened her shoulders and gripped the steering wheel harder as they approached the shared driveway to their houses. The sooner she got away from him, the better.

She forced a grin onto her face as she turned up to his house. "I'll drop you off and then I'm going to take Mutt for a walk." Hopefully, she could keep some of her dignity intact. "Thank you for last night. It was very pleasant."

Liam shot her a glance and opened his door. "I'll see you later, then."

"Yes, you will." She kept the bright smile on her face until she backed down the drive and turned into the gate of Cliff Cottage.

***

Very pleasant?

God, that was as bad as her telling him she'd had a nice time. Liam pushed the front door open and strode across the tiled foyer. He was falling for Georgie and should really pull back. It had been a magical night together, but she'd soon be gone. He shrugged as he headed for the study. Immerse himself in Nepal; that was the solution. He had a hero to sort out today. He'd cope once she was gone. He'd have to. Once she left, he would settle into his novels and his house and he'd forget about her. Liam tried to push away the thought of Georgie sleeping in his arms, but it wouldn't go. All he could see was her lustrous auburn hair splayed across his chest as she'd lain beside him.

What the hell was he thinking? No more pondering emotions or red-haired beauties. Liam shrugged off his suit jacket and switched on his computer. He'd get changed later, when he broke for a coffee. The computer whirred to life and he accessed the cloud drive where he'd last saved his work. As he scrolled through the last chapters he'd written, Georgie's face stayed with him. Then the feelings that had consumed him for the past twenty-four hours turned into letters and words and his fingers flew over the keyboard. But he wasn't going to hold her back. He pulled a face as he typed. This time the tables were turned. For once, he was the needy person, but he couldn't keep Georgie from doing what she wanted. If she didn't go on this trip, because he asked her to stay, she'd end up resenting him later. It would be like Vanessa all over again.

In a way, it was like a purging. Liam knew he couldn't afford to trust his heart, no matter what he thought he felt for Georgie. He'd learned that the hard way.

God, even the name of this book is *Guardian of the Village*. It didn't matter that his hero was high up in the lofty Himalayas. His own heart was in just as much jeopardy here in Hideaway Bay.

He'd be guarding it until she left on her trip, that's for sure.

Liam stood and frowned at his watch as the sound of a door closing caught his attention. He stretched, surprised to see how long he'd been at the computer. It was mid-afternoon. Georgie was late starting work. He'd managed to operate on two levels while he'd worked. The story had flowed and he was more than satisfied with its progress. But he was less than satisfied with the emotions that ran through him. No matter how hard he tried, he couldn't shift them.

Georgie was firmly embedded in his head, but he'd just have to get used to the idea of her leaving, though he couldn't understand why she was so set on moving away. She was as much a part of this community as the cliffs along the beach. He was sure she wasn't being true to herself. But Liam had already experienced enough dishonesty with Vanessa.

Whatever happened with Georgie, however he felt, whatever she thought, he was going to be honest. Before he went upstairs to the study, he switched on the coffeemaker and went to get changed into his jeans. Liam tipped his head to the side and listened as he headed back to the kitchen. It was completely quiet, apart from the burbling of the coffee machine and the noise of the waves breaking on the rocks at the bottom of the cliff. There was no sound coming from above.

Shrugging, he poured two coffees and headed up the stairs, prepared to be completely honest with Georgie. If she blew him off, so be it. Balancing the coffee cups in one hand, he pushed open the door and looked around the room. The room was empty. The closing door that had disturbed him must have been her leaving.

He'd do some more writing and then he'd go down to the cottage to see her.

Maybe.

Chapter Nineteen

Georgie was being a coward. As soon as she finished the trim on the middle shelf, she packed up quietly and then jumped into the ute. She headed for Thelma and Mitzi's house, even though it was only mid-afternoon. The more time she spent away from Liam the better. No more nights together. She'd focus on his bookshelves, get them finished, and get ready for her trip. Time to ease back before it was too hard to leave and she couldn't. They were good together and they'd had fun, but she was leaving and he wasn't going to entice her to stay.

"Georgie! We haven't seen you for ages."

She shot a dry smile at Thelma. "All of three days. I was here on Sunday, remember?"

"But you've been busy with your young man. So we quite understand if you're too busy to call on us, don't we, Mitzi?"

"You two are incorrigible!" Georgie couldn't help the laugh that escaped as she hugged Thelma. "I'm here now, so what's for dinner?"

Conversation was lively as she sat in the kitchen and watched her friends whip up a meal.

"It's a shame you didn't bring Liam with you." Thelma looked sideways at Mitzi as she stirred the pot of soup she'd taken from the refrigerator.

"I know what the pair of you are up to." Georgie forced a smile on her face but shook her head. "It's not going to happen. I'm leaving in less than two weeks."

Two wrinkled faces fell with a collective sigh. Thelma pulled out a chair and sat beside her. "We so hoped that you and Liam would get together. It would have been a perfect ending. Things would have come full circle for us."

"What do you mean?"

Mitzi put the spoon on to the sink and came to sit at the table. "Because of Joe." Her voice was soft. "Liam's Uncle Joe and I were dating. He used to drive me around in the Fireflite. And then he went to Vietnam." She wiped a tear away and Georgie reached out to her and held her soft hand. "I waited for him to come back, but I was foolish. He was the love of my life and I didn't tell him before he went away. When he came back, he had a wife." Georgie squeezed Mitzi's fingers as her voice wavered. "I left it too late. Don't you dare make the same mistake."

Thelma chimed in. "We thought it would be perfect, if you, part of our family, and Liam got together and closed the circle."

Georgie shook her head. "Oh, you sweet things. I'm sorry, but it's not going to happen. Liam doesn't need me in his life. He's a famous author. He has his career, and besides, it wasn't that long ago that his wife died."

She stared at the two expectant faces across the table. "And I'm about to leave on my big adventure. I can't fall in love just because you want me to." She kept her voice steady and the smile on her face. There was no way anyone would ever know she *had* fallen in love with the man. Not even Sienna. It was her secret and if she was going to get over him and leave…no one else was going to know how she felt. No more wearing her heart on her sleeve.

Yes, she'd finally admitted it to herself. She had fallen in love…again. But no, it wasn't again. This was the first time in her life she had experienced this feeling. All the other times she'd just thought it was love. Now she knew the difference. Even more reason for not taking the risk of being the one left behind. It had hurt her ego the other times; if Liam knew how she felt and left her, this time her heart would be shattered.

"I'm off to see the world, and I promise I'll send you a postcard from every stop I make. Now is that soup almost done? I'm starving."

Yes, I carried that off perfectly. All she had to do was keep

543

it together until she left. Be jolly, happy Georgie, and get her bags packed. She could cry as much as she liked on her way to Hawaii.

***

For the first time since he'd moved into the house on the cliff, Liam regretted not having a car at his disposal. The cottage below sat in darkness. It would have been good to have jumped in a car and gone for a drive along the coast. He was pleased he'd be able to pick his Porsche up next week. As he thought of going up to the city, he realised he hadn't called Sarah about the cancelled meeting with the editor.

He went in search of his mobile and found it on the floor beside his computer. He had been altogether too vague since he'd met Georgie, but at least he'd been back in his creative zone. Having a break from both tonight might be good.

"Sarah?" His agent picked up straightaway. "It's me, Liam."

"Good to hear from you. I was going to call you tomorrow." Her voice was wary. "So how did the meeting with the editor go? I've been waiting for you to call."

"Sorry. I've been…a bit busy. Larissa didn't show—her flight was cancelled. She's rescheduled for next week." Liam wandered over to the window and looked down the hill. Still no lights on at the cottage.

"So are we."

"We?"

"Mike and me." Sarah spoke quickly. "We're staying at the Fairmont in Caloundra. Look, we're just out for dinner. I'll call later and we'll organise a time to meet up. I'll come to the meeting with you."

"Great." Liam meant it. It would be good to catch up with his friends. "Oh. And Sarah?" He tried not to sound too smug. "First ten chapters are finished and I've got another book to show her, too. A short one."

But the first thing he was going to do was sort out his feelings for Georgie. He knew he couldn't fight them any longer. For the first time in many months, Liam was happy. Happy where he was and with what he was doing. The one thing to complete his happiness would be to have Georgie by his side. All he had to do was convince her of that. He'd give her time to miss him, and he'd put the days to good use. One thing about falling in love: his muse was back with a vengeance.

***

The days passed quickly for Georgie. She was up early each morning, worked all day, and was home in the early afternoon. She went out every afternoon and stayed out for dinner, catching up with her friends and saying good-bye. Thelma and Mitzi wanted to put on a farewell party for her but she refused, trying to be gentle when she saw their disappointment.

Liam had stayed in his study each day, and Georgie wondered why he was avoiding her. Hopefully, he'd decided to move on and that the couple of nights they had spent together were just a casual...casual what? She couldn't face another night with him and then leave. She was barely keeping it together now. Putting on such a brave "happy Georgie" front with her friends was taking its toll. But despite being so tired, sleep was a long time coming each night.

She decided to work all weekend and was putting the last trim on the bookshelf along the far wall on Sunday afternoon when there was a tap on the door. She jumped down from the stepladder and smoothed her hair back as she crossed the room, schooling her expression into a friendly smile.

The numbness of the last few days deepened when she opened the door. She had put her feelings on ice. Liam leaned against the doorjamb and looked at her, casual and...well...just gorgeous. His signature white shirt was unbuttoned, but he wore a white T-shirt beneath. Fighting to keep a friendly and welcoming expression— tradesperson to client—on her face, Georgie tucked the hammer into her work belt.

"Hi, stranger. You've been busy writing?"

He looked at her and those sexy blue eyes didn't blink. Goose bumps prickled Georgie's skin from her neck all the way down her arms. Her fingers shook, and she ran her hands up and down her arms briskly.

"Gosh, that breeze is strong coming down the corridor." She turned away from him and walked over to the open window and pulled it down. Her back was to him and she closed her eyes. "Could you close the door, please?"

Keep calm, stop babbling. Play it cool.

Slow footsteps followed her across the room, and she opened her eyes and picked up a handful of nails. "Do you mind if I keep working?"

Liam still hadn't spoken a word.

Georgie placed one nail at the edge of the fancy trim and pulled the hammer from her belt. "Shelves are looking good. I hope you're happy with them." She felt him behind her before his breath brushed the back of her bare neck. Her hair was twisted in a high ponytail. "How is the book coming along?" God, the cheeriness in her voice sounded false even to her.

"Would you have dinner with me tonight?" Liam's voice was soft and his mouth must have been awfully close, because his breath now warmed her ear.

Yes, oh yes. No, I can't. Oh God, help me.

"Ah, I'm not sure what my plans are." She put another nail between her lips and dug into her belt for a couple more, feeling very clever. Even if he wanted to kiss her, he couldn't.

Gentle hands reached across; one took the hammer from her grasp, and the other slid slowly to her waist and turned her around. She looked up at him, the cold nail pressing into her lip. Liam's eyes were dancing with mirth, and he reached up and took

546

it from between her lips.

"If you think that is going to stop you from talking to me, you're wrong." He led her across to the wide windowsill and gently pushed her down until she was looking up at him. He put the hammer on the floor before he leaned over in front of her, one hand on each side of her on the windowsill. "I've given you a few days to work in peace, although it's been hard to stay away."

The look on Liam's face almost broke her determination to resist him, and she swallowed before she opened her mouth, but he shook his head. "I want *you* to listen to me. Don't talk."

Her skin was tight, and all Georgie wanted was to feel Liam stroking her skin, holding her. Her traitorous body was clamouring for him. His hands were still beside her and his face was a whisper away, but he didn't touch her. Her heart panicked in her chest as the ice began to crack.

No.

"You are beautiful, Georgie." When she screwed up her nose in dissent, Liam shook his head. "And I mean inside and out. Your lovely hair, your milk-white skin. Green witch eyes that see into my soul; eyes that I know understand me. A mouth that tempts me"—he smiled and she trembled—"even with nails in it."

The ice around her heart cracked a little more. Georgie swore she could feel the warmth spreading through her chest. His lips hovered above hers but did not come closer.

"You are caring, patient, and sweet, and you give so much of yourself to others."

The warmth of his skin surrounded her but still he didn't touch her.

"In your smile, I see someone so gorgeous, and when you smile at me"—finally he lifted his hand, but he put it on his heart—"this is where I feel it."

Cautious optimism fluttered through her. Almost...almost...she could believe he meant what he was saying to her. She leaned into him.

"One word." His voice was deep and mellow, and his expression was dreamy as he held her gaze.

Oh my God, if he used the L-word, Georgie knew she'd melt into a puddle at his feet. She widened her eyes and waited.

"Yes...just say yes." His breath brushed her lips.

Georgie's voice shook. "I don't know what the question is."

"Spend the night with me? I'll cook dinner and then we'll talk some more. Okay?" Liam stepped back and Georgie nodded before she managed to croak out a yes. He turned quickly and threw a smiling glance back at her when he reached the door.

"Seven o'clock, okay?"

She nodded again, feeling like one of those dolls with the bobbing head.

"And Georgie, wear that green dress you had on the other day. I'll put the fire on."

The door closed behind him and Georgie put her hands to her cheeks. She wouldn't need a fire. The blood pumping through her body would be enough to keep both of them warm.

Mutt started howling as Georgie closed the gate behind her. Having time to think this afternoon had not been good. The way Liam had looked at her and the words he had spoken had planted a tiny seed of hope within her. Her distrust began to lift, and she'd smiled at herself in Ana's mirror as she'd taken extra care with her appearance. A little kernel of an idea began to take shape in her head. He'd asked her to put her trip off a while, but maybe he could come with her?

She pulled her shawl around her shoulders as she walked slowly up the hill, and the wind caught the green dress Liam had asked her to wear, pushing it against her legs. The temperature had dropped; a storm was brewing over the sea. Her heart fluttered a little as she stood outside his door, and she chastised herself. This was crazy. She'd walked through this door every day for the past three weeks. There was no need to feel nervous.

The door opened before she could knock.

"Quick, come in out of that wind." Liam looked up at the threatening sky and then down at her dress. He grinned and ushered her inside, a gentle hand on her back. "I've just got to check on something in the kitchen." He cocked his head to the side. "Is that Mutt I hear?"

Georgie relaxed a little as she looked up at him. He was babbling as much as she did when she was nervous. She tipped her head to the side. "No, just the wind. He's safely inside the cottage."

They sat in front of the fire while they ate, and Liam kept the conversation casual. Finally, after he'd brought in a tray with coffee and chocolates, he slid over next to her and took her hand.

"So?" he said.

"So, what?" Georgie reached for her coffee. She'd managed to talk normally through the meal, and tried not to appear too nervous although every time she caught Liam looking at her a fresh tremble would run down her back.

"So did you think about what I said this afternoon?"

"Y…e…s," she said slowly.

"And?"

"And what?"

"Oh, for goodness' sake, Georgie, you are the most frustrating woman." He put his hand to his heart and grinned at her. Her heart rate kicked up a notch. It was altogether unfair that a man could be so good-looking.

She shook her head. "Liam, I don't know what you want from me. What you said this afternoon was really sweet, but you've forgotten I'm leaving."

Liam took the coffee cup from her hand. "No, I haven't. I

549

wouldn't ask you not to go. I'd never do that."

His blue eyes held hers, and Georgie's determination to make her own way in the world slipped a little more. "I've got a better idea." Georgie swallowed and stared back at him. "Why don't you come with me?"

Liam shook his head slowly. "Thanks, but I'm not going anywhere. I just got here and besides…"

"Besides what?"

"I like being settled. My days of travel are over."

"And mine are just beginning." Even though Georgie's smile was bright, Liam's words cut deep, but there was no way she was going to let him see how much he hurt her. They could have time together before she left, and she would stay strong. No man was ever going to see how vulnerable she was. Never again.

"I'll send you a postcard so you can see what you're missing out on." Georgie stared at Liam and held out her hand. "I'm cold. I think we'll be warmer in your bedroom?" She was proud of the coquettish smile she managed to summon up, hiding the hurt that had settled in her chest at his instant refusal of her suggestion to come with her.

Three hours later, Georgie stood at the window of Liam's bedroom looking out over the ocean. The storm had blown itself out, not that they had heard much of it… Liam had whispered sweet nothings in her ear before taking her to delightful places. Now the night sky was filled with stars, and the silver sheen from the rising moon polished the ocean. Hugging her arms around herself, Georgie stared out at the water. It was going to be so hard to leave, but she was going to. When Liam had dismissed her suggestion that he go with her, her world had fallen to pieces, but she'd been strong and hidden her feelings. She was leaving.

It was still ten days until she left and she would spend the time with Liam. Maybe when she was old and grey like Thelma and Mitzi, it would be a story to tell. Georgie smiled and walked across the soft carpet back to the bed where Liam lay sleeping.

Chapter Twenty

Georgie tooted the horn of the old ute and glanced down at her watch. If Liam didn't hurry up, he'd miss his appointment. He was meeting his new editor in Brisbane and then picking up his new Porsche. She was going to the city for some final shopping before she packed.

She looked up with a smile as Liam came out of the house and slammed the door. He was wearing a pale grey suit and a white shirt with his hair loose on his collar. God, she was going to miss him. Georgie swallowed and dug deep for strength.

He looked down at the suit with a grin as he put an envelope on the seat between them. "Second time in two weeks I've had my suit out, but I have to impress the new editor."

"And you'll sure look the part in the new car." Georgie loved to tease him. Sometimes she wondered if she was making the wrong decision, and then she remembered her mantra.

Independence.

The traffic on the motorway was heavy, and they were late getting into the city.

"Just drop me off at the hotel." Liam leaned over and kissed her before he opened the door. "I'll take you for a spin in the Porsche this afternoon."

"I'll look forward to it—*after* I get some work done on your shelves. Have a good meeting."

Liam waited on the kerb until she drove off, and Georgie sighed as she glanced in the rear view mirror and saw him standing there watching her. It was getting harder by the day; the more time they spent together, the harder it was going to be to leave him. Georgie waited for the light to change and frowned as she looked down at the seat. Shoot. Liam had had left his envelope on the seat.

As soon as the light changed, she did a U-turn and headed back to the hotel. She pulled into the drop-off area beneath the ornate grey arches and jumped out.

"I'll only be one minute." The concierge nodded and she grabbed the envelope and ran across to the door. Luckily, she'd dressed for a trip to the city and didn't feel out of place in the luxurious foyer. Georgie's heels clicked on the marble floor as she crossed toward the main desk along the wall and looked around. Her professional eye appreciated the marble columns rising to the fancy gilded ceiling.

Liam was standing by the elevator door and Georgie opened her mouth to call out to him, but the sound died in her throat as he held his arms out to an elegant blonde woman who stepped from the elevator. Liam had told her he'd never even met the editor his publisher had sent to Brisbane.

Georgie took a shuddering breath as pain sliced through her. The woman he was holding had her hands on either side of his face and he was smiling down at her, his face alight. It was the same way he'd looked at Georgie only hours ago. As she watched, he lowered his head and the woman lifted her face to his as she slid her arms around him. Georgie turned and ran, unable to watch for a second longer. It felt as though the breath had left her chest and her heart was surrounded by ice. She pushed her way through a crowd of people coming through the door, not caring as she forced her way through. A roaring sound filled her ears and she jumped into the truck and tried to turn the key, but her hands were shaking too much. Georgie took a deep breath and wiped away the tears that were filling her eyes, making it impossible to see clearly. Taking a deep breath, she forced her hand to stop shaking long enough to start the truck.

She drove into the traffic not knowing where she was going, trying to force away the feeling that she was going to throw up.

It had happened again, but this time her heart was in tatters. She had ever experienced the heart-wrenching grief that consumed her. It was a physical pain, and she didn't know how to make it go away.

***

Georgie had managed to get a couple of hours' sleep. Now Thelma and Mitzi comforted her with shoulder pats and hugs as she'd sat at their kitchen table drinking coffee. After going back to Ana's house and packing up as quickly as she could, Georgie had called in at Uncle Renzo's house and dropped off Mutt and Sooky, but she needed a female shoulder—or two—to cry on. Ana's ute was now parked in the garage next to the Fireflite and Aldo was picking her up shortly and taking her to Brisbane in his taxi.

For no fare, of course. Even the thought of his kindness brought a fresh wave of tears to Georgie's eyes and started Thelma and Mitzi fussing over her again. Her gaze fell on a pile of magazines on the table and before Mitzi could move it away, she spotted Liam's face on the front cover.

"I should have known what I was letting myself in for, right?" She sniffed and pushed the magazine away. At least the woman in the photo with him wasn't the one she'd seen in the hotel. Of course not; he was famous. Someone that famous would have a woman in every city. Georgie knew she was being unfair, but she'd seen him with her own eyes. The enormity of what she'd seen, and more importantly, of how gullible she'd been to trust him, settled like a chill in her body. The terrible picture of Liam about to kiss that woman would not leave her mind.

Mitzi wrung her hands as she stared at Georgie, her eyes filling with tears. "I can't believe it, Georgie. I saw the way Liam looked at you."

Georgie shook her head. "I saw him with my own eyes." Her phone beeped, and she picked it up and read the message.

Will see you at the airport. Love Sienna and Jack xxx

Georgie's eyes filled again. Of course Thelma and Mitzi had rung Sienna when she'd turned up yesterday afternoon looking for somewhere to spend the night. She'd spent an hour crying on the phone to Sienna. The whole world probably knew by now what a gullible fool she was.

A gullible, unlovable fool. With no chance of ever being part of a couple. She just didn't have it in her. No wonder Liam hadn't wanted to come to Hawaii with her.

Thelma passed Georgie the box of tissues as she sniffed again.

Chapter Twenty-One

Liam was late getting back to the coast. He'd tried to call Georgie to tell her he'd been delayed because the car delivery had been delayed, and then the traffic had been heavy due to an accident on the motorway, but she hadn't picked up. It was dark by the time he pulled into the old garage at his house where the pink Fireflite had resided for many years. He looked down the hill but the cottage was dark. Georgie must have gone visiting again. Liam was looking forward to becoming a part of this community and a part of her life. He'd invited Sarah and Mike down tomorrow. He couldn't wait for them to meet Georgie and see his new place.

"You look amazing." When Sarah had finally stopped hugging him, she'd stepped back and looked him up and down with a smile. "In fact, you look too good, Liam. Where has the suffering writer look gone?" Later, when he told her he'd met someone, Sarah had smiled.

The meeting with Larissa, the new editor, had gone well. They'd all laughed when he realised he'd forgotten his manuscript.

"Damn. I've left my notes and my flash drive in Georgie's car." Luckily, Larissa had been happy with the chapters he'd emailed earlier, and when they'd finished discussing business, Sarah had called up to their room and Mike had come back down and joined them for a quick drink.

Liam waited up for Georgie till almost midnight before he went to bed. She must have decided to stay down at the cottage rather than disturb him. It would be the first night in a week they had been apart, and he went to bed disappointed that she hadn't called.

***

He slept soundly and headed down the hill to the cottage first thing. He wanted to make sure Georgie would be around to meet Mike and Sarah after lunch.

The gate to the road was padlocked and Liam frowned as he stared at the house. There was no sign of the old ute or Mutt, and the house blinds were all drawn. Liam strode across the lawn and ran up the steps. The house was locked up, but he still knocked on the door as an uneasy feeling overtook him. The place looked as though it had been closed up. Georgie had never closed the blinds or locked the gate the whole time he'd lived up the hill.

He hurried back up the hill, pleased he'd grabbed the keys to his new car before he'd headed out. Liam jumped in and drove to Maleny, keeping an eye out for the old ute, but there was no sign of it at the hardware store or parked in the main street. Frowning, he turned onto the road that led down to Thelma and Mitzi's cottage. *Maybe Georgie had gone to visit and stayed there for the night?*

As soon as he turned into the driveway he knew something was not right. The two elderly ladies were sitting on their front porch. Mitzi was dabbing at her eyes with a lace-edged handkerchief. Thelma rose slowly to her feet, her arms folded. There was not a welcoming smile to be seen.

"Liam." Thelma nodded and Mitzi blew her nose. "Why are you here?" Thelma gestured for her sister to sit back down as Mitzi rose shakily to her feet.

"I'm looking for Georgie. Have you seen her?"

"Why?"

"There's somebody I want her to meet."

"*Hmm.* Is there?" Thelma's voice was cold and Liam scratched his head.

"So do you know where she is?"

Mitzi grabbed Thelma's arm and her voice was soft. "Tell him, Thel."

"She's at the airport. The poor darling was so upset, she decided to leave early."

"Upset?" Lima looked from one to the other. "Why was she upset? What happened?"

"See, I told you." Mitzi stood up this time and walked across to the step to stand beside Liam. "I knew it couldn't be true. I tried to tell her that."

Thelma's voice was low and she frowned at her sister. "So why were you in a clinch with a woman you'd never met when Georgie went back to the hotel to give you your manuscript?"

Suddenly it was blindingly obvious what had happened. Liam swore and Mitzi gasped.

Of all the things to happen.

***

Liam drove back to the coast and as far as the lookout. He parked the car and stared out over the ocean, his thoughts swirling through his head. Georgie's seeing him hugging Sarah had set off a chain of events that may have saved him from making a terrible mistake—the same one he'd made before. Vanessa had been needy, and he'd sworn he would never get caught by a needy woman again. He'd thought he'd fallen for Georgie, and she'd fought him every step of the way, but like the soft-hearted romantic he was, he hadn't listened. Now Liam forced himself to step back and think about what he had really wanted when he came here to Hideaway Bay. What he'd wanted and where he'd ended up.

Where he wanted to be.

Find the muse. Write my books. Okay, that was done and he was happy.

Have my privacy. Be a recluse like Uncle Joe had been. He hadn't had that. A red-haired carpenter had breached his privacy as soon as he'd arrived. And she'd introduced him to the community and to her family. *And I loved every minute of it.*

558

Never travel again. The horror that had filled him when he had been in Nepal and heard of Vanessa's death had firmed his resolve to settle and never travel overseas again. Liam knew that fear was irrational, but it had been real to him. He'd almost burned his passport.

Spend my days alone writing. Liam thought of the nights Georgie had spent in his bed, how she'd shown him the sights of Brisbane. The joy on her face as she'd chased the dog on the beach, the little wrinkle on her forehead when she was measuring his bookshelves. The feeling that filled him when he held her in his arms.

Liam didn't want to be alone. Knowing he'd hurt Georgie, even if unintentionally, was worse than any of his other fears.

Never have anyone need him again. Georgie was vulnerable, and he knew she'd been hurt even though she hadn't told him.

Liam opened the car door and climbed out of the car. He stood looking out to the bay as he came to a decision.

He hadn't been able to give Vanessa what she'd wanted, and he knew now it was because he'd never loved her. When he'd arrived in Hideaway Bay he'd been closed down, and what he'd believed had been right for him had been turned around by a green-eyed, red-haired woman who had bewitched him.

He loved Georgie Sacchi and he was not going to let her go.

No matter what it took.

Chapter Twenty-Two

Georgie walked toward the coffee shop at Brisbane International Airport where she'd arranged to meet Sienna and Jack. Her head was bowed and she lugged her carry-on bag over her shoulder, not watching where she was going. She barrelled straight into the tall man standing in front of her.

"Sorry," she muttered and stepped to the side to go around him. When he moved to block her way, Georgie looked up and she gasped. Blue eyes stared down at her and his lips lifted in a smile. She almost smiled back before reality hit her.

Liam? Here?

"What the hell are you doing here?" She looked around, desperate to get away from him before she made a fool of herself.

Liam took her arm and she tried to shake it off.

"Let me through, please." She tried to keep her voice cold and not look at him. As she looked down she saw the bag on the floor next to him. Lifting her head, she frowned at him. "Where are you going?"

"Hawaii." A tender smile curved his lips "If you'll let me come with you."

"What?" she said stupidly. "Why would you want to come with me? You said you've had enough adventures."

"Because I love you?" He took the bag off her shoulder as he looked down at her. "And because I can sit next to you on the plane and tell you that over and over again." Georgie stiffened as his arms went around her. "After I explain what you saw at the hotel."

"What did you say?" As much as she tried to fight it, a little burst of joy bubbled in her chest as Liam leaned his cheek against

560

hers.

"I said I love you. And I'm not letting you go anywhere without me. I'll travel the world with you. Wherever you want to go."

Georgie stepped out of his hold and wiped her eyes with the back of her hand. Liam hadn't shaved, and his hair was loose around his collar. She looked at him, really looked at him. Not only had his face lost the gauntness that it had held the first time she'd seen him on the beach, his eyes held an expression that hadn't been there, either. It was the way he was looking at her. All the feelings that clamoured inside Georgie were mirrored in Liam's face.

"The woman I was hugging at the Fairmont was my agent, Sarah. I hadn't seen her since Vanessa's funeral. If you'd waited a minute longer, you would have seen her husband, Mike, come over and thump me on the back while I was hugging her." He looked down at her and raised his hand to cup her cheek. "Mike and Sarah are my best friends, and they were coming down to the bay today to meet you. I told them I'd fallen in love with a green-eyed woman who bewitched me." A grin crossed his face. "You'll have to tell me where we're going after Hawaii so I can organise for them to meet us."

"How about Machu Picchu?"

Georgie spun around as Sienna's voice came from behind. "I hope you've got that on your tickets. We have a date there for our birthday in a few months."

"Tickets?" She looked at Liam, who pulled a travel wallet out of his shirt pocket.

"Do you know how hard it is to buy a round-the-world ticket with only a couple of hours to get to the airport?" Liam's grin got wider and he pulled her back to him. "And organise Thelma and Mitzi to look after the house for a few months?'

Georgie's heart started beating again. The ice was melting

and warmth filled her veins as she looked around. Sienna and Jack both had smiles on their faces, and Liam was still looking down at her intently.

Oh my God. Georgie hugged the feeling to her before she spoke. Liam loved her? Liam was going to come on her trip with her. And the whole trip? Not just Hawaii? With *her*? Unlovable Georgie?

This man who was holding her like he'd never let her go? This man *loved* her. Happiness flooded through Georgie and she put her hands on either side of Liam's unshaven cheeks.

"I jumped to conclusions, didn't I?" Georgie let the love flow through her.

"You need to—"

"*Ssh*. My turn." Georgie trailed her hand across the stubble on Liam's chin and put one finger against his lips. "I haven't told you that I love you yet. That's pretty important for you to know, if you're coming with me."

The last thing Georgie saw before she closed her eyes for Liam to kiss her was Sienna wiping her eyes. "Now we've made Sienna cry. And she never cries."

Epilogue

The mist hung low over the lush green mountains and a gentle rain had brushed their faces as the small group walked barefoot on the damp grass. Soft music surrounded them and the guests smiled as the bridal party appeared over the hill. Thelma and Mitzi dabbed at their eyes with lace handkerchiefs, but their emotion soon turned to gentle laughter as Faith dropped her mother's hand and sat on the wet grass and began to tip out the rose petals in the basket she'd been carrying.

"Faith, come on. You can play later." Ana smiled apologetically at Georgie as she picked her little daughter up from the grass and settled her on her hip. "Sorry, the joys of two-year-old flower girls."

Georgie leaned down and kissed the soft cheek of the little girl as Sienna waited for them to catch up. "She's fine; nothing is going to spoil this day."

Sienna smiled at her cousin. "And you've done it, sis. Your childhood dream. First married out of the three of us...and before your thirtieth birthday. One day to go...you just made it," she said drily.

Georgie stood beside Sienna as Ana followed them with Faith. "Only just, sis. It doesn't seem like almost a year since our last birthday, does it? And Ana's next." Ana and Blake had set the date for their own wedding.

The gathering was small. The guests sat in two rows of silk-covered chairs on a grassed terrace, where petals were strewn on the ground in heart shapes. The area was protected from the breeze by a polished dry stone wall. Joe and Magda sat behind Thelma and Mitzi; Sarah and Mike were beside Uncle Renzo and

Aunt Lucia.

"Well, you two got to Machu Picchu like you planned, but I bet you never thought it would be for your wedding," Ana said.

Georgie smiled at her two best friends and her heart filled. Everyone she loved was here to see her take her wedding vows with Liam. She looked ahead, past the chairs to where he stood waiting with Jack, Blake, and the celebrant, in front of a small altar. A magnificent vista of mist-covered mountains formed a dramatic backdrop behind Liam, who stood tall and proud. He held her eyes with his, his white silk shirt billowing in the gentle breeze over his loose white trousers.

The music swelled and Georgie stepped ahead. The others could catch up; Liam was waiting for her. She smiled as he took her hand and spoke softly.

"Hello, my beautiful Georgie."

Later that night in the hotel at the base of the mountain, Georgie rested her head on Liam's shoulder. She closed her eyes and let out a soft sigh as his lips brushed her cheek softly and they moved slowly together on the dance floor.

"You didn't tell me all the news, Mrs. Wyndham," he said softly.

"What news?" She opened her eyes and looked up at this man she loved with all of her heart.

"Look." He nodded in the direction of Sienna and Jack. Jack's hand was resting on the almost-unnoticeable bump on Sienna's tummy, and Georgie smiled.

"She didn't want to take away from our day. She's telling everyone tomorrow."

"I think it's too late." Liam smiled as Thelma and Mitzi threw their arms around Sienna. "They don't miss a trick, do they?"

"I adore them. It was so good that they all came to our

wedding." Georgie had missed her family and friends as she'd toured the world with Liam, but the six months they had travelled together had been an experience she would always cherish.

"I've got the tickets for our honeymoon destination in our room." His sexy smile spread across his face, and the inevitable warmth turned Georgie's bones deliciously loose.

"Maybe you should take me to the suite and show me?" Georgie lifted her hands to his cheeks and rested her lips against her husband's. "Where are we going?"

"There's a house on the hill at Hideaway Bay waiting for us." He grinned down at her. "And there are some bookshelves to be finished. Don't know where we can find a good tradesperson, do you?"

T
THE END

Also by Annie Seaton

Whitsunday Dawn
Undara
Osprey Reef

Porter Sisters Series

Kakadu Sunset

Daintree

Diamond Sky

Hidden Valley

Larapinta(2022)

Pentecost Island Series (2020)

Pippa

Eliza

Nell

Tamsin

Evie

Cherry

Odessa

Sienna

Tess

Isla

Sunshine Coast Series

Waiting for Ana

The Trouble with Jack

Healing His Heart

Bondi Beach Love Series

Beach House

Beach Music

Beach Walk

Beach Dreams

The House on the Hill

Second Chance Bay Series

Her Outback Playboy

Her Outback Protector

Her Outback Haven

Her Outback Paradise

Love Across Time Series

Come Back to Me

Follow Me

Finding Home

The Threads that Bind

Others

The Trouble with Paradise

Deadly Secrets

Adventures in Time

Silver Valley Witch

The Emerald Necklace

Worth the Wait

Ten Days in Paradise

Baby It's Hot Outside

About Annie

Annie lives in Australia, on the beautiful north coast of New South Wales. She sits in her writing chair and looks out over the tranquil Pacific Ocean. She has fulfilled her lifelong dream of becoming an author and is producing books at a prolific rate.

She writes contemporary romance and loves telling the stories that always have a happily ever after. She lives with her very own hero of many years and they share their home with Toby, the naughtiest dog in the universe, and Barney, the rag doll kitten, who hides when the grandchildren come to visit.

Stay up to date with her latest releases at her website: **http://www.annieseaton.net**

If you would like to stay up to date with Annie's releases, subscribe to her newsletter on her website.

Awards:

Book of the Year (Whitsunday Dawn) - Ausrom Readers' Choice Awards 2018.

Finalist (Whitsunday Dawn) – ARRA romantic suspense.

Finalist - NZ KORU award 2018 and 2020.

Winner - Best Established Author of the Year 2017 AUSROM.

Longlisted - Sisters in Crime Davitt Awards 2016, 2017, 2018, 2019.

Finalist (Kakadu Sunset) - Book of the Year, Long

Romance, RWA Ruby awards 2016.

Winner - Best Established Author of the Year 2015 AUSROM.

Winner - Author of the Year 2014 AUSROM.